The Faerie Queene, Books Three and Four

(Bk. 3 & 4)

D1033620

Edmund Spenser

CLASSIC BOOKS INTERNATIONAL

TABLE OF CONTENTS

THE THIRD BOOKE OF THE FAERIE QVEENE.
Contayning,

THE LEGEND OF BRITOMARTIS.

OR

Of Chastitie.

IT falles me here to write of Chastity, That fairest vertue, farre aboue the rest; For which what needs me fetch
from Faery Forreine ensamples, it to haue exprest? Sith it is
shrined in my Soueraines brest, And form'd so liuely in each
perfect part That to all Ladies, which haue it profest, Need
but behold the pourtraict of her hart, If pourtrayd it might be
by any liuing art. But liuing art may not least part expresse,
Nor life-resembling pencill it can paint, All were it Zeuxis or
Praxiteles: His daedale hand would faile, and greatly faint,
And her perfections with his error taint: Ne Poets wit, that
passeth Painter farre In picturing the parts of beautie daint,
So hard a workmanship aduenture darre, For fear through
want of words her excellence to marre.

How then shall I, Apprentice of the skill, That whylome
in diuinest wits did raine, Presume so high to stretch mine
humble quill? Yet now my lucklesse lot doth me constraine
Hereto perforce. But ô dred Soueraine Thus farre forth pardon, sith that choicest wit Cannot your glorious pourtraict
figure plaine That I in colourd showes may shadow it, And
antique praises vnto present persons fit.

But if in liuing colours, and right hew, Your selfe you couet to see pictured, Who can it doe more liuely, or more trew,
Then that sweet verse, with Nectar sprinckeled, In which a
gracious seruant pictured His Cynthia, his heauens fairest
light? That with his melting sweetnesse rauished, And with
the wonder of her beames bright, My senses lulled are in
slomber of delight.

But let that same delitious Poet lend A little leaue vnto
a rusticke Muse To sing his mistresse prayse, and let him
mend, If ought amis her liking may abuse: Ne let his fairest

Cynthia refuse, In mirrours more then one her selfe to see, But either Gloriana let her chuse, Or in Belphoebe fashioned to bee: In th'one her rule, in th'other her rare chastitee.

Canto I.

Guyon encountreth Britomart, faire Florimell is chaced: Duessaes traines and Malecastaes champions are defaced.

T He famous Briton Prince and Faerie knight, After long wayes and perilous paines endured, Hauing their wearie limbes to perfect plight Restord, and sory wounds right well recured, Of the faire Alma greatly were procured, To make there lenger soiourne and abode; But when thereto they might not be allured, From seeking praise, and deeds of armes abrode, They courteous conge tooke, and forth together yode. But the captiu'd Acrasia he sent, Because of trauell long, a nigher way, With a strong gard, all reskew to preuent, And her to Faerie court safe to conuay, That her for witnesse of his hard assay, Vnto his Faerie Queene he might present: But he him selfe betooke another way, To make more triall of his hardiment, And seeke aduentures, as he with Prince Arthur went.

Long so they trauelled through wastefull wayes, Where daungers dwelt, and perils most did wonne, To hunt for glorie and renowmed praise; Full many Countries they did ouerronne, From the vprising to the setting Sunne, And many hard aduentures did atchieue; Of all the which they honour euer wonne, Seeking the weake oppressed to relieue, And to recouer right for such, as wrong did grieue.

At last as through an open plaine they yode, They spide a knight, that towards pricked faire, And him beside an aged Squire there rode, That seem'd to couch vnder his shield three-square, As if that age bad him that burden spare, And yield it those, that stouter could it wield: He them espying, gan himselfe prepare, And on his arme addresse his goodly shield That bore a Lion passant in a golden field.

Which seeing good Sir Guyon, deare besought The Prince of grace, to let him runne that turne. He graunted: then the

Faery quickly raught His poinant speare, and sharpely gan to spurne His fomy steed, whose fierie feete did burne The verdant grasse, as he thereon did tread; Ne did the other backe his foot returne, But fiercely forward came withouten dread, And bent his dreadfull speare against the others head.

They bene ymet, and both their points arriued, But Guyon droue so furious and fell, That seem'd both shield & plate it would haue riued; Nathelesse it bore his foe not from his sell, But made him stagger, as he were not well: But Guyon selfe, ere well he was aware, Nigh a speares length behind his crouper fell, Yet in his fall so well him selfe he bare, That mischieuous mischance his life & limbes did spare.

Great shame and sorrow of that fall he tooke; For neuer yet, sith warlike armes he bore, And shiuering speare in bloudie field first shooke, He found himselfe dishonored so sore. Ah gentlest knight, that euer armour bore, Let not thee grieue dismounted to haue beene, And brought to ground, that neuer wast before; For not thy fault, but secret powre vnseene, That speare enchaunted was, which layd thee on the greene.

But weenedst thou what wight thee ouerthrew, Much greater griefe and shamefuller regret For thy hard fortune then thou wouldst renew, That of a single damzell thou wert met On equall plaine, and there so hard beset; Euen the famous Britomart it was, Whom straunge aduenture did from Britaine fet, To seeke her louer (loue farre sought alas,) Whose image she had seene in Venus looking glas.

Full of disdainefull wrath, he fierce vprose, For to reuenge that foule reprochfull shame, And snatching his bright sword began to close With her on foot, and stoutly forward came; Die rather would he, then endure that same. Which when his Palmer saw, he gan to feare His toward perill and vntoward blame, Which by that new rencounter he should reare: For death sate on the point of that enchaunted speare.

And hasting towards him gan faire perswade, Not to prouoke misfortune, nor to weene His speares default to mend with cruell blade; For by his mightie Science he had seene The secret vertue of that weapon keene, That mortall puissance mote not withstond: Nothing on earth mote alwaies happie beene. Great hazard were it, and aduenture fond, To loose long gotten honour with one euill hond.

By such good meanes he him discounselled, From prosecuting his reuenging rage; And eke the Prince like treaty handeled, His wrathfull will with reason to asswage, And laid the blame, not to his carriage, But to his starting steed, that swaru'd asyde, And to the ill purueyance of his page, That had his furnitures not firmely tyde: So is his angry courage fairely pacifyde.

Thus reconcilement was betweene them knit, Through goodly temperance, and affection chaste, And either vowd with all their power and wit, To let not others honour be defaste, Of friend or foe, who euer it embaste, Ne armes to beare against the others syde: In which accord the Prince was also plaste, And with that golden chaine of concord tyde. So goodly all agreed, they forth yfere did ryde.

O goodly vsage of those antique times, In which the sword was seruant vnto right; When not for malice and contentious crimes, But all for praise, and proofe of manly might, The martiall brood accustomed to fight: Then honour was the meed of victorie, And yet the vanquished had no despight: Let later age that noble vse enuie, Vile rancour to auoid, and cruell surquedrie.

Long they thus trauelled in friendly wise, Through countries waste, and eke well edifyde, Seeking aduentures hard, to exercise Their puissance, whylome full dernely tryde: At length they came into a forrest wyde, Whose hideous horror and sad trembling sound Full griesly seem'd: therein they long did ryde, Yet tract of liuing creatures none they found, Saue Beares, Lions, & Buls, which romed them around.

All suddenly out of the thickest brush, Vpon a milkwhite Palfrey all alone, A goodly Ladie did foreby them rush, Whose face did seeme as cleare as Christall stone, And eke through feare as white as whales bone: Her garments all were wrought of beaten gold, And all her steed with tinsell trappings shone, Which fled so fast, that nothing mote him hold, And scarse them leasure gaue, her passing to behold.

Still as she fled, her eye she backward threw, As fearing euill, that pursewd her fast; And her faire yellow locks behind her flew, Loosely disperst with puffe of euery blast: All as a blazing starre doth farre outcast His hearie beames, and flaming lockes dispred, At sight whereof the people stand aghast: But the sage wisard telles, as he has red, That it importunes death and dolefull drerihed.

So as they gazed after her a while, Lo where a griesly Foster forth did rush, Breathing out beastly lust her to defile: His tyreling iade he fiercely forth did push, Through thicke and thin, both ouer banke and bush In hope her to attaine by hooke or crooke, That from his gorie sides the bloud did gush: Large were his limbes, and terrible his looke, And in his clownish hand a sharp bore speare he shooke.

Which outrage when those gentle knights did see, Full of great enuie and fell gealosy, They stayd not to auise, who first should bee, But all spurd after fast, as they mote fly, To reskew her from shamefull villany. The Prince and Guyon equally byliue Her selfe pursewd, in hope to win thereby Most goodly meede, the fairest Dame aliue: But after the foule foster Timias did striue.

The whiles faire Britomart, whose constant mind, Would not so lightly follow beauties chace, Ne reckt of Ladies Loue, did stay behind, And them awayted there a certaine space, To weet if they would turne backe to that place: But when she saw them gone, she forward went, As lay her iourney, through that perlous Pace, With stedfast courage and stout hardiment; Ne euill thing she fear'd, ne euill thing she ment.

At last as nigh out of the wood she came, A stately Castle farre away she spyde, To which her steps directly she did frame. That Castle was most goodly edifyde, And plaste for pleasure nigh that forrest syde: But faire before the gate a spatious plaine, Mantled with greene, it selfe did spredden wyde, On which she saw sixe knights, that did darraine Fierce battell against one, with cruell might and maine.

Mainly they all attonce vpon him laid, And sore beset on euery side around, That nigh he breathlesse grew, yet nought dismaid, Ne euer to them yielded foot of ground All had he lost much bloud through many a wound, But stoutly dealt his blowes, and euery way To which he turned in his wrathfull stound, Made them recoile, and fly from dred decay, That none of all the sixe before, him durst assay.

Like dastard Curres, that hauing at a bay The saluage beast embost in wearie chace, Dare not aduenture on the stubborne pray, Ne byte before, but rome from place to place, To get a snatch, when turned is his face. In such distresse and doubtfull ieopardy, When Britomart him saw, she ran a pace Vnto his reskew, and with earnest cry, Bad those same sixe forbeare that single enimy.

But to her cry they list not lenden eare, Ne ought the more their mightie strokes surceasse, But gathering him round about more neare, Their direfull rancour rather did encreasse; Till that she rushing through the thickest preasse, Perforce disparted their compacted gyre, And soone compeld to hearken vnto peace: Tho gan she myldly of them to inquyre The cause of their dissention and outrageous yre.

Whereto that single knight did answere frame; These sixe would me enforce by oddes of might, To chaunge my liefe, and loue another Dame, That death me liefer were, then such despight, So vnto wrong to yield my wrested right: For I loue one, the truest one on ground, Ne list me chaunge; she th'Errant Damzell hight, For whose deare sake full many a bitter stownd, I haue endur'd, and tasted many a bloudy wound.

Certes (said she) then bene ye sixe to blame, To weene your wrong by force to iustifie: For knight to leaue his Ladie were great shame, That faithfull is, and better were to die.

All losse is lesse, and lesse the infamie, Then losse of loue to him, that loues but one; Ne may loue be compeld by maisterie; For soone as maisterie comes, sweet loue anone Taketh his nimble wings, and soone away is gone.

Then spake one of those sixe, There dwelleth here Within this castle wall a Ladie faire, Whose soueraine beautie hath no liuing pere, Thereto so bounteous and so debonaire, That neuer any mote with her compaire. She hath ordaind this law, which we approue, That euery knight, which doth this way repaire, In case he haue no Ladie, nor no loue, Shall doe vnto her seruice neuer to remoue.

But if he haue a Ladie or a Loue, Then must he her forgoe with foule defame, Or else with vs by dint of sword approue, That she is fairer, then our fairest Dame, As did this knight, before ye hither came. Perdie (said Britomart) the choise is hard: But what reward had he, that ouercame? He should aduaunced be to high regard, (Said they) and haue our Ladies loue for his reward.

Therefore a read Sir, if thou haue a loue. Loue haue I sure, (quoth she) but Lady none; Yet will I not fro mine owne loue remoue, Ne to your Lady will I seruice done, But wreake your wrongs wrought to this knight alone, And proue his cause. With that her mortall speare She mightily auentred towards one, And downe him smot, ere well aware he weare, Then to the next she rode, & downe the next did beare.

Ne did she stay, till three on ground she layd, That none of them himselfe could reare againe; The fourth was by that other knight dismayd, All were he wearie of his former paine, That now there do but two of six remaine; Which two did yield, before she did them smight. Ah (said she then) now may ye all see plaine, That truth is strong, and trew loue most of might, That for his trusty seruaunts doth so strongly fight.

Too well we see, (said they) and proue too well Our faulty weaknesse, and your matchlesse might: For thy, faire Sir, yours be the Damozell, Which by her owne law to your lot doth light, And we your liege men faith vnto you plight. So vnderneath her feet their swords they mard, And after her besought, well as they might, To enter in, and reape the dew reward: She graunted, and then in they all together far'd.

Long were it to describe the goodly frame, And stately port of Castle Ioyeous, (For so that Castle hight by commune name) Where they were entertaind with curteous And comely glee of many gracious Faire Ladies, and of many a gentle knight, Who through a Chamber long and spacious, Eftsoones them brought vnto their Ladies sight, That of them cleeped was the Lady of delight.

But for to tell the sumptuous aray Of that great chamber, should be labour lost: For liuing wit, I weene, cannot display The royall riches and exceeding cost, Of euery pillour and of euery post; Which all of purest bullion framed were, And with great pearles and pretious stones embost, That the bright glister of their beames cleare Did sparckle forth great light, and glorious did appeare.

These straunger knights through passing, forth were led Into an inner rowme, whose royaltee And rich purueyance might vneath be red; Mote Princes place beseeme so deckt to bee. Which stately manner when as they did see, The image of superfluous riotize, Exceeding much the state of meane degree, They greatly wondred, whence so sumptuous guize Might be maintaynd, and each gan diuersely deuize.

The wals were round about apparelled With costly clothes of Arras and of Toure, In which with cunning hand was pourtrahed The loue of Venus and her Paramoure The faire Adonis, turned to a flowre, A worke of rare deuice, and wondrous wit. First did it shew the bitter balefull stowre, Which her assayd with many a feruent fit, When first her tender hart was with his beautie smit.

Then with what sleights and sweet allurements she Entyst the Boy, as well that art she knew, And wooed him her Paramoure to be; Now making girlonds of each flowre that grew, To crowne his golden lockes with honour dew; Now

leading him into a secret shade From his Beauperes, and
from bright heauens vew, Where him to sleepe she gently
would perswade, Or bathe him in a fountaine by some couert
glade.

And whilst he slept, she ouer him would spred Her mantle, colour'd like the starry skyes, And her soft arme lay
vnderneath his hed, And with ambrosiall kisses bathe his
eyes; And whilest he bath'd, with her two crafty spyes, She
secretly would search each daintie lim, And throw into the
well sweet Rosemaryes, And fragrant violets, and Pances
trim, And euer with sweet Nectar she did sprinkle him.

So did she steale his heedelesse hart away, And ioyd his
loue in secret vnespyde. But for she saw him bent to cruell
play, To hunt the saluage beast in forrest wyde, Dreadfull
of daunger, that mote him betyde, She oft and oft aduiz'd
him to refraine From chase of greater beasts, whose brutish
pryde Mote breede him scath vnwares: but all in vaine; For
who can shun the chaunce, that dest'ny doth ordaine?

Lo, where beyond he lyeth languishing, Deadly engored
of a great wild Bore, And by his side the Goddesse groueling
Makes for him endlesse mone, and euermore With her soft
garment wipes away the gore, Which staines his snowy skin
with hatefull hew: But when she saw no helpe might him
restore, Him to a dainty flowre she did transmew, Which in
that cloth was wrought, as if it liuely grew.

So was that chamber clad in goodly wize, And round
about it many beds were dight, As whilome was the antique
worldes guize, Some for vntimely ease, some for delight, As
pleased them to vse, that vse it might: And all was full of
Damzels, and of Squires, Dauncing and reueling both day
and night, And swimming deepe in sensuall desires, And Cupid still emongst them kindled lustfull fires.

And all the while sweet Musicke did diuide Her looser
notes with Lydian harmony; And all the while sweet birdes
thereto applide Their daintie layes and dulcet melody,
Ay caroling of loue and iollity, That wonder was to heare

their trim consort. Which when those knights beheld, with scornefull eye, They sdeigned such lasciuious disport, And loath'd the loose demeanure of that wanton sort.

Thence they were brought to that great Ladies vew, Whom they found sitting on a sumptuous bed, That glistred all with gold and glorious shew, As the proud Persian Queenes accustomed: She seemd a woman of great bountihed, And of rare beautie, sauing that askaunce Her wanton eyes, ill signes of womanhed, Did roll too highly, and too often glaunce, Without regard of grace, or comely amenaunce.

Long worke it were, and needlesse to deuize Their goodly entertainement and great glee: She caused them be led in curteous wize Into a bowre, disarmed for to bee, And cheared well with wine and spiceree: The Redcrosse Knight was soone disarmed there, But the braue Mayd would not disarmed bee, But onely vented vp her vmbriere, And so did let her goodly visage to appere.

As when faire Cynthia, in darkesome night, Is in a noyous cloud enueloped, Where she may find the substaunce thin and light, Breakes forth her siluer beames, and her bright hed Discouers to the world discomfited; Of the poore traueller, that went astray, With thousand blessings she is heried; Such was the beautie and the shining ray, With which faire Britomart gaue light vnto the day.

And eke those six, which lately with her fought, Now were disarmd, and did them selues present Vnto her vew, and company vnsoght; For they all seemed curteous and gent, And all sixe brethren, borne of one parent, Which had them traynd in all ciuilitee, And goodly taught to tilt and turnament; Now were they liegemen to this Lady free, And her knights seruice ought, to hold of her in fee.

The first of them by name Gardante hight, A iolly person, and of comely vew; The second was Parlante, a bold knight, And next to him Iocante did ensew; Basciante did him selfe most curteous shew; But fierce Bacchante seemd too fell and keene; And yet in armes Noctante greater grew: All were

faire knights, and goodly well beseene, But to faire Britomart they all but shadowes beene.

For she was full of amiable grace, And manly terrour
mixed therewithall, That as the one stird vp affections bace,
So th'other did mens rash desires apall, And hold them backe,
that would in errour fall; As he, that hath espide a vermeill
Rose, To which sharpe thornes and breres the way forstall,
Dare not for dread his hardy hand expose, But wishing it far
off, his idle wish doth lose.

Whom when the Lady saw so faire a wight. All ignoraunt
of her contrary sex, (For she her weend a fresh and lusty
knight) She greatly gan enamoured to wex, And with vaine
thoughts her falsed fancy vex: Her fickle hart conceiued
hasty fire, Like sparkes of fire, which fall in sclender flex,
That shortly brent into extreme desire, And ransackt all her
veines with passion entire.

Eftsoones she grew to great impatience And into termes
of open outrage brust, That plaine discouered her incontinence, Ne reckt she, who her meaning did mistrust; For she
was giuen all to fleshly lust, And poured forth in sensuall
delight, That all regard of shame she had discust, And meet
respect of honour put to flight: So shamelesse beauty soone
becomes a loathy sight.

Faire Ladies, that to loue captiued arre, And chaste desires do nourish in your mind, Let not her fault your sweet
affections marre, Ne blot the bounty of all womankind;
'Mongst thousands good one wanton Dame to find: Emongst
the Roses grow some wicked weeds; For this was not to loue,
but lust inclind; For loue does alwayes bring forth bounteous
deeds, And in each gentle hart desire of honour breeds.

Nought so of loue this looser Dame did skill, But as a
coale to kindle fleshly flame, Giuing the bridle to her wanton
will, And treading vnder foote her honest name: Such loue is
hate, and such desire is shame. Still did she roue at her with
crafty glaunce Of her false eyes, that at her hart did ayme,
And told her meaning in her countenaunce; But Britomart

dissembled it with ignoraunce.

Supper was shortly dight and downe they sat, Where
they were serued with all sumptuous fare, Whiles fruitfull
Ceres, and Lyæus fat Pourd out their plenty, without spight
or spare: Nought wanted there, that dainty was and rare;
And aye the cups their bancks did ouerflow, And aye betweene the cups, she did prepare Way to her loue, and secret
darts did throw; But Britomart would not such guilfull mes-
sage know.

So when they slaked had the feruent heat Of appetite
with meates of euery sort, The Lady did faire Britomart entreat, Her to disarme, and with delightfull sport To loose
her warlike limbs and strong effort, But when she mote not
thereunto be wonne, (For she her sexe vnder that straunge
purport Did vse to hide, and plaine apparaunce shonne:) In
plainer wise to tell her grieuaunce she begonne.

And all attonce discouered her desire With sighes, and
sobs, and plaints, & piteous griefe, The outward sparkes of
her in burning fire; Which spent in vaine, at last she told her
briefe, That but if she did lend her short reliefe, And do her
comfort, she mote algates dye. But the chaste damzell, that
had neuer priefe Of such malengine and fine forgerie, Did
easily beleeue her strong extremitie.

Full easie was for her to haue beliefe, Who by self-feeling
of her feeble sexe, And by long triall of the inward griefe,
Wherewith imperious loue her hart did vexe, Could iudge
what paines do louing harts perplexe. Who meanes no guile,
be guiled soonest shall, And to faire semblaunce doth light
faith annexe; The bird, that knowes not the false fowlers call,
Into his hidden net full easily doth fall.

For thy, she would not in discourteise wise, Scorne the
faire offer of good will profest; For great rebuke it is, loue
to despise, Or rudely sdeigne a gentle harts request; But
with faire countenaunce, as beseemed best, Her entertaynd;
nath'lesse she inly deemd Her loue too light, to wooe a wandring guest: Which she misconstruing, thereby esteemd That

from like inward fire that outward smoke had steemd.

Therewith a while she her flit fancy fed, Till she mote winne fit time for her desire, But yet her wound still inward freshly bled, And through her bones the false instilled fire Did spred it selfe, and venime close inspire. Tho were the tables taken all away, And euery knight, and euery gentle Squire Gan choose his dame with Basciomani gay, With whom he meant to make his sport & courtly play.

Some fell to daunce, some fell to hazardry, Some to make loue, some to make meriment, As diuerse wits to diuers things apply; And all the while faire Malecasta bent Her crafty engins to her close intent. By this th'eternall lampes, wherewith high Ioue Doth light the lower world, were halfe yspent, And the moist daughters of huge Atlas stroue Into the Ocean deepe to driue their weary droue.

High time it seemed then for euery wight Them to betake vnto their kindly rest; Eftsoones long waxen torches weren light, Vnto their bowres to guiden euery guest: Tho when the Britonesse saw all the rest Auoided quite, she gan her selfe despoile, And safe commit to her soft fethered nest, Where through long watch, & late dayes weary toile, She soundly slept, & carefull thoughts did quite assoile.

Now whenas all the world in silence deepe Yshrowded was, and euery mortall wight Was drowned in the depth of deadly sleepe, Faire Malecasta, whose engrieued spright Could find no rest in such perplexed plight, Lightly arose out of her wearie bed, And vnder the blacke vele of guilty Night, Her with a scarlot mantle couered, That was with gold and Ermines faire enueloped.

Then panting soft, and trembling euerie ioynt, Her fearfull feete towards the bowre she moued; Where she for secret purpose did appoynt To lodge the warlike mayd vnwisely loued, And to her bed approching, first she prooued, Whether she slept or wakt, with her soft hand She softly felt, if any member mooued, And lent her wary eare to vnderstand, If any puffe of breath, or signe of sence she fand.

Which whenas none she fond, with easie shift, For feare least her vnwares she should abrayd, Th'embroderd quilt she lightly vp did lift, And by her side her selfe she softly layd, Of euery finest fingers touch affrayd; Ne any noise she made, ne word she spake, But inly sigh'd. At last the royall Mayd Out of her quiet slomber did awake, And chaungd her weary side, the better ease to take.

Where feeling one close couched by her side, She lightly lept out of her filed bed, And to her weapon ran, in minde to gride The loathed leachour. But the Dame halfe ded Through suddein feare and ghastly drerihed, Did shrieke alowd, that through the house it rong, And the whole family therewith adred, Rashly out of their rouzed couches sprong, And to the troubled chamber all in armes did throng.

And those six Knights that Ladies Champions, And eke the Redcrosse knight ran to the stownd, Halfe armd and halfe vnarmd, with them attons: Where when confusedly they came, they fownd Their Lady lying on the sencelesse grownd; On th'other side, they saw the warlike Mayd All in her snow-white smocke, with locks vnbownd, Threatning the point of her auenging blade, That with so troublous terrour they were all dismayde.

About their Lady first they flockt arownd, Whom hauing laid in comfortable couch, Shortly they reard out of her frosen swownd; And afterwards they gan with fowle reproch To stirre vp strife, and troublous contecke broch: But by ensample of the last dayes losse, None of them rashly durst to her approch, Ne in so glorious spoile themselues embosse; Her succourd eke the Champion of the bloudy Crosse.

But one of those sixe knights, Gardante hight, Drew out a deadly bow and arrow keene, Which forth he sent with felonous despight, And fell intent against the virgin sheene: The mortall steele stayd not, till it was seene To gore her side, yet was the wound not deepe, But lightly rased her soft silken skin, That drops of purple bloud thereout did weepe, Which did her lilly smock with staines of vermeil steepe.

Wherewith enrag'd she fiercely at them flew, And with her flaming sword about her layd, That none of them foule mischiefe could eschew, But with her dreadfull strokes were all dismayd: Here, there, and euery where about her swayd Her wrathfull steele, that none mote it abide; And eke the Redcrosse knight gaue her good aid, Ay ioyning foot to foot, and side to side, That in short space their foes they haue quite terrifide.

Tho whenas all were put to shamefull flight, The noble Britomartis her arayd, And her bright armes about her body dight: For nothing would she lenger there be stayd, Where so loose life, and so vngentle trade Was vsd of Knights and Ladies seeming gent: So earely ere the grosse Earthes grye-sy shade Was all disperst out of the firmament, They tooke their steeds, & forth vpō their iourney went.

Cant. II.

The Redcrosse knight to Britomart describeth Artegall: The wondrous myrrhour, by which she in loue with him did fall.

H Ere haue I cause, in men iust blame to find, That in their proper prayse too partiall bee, And not indifferent to woman kind, To whom no share in armes and cheualrie They do impart, ne maken memorie Of their braue gestes and prowesse martiall; Scarse do they spare to one or two or three, Rowme in their writs; yet the same writing small Does all their deeds deface, and dims their glories all. But by record of antique times I find, That women wont in warres to beare most sway, And to all great exploits them selues inclind: Of which they still the girlond bore away, Till enui-ous Men fearing their rules decay, Gan coyne streight lawes to curb their liberty; Yet sith they warlike armes haue layd away: They haue exceld in artes and pollicy, That now we foolish men that prayse gin eke t'enuy.

Of warlike puissaunce in ages spent, Be thou faire Brit-omart, whose prayse I write, But of all wisedome be thou precedent, O soueraigne Queene, whose prayse I would endite, Endite I would as dewtie doth excite; But ah my rimes too rude and rugged arre, When in so high an obiect they do lite, And striuing, fit to make, I feare do marre: Thy selfe thy prayses tell, and make them knowen farre.

She trauelling with Guyon by the way, Of sundry things faire purpose gan to find, T'abridg their iourney long, and lingring day; Mongst which it fell into that Faeries mind, To aske this Briton Mayd, what vncouth wind, Brought her into those parts, and what inquest Made her dissemble her disguised kind: Faire Lady she him seemd, like Lady drest, But fairest knight aliue, when armed was her brest.

Thereat she sighing softly, had no powre To speake a while, ne ready answere make, But with hart-thrilling throbs and bitter stowre, As if she had a feuer fit, did quake, And euery daintie limbe with horrour shake; And euer and anone the rosy red, Flasht through her face, as it had been a flake Of lightning, through bright heauen fulmined; At last the passion past she thus him answered.

Faire Sir, I let you weete, that from the howre I taken was from nourses tender pap, I haue beene trained vp in warlike stowre, To tossen speare and shield, and to affrap The warlike ryder to his most mishap; Sithence I loathed haue my life to lead, As Ladies wont, in pleasures wanton lap, To finger the fine needle and nyce thread; Me leuer were with point of foemans speare be dead.

All my delight on deedes of armes is set, To hunt out perils and aduentures hard, By sea, by land, where so they may be met, Onely for honour and for high regard, Without respect of richesse or reward. For such intent into these parts I came, Withouten compasse, or withouten card, Far fro my natiue soyle, that is by name The greater Britaine, here to seeke for prayse and fame.

Fame blazed hath, that here in Faery lond Do many famous Knightes and Ladies wonne, And many straunge aduentures to be fond, Of which great worth and worship may be wonne; Which I to proue, this voyage haue begonne.

But mote I weet of you, right curteous knight, Tydings of one, that hath vnto me donne Late foule dishonour and reprochfull spight, The which I seeke to wreake, and Arthegall he hight.

The word gone out, she backe againe would call, As her repenting so to haue missayd, But that he it vp-taking ere the fall, Her shortly answered; Faire martiall Mayd Certes ye misauised beene, t'vpbrayd A gentle knight with so vnknightly blame: For weet ye well of all, that euer playd At tilt or tourney, or like warlike game, The noble Arthegall hath euer borne the name.

For thy great wonder were it, if such shame Should euer enter in his bounteous thought, Or euer do, that mote deseruen blame: The noble courage neuer weeneth ought, That may vnworthy of it selfe be thought. Therefore, faire Damzell, be ye well aware, Least that too farre ye haue your sorrow sought: You and your countrey both I wish welfare, And honour both; for each of other worthy are.

The royall Mayd woxe inly wondrous glad, To heare her Loue so highly magnifide, And ioyd that euer she affixed had, Her hart on knight so goodly glorifide, How euer finely she it faind to hide: The louing mother, that nine monethes did beare, In the deare closet of her painefull side, Her tender babe, it seeing safe appeare, Doth not so much reioyce, as she reioyced theare.

But to occasion him to further talke, To feed her humour with his pleasing stile, Her list in strifull termes with him to balke, And thus replide, How euer, Sir, ye file Your curteous tongue, his prayses to compile, It ill beseemes a knight of gentle sort, Such as ye haue him boasted, to beguile A simple mayd, and worke so haynous tort, In shame of knighthood, as I largely can report.

Let be therefore my vengeaunce to disswade, And read, where I that faytour false may find. Ah, but if reason faire might you perswade, To slake your wrath, and mollifie your mind, (Said he) perhaps ye should it better find: For hardy thing it is, to weene by might, That man to hard conditions to bind, Or euer hope to match in equall fight, Whose prowesse paragon saw neuer liuing wight.

Ne soothlich is it easie for to read, Where now on earth, or how he may be found; For he ne wonneth in one certaine stead, But restlesse walketh all the world around, Ay doing things, that to his fame redound, Defending Ladies cause, and Orphans right, Where so he heares, that any doth confound Them comfortlesse, through tyranny or might: So is his soueraine honour raisde to heauens hight.

His feeling words her feeble sence much pleased, And softly sunck into her molten hart; Hart that is inly hurt, is greatly eased With hope of thing, that may allegge his smart; For pleasing words are like to Magick art, That doth the charmed Snake in slomber lay: Such secret ease felt gentle Britomart, Yet list the same efforce with faind gainesay; So dischord oft in Musick makes the sweeter lay.

And said, Sir knight, these idle termes forbeare, And sith it is vneath to find his haunt, Tell me some markes, by which he may appeare, If chaunce I him encounter parauaunt; For perdie one shall other slay, or daunt: What shape, what shield, what armes, what steed, what sted, And what so else his person most may vaunt? All which the Redcrosse knight to point ared, And him in euery part before her fashioned.

Yet him in euery part before she knew, How euer list her now her knowledge faine, Sith him whilome in Britaine she did vew, To her reuealed in a mirrhour plaine, Whereof did grow her first engraffed paine; Whose root and stalke so bitter yet did tast, That but the fruit more sweetnesse did containe, Her wretched dayes in dolour she mote wast, And yield the pray of loue to lothsome death at last.

By strange occasion she did him behold, And much more strangely gan to loue his sight, As it in bookes hath written bene of old. In Deheubarth that now South-wales is hight, What time king Ryence raign'd, and dealed right, The great Magitian Merlin had deuiz'd, By his deepe science, and hell-dreaded might, A looking glasse, right wondrously aguiz'd, Whose vertues through the wyde world soone were solemniz'd.

It vertue had, to shew in perfect sight, What euer thing was in the world contaynd, Betwixt the lowest earth and heauens hight, So that it to the looker appertaynd; What euer foe had wrought, or frend had faynd, Therein discouered was, ne ought mote pas, Ne ought in secret from the same remaynd; For thy it round and hollow shaped was, Like to the world it selfe, and seem'd a world of glas.

Who wonders not, that reades so wonderous worke? But who does wonder, that has red the Towre, Wherein th'Ægyptian Phao long did lurke From all mens vew, that none might her discoure, Yet she might all men vew out of her bowre? Great Ptolomæe it for his lemans sake Ybuilded all of glasse, by Magicke powre, And also it impregnable did make; Yet when his loue was false, he with a peaze it brake.

Such was the glassie globe that Merlin made, And gaue vnto king Ryence for his gard, That neuer foes his kingdome might inuade, But he it knew at home before he hard Tydings thereof, and so them still debar'd. It was a famous Present for a Prince, And worthy worke of infinite reward, That treasons could bewray, and foes conuince; Happie this Realme, had it remained euer since.

One day it fortuned, faire Britomart Into her fathers closet to repayre; For nothing he from her reseru'd apart, Being his onely daughter and his hayre; Where when she had espyde that mirrhour fayre, Her selfe a while therein she vewd in vaine; Tho her auizing of the vertues rare, Which thereof spoken were, she gan againe Her to bethinke of, that mote to her selfe pertaine.

But as it falleth, in the gentlest harts Imperious Loue hath highest set his throne, And tyrannizeth in the bitter smarts Of them, that to him buxome are and prone: So thought this Mayd (as maydens vse to done) Whom fortune for her husband would allot, Not that she lusted after any one; For she was pure from blame of sinfull blot, Yet wist her life at last must lincke in that same knot.

Eftsoones there was presented to her eye A comely knight, all arm'd in complete wize, Through whose bright ventayle lifted vp on hye His manly face, that did his foes agrize, And friends to termes of gentle truce entize, Lookt foorth, as Phoebus face out of the east, Betwixt two shadie mountaines doth arize; Portly his person was, and much increast Through his Heroicke grace, and honorable gest.

His crest was couered with a couchant Hound, And all his armour seem'd of antique mould, But wondrous massie and assured sound, And round about yfretted all with gold, In which there written was with cyphers old, Achilles armes, which Arthegall did win. And on his shield enueloped seuenfold He bore a crowned litle Ermilin, That deckt the azure field with her faire pouldred skin.

The Damzell well did vew his personage, And liked well, ne further fastned not, But went her way; ne her vnguilty age Did weene, vnwares, that her vnlucky lo t Lay hidden in the bottome of the pot; Of hurt vnwist most daunger doth redound: But the false Archer, which that arrow shot So slyly, that she did not feele the wound, Did smyle full smoothly at her weetlesse wofull stound.

Thenceforth the feather in her loftie crest, Ruffed of loue, gan lowly to auaile, And her proud portance, and her princely gest, With which she earst tryumphed, now did quail Sad, solemne, sowre, and full of fancies fraile She woxe; yet wist she neither how, nor why, She wist not, silly Mayd, what she did aile, Yet wist, she was not well at ease perdy, Yet thought it was not loue, but some melancholy.

So soone as Night had with her pallid hew Defast the beautie of the shining sky, And reft from men the worlds desired vew, She with her Nourse adowne to sleepe did lye; But sleepe full farre away from her did fly: In stead thereof sad sighes, and sorrowes deepe Kept watch and ward about her warily, That nought she did but wayle, and often steepe He daintie couch with teares, which closely she did weepe.

And if that any drop of slombring rest Did chaunce to still into her wearie spright, When feeble nature felt her selfe opprest, Streight way with dreames, and with fantasticke sight Of dreadfull things the same was put to flight, That oft out of her bed she did astart, As one with vew of ghastly feends affright: Tho gan she to renew her former smart, And thinke of that faire visage, written in her hart.

One night, when she was tost with such vnrest, Her aged Nurse, whose name was Glauce hight, Feeling her leape out of her loathed nest, Betwixt her feeble armes her quickly keight, And downe againe in her warme bed her dight; Ah my deare daughter, ah my dearest dread, What vncouth fit (said she) what euill plight Hath thee opprest, and with sad drearyhead Chaunged thy liuely cheare, and liuing made thee dead?

For not of nought these suddeine ghastly feares All night afflict thy naturall repose, And all the day, when as thine equall peares, Their fit disports with faire delight doe chose, Thou in dull corners doest thy selfe inclose, Ne tastest Princes pleasures, ne doest spred Abroad thy fresh youthes fairest flowre, but lose Both leafe and fruit, both too vntimely shed, As one in wilfull bale for euer buried.

The time, that mortall men their weary cares Do lay away, and all wilde beastes do rest, And euery riuer eke his course forbeares Then doth this wicked euill thee infest, And riue with thousand throbs thy thrilled brest; Like an huge Aetn' of deepe engulfed griefe, Sorrow is heaped in thy hollow chest, Whence forth it breakes in sighes and anguish rife, As smoke and sulphure mingled with confused strife.

Aye me, how much I feare, least loue it bee; But if that loue it be, as sure I read By knowen signes and passions, which I see, Be it worthy of thy race and royall sead, Then I auow by this most sacred head Of my deare foster child, to ease thy griefe, And win thy will: Therefore away doe dread; For death nor daunger from thy dew reliefe Shall me debarre, tell me therefore my liefest liefe.

So hauing said, her twixt her armes twaine She straightly straynd, and colled tenderly, And euery trembling ioynt, and euery vaine She softly felt, and rubbed busily, To doe the frosen cold away to fly; And her faire deawy eies with kisses deare She oft did bath, and oft againe did dry; And euer her importund, not to feare To let the secret of her hart to her appeare.

The Damzell pauzd, and then thus fearefully; Ah Nurse, what needeth thee to eke my paine? Is not enough, that I alone doe dye, But it must doubled be with death of twaine? For nought for me but death there doth remaine. O daughter deare (said she) despaire no whit; For neuer sore, but might a salue obtaine: That blinded God, which hath ye blindly smit, Another arrow hath your louers hart to hit.

But mine is not (quoth she) like others wound; For which no reason can find remedy. Was neuer such, but mote the like be found, (Said she) and though no reason may apply Salue to your sore, yet loue can higher stye, Then reasons reach, and oft hath wonders donne. But neither God of loue, nor God of sky Can doe (said she) that, which cannot be donne. Things oft impossible (quoth she) seeme, ere begonne.

These idle words (said she) doe nought asswage My stubborne smart, but more annoyance breed, For no no vsuall fire, no vsuall rage It is, ô Nurse, which on my life doth feed, And suckes the bloud, which from my hart doth bleed. But since thy faithfull zeale lets me not hyde My crime, (if crime it be) I will it reed. Nor Prince, nor pere it is, whose loue hath gryde My feeble brest of late, and launched this wound wyde.

Nor man it is, nor other liuing wight; For then some hope I might vnto me draw, But th'only shade and semblant of a knight, Whose shape or person yet I neuer saw, Hath me subiected to loues cruell law: The same one day, as me misfortune led, I in my fathers wondrous mirrhour saw, And pleased with that seeming goodly-hed, Vnwares the hidden hooke with baite I swallowed.

Sithens it hath infixed faster hold Within my bleeding bowels, and so sore Now ranckleth in this same fraile fleshly mould, That all mine entrailes flow with poysnous gore, And th'vlcer groweth daily more and more; Ne can my running sore find remedie, Other then my hard fortune to deplore, And languish as the leafe falne from the tree, Till death make one end of my dayes and miserie.

Daughter (said she) what need ye be dismayd, Or why make ye such Monster of your mind? Of much more vncouth thing I was affrayd; Of filthy lust, contrarie vnto kind: But this affection nothing straunge I find; For who with reason can you aye reproue, To loue the semblant pleasing most your mind, And yield your heart, whence ye cannot remoue? No guilt in you, but in the tyranny of loue.

Not so th'Arabian Myrrhe did set her mind; Nor so did Biblis spend her pining hart, But lou'd their natiue flesh against all kind, And to their purpose vsed wicked art: Yet playd Pasiphaë a more monstrous part, That lou'd a Bull, and learnd a beast to bee; Such shamefull lusts who loaths not, which depart From course of nature and of modestie? Sweet loue such lewdnes bands from his faire companie.

But thine my Deare (welfare thy heart my deare) Though strange beginning had, yet fixed is On one, that worthy may perhaps appeare; And certes seemes bestowed not amis: Ioy thereof haue thou and eternall blis. With that vpleaning on her elbow weake, Her alablaster brest she soft did kis, Which all that while she felt to pant and quake, As it an Earth-quake were; at last she thus bespake.

Beldame, your words doe worke me litle ease; For though my loue be not so lewdly bent, As those ye blame, yet may it nought appease My raging smart, ne ought my flame relent, But rather doth my helpelesse griefe augment. For they, how euer shamefull and vnkind, Yet did possesse their horrible intent: Short end of sorrowes they thereby did find; So was their fortune good, though wicked were their mind.

But wicked fortune mine, though mind be good, Can haue no end, nor hope of my desire, But feed on shadowes, whiles I die for food, And like a shadow wexe, whiles with entire Affection, I doe languish and expire. I fonder, then Cephisus foolish child, Who hauing vewed in a fountaine shere His face, was with the loue thereof beguild; I fonder loue a shade, the bodie farre exild.

Nought like (quoth she) for that same wretched boy Was of himselfe the idle Paramoure; Both loue and louer, without hope of ioy, For which he faded to a watry flowre. But better fortune thine, and better howre, Which lou'st the shadow of a warlike knight; No shadow, but a bodie hath in powre: That bodie, wheresoeuer that it light, May learned be by cyphers, or by Magicke might.

But if thou may with reason yet represse The growing euill, ere it strength haue got, And thee abandond wholly doe possesse, Against it strongly striue, and yield thee not, Till thou in open field adowne be smot. But if the passion may-ster thy fraile might, So that needs loue or death must be thy lot, Then I auow to thee, by wrong or right To compasse thy desire, and find that loued knight.

Her chearefull words much cheard the feeble spright Of the sicke virgin, that her downe she layd In her warme bed to sleepe, if that she might; And the old-woman carefully dis-playd The clothes about her round with busie ayd; So that at last a little creeping sleepe Surprisd her sense: she therewith well apayd, The drunken lampe downe in the oyle did steepe, And set her by to watch, and set her by to weepe.

Earely the morrow next, before that day His ioyous face did to the world reueale, They both vprose and tooke their readie way Vnto the Church, their prayers to appeale, With great deuotion, and with litle zeale: For the faire Damzell from the holy herse Her loue-sicke hart to other thoughts did steale; And that old Dame said many an idle verse, Out of her daughters hart fond fancies to reuerse.

Returned home, the royall Infant fell Into her former fit;

for why, no powre Nor guidance of her selfe in her did dwell.
But th'aged Nurse her calling to her bowre, Had gathered
Rew, and Sauine, and the flowre Of Camphara, and Cala-
mint, and Dill, All which she in a earthen Pot did poure, And
to the brim with Colt wood did it fill, And many drops of
milke and bloud through it did spill.

Then taking thrise three haires from off her head, Them
trebly breaded in a threefold lace, And round about the pots
mouth, bound the thread, And after hauing whispered a
space Certaine sad words, with hollow voice and bace, She
to the virgin said, thrise said she it; Come daughter come,
come; spit vpon my face, Spit thrise vpon me, thrise vpon me
spit; Th'vneuen number for this businesse is most fit.

That sayd, her round about she from her turnd, She
turned her contrarie to the Sunne, Thrise she her turnd contrary, and returnd, All contrary, for she the right did shunne,
And euer what she did, was streight vndonne. So thought
she to vndoe her daughters loue: But loue, that is in gentle
brest begonne, No idle charmes so lightly may remoue, That
well can witnesse, who by triall it does proue.

Ne ought it mote the noble Mayd auayle, Ne slake the
furie of her cruell flame, But that she still did waste, and still
did wayle, That through long languour, and hart-burning
brame She shortly like a pyned ghost became, Which long
hath waited by the Stygian strond. That when old Glauce
saw, for feare least blame Of her miscarriage should in her
be fond, She wist not how t'amend, nor how it to withstond.

Cant. III.

Merlin bewrayes to Britomart, the state of Artegall.
And shewes the famous Progeny which from them springen
shall.

M Ost sacred fire, that burnest mightily In liuing brests,
ykindled first aboue, Emongst th'eternall spheres and lamp-
ing sky, And thence pourd into men, which men call Loue;
Not that same, which doth base affections moue In brutish
minds, and filthy lust inflame, But that sweet fit, that doth

true beautie loue, And choseth vertue for his dearest Dame, Whence spring all noble deeds and neuer dying fame: Well did Antiquitie a God thee deeme, That ouer mortall minds hast so great might, To order them, as best to thee doth seeme, And all their actions to direct aright; The fatall purpose of diuine foresight, Thou doest effect in destined descents, Through deepe impression of thy secret might, And stirredst vp th'Heroes high intents, Which the late world admyres for wondrous monimets.

But thy dread darts in none doe triumph more, Ne brauer proofe in any, of thy powre Shew'dst thou, then in this royall Maid of yore, Making her seeke an vnknowne Paramoure, From the worlds end, through many a bitter stowre: From whose two loynes thou afterwards did rayse Most famous fruits of matrimoniall bowre, Which through the earth haue spred their liuing prayse, That fame in trompe of gold eternally displayes.

Begin then, ô my dearest sacred Dame, Daughter of Phoebus and of Memorie, That doest ennoble with immortall name The warlike Worthies, from antiquitie, In thy great volume of Eternitie: Begin, ô Clio, and recount from hence My glorious Soueraines goodly auncestrie, Till that by dew degrees and long pretence, Thou haue it lastly brought vnto her Excellence.

Full many wayes within her troubled mind, Old Glauce cast, to cure this Ladies griefe: Full many waies she sought, but none could find, Nor herbes, nor charmes, nor counsell, that is chiefe And choisest med'cine for sicke harts reliefe: For thy great care she tooke, and greater feare, Least that it should her turne to foule repriefe, And sore reproch, when so her father deare Should of his dearest daughters hard misfortune heare.

At last she her auisd, that he, which made That mirrhour, wherein the sicke Damosell So straungely vewed her straunge louers shade, To weet, the learned Merlin, well could tell, Vnder what coast of heauen the man did dwell, And by what meanes his loue might best be wrought: For though beyond the Africk Ismaell, Or th'Indian Peru he were, she thought Him forth through infinite endeuour to haue sought.

Forthwith themselues disguising both in straunge And base attyre, that none might them bewray, To Maridunum, that is now by chaunge Of name Cayr-Merdin cald, they tooke their way: There the wise Merlin whylome wont (they say) To make his wonne, low vnderneath the ground, In a deepe delue, farre from the vew of day, That of no liuing wight he mote be found, When so he counseld with his sprights encõpast round.

And if thou euer happen that same way To trauell, goe to see that dreadfull place: It is an hideous hollow caue (they say) Vnder a rocke that lyes a little space From the swift Barry, tombling downe apace, Emongst the woodie hilles of Dyneuowre: But dare thou not, I charge, in any cace, To enter into that same balefull Bowre, For fear the cruell Feends should thee vnwares deuowre.

But standing high aloft, low lay thine eare, And there such ghastly noise of yron chaines, And brasen Caudrons thou shalt rombling heare, Which thousand sprights with long enduring paines Doe tosse, that it will stonne thy feeble braines, And oftentimes great grones, and grieuous stounds, When too huge toile and labour them constraines: And oftentimes loud strokes, and ringing sounds From vnder that deepe Rocke most horribly rebounds.

The cause some say is this: A litle while Before that Merlin dyde, he did intend, A brasen wall in compas to compile About Cairmardin, and did it commend Vnto these Sprights, to bring to perfect end. During which worke the Ladie of the Lake, Whom long he lou'd, for him in hast did send, Who thereby forst his workemen to forsake, Them bound till his returne, their labour not to slake.

In the meane time through that false Ladies traine, He was surprisd, and buried vnder beare, Ne euer to his worke returnd againe: Nath'lesse those feends may not their worke forbeare, So greatly his commaundement they feare, But there doe toyle and trauell day and night, Vntill that brasen wall they vp doe reare: For Merlin had in Magicke more insight, Then euer him before or after liuing wight.

For he by words could call out of the sky Both Sunne and Moone, and make them him obay: The land to sea, and sea to maineland dry, And darkesome night he eke could turne to day: Huge hostes of men he could alone dismay, And hostes of men of meanest things could frame, When so him list his enimies to fray: That to this day for terror of his fame, The feends do quake, when any him to them does name.

And sooth, men say that he was not the sonne Of mortall Syre, or other liuing wight, But wondrously begotten, and begonne By false illusion of a guilefull Spright, On a faire Ladie Nonne, that whilome hight Matilda, daughter to Pubidius, Who was the Lord of Mathrauall by right, And coosen vnto king Ambrosius: Whence he indued was with skill so maruellous.

They here ariuing, staid a while without, Ne durst aduenture rashly in to wend, But of their first intent gan make new dout For dread of daunger, which it might portend: Vntill the hardie Mayd (with loue to frend) First entering, the dreadfull Mage there found Deepe busied bout worke of wondrous end, And writing strange characters in the ground, With which the stubborn feends he to his seruice bound.

He nought was moued at their entrance bold: For of their comming well he wist afore, Yet list them bid their businesse to vnfold, As if ought in this world in secret store Were from him hidden, or vnknowne of yore. Then Glauce thus, Let not it thee offend, That we thus rashly through thy darkesome dore, Vnwares haue prest: for either fatall end, Or other mightie cause vs two did hither send.

He bad tell on; and then she thus began. Now haue three Moones with borrow'd brothers light, Thrice shined faire, and thrice seem'd dim and wan, Sith a sore euill, which this virgin bright Tormenteth, and doth plonge in dolefull plight, First rooting tooke; but what thing it mote bee, Or whence it sprong, I cannot read aright: But this I read, that but if remedee Thou her afford, full shortly I her dead shall see.

Therewith th'Enchaunter softly gan to smyle At her smooth speeches, weeting inly well, That she to him dissembled womanish guyle, And to her said, Beldame, by that ye tell, More need of leach-craft hath your Damozell, Then of my skill: who helpe may haue elsewhere, In vaine seekes wonders out of Magicke spell. Th'old woman wox half blanck, those words to heare; And yet was loth to let her purpose plaine appeare.

And to him said, If any leaches skill, Or other learned meanes could haue redrest This my deare daughters deepe engraffed ill, Certes I should be loth thee to molest: But this sad euill, which doth her infest, Doth course of naturall cause farre exceed, And housed is within her hollow brest, That either seemes some cursed witches deed, Or euill spright, that in her doth such torment breed.

The wisard could no lenger beare her bord, But brusting forth in laughter, to her sayd; Glauce, what needs this colourable word, To cloke the cause, that hath it selfe bewrayd? Ne ye faire Britomartis, thus arayd, More hidden are, then Sunne in cloudy vele; Whom thy good fortune, hauing fate obayd, Hath hither brought, for succour to appele; The which the powres to thee are pleased to reuele.

The doubtfull Mayd, seeing her selfe descryde, Was all abasht, and her pure yuory Into a cleare Carnation suddeine dyde; As faire Aurora rising hastily, Doth by her blushing tell, that she did lye All night in old Tithonus frosen bed, Whereof she seemes ashamed inwardly. But her old Nourse was nought dishartened, But vauntage made of that, which Merlin had ared.

And sayd, Sith then thou knowest all our griefe, (For what doest not thou know?) of grace I pray, Pitty our plaint, and yield vs meet reliefe. With that the Prophet still awhile did stay, And then his spirite thus gan forth display; Most noble Virgin, that by fatall lore Hast learn'd to loue, let no whit thee dismay The hard begin, that meets thee in the dore, And with sharpe fits thy tender hart oppresseth sore.

For so must all things excellent begin, And eke enrooted deepe must be that Tree, Whose big embodied braunches shall not lin, Till they to heauens hight forth stretched bee. For from thy wombe a famous Progenie Shall spring, out of the auncient Troian blood, Which shall reuiue the sleeping memorie Of those same antique Peres, the heauens brood, Which Greece and Asian riuers stained with their blood.

Renowmed kings, and sacred Emperours, Thy fruitfull Ofspring, shall from thee descend; Braue Captaines, and most mighty warriours, That shall their conquests through all lands extend, And their decayed kingdomes shall amend: The feeble Britons, broken with long warre, They shall vpreare, and mightily defend Against their forrein foe, that comes from farre, Till vniuersall peace compound all ciuill iarre.

It was not, Britomart, thy wandring eye, Glauncing vn-wares in charmed looking glas, But the streight course of heauenly destiny, Led with eternall prouidence, that has Guided thy glaunce, to bring his will to pas: Ne is thy fate, ne is thy fortune ill, To loue the prowest knight, that euer was. Therefore submit thy wayes vnto his will, And do by all dew meanes thy destiny fulfill.

But read (said Glauce) thou Magitian What meanes shall she out seeke, or what wayes take? How shall she know, how shall she find the man? Or what needs her to toyle, sith fates can make Way for themselues, their purpose to partake? Then Merlin thus; Indeed the fates are firme, And may not shrinck, though all the world do shake: Yet ought mens good endeuours them confirme, And guide the heauenly causes to their constant terme.

The man whom heauens haue ordaynd to bee The spouse of Britomart, is Arthegall: He wonneth in the land of Fay-eree, Yet is no Fary borne, ne sib at all To Elfes, but sprong of seed terrestriall, And whilome by false Faries stolne away,

Whiles yet in infant cradle he did crall; Ne other to himselfe is knowne this day, But that he by an Elfe was gotten of a Fay.

But sooth he is the sonne of Gorlois, And brother vnto Cador Cornish king, And for his warlike feates renowmed is, From where the day out of the sea doth spring, Vntill the closure of the Euening. From thence, him firmely bound with faithfull band, To this his natiue soyle thou backe shalt bring, Strongly to aide his countrey, to withstand The powre of forrein Paynims, which inuade thy land.

Great aid thereto his mighty puissaunce, And dreaded name shall giue in that sad day: Where also proofe of thy prow valiaunce Thou then shalt make, t'increase thy louers pray. Long time ye both in armes shall beare great sway, Till thy wombes burden thee from them do call, And his last fate him from thee take away, Too rathe cut off by practise criminall Of secret foes, that him shall make in mischiefe fall.

Where thee yet shall he leaue for memory Of his late puissaunce, his Image dead, That liuing him in all actiuity To thee shall represent. He from the head Of his coosin Constantius without dread Shall take the crowne, that was his fathers right, And therewith crowne himselfe in th'others stead: Then shall he issew forth with dreadfull might, Against his Saxon foes in bloudy field to fight.

Like as a Lyon, that in drowsie caue Hath long time slept, himselfe so shall he shake, And comming forth, shall spred his banner braue Ouer the troubled South, that it shall make The warlike Mertians for feare to quake: Thrise shall he fight with them, and twise shall win, But the third time shall faire accordaunce make: And if he then with victorie can lin, He shall his dayes with peace bring to his earthly In.

His sonne, hight Vortipore, shall him succeede In kingdome, but not in felicity; Yet shall he long time warre with happy speed, And with great honour many battels try: But at the last to th'importunity Of froward fortune shall be forst to yield. But his sonne Malgo shall full mightily Auenge his fathers losse, with speare and shield, And his proud foes discomfit in victorious field.

Behold the man, and tell me Britomart, If ay more goodly creature thou didst see; How like a Gyaunt in each manly part Beares he himselfe with portly maiestee, That one of th'old Heroes seemes to bee: He the six Islands, comprouinciall In auncient times vnto great Britainee, Shall to the same reduce, and to him call Their sundry kings to do their homage seuerall.

All which his sonne Careticus awhile Shall well defend, and Saxons powre suppresse, Vntill a straunger king from vnknowne soyle Arriuing, him with multitude oppresse; Great Gormond, hauing with huge mightinesse Ireland subdewd, and therein fixt his throne, Like a swift Otter, fell through emptinesse, Shall ouerswim the sea with many one Of his Norueyses, to assist the Britons fone.

He in his furie all shall ouerrunne, And holy Church with faithlesse hands deface, That thy sad people vtterly fordonne, Shall to the vtmost mountaines fly apace: Was neuer so great wast in any place, Nor so fowle outrage doen by liuing men: For all thy Cities they shall sacke and race, And the greene grasse, that groweth, they shall bren, That euen the wild beast shall dy in starued den.

Whiles thus thy Britons do in languour pine, Proud Etheldred shall from the North arise, Seruing th'ambitious will of Augustine, And passing Dee with hardy enterprise, Shall backe repulse the valiaunt Brockwell twise, And Bangor with massacred Martyrs fill; But the third time shall rew his foolhardise: For Cadwan pittying his peoples ill, Shall stoutly him defeat, and thousand Saxons kill.

But after him, Cadwallin mightily On his sonne Edwin all those wrongs shall wreake; Ne shall auaile the wicked sorcery Of false Pellite, his purposes to breake, But him shall slay, and on a gallowes bleake Shall giue th'enchaunter his vnhappy hire; Then shall the Britons, late dismayd and weake, From their long vassalage gin to respire, And on their

Paynim foes auenge their ranckled ire.

Ne shall he yet his wrath so mitigate, Till both the sonnes of Edwin he haue slaine, Offricke and Osricke, twinnes vnfortunate, Both slaine in battell vpon Layburne plaine, Together with the king of Louthiane, Hight Adin, and the king of Orkeny, Both ioynt partakers of the fatall paine: But Penda, fearefull of like desteny, Shall yield him selfe his liegeman, and sweare fealty.

Him shall he make his fatall Instrument, T'afflict the other Saxons vnsubdewd; He marching forth with fury insolent Against the good king Oswald, who indewd With heauenly powre, and by Angels reskewd, All holding crosses in their hands on hye, Shall him defeate withouten bloud imbrewd: Of which, that field for endlesse memory, Shall Heuenfield be cald to all posterity.

Where at Cadwallin wroth, shall forth issew, And an huge hoste into Northumber lead, With which he godly Oswald shall subdew, And crowne with martyrdome his sacred head. Whose brother Oswin, daunted with like dread, With price of siluer shall his kingdome buy, And Penda, seeking him adowne to tread, Shall tread adowne, and do him fowly dye, But shall with gifts his Lord Cadwallin pacify.

Then shall Cadwallin dye, and then the raine Of Britons eke with him attonce shall dye; Ne shall the good Cadwallader with paine, Or powre, be hable it to remedy, When the full time prefixt by destiny, Shalbe expird of Britons regiment. For heauen it selfe shall their successe enuy, And them with plagues and murrins pestilent Consume, till all their warlike puissaunce be spent.

Yet after all these sorrowes, and huge hills Of dying people, during eight yeares space, Cadwallader not yielding to his ills, From Armoricke, where long in wretched cace He liu'd, returning to his natiue place, Shalbe by vision staid from his intent: For th'heauens haue decreed, to displace The Britons, for their sinnes dew punishment, And to the Saxons ouer-giue their gouernment.

Then woe, and woe, and euerlasting woe, Be to the Briton babe, that shalbe borne, To liue in thraldome of his fathers foe; Late King, now captiue, late Lord, now forlorne, The worlds reproch, the cruell victors scorne, Banisht from Princely bowre to wastfull wood: O who shall helpe me to lament, and mourne The royall seed, the antique Troian blood, Whose Empire lenger here, then euer any stood.

The Damzell was full deepe empassioned, Both for his griefe, and for her peoples sake, Whose future woes so plaine he fashioned, And sighing sore, at length him thus bespake; Ah but will heauens fury neuer slake, Nor vengeaunce huge relent it selfe at last? Will not long misery late mercy make, But shall their name for euer be defast, And quite from of th'earth their memory be rast?

Nay but the terme (said he) is limited, That in this thraldome Britons shall abide, And the iust reuolution measured, That they as Straungers shalbe notifide. For twise foure hundreth yeares shalbe supplide, Ere they to former rule restor'd shalbee, And their importune fates all satisfide: Yet during this their most obscuritee, Their beames shall oft breake forth, that men them faire may see.

For Rhodoricke, whose surname shalbe Great, Shall of him selfe a braue ensample shew, That Saxon kings his friendship shall intreat; And Howell Dha shall goodly well indew The saluage minds with skill of iust and trew; Then Griffyth Conan also shall vp reare His dreaded head, and the old sparkes renew Of natiue courage, that his foes shall feare, Least backe againe the kingdome he from them should beare.

Ne shall the Saxons selues all peaceably Enioy the crowne, which they from Britons wonne First ill, and after ruled wickedly: For ere two hundred yeares be full outronne, There shall a Rauen far from rising Sunne, With his wide wings vpon them fiercely fly, And bid his faithlesse chickens ouerronne The fruitfull plaines, and with fell cruelty, In their auenge, tread downe the victours surquedry.

Yet shall a third both these, and thine subdew; There shall a Lyon from the sea-bord wood Of Neustria come roring, with a crew Of hungry whelpes, his battailous bold brood, Whose clawes were newly dipt in cruddy blood, That from the Daniske Tyrants head shall rend Th'vsurped crowne, as if that he were wood, And the spoile of the countrey conquered Emongst his young ones shall diuide with bountyhed.

Tho when the terme is full accomplishid, There shall a sparke of fire, which hath long-while Bene in his ashes raked vp, and hid, Be freshly kindled in the fruitfull Ile Of Mona, where it lurked in exile; Which shall breake forth into bright burning flame, And reach into the house, that beares the stile Of royall maiesty and soueraigne name; So shall the Briton bloud their crowne againe reclame.

Thenceforth eternall vnion shall be made Betweene the nations different afore, And sacred Peace shall louingly perswade The warlike minds, to learne her goodly lore, And ciuile armes to exercise no more: Then shall a royall virgin raine, which shall Stretch her white rod ouer the Belgicke shore, And the great Castle smite so sore with all, That it shall make him shake, and shortly learne to fall.

But yet the end is not. There Merlin stayd, As ouercomen of the spirites powre, Or other ghastly spectacle dismayd, That secretly he saw, yet note discoure: Which suddein fit, and halfe extatick stoure When the two fearefull women saw, they grew Greatly confused in behauioure; At last the fury past, to former hew Hee turnd againe, and chearefull looks as earst did shew.

Then, when them selues they well instructed had Of all, that needed them to be inquird, They both conceiuing hope of comfort glad, With lighter hearts vnto their home retird; Where they in secret counsell close conspird, How to effect so hard an enterprize, And to possesse the purpose they desird: Now this, now that twixt them they did deuise, And diuerse plots did frame, to maske in strange disguise.

At last the Nourse in her foolhardy wit Conceiu'd a bold

deuise, and thus bespake; Daughter, I deeme that counsell aye most fit, That of the time doth dew aduauntage take; Ye see that good king Vther now doth make Strong warre vpon the Paynim brethren, hight Octa and Oza, whom he lately brake Beside Cayr Verolame, in victorious fight, That now all Britanie doth burne in armes bright.

That therefore nought our passage may empeach, Let vs in feigned armes our selues disguize, And our weake hands (whom need new strength shall teach) The dreadfull speare and shield to exercize: Ne certes daughter that same war-like wize I weene, would you misseeme; for ye bene tall, And large of limbe, t'atchieue an hard emprize, Ne ought ye want, but skill, which practize small Will bring, and shortly make you a mayd Martiall.

And sooth, it ought your courage much inflame, To heare so often, in that royall hous, From whence to none inferiour ye came, Bards tell of many women valorous Which haue full many feats aduenturous Performd, in paragone of proud-est men: The bold Bunduca, whose victorious Exploits made Rome to quake, stout Guendolen, Renowmed Martia, and re-doubted Emmilen.

And that, which more then all the rest may sway, Late dayes ensample, which these eyes beheld, In the last field before Meneuia Which Vther with those forrein Pagans held, I saw a Saxon Virgin, the which feld Great Vlfin thrise vpon the bloudy plaine, And had not Carados her hand withheld From rash reuenge, she had him surely slaine, Yet Carados himselfe from her escapt with paine.

Ah read, (quoth Britomart) how is she hight? Faire Ange-la (quoth she) men do her call, No whit lesse faire, then ter-rible in fight: She hath the leading of a Martiall And mighty people, dreaded more then all The other Saxons, which do for her sake And loue, themselues of her name Angles call. Therefore faire Infant her ensample make Vnto thy selfe, and equall courage to thee take.

Her harty words so deepe into the mynd Of the young

Damzell sunke, that great desire Of warlike armes in her forthwith they tynd, And generous stout courage did inspire, That she resolu'd, vnweeting to her Sire, Aduent'rous knighthood on her selfe to don, And counseld with her Nourse, her Maides attire To turne into a massy habergeon, And bad her all things put in readinesse anon.

Th'old woman nought, that needed, did omit; But all things did conueniently puruay: It fortuned (so time their turne did fit) A band of Britons ryding on forray Few dayes before, had gotten a great pray Of Saxon goods, emongst the which was seene A goodly Armour, and full rich aray, Which long'd to Angela, the Saxon Queene, All fretted round with gold, and goodly well beseene.

The same, with all the other ornaments, King Ryence caused to be hanged hy In his chiefe Church, for endlesse moniments Of his successe and gladfull victory: Of which her selfe auising readily, In th'euening late old Glauce thither led Faire Britomart, and that same Armory Downe taking, her therein appareled, Well as she might, and with braue bauldrick garnished.

Beside those armes there stood a mighty speare, Which Bladud made by Magick art of yore, And vsd the same in battell aye to beare; Sith which it had bin here preseru'd in store, For his great vertues proued long afore: For neuer wight so fast in sell could sit, But him perforce vnto the ground it bore: Both speare she tooke, and shield, which hong by it: Both speare & shield of great powre, for her purpose fit.

Thus when she had the virgin all arayd, Another harnesse, which did hang thereby, About her selfe she dight, that the young Mayd She might in equall armes accompany, And as her Squire attend her carefully: Tho to their ready Steeds they clombe full light, And through back wayes, that none might them espy, Couered with secret cloud of silent night, Themselues they forth conuayd, & passed forward right.

Ne rested they, till that to Faery lond They came, as Merlin them directed late: Where meeting with this Redcrosse knight, she fond Of diuerse things discourses to dilate, But most of Arthegall, and his estate. At last their wayes so fell, that they mote part Then each to other well affectionate, Friendship professed with vnfained hart, The Redcrosse knight diuerst, but forth rode Britomart.

Cant. IIII.

Bold Marinell of Britomart, Is throwne on the Rich strond: Faire Florimell of Arthur is Long followed, but not fond.

VV Here is the Antique glory now become, That whilome wont in women to appeare? Where be the braue atchieuements doen by some? Where be the battels, where the shield and speare, And all the conquests, which them high did reare, That matter made for famous Poets verse, And boastfull men so oft abasht to heare? Bene they all dead, and laid in dolefull herse? Or doen they onely sleepe, and shall againe reuerse? If they be dead, then woe is me therefore: But if they sleepe, ô let them soone awake: For all too long I burne with enuy sore, To heare the warlike feates, which Homere spake Of bold Penthesilee, which made a lake Of Greekish bloud so oft in Troian plaine; But when I read, how stout Debora strake Proud Sisera, and how Camill' hath slaine The huge Orsilochus, I swell with great disdaine.

Yet these, and all that else had puissaunce, Cannot with noble Britomart compare, Aswell for glory of great valiaunce, As for pure chastitie and vertue rare, That all her goodly deeds do well declare. Well worthy stock, from which the branches sprong, That in late yeares so faire a blossome bare, As thee, ô Queene, the matter of my song, Whose lignage from this Lady I deriue along.

Who when through speaches with the Redcrosse knight, She learned had th'estate of Arthegall, And in each point her selfe informd aright, A friendly league of loue perpetuall She with him bound, and Congé tooke withall. Then he forth on his iourney did proceede, To seeke aduentures, which mote him befall, And win him worship through his warlike deed,

Which alwayes of his paines he made the chiefest meed.

But Britomart kept on her former course, Ne euer dofte
her armes, but all the way Grew pensiue through that amorous discourse, By which the Redcrosse knight did earst
display Her louers shape, and cheualrous aray; A thousand
thoughts she fashioned in her mind, And in her feigning fancie did pourtray Him such, as fittest she for loue could find,
Wise, warlike, personable, curteous, and kind.

With such selfe-pleasing thoughts her wound she fed,
And thought so to beguile her grieuous smart; But so her
smart was much more grieuous bred, And the deepe wound
more deepe engord her hart, That nought but death her dolour mote depart. So forth she rode without repose or rest,
Searching all lands and each remotest part, Following the
guidaunce of her blinded guest, Till that to the sea-coast at
length she her addrest.

There she alighted from her light-foot beast, And sitting
downe vpon the rocky shore, Bad her old Squire vnlace her
lofty creast; Tho hauing vewd a while the surges hore, That
gainst the craggy clifts did loudly rore, And in their raging
surquedry disdaynd, That the fast earth affronted them so
sore, And their deuouring couetize restraynd, Thereat she
sighed deepe, and after thus complaynd.

Huge sea of sorrow, and tempestuous griefe, Wherein my
feeble barke is tossed long, Far from the hoped hauen of reliefe, Why do thy cruell billowes beat so strong, And thy moyst
mountaines each on others throng, Threatning to swallow vp
my fearefull life? O do thy cruell wrath and spightfull wrong
At length allay, and stint thy stormy strife, Which in these
troubled bowels raignes, & rageth rife.

For else my feeble vessell crazd, and crackt Through
thy strong buffets and outrageous blowes, Cannot endure,
but needs it must be wrackt On the rough rocks, or on the
sandy shallowes, The whiles that loue it steres, and fortune
rowes; Loue my lewd Pilot hath a restlesse mind And fortune Boteswaine no assuraunce knowes, But saile withouten

starres gainst tide and wind: How can they other do, sith both are bold and blind?

Thou God of winds, that raignest in the seas, That raignest also in the Continent, At last blow vp some gentle gale of ease, The which may bring my ship, ere it be rent, Vnto the gladsome port of her intent: Then when I shall my selfe in safety see, A table for eternall moniment Of thy great grace, and my great ieopardee, Great Neptune, I auow to hallow vnto thee.

Then sighing softly sore, and inly deepe, She shut vp all her plaint in priuy griefe; For her great courage would not let her weepe, Till that old Glauce gan with sharpe repriefe, Her to restraine, and giue her good reliefe, Through hope of those, which Merlin had her told Should of her name and nation be chiefe, And fetch their being from the sacred mould Of her immortall wombe, to be in heauen enrold.

Thus as she her recomforted, she spyde, Where farre away one all in armour bright, With hastie gallop towards her did ryde; Her dolour soone she ceast, and on her dight Her Helmet, to her Courser mounting light: Her former sorrow into suddein wrath, Both coosen passions of distroubled spright, Conuerting, forth she beates the dustie path; Loue and despight attonce her courage kindled hath.

As when a foggy mist hath ouercast The face of heauen, and the cleare aire engrost, The world in darkenesse dwels, till that at last The watry Southwinde from the seabord cost Vpblowing, doth disperse the vapour lo'st, And poures it selfe forth in a stormy showre; So the faire Britomart hauing disclo'st Her clowdy care into a wrathfull stowre, The mist of griefe dissolu'd, did into vengeance powre.

Eftsoones her goodly shield addressing faire, That mortall speare she in her hand did take, And vnto battell did her selfe prepaire. The knight approching, sternely her bespake; Sir knight, that doest thy voyage rashly make By this forbidden way in my despight, Ne doest by others death ensample take, I read thee soone retyre, whiles thou hast might, Least afterwards it be too late to take thy flight.

Ythrild with deepe disdaine of his proud threat, She shortly thus; Fly they, that need to fly; Words fearen babes. I meane not thee entreat To passe; but maugre thee will passe or dy. Ne lenger stayd for th'other to reply, But with sharpe speare the rest made dearly knowne. Strongly the straunge knight ran, and sturdily Strooke her full on the brest, that made her downe Decline her head, & touch her crouper with her crowne.

But she againe him in the shield did smite, With so fierce furie and great puissaunce, That through his threesquare scuchin percing quite, And through his mayled hauberque, by mischaunce The wicked steele through his left side did glaunce; Him so transfixed she before her bore Beyond his croupe, the length of all her launce, Till sadly soucing on the sandie shore, He tombled on an heape, and wallowd in his gore.

Like as the sacred Oxe, that carelesse stands, With gilden hornes, and flowry girlonds crownd, Proud of his dying honor and deare bands, Whiles th'altars fume with frankincense arownd, All suddenly with mortall stroke astownd, Doth groueling fall, and with his streaming gore Distaines the pillours, and the holy grownd, And the faire flowres, that decked him afore; So fell proud Marinell vpon the pretious shore.

The martiall Mayd stayd not him to lament, But forward rode, and kept her readie way Along the strond, which as she ouer-went, She saw bestrowed all with rich aray Of pearles and pretious stones of great assay, And all the grauell mixt with golden owre; Whereat she wondred much, but would not stay For gold, or perles, or pretious stones an howre, But them despised all; for all was in her powre.

Whiles thus he lay in deadly stonishment, Tydings hereof came to his mothers eare; His mother was the blacke-browd Cymoent, The daughter of great Nereus, which did beare This warlike sonne vnto an earthly peare, The famous Dumarin; who on a day Finding the Nymph a sleepe in secret wheare, As he by chaunce did wander that same way, Was taken with her loue, and by her closely lay.

There he this knight of her begot, whom borne She of his father Marinell did name, And in a rocky caue as wight forlorne, Long time she fostred vp, till he became A mightie man at armes, and mickle fame Did get through great aduentures by him donne: For neuer man he suffred by that same Rich strond to trauell, whereas he did wonne, But that he must do battell with the Sea-nymphes sonne.

An hundred knights of honorable name He had subdew'd and them his vassals made, That through all Farie lond his noble fame Now blazed was, and feare did all inuade, That none durst passen through that perilous glade. And to aduance his name and glorie more, Her Sea-god syre she dearely did perswade, T'endow her sonne with threasure and rich store, Boue all the sonnes, that were of earthly wombes ybore.

The God did graunt his daughters deare demaund, To doen his Nephew in all riches flow; Eftsoones his heaped waues he did commaund, Out of their hollow bosome forth to throw All the huge threasure, which the sea below Had in his greedie gulfe deuoured deepe, And him enriched through the ouerthrow And wreckes of many wretches, which did weepe, And often waile their wealth, which he from them did keepe.

Shortly vpon that shore there heaped was, Exceeding riches and all pretious things, The spoyle of all the world, that it did pas The wealth of th'East, and pompe of Persian kings; Gold, amber, yuorie, perles, owches, rings, And all that else was pretious and deare, The sea vnto him voluntary brings, That shortly he a great Lord did appeare, As was in all the lond of Faery, or elsewheare.

Thereto he was a doughtie dreaded knight, Tryde often to the scath of many deare, That none in equall armes him matchen might, The which his mother seeing, gan to feare

Least his too haughtie hardines might reare Some hard mishap, in hazard of his life: For thy she oft him counseld to forbeare The bloudie battell, and to stirre vp strife, But after all his warre, to rest his wearie knife.

And for his more assurance, she inquir'd One day of Proteus by his mightie spell, (For Proteus was with prophecie inspir'd) Her deare sonnes destinie to her to tell, And the sad end of her sweet Marinell. Who through foresight of his eternall skill, Bad her from womankind to keepe him well: For of a woman he should haue much ill, A virgin strange and stout him should dismay, or kill.

For thy she gaue him warning euery day, The loue of women not to entertaine; A lesson too too hard for liuing clay, From loue in course of nature to refraine: Yet he his mothers lore did well retaine, And euer from faire Ladies loue did fly; Yet many Ladies faire did oft complaine, That they for loue of him would algates dy: Dy, who so list for him, he was loues enimy.

But ah, who can deceiue his destiny, Or weene by warning to auoyd his fate? That when he sleepes in most security, And safest seemes, him soonest doth amate, And findeth dew effect or soone or late. So feeble is the powre of fleshly arme. His mother bad him womens loue to hate, For she of womans force did feare no harme; So weening to haue arm'd him, she did quite disarme.

This was that woman, this that deadly wound, That Proteus prophecide should him dismay, The which his mother vainely did expound, To be hart-wounding loue, which should assay To bring her sonne vnto his last decay. So tickle be the termes of mortall state, And full of subtile sophismes, which do play With double senses, and with false debate, T'approue the vnknowen purpose of eternall fate.

Too true the famous Marinell it fownd, Who through late triall, on that wealthy Strond Inglorious now lies in senselesse swownd, Through heauy stroke of Britomartis hond. Which when his mother deare did vnderstond, And heauy tydings heard, whereas she playd Amongst her watry sisters by a pond, Gathering sweet daffadillyes, to haue made Gay girlonds, from the Sun their forheads faire to shade.

Eftsoones both flowres and girlonds farre away She flong, and her faire deawy lockes yrent, To sorrow huge she turnd her former play, And gamesom merth to grieuous dreriment: She threw her selfe downe on the Continent, Ne word did speake, but lay as in a swowne, Whiles all her sisters did for her lament, With yelling outcries, and with shrieking sowne; And euery one did teare her girlond from her crowne.

Soone as she vp out of her deadly fit Arose, she bad her charet to be brought, And all her sisters, that with her did sit, Bad eke attonce their charets to be sought; Tho full of bitter griefe and pensiue thought, She to her wagon clombe; clombe all the rest, And forth together went, with sorrow fraught. The waues obedient to their beheast, Them yielded readie passage, and their rage surceast.

Great Neptune stood amazed at their sight, Whiles on his broad round backe they softly slid And eke himselfe mournd at their mournfull plight, Yet wist not what their wailing ment, yet did For great compassion of their sorrow, bid His mightie waters to them buxome bee; Eftsoones the roaring billowes still abid, And all the griesly Monsters of the See Stood gaping at their gate, and wondred them to see.

A teme of Dolphins raunged in aray, Drew the smooth charet of sad Cymoent; They were all taught by Triton, to obay To the long raynes, at her commaundement: As swift as swallowes, on the waues they went, That their broad flaggie finnes no fome did reare, Ne bubbling roundell they behind them sent; The rest of other fishes drawen weare, Which with their finny oars the swelling sea did sheare.

Soone as they bene arriu'd vpon the brim Of the Rich strond, their charets they forlore, And let their temed fishes softly swim Along the margent of the fomy shore, Least they their finnes should bruze, and surbate sore Their tender feet vpon the stony ground: And comming to the place, where all in gore And cruddy bloud enwallowed they found The lucklesse Marinell, lying in deadly swound;

His mother swowned thrise, and the third time Could scarce recouered be out of her paine; Had she not bene deuoyd of mortall slime, She should not then haue bene reliu'd againe, But soone as life recouered had the raine, She made so piteous mone and deare wayment, That the hard rocks could scarse from teares refraine, And all her sister Nymphes with one consent Supplide her sobbing breaches with sad complement.

Deare image of my selfe (she said) that is, The wretched sonne of wretched mother borne, Is this thine high aduauncement, ô is this Th'immortall name, with which thee yet vnborne Thy Gransire Nereus promist to adorne? Now lyest thou of life and honor reft; Now lyest thou a lumpe of earth forlorne, Ne of thy late life memory is left, Ne can thy irreuocable destiny be weft?

Fond Proteus, father of false prophecis, And they more fond, that credit to thee giue, Not this the worke of womans hand ywis, That so deepe wound through these deare members driue. I feared loue: but they that loue do liue, But they that die, doe neither loue nor hate. Nath'lesse to thee thy folly I forgiue, And to my selfe, and to accursed fate The guilt I doe ascribe: deare wisedome bought too late.

O what auailes it of immortall seed To beene ybred and neuer borne to die? Farre better I it deeme to die with speed, Then waste in woe and wailefull miserie. Who dyes the vtmost dolour doth abye, But who that liues, is left to waile his losse: So life is losse, and death felicitie. Sad life worse then glad death: and greater crosse To see friends graue, the dead the graue selfe to engrosse.

But if the heauens did his dayes enuie, And my short blisse maligne, yet mote they well Thus much afford me, ere that he did die That the dim eyes of my deare Marinell I mote haue closed, and him bed farewell, Sith other offices for mother meet They would not graunt. Yet maulgre them farewell, my sweetest sweet; Farewell my sweetest sonne, sith we no more shall meet.

Thus when they all had sorrowed their fill, They softly gan to search his griesly wound: And that they might him handle more at will, They him disarm'd, and spredding on the ground Their watchet mantles frindgd with siluer round, They softly wipt away the gelly blood From th'orifice; which hauing well vpbound, They pourd in soueraine balme, and Nectar good, Good both for earthly med'cine, and for heauenly food.

Tho when the lilly handed Liagore, (This Liagore whylome had learned skill In leaches craft, by great Appolloes lore, Sith her whylome vpon high Pindus hill, He loued, and at last her wombe did fill With heauenly seed, whereof wise Pæon sprong) Did feele his pulse, she knew their staied still Some litle life his feeble sprites emong; Which to his mother told, despeire she from her flong.

Tho vp him taking in their tender hands, They easily vnto her charet beare: Her teme at her commaundement quiet stands, Whiles they the corse into her wagon reare, And strow with flowres the lamentable beare: Then all the rest into their coches clim, And through the brackish waues their passage sheare; Vpon great Neptunes necke they softly swim, And to her watry chamber swiftly carry him.

Deepe in the bottome of the sea, her bowre Is built of hollow billowes heaped hye, Like to thicke cloudes, that threat a stormy showre, And vauted all within, like to the sky, In which the Gods do dwell eternally: There they him laid in easie couch well dight; And sent in haste for Tryphon, to apply Salues to his wounds, and medicines of might: For Tryphon of sea gods the soueraine leach is hight.

The whiles the Nymphes sit all about him round, Lamenting his mishap and heauy plight; And oft his mother vewing his wide wound, Cursed the hand, that did so deadly smight Her dearest sonne, her dearest harts delight. But none of all those curses ouertooke The warlike Maid, th'ensample of

that might, But fairely well she thriu'd, and well did brooke
Her noble deeds, ne her right course for ought forsooke.

Yet did false Archimage her still pursew, To bring to passe his mischieuous intent, Now that he had her singled from
the crew Of courteous knights, the Prince, and Faery gent,
Whom late in chace of beautie excellent She left, pursewing
that same foster strong; Of whose foule outrage they impatient, And full of fiery zeale, him followed long, To reskew
her from shame, and to reuenge her wrong.

Through thick and thin, through mountaines & through
plains, Those two great chãpions did attonce pursew The
fearefull damzell, with incessant paines: Who from them
fled, as light-foot hare from vew Of hunter swift, and sent of
houndes trew. At last they came vnto a double way, Where,
doubtfull which to take, her to reskew, Themselues they did
dispart, each to assay, Whether more happie were, to win so
goodly pray.

But Timias, the Princes gentle Squire, That Ladies loue
vnto his Lord forlent, And with proud enuy, and indignant
ire, After that wicked foster fiercely went. So beene they three
three sundry wayes ybent. But fairest fortune to the Prince
befell, Whose chaunce it was, that soone he did repent, To
take that way, in which that Damozell Was fled afore, affraid
of him, as feend of hell.

At last of her farre off he gained vew: Then gan he freshly
pricke his fomy steed, And euer as he nigher to her drew, So
euermore he did increase his speed, And of each turning still
kept warie heed: Aloud to her he oftentimes did call, To doe
away vaine doubt, and needlesse dreed: Full myld to her he
spake, and oft let fall Many meeke wordes, to stay and comfort her withall.

But nothing might relent her hastie flight; So deepe the
deadly feare of that foule swaine Was earst impressed in her
gentle spright: Like as a fearefull Doue, which through the
raine, Of the wide aire her way does cut amaine, Hauing farre
off espyde a Tassell gent, Which after her his nimble wings

doth straine, Doubleth her haste for feare to be for-hent, And with her pineons cleaues the liquid firmament.

With no lesse haste, and eke with no lesse dreed, That fearefull Ladie fled from him, that ment To her no euill thought, nor euill deed; Yet former feare of being fowly shent, Carried her forward with her first intent: And though oft looking backward, well she vewd, Her selfe freed from that foster insolent, And that it was a knight, which now her sewd, Yet she no lesse the knight feard, then that villein rude.

His vncouth shield and straunge armes her dismayd, Whose like in Faery lond were seldome seene, That fast she from him fled, no lesse affrayd, Then of wilde beastes if she had chased beene: Yet he her followd still with courage keene, So long that now the golden Hesperus Was mounted high in top of heauen sheene, And warnd his other brethren ioyeous, To light their blessed lamps in Ioues eternall hous.

All suddenly dim woxe the dampish ayre, And griesly shadowes couered heauen bright, That now with thousand starres was decked fayre; Which when the Prince beheld, a lothfull sight, And that perforce, for want of lenger light, He mote surcease his suit, and lose the hope Of his long labour, he gan fowly wyte His wicked fortune, that had turnd aslope, And cursed night, that reft from him so goodly scope.

Tho when her wayes he could no more descry, But to and fro at disauenture strayd; Like as a ship, whose Lodestarre suddenly Couered with cloudes, her Pilot hath dismayd; His wearisome pursuit perforce he stayd, And from his loftie steed dismounting low, Did let him forage. Downe himselfe he layd Vpon the grassie ground, to sleepe a throw; The cold earth was his couch, the hard steele his pillow.

But gentle Sleepe enuyde him any rest; In stead thereof sad sorrow, and disdaine Of his hard hap did vexe his noble brest, And thousand fancies bet his idle braine With their light wings, the sights of semblants vaine: Oft did he wish, that Lady faire mote bee His Faery Queene, for whom he

did complaine: Or that his Faery Queene were such, as shee:
And euer hastie Night he blamed bitterlie.

Night thou foule Mother of annoyance sad, Sister of
heauie death, and nourse of woe, Which wast begot in heau-
en, but for thy bad And brutish shape thrust downe to hell
below, Where by the grim floud of Cocytus slow Thy dwelling
is, in Herebus blacke hous, (Blacke Herebus thy husband is
the foe Of all the Gods) where thou vngratious, Halfe of thy
dayes doest lead in horrour hideous.

What had th'eternall Maker need of thee, The world in
his continuall course to keepe, That doest all things deface,
ne lettest see The beautie of his worke? Indeed in sleepe
The slouthfull bodie, that doth loue to steepe His lustlesse
limbes, and drowne his baser mind, Doth praise thee oft, and
oft from Stygian deepe Calles thee, his goddesse in his error
blind, And great Dame Natures handmaide, chearing euery
kind.

But well I wote, that to an heauy hart Thou art the
root and nurse of bitter cares, Breeder of new, renewer of
old smarts: In stead of rest thou lendest rayling teares, In
stead of sleepe thou sendest troublous feares, And dreadfull
visions, in the which aliue The drearie image of sad death
appeares: So from the wearie spirit thou doest driue Desired
rest, and men of happinesse depriue.

Vnder thy mantle blacke there hidden lye, Light-shon-
ning theft, and traiterous intent, Abhorred bloudshed, and
vile felony, Shamefull deceipt, and daunger imminent; Foule
horror, and eke hellish dreriment: All these I wote in thy
protection bee, And light doe shonne, for feare of being shent:
For light ylike is loth'd of them and thee, And all that lewdnesse loue, doe hate the light to see.

For day discouers all dishonest wayes, And sheweth each
thing, as it is indeed: The prayses of high God he faire displayes, And his large bountie rightly doth areed. Dayes dearest children be the blessed seed, Which darknesse shall subdew, and heauen win; Truth is his daughter; he her first did

breed, Most sacred virgin, without spot of sin. Our life is day, but death with darknesse doth begin.

O when will day then turne to me againe, And bring with him his long expected light? O Titan, haste to reare thy ioyous waine: Speed thee to spred abroad thy beames bright? And chase away this too long lingring night, Chase her away, from whence she came, to hell. She, she it is, that hath me done despight: There let her with the damned spirits dwell, And yeeld her roome to day, that can it gouerne well.

Thus did the Prince that wearie night outweare, In restlesse anguish and vnquiet paine: And earely, ere the morrow did vpreare His deawy head out of the Ocean maine, He vp arose, as halfe in great disdaine, And clombe vnto his steed. So forth he went, With heauie looke and lumpish pace, that plaine In him bewraid great grudge and maltalent: His steed eke seem'd t'apply his steps to his intent.

Cant. V.

Prince Arthur heares of Florimell: three fosters Timias wound, Belphebe finds him almost dead, and reareth out of sownd.

VV Onder it is to see, in diuerse minds, How diuersly loue doth his pageants play, And shewes his powre in variable kinds: The baser wit, whose idle thoughts alway Are wont to cleaue vnto the lowly clay, It stirreth vp to sensuall desire, And in lewd slouth to wast his carelesse day: But in braue sprite it kindles goodly fire, That to all high desert and honour doth aspire. Ne suffereth it vncomely idlenesse, In his free thought to build her sluggish nest: Ne suffereth it thought of vngentlenesse, Euer to creepe into his noble brest, But to the highest and the worthiest Lifteth it vp, that else would lowly fall: It lets not fall, it lets it not to rest: It lets not scarse this Prince to breath at all, But to his first poursuit him forward still doth call.

Who long time wandred through the forrest wyde, To finde some issue thence, till that at last He met a Dwarfe, that seemed terrifyde With some late perill, which he hard-

ly past, Or other accident, which him aghast; Of whom he
asked, whence he lately came, And whither now he trauelled
so fast: For sore he swat, and running through that same
Thicke forest, was bescratcht, & both his feet nigh lame.

Panting for breath, and almost out of hart, The Dwarfe
him answerd, Sir, ill mote I stay To tell the same. I lately did
depart From Faery court, where I haue many a day Serued a
gentle Lady of great sway, And high accompt throughout all
Elfin land, Who lately left the same, and tooke this way: Her
now I seeke, and if ye vnderstand Which way she fared hath,
good Sir tell out of hand.

What mister wight (said he) and how arayd? Royally clad
(quoth he) in cloth of gold, As meetest may beseeme a noble mayd; Her faire lockes in rich circlet be enrold, A fairer
wight did neuer Sunne behold, And on a Palfrey rides more
white then snow, Yet she her selfe is whiter manifold: The
surest signe, whereby ye may her know, Is, that she is the
fairest wight aliue, I trow.

Now certes swaine (said he) such one I weene, Fast flying
through this forest from her fo, A foule ill fauoured foster,
I haue seene; Her selfe, well as I might, I reskewd tho, But
could not stay; so fast she did foregoe, Carried away with
wings of speedy feare. Ah dearest God (quoth he) that is
great woe, And wondrous ruth to all, that shall it heare. But
can ye read Sir, how I may her find, or where.

Perdy me leuer were to weeten that, (Said he) then ran-
some of the richest knight, Or all the good that euer yet I gat:
But froward fortune, and too forward Night Such happinesse
did, maulgre, to me spight, And fro me reft both life and light
attone. But Dwarfe aread, what is that Lady bright, That
through this forest wandreth thus alone; For of her errour
straunge I haue great ruth and mone.

That Lady is (quoth he) where so she bee, The bountiest
virgin, and most debonaire, That euer liuing eye I weene did
see; Liues none this day, that may with her compare In stedfast chastitie and vertue rare, The goodly ornaments of beau-

tie bright; And is ycleped Florimell the faire, Faire Florimell belou'd of many a knight, Yet she loues none but one, that Marinell is hight.

A Sea-nymphes sonne, that Marinell is hight, Of my deare Dame is loued dearely well; In other none, but him, she sets delight, All her delight is set on Marinell; But he sets nought at all by Florimell: For Ladies loue his mother long ygoe Did him, they say, forwarne through sacred spell. But fame now flies, that of a forreine foe He is yslaine, which is the ground of all our woe.

Fiue dayes there be, since he (they say) was slaine, And foure, since Florimell the Court for-went, And vowed neuer to returne againe, Till him aliue or dead she did inuent. Therefore, faire Sir, for loue of knighthood gent, And honour of trew Ladies, if ye may By your good counsell, or bold hardiment, Or succour her, or me direct the way; Do one, or other good, I you most humbly pray.

So may ye gaine to you full great renowme, Of all good Ladies through the world so wide, And haply in her hart find highest rowme, Of whom ye seeke to be most magnifide: At least eternall meede shall you abide. To whom the Prince; Dwarfe, comfort to thee take, For till thou tidings learne, what her betide, I here auow thee neuer to forsake. Ill weares he armes, that nill them vse for Ladies sake.

So with the Dwarfe he backe return'd againe, To seeke his Lady, where he mote her find; But by the way he greatly gan complaine The want of his good Squire late left behind, For whom he wondrous pensiue grew in mind, For doubt of daunger, which mote him betide; For him he loued aboue all mankind, Hauing him trew and faithfull euer tride, And bold, as euer Squire that waited by knights side.

Who all this while full hardly was assayd Of deadly daunger, which to him betid; For whiles his Lord pursewd that noble Mayd, After that foster fowle he fiercely rid, To bene auenged of the shame, he did To that faire Damzell: Him he chaced long Through the thicke woods, wherein he would

haue hid His shamefull head from his auengement strong.
And oft him threatned death for his outrageous wrong.

Nathlesse the villen sped him selfe so well, Whether
through swiftnesse of his speedy beast, Or knowledge of those
woods, where he did dwell, That shortly he from daunger
was releast, And out of sight escaped at the least; Yet not escaped from the dew reward Of his bad deeds, which dayly he
increast, Ne ceased not, till him oppressed hard The heauy
plague, that for such leachours is prepard.

For soone as he was vanisht out of sight, His coward courage gan emboldned bee, And cast t'auenge him of that fowle
despight, Which he had borne of his bold enimee. Tho to his
brethren came: for they were three Vngratious children of
one gracelesse sire, And vnto them complained, how that he
Had vsed bene of that foolehardy Squire; So them with bitter
words he stird to bloudy ire.

Forthwith themselues with their sad instruments Of
spoyle and murder they gan arme byliue, And with him forth
into the forest went, To wreake the wrath, which he did earst
reuiue In their sterne brests, on him which late did driue
Their brother to reproch and shamefull flight: For they had
vow'd, that neuer he aliue Out of that forest should escape
their might; Vile rancour their rude harts had fild with such
despight.

Within that wood there was a couert glade, Foreby a narrow foord, to them well knowne, Through which it was vneath
for wight to wade; And now by fortune it was ouerflowne:
By that same way they knew that Squire vnknowne Mote
algates passe; for thy, themselues they set There in await,
with thicke woods ouer growne, And all the while their malice they did whet With cruell threats, his passage through
the ford to let.

It fortuned, as they deuized had, The gentle Squire came
ryding that same way, Vnweeting of their wile and treason
bad, And through the ford to passen did assay; But that fierce
foster, which late fled away, Stoutly forth stepping on the

further shore, Him boldly bad his passage there to stay, Till he had made amends, and full restore For all the damage, which he had him doen afore.

With that at him a quiu'ring dart he threw, With so fell force and villeinous despighte, That through his haberieon the forkehead flew, And through the linked mayles empierced quite, But had no powre in his soft flesh to bite: That stroke the hardy Squire did sore displease, But more that him he could not come to smite; For by no meanes the high banke he could sease, But labour'd long in that deepe ford with vaine disease.

And still the foster with his long bore-speare Him kept from landing at his wished will; Anone one sent out of the thicket neare A cruell shaft, headed with deadly ill, And fethered with an vnlucky quill; The wicked steele stayd not, till it did light In his left thigh, and deepely did it thrill: Exceeding griefe that wound in him empight, But more that with his foes he could not come to fight.

At last through wrath and vengeaunce making way, He on the bancke arriu'd with mickle paine, Where the third brother him did sore assay, And droue at him with all his might and maine A forrest bill, which both his hands did straine; But warily he did auoide the blow, And with his speare requited him againe, That both his sides were thrilled with the throw, And a large streame of bloud out of the wound did flow.

He tombling downe, with gnashing teeth did bite The bitter earth, and bad to let him in Into the balefull house of endlesse night, Where wicked ghosts do waile their former sin. Tho gan the battell freshly to begin; For nathemore for that spectacle bad, Did th'other two their cruell vengeaunce blin, But both attonce on both sides him bestad, And load vpon him layd, his life for to haue had.

Tho when that villain he auiz'd, which late Affrighted had the fairest Florimell, Full of fiers fury, and indignant hate, To him he turned, and with rigour fell Smote him so rudely on the Pannikell, That to the chin he cleft his head in twaine: Downe on the ground his carkas groueling fell; His sinfull soule with desperate disdaine, Out of her fleshly ferme fled to the place of paine.

That seeing now the onely last of three, Who with that wicked shaft him wounded had, Trembling with horrour, as that did foresee The fearefull end of his auengement sad, Through which he follow should his brethren bad, His bootelesse bow in feeble hand vpcaught, And therewith shot an arrow at the lad; Which faintly fluttring, scarce his helmet raught, And glauncing fell to ground, but him annoyed naught.

With that he would haue fled into the wood; But Timias him lightly ouerhent, Right as he entring was into the flood, And strooke at him with force so violent, That headlesse him into the foord he sent: The carkas with the streame was carried downe, But th'head fell backeward on the continent. So mischief fel vpon the meaners crowne; They three be dead with shame, the Squire liues with renowne.

He liues, but takes small ioy of his renowne; For of that cruell wound he bled so sore, That from his steed he fell in deadly swowne; Yet still the bloud forth gusht in so great store, That he lay wallowd all in his owne gore. Now God thee keepe, thou gentlest Squire aliue, Else shall thy louing Lord thee see no more, But both of comfort him thou shalt depriue, And eke thy selfe of honour, which thou didst atchiue.

Prouidence heauenly passeth liuing thought, And doth for wretched mens reliefe make way; For loe great grace or fortune thither brought Comfort to him, that comfortlesse now lay. In those same woods, ye well remember may, How that a noble hunteresse did wonne, She, that base Braggadochio did affray, And made him fast out of the forrest runne; Belphoebe was her name, as faire as Phoebus sunne.

She on a day, as she pursewd the chace Of some wild beast, which with her arrowes keene She wounded had, the same along did trace By tract of bloud, which she had freshly seene, To haue besprinckled all the grassy greene; By the great persue, which she there perceau'd, Well hoped she the beast engor'd had beene, And made more hast, the life to haue bereau'd: But ah, her expectation greatly was deceau'd.

Shortly she came, whereas that woefull Squire With bloud deformed, lay in deadly swownd: In whose faire eyes, like lamps of quenched fire, The Christall humour stood congealed rownd; His locks, like faded leaues fallen to grownd, Knotted with bloud, in bounches rudely ran, And his sweete lips, on which before that stownd The bud of youth to blossome faire began, Spoild of their rosie red, were woxen pale and wan.

Saw neuer liuing eye more heauy sight, That could haue made a rocke of stone to rew, Or riue in twaine: which when that Lady bright Besides all hope with melting eyes did vew, All suddeinly abasht she chaunged hew, And with sterne horrour backward gan to start: But when she better him beheld, she grew Full of soft passion and vnwonted smart: The point of pitty perced through her tender hart.

Meekely she bowed downe, to weete if life Yet in his frosen members did remaine, And feeling by his pulses beating rife, That the weake soule her seat did yet retaine, She cast to comfort him with busie paine: His double folded necke she reard vpright, And rubd his temples, and each trembling vaine; His mayled haberieon she did vndight, And from his head his heauy burganet did light.

Into the woods thenceforth in hast she went, To seeke for hearbes, that mote him remedy; For she of hearbes had great intendiment, Taught of the Nymphe, which from her infancy Her nourced had in trew Nobility: There, whether it diuine Tobacco were, Or Panachæa, or Polygony, She found, and brought it to her patient deare Who al this while lay bleeding out his hart-bloud neare.

The soueraigne weede betwixt two marbles plaine She pownded small, and did in peeces bruze, And then atweene her lilly handes twaine, Into his wound the iuyce thereof did scruze, And round about, as she could well it vze, The flesh therewith she suppled and did steepe, T'abate all spasme, and soke the swelling bruze, And after hauing searcht the intuse deepe, She with her scarfe did bind the wound frō cold to keepe.

By this he had sweete life recur'd againe, And groning inly deepe, at last his eyes, His watry eyes, drizling like deawy raine, He vp gan lift toward the azure skies, From whence descend all hopelesse remedies: Therewith he sigh'd, and turning him aside, The goodly Mayd full of diuinities, And gifts of heauenly grace he by him spide, Her bow and gilden quiuer lying him beside.

Mercy deare Lord (said he) what grace is this, That thou hast shewed to me sinfull wight, To send thine Angell from her bowre of blis, To comfort me in my distressed plight? Angell, or Goddesse do I call thee right? What seruice may I do vnto thee meete, That hast from darkenesse me returnd to light, And with thy heauenly salues and med'cines sweete, Hast drest my sinfull wounds? I kisse thy blessed feete.

Thereat she blushing said, Ah gentle Squire, Nor Goddesse I, nor Angell, but the Mayd, And daughter of a woody Nymphe, desire No seruice, bu tthy safety and ayd; Which if thou gaine, I shalbe well apayd. We mortall wights, whose liues and fortunes bee To commun accidents still open layd, Are bound with commun bond of frailtee, To succour wretched wights, whom we captiued see.

By this her Damzels, which the former chace Had vndertaken after her, arriu'd, As did Belphoebe, in the bloudy place, And thereby deemd the beast had bene depriu'd Of life, whom late their Ladies arrow ryu'd: For thy, the bloudy tract they follow fast, And euery one to runne the swiftest stryu'd; But two of them the rest far ouerpast, And where their Lady was, arriued at the last.

Where when they saw that goodly boy, with blood Defowled, and their Lady dresse his wownd, They wondred much, and shortly vnderstood, How him in deadly case their Lady fownd, And reskewed out of the heauy stownd.

Eftsoones his warlike courser, which was strayd Farre in the woods, whiles that he lay in swownd, She made those Damzels search, which being stayd, They did him set thereon, and forthwith them conuayd.

Into that forest farre they thence him led, Where was their dwelling, in a pleasant glade, With mountaines round about enuironed, And mighty woods, which did the valley shade, And like a stately Theatre it made, Spreading it selfe into a spatious plaine. And in the midst a little riuer plaide Emongst the pumy stones, which seemd to plaine With gentle murmure, that his course they did restraine.

Beside the same a dainty place there lay, Planted with mirtle trees and laurels greene, In which the birds song many a louely lay Of gods high prayse, and of their loues sweet teene, As it an earthly Paradize had beene: In whose enclosed shadow there was pight A faire Pauilion, scarcely to be seene, The which was all within most richly dight, That greatest Princes liuing it mote well delight.

Thither they brought that wounded Squire, and layd In easie couch his feeble limbes to rest, He rested him a while, and then the Mayd His ready wound with better salues new drest; Dayly she dressed him, and did the best His grieuous hurt to garish, that she might, That shortly she his dolour hath redrest, And his foule sore reduced to faire plight: It she reduced, but himselfe destroyed quight.

O foolish Physick, and vnfruitfull paine, That heales vp one and makes another wound: She his hurt thigh to him recur'd againe, But hurt his hart, the which before was sound, Through an vnwary dart, which did rebound From her faire eyes and gracious countenaunce. What bootes it him from death to be vnbound, To be captiued in endlesse duraunce Of sorrow and despaire without aleggeaunce?

Still as his wound did gather, and grow hole, So still his hart woxe sore, and health decayd: Madnesse to saue a part, and lose the whole. Still whenas he beheld the heauenly Mayd, Whiles dayly plaisters to his wound she layd, So

still his Malady the more increast, The whiles her matchlesse beautie him dismayd. Ah God, what other could he do
at least, But loue so faire a Lady, that his life release?

Long while he stroue in his courageous brest, With reason dew the passion to subdew, And loue for to dislodge
out of his nest: Still when her excellencies he did vew, Her
soueraigne bounty, and celestiall hew, The same to loue he
strongly was constraind: But when his meane estate he did
reuew, He from such hardy boldnesse was restraind, And of
his lucklesse lot and cruell loue thus plaind.

Vnthankfull wretch (said he) is this the meed, With which
her soueraigne mercy thou doest quight? Thy life she saued
by her gracious deed, But thou doest weene with villeinous
despight, To blot her honour, and her heauenly light. Dye
rather, dye, then so disloyally Deeme of her high desert, or
seeme so light: Faire death it is to shonne more shame, to dy:
Dye rather, dy, then euer loue disloyally.

But if to loue disloyalty it bee, Shall I then hate her, that
from deathes dore Me brought? ah farre be such reproch fro
mee. What can I lesse do, then her loue therefore, Sith I her
dew reward cannot restore: Dye rather, dye, and dying do
her serue, Dying her serue, and liuing her adore; Thy life she
gaue, thy life she doth deserue: Dye rather, dye, then euer
from her seruice swerue.

But foolish boy, what bootes thy seruice bace To her, to
whom the heauens do serue and sew? Thou a meane Squire,
of meeke and lowly place, She heauenly borne, and of celestiall hew. How then? of all loue taketh equall vew: And doth
not highest God vouchsafe to take The loue and seruice of
the basest crew? If she will not, dye meekly for her sake; Dye
rather, dye, then euer so faire loue forsake.

Thus warreid he long time against his will, Till that
through weaknesse he was forst at last, To yield himselfe
vnto the mighty ill: Which as a victour proud, gan ransack
fast His inward parts, and all his entrayles wast, That neither bloud in face, nor life in hart It left, but both did quite

drye vp, and blast; As percing leuin, which the inner part Of euery thing consumes, and calcineth by art.

Which seeing faire Belphoebe, gan to feare, Least that his wound were inly well not healed, Or that the wicked steele empoysned were: Litle she weend, that loue he close concealed; Yet still he wasted, as the snow congealed, When the bright sunne his beams thereon doth beat; Yet neuer he his hart to her reuealed, But rather chose to dye for sorrow great, Then with dishonorable termes her to entreat.

She gracious Lady, yet no paines did spare, To do him ease, or do him remedy: Many Restoratiues of vertues rare, And costly Cordialles she did apply, To mitigate his stubborne mallady: But that sweet Cordiall, which can restore A loue-sick hart, she did to him enuy; To him, and to all th'vnworthy world forlore She did enuy that soueraigne salue, in secret store.

That dainty Rose, the daughter of her Morne, More deare then life she tendered, whose flowre The girlond of her honour did adorne: Ne suffred she the Middayes scorching powre, Ne the sharp Northerne wind thereon to showre, But lapped vp her silken leaues most chaire, When so the froward skye began to lowre: But soone as calmed was the Christall aire, She did it faire dispred, and let to florish faire.

Eternall God in his almighty powre, To make ensample of his heauenly grace, In Paradize whilome did plant this flowre, Whence he it fetcht out of her natiue place, And did in stocke of earthly flesh enrace, That mortall men her glory should admire In gentle Ladies brest, and bounteous race Of woman kind it fairest flowre doth spire, And beareth fruit of honour and all chast desire.

Faire ympes of beautie, whose bright shining beames Adorne the world with like to heauenly light, And to your willes both royalties and Realmes Subdew, through conquest of your wondrous might, With this faire flowre your goodly girlonds dight, Of chastity and vertue virginall, That shall embellish more your beautie bright, And crowne your heades with heauenly coronall, Such as the Angels weare before Gods tribunall.

To youre faire selues a faire ensample frame, Of this faire virgin, this Belphoebe faire, To whom in perfect loue, and spotlesse fame, Of chastitie, none liuing may compaire: Ne poysnous Enuy iustly can empaire The prayse of her fresh flowring Maidenhead; For thy, she standeth on the highest staire Of th'honorable stage of womanhead, That Ladies all may follow her ensample dead.

In so great prayse of stedfast chastity, Nathlesse she was so curteous and kind, Tempred with grace, and goodly modesty, That seemed those two vertues stroue to find The higher place in her Heroick mind: So striuing each did other more augment, And both encreast the prayse of woman kind, And both encreast her beautie excellent; So all did make in her a perfect complement.

Cant. VI.

The birth of faire Belphoebe and Of Amoret is told. The Gardins of Adonis fraught With pleasures manifold.

VV Ell may I weene, faire Ladies, all this while Ye wonder, how this noble Damozell So great perfections did in her compile, Sith that in saluage forests she did dwell, So farre from court and royall Citadell, The great schoolmistresse of all curtesy: Seemeth that such wild woods should far expell All ciuill vsage and gentility, And gentle sprite deforme with rude rusticity. But to this faire Belphoebe in her berth The heauens so fauourable were and free, Looking with myld aspect vpon the earth, In th'Horoscope of her natiuitee, That all the gifts of grace and chastitee On her they poured forth of plenteous horne; Ioue laught on Venus from his soueraigne see, And Phoebus with faire beames did her adorne, And all the Graces rockt her cradle being borne.

Her berth was of the wombe of Morning dew, And her conception of the ioyous Prime, And all her whole creation did her shew Pure and vnspotted from all loathly crime, That is ingenerate in fleshly slime. So was this virgin borne, so was she bred, So was she trayned vp from time to time, In all chast vertue, and true bounti-hed Till to her dew perfection she was ripened.

Her mother was the faire Chrysogonee, The daughter of Amphisa, who by race A Faerie was, yborne of high degree, She bore Belphoebe, she bore in like cace Faire Amoretta in the second place: These two were twinnes, & twixt them two did share The heritage of all celestiall grace. That all the rest it seem'd they robbed bare Of bountie, and of beautie, and all vertues rare.

It were a goodly storie, to declare, By what straunge accident faire Chrysogone Conceiu'd these infants, and how them she bare, In this wild forrest wandring all alone, After she had nine moneths fulfild and gone: For not as other wemens commune brood, They were enwombed in the sacred throne Of her chaste bodie, nor with commune food, As other wemens babes, they sucked vitall blood.

But wondrously they were begot, and bred Through influence of th'heauens fruitfull ray, As it in antique bookes is mentioned. It was vpon a Sommers shynie day, When Titan faire his beames did display, In a fresh fountaine, farre from all mens vew, She bath'd her brest, the boyling heat t'allay; She bath'd with roses red, and violets blew, And all the sweetest flowres, that in the forrest grew.

Till faint through irkesome wearinesse, adowne Vpon the grassie ground her selfe she layd To sleepe, the whiles a gentle slombring swowne Vpon her fell all naked bare displayd; The sunne-beames bright vpon her body playd, Being through former bathing mollifide, And pierst into her wombe, where they embayd With so sweet sence and secret power vnspide, That in her pregnant flesh they shortly fructifide.

Miraculous may seeme to him, that reades So straunge ensample of conception; But reason teacheth that the fruitfull seades Of all things liuing, through impression Of the sun-beames in moyst complexion, Doe life conceiue and quickned are by kynd: So after Nilus invndation, Infinite shapes of

creatures men do fynd, Informed in the mud, on which the
Sunne hath shynd.

Great father he of generation Is rightly cald, th'author
of life and light; And his faire sister for creation Ministreth
matter fit, which tempred right With heate and humour,
breedes the liuing wight. So sprong these twinnes in wombe
of Chrysogone, Yet wist she nought thereof, but sore affright,
Wondred to see her belly so vpblone, Which still increast, till
she her terme had full outgone.

Whereof conceiuing shame and foule disgrace, Albe her
guiltlesse conscience her cleard, She fled into the wildernesse a space, Till that vnweeldy burden she had reard, And
shund dishonor, which as death she feard: Where wearie of
long trauell, downe to rest Her selfe she set, and comfortably
cheard; There a sad cloud of sleepe her ouerkest, And seized
euery sense with sorrow sore opprest.

It fortuned, faire Venus hauing lost Her little sonne, the
winged god of loue, Who for some light displeasure, which
him crost, Was from her fled, as flit as ayerie Doue, And left
her blisfull bowre of ioy aboue, (So from her often he had fled
away, When she for ought him sharpely did reproue, And
wandred in the world in strange aray, Disguiz'd in thousand
shapes, that none might him bewray.)

Him for to seeke, she left her heauenly hous, The house of
goodly formes and faire aspects, Whence all the world deriues
the glorious Features of beautie, and all shapes select, With
which high God his workmanship hath deckt; And searched
euery way, through which his wings Had borne him, or his
tract she mote detect: She promist kisses sweet, and sweeter
things Vnto the man, that of him tydings to her brings.

First she him sought in Court, where most he vsed Whylome to haunt, but there she found him not; But many there
she found, which sore accused His falsehood, and with foule
infamous blot His cruell deedes and wicked wyles did spot:
Ladies and Lords she euery where mote heare Complayning,
how with his empoysned shot Their wofull harts he wounded

had whyleare, And so had left them languishing twixt hope and feare.

She then the Citties sought from gate to gate, And euery one did aske, did he him see; And euery one her answerd, that too late He had him seene, and felt the crueltie Of his sharpe darts and whot artillerie; And euery one threw forth reproches rife Of his mischieuous deedes, and said, that hee Was the disturber of all ciuill life, The enimy of peace, and author of all strife.

Then in the countrey she abroad him sought, And in the rurall cottages inquired, Where also many plaints to her were brought, How he their heedlesse harts with loue had fyred, And his false venim through their veines inspyred; And eke the gentle shepheard swaynes, which sat Keeping their flee-cie flockes, as they were hyred, She sweetly heard complaine, both how and what Her sonne had to them doen; yet she did smile thereat.

But when in none of all these she him got, She gan auize, where else he mote him hyde: At last she her bethought, that she had not Yet sought the saluage woods and forrests wyde, In which full many louely Nymphes abyde, Mongst whom might be, that he did closely lye, Or that the loue of some of them him tyde: For thy, she thither cast her course t'apply, To search the secret haunts of Dianes company.

Shortly vnto the wastefull woods she came, Whereas she found the Goddesse with her crew, After late chace of their embrewed game, Sitting beside a fountaine in a rew, Some of them washing with the liquid dew From off their dainty limbes the dustie sweat, And soyle which did deforme their liuely hew; Others lay shaded from the scorching heat; The rest vpon her person gaue attendance great.

She hauing hong vpon a bough on high Her bow and painted quiuer, had vnlaste Her siluer buskins from her nim-ble thigh, And her lancke loynes vngirt, and brests vnbraste, After her heat the breathing cold to taste; Her golden lockes, that late in tresses bright Embreaded were for hindring of her haste, Now loose about her shoulders hong vndight, And were with sweet Ambrosia all besprinckled light.

Soone as she Venus saw behind her backe, She was asham'd to be so loose surprized, And woxe halfe wroth against her damzels slacke, That had not her thereof before auized, But suffred her so carelesly disguized Be ouertaken. Soone her garments loose Vpgath'ring, in her bosome she comprized, Well as she might, and to the Goddesse rose, Whiles all her Nymphes did like a girlond her enclose.

Goodly she gan faire Cytherea greet, And shortly asked her, what cause her brought Into that wildernesse for her vnmeet, From her sweet bowres, and beds with pleasures fraught: That suddein change she strange aduenture thought. To whom halfe weeping, she thus answered, That she her dearest sonne Cupido sought, Who in his frowardnesse from her was fled; That she repented sore, to haue him angered.

Thereat Diana gan to smile, in scorne Of her vaine plaint, and to her scoffing sayd; Great pittie sure, that ye be so forlorne Of your gay sonne, that giues ye so good ayd To your disports: ill mote ye bene apayd. But she was more engrieued, and replide; Faire sister, ill beseemes it to vpbrayd A dolefull heart with so disdainfull pride; The like that mine, may be your paine another tide.

As you in woods and wanton wildernesse Your glory set, to chace the saluage beasts, So my delight is all in ioyfulnesse, In beds, in bowres, in banckets, and in feasts: And ill becomes you with your loftie creasts, To scorne the ioy, that Ioue is glad to seeke; We both are bound to follow heauens beheasts, And tend our charges with obeisance meeke: Spare, gentle sister, with reproch my paine to eeke.

And tell me, if that ye my sonne haue heard, To lurke emongst your Nymphes in secret wize; Or keepe their cabins: much I am affeard, Least he like one of them him selfe disguize, And turne his arrowes to their exercize: So may he long himselfe full easie hide: For he is faire and fresh in face and guize, As any Nymph (let not it be enuyde,) So saying euery Nymph full narrowly she eyde.

But Phoebe therewith sore was angered, And sharply said; Goe Dame, goe seeke your boy, Where you him lately left, in Mars his bed; He comes not here, we scorne his foolish ioy, Ne lend we leisure to his idle toy: But if I catch him in this company, By Stygian lake I vow, whose sad annoy The Gods doe dread, he dearely shall abye: Ile clip his wanton wings, that he no more shall fly.

Whom when as Venus saw so sore displeased, She inly sory was, and gan relent, What she had said: so her she soone appeased, With sugred words and gentle blandishment, Which as a fountaine from her sweet lips went, And welled goodly forth, that in short space She was well pleasd, and forth her damzels sent, Through all the woods, to search from place to place, If any tract of him or tydings they mote trace.

To search the God of loue, her Nymphes she sent Throughout the wandring forrest euery where: And after them her selfe eke with her went To seeke the fugitiue, both farre and nere, So long they sought, till they arriued were In that same shadie couert, whereas lay Faire Crysogone in slombry traunce whilere: Who in her sleepe (a wondrous thing to say) Vnwares had borne two babes, as faire as springing day.

Vnwares she them conceiu'd, vnwares she bore: She bore withouten paine, that she conceiued Withouten pleasure: ne her need implore Lucinaes aide: which when they both perceiued, They were through wonder nigh of sense bereaued, And gazing each on other, nought bespake: At last they both agreed, her seeming grieued Out of her heauy swowne not to awake, But from her louing side the tender babes to take.

Vp they them tooke, each one a babe vptooke, And with them carried, to be fostered; Dame Phoebe to a Nymph her babe betooke, To be vpbrought in perfect Maydenhed, And of her selfe her name Belphoebe red: But Venus hers thence farre away conuayd, To be vpbrought in goodly womanhed, And in her litle loues stead, which was strayd, Her Amoretta cald, to comfort her dismayd.

She brought her to her ioyous Paradize, Where most she wonnes, whe she on earth does dwel. So faire a place, as Nature can deuize: Whether in Paphos, or Cytheron hill, Or it in Gnidus be, I wote not well; But well I wote by tryall, that this same All other pleasant places doth excell, And called is by her lost louers name, The Gardin of Adonis, farre renowmd by fame.

In that same Gardin all the goodly flowres, Wherewith dame Nature doth her beautifie, And decks the girlonds of her paramoures, Are fetcht: there is the first seminarie Of all things, that are borne to liue and die, According to their kindes. Long worke it were, Here to account the endlesse progenie Of all the weedes, that bud and blossome there; But so much as doth need, must needs be counted here.

It sited was in fruitfull soyle of old, And girt in with two walles on either side; The one of yron, the other of bright gold, That none might thorough breake, nor ouer-stride: And double gates it had, which opened wide, By which both in and out men moten pas; Th'one faire and fresh, the other old and dride: Old Genius the porter of them was, Old Genius, the which a double nature has.

He letteth in, he letteth out to wend, All that to come into the world desire; A thousand thousand naked babes attend About him day and night, which doe require, That he with fleshly weedes would them attire: Such as him list, such as eternall fate Ordained hath, he clothes with sinfull mire, And sendeth forth to liue in mortall state, Till they againe returne backe by the hinder gate.

After that they againe returned beene, They in that Gardin planted be againe; And grow afresh, as they had neuer seene Fleshly corruption, nor mortall paine. Some thousand yeares so doen they there remaine; And then of him are clad with other hew, Or sent into the chaungefull world againe, Till thither they returne, where first they grew: So like a wheele around they runne from old to new.

Ne needs there Gardiner to set, or sow, To plant or prune: for of their owne accord All things, as they created were, doe grow, And yet remember well the mightie word, Which first was spoken by th'Almightie lord, That bad them to increase and multiply: Ne doe they need with water of the ford, Or of the clouds to moysten their roots dry; For in themselues eternall moisture they imply.

Infinite shapes of creatures there are bred, And vncouth formes, which none yet euer knew, And euery sort is in a sundry bed Set by it selfe, and ranckt in comely rew: Some fit for reasonable soules t'indew, Some made for beasts, some made for birds to weare, And all the fruitfull spawne of fishes hew In endlesse rancks along enraunged were, That seem'd the Ocean could not containe them there.

Daily they grow, and daily forth are sent Into the world, it to replenish more; Yet is the stocke not lessened, nor spent, But still remaines in euerlasting store, As it at first created was of yore. For in the wide wombe of the world there lyes, In hatefull darkenesse and in deepe horrore, An huge eternall Chaos, which supplyes The substances of natures fruitfull progenyes.

All things from thence doe their first being fetch, And borrow matter, whereof they are made, Which when as forme and feature it does ketch, Becomes a bodie, and doth then inuade The state of life, out of the griesly shade. That substance is eterne, and bideth so, Ne when the life decayes, and forme does fade, Doth it consume, and into nothing go, But chaunged is, and often altred to and fro.

The substance is not chaunged, nor altered, But th'only forme and outward fashion; For euery substance is conditioned To change her hew, and sundry formes to don, Meet for her temper and complexion: For formes are variable and decay, By course of kind, and by occasion; And that faire flowre of beautie fades away, As doth the lilly fresh before the sunny ray.

Great enimy to it, and to all the rest, That in the Gardin of Adonis springs, Is wicked Time, who with his scyth addrest, Does mow the flowring herbes and goodly things, And all their glory to the ground downe flings, Where they doe wither, and are fowly mard: He flyes about, and with his flaggy wings Beates downe both leaues and buds without regard, Ne euer pittie may relent his malice hard.

Yet pittie often did the gods relent, To see so faire things mard, and spoyled quight: And their great mother Venus did lament The losse of her deare brood, her deare delight: Her hart was pierst with pittie at the sight, When walking through the Gardin, them she spyde, Yet no'te she find redresse for such despight. For all that liues, is subiect to that law: All things decay in time, and to their end do draw.

But were it not, that Time their troubler is, All that in this delightfull Gardin growes, Should happie be, and haue immortall blis: For here all plentie, and all pleasure flowes, And sweet loue gentle fits emongst them throwes, Without fell rancor, or fond gealosie; Franckly each paramour his leman knowes, Each bird his mate, ne any does enuie Their goodly meriment, and gay felicitie.

There is continuall spring, and haruest there Continuall, both meeting at one time: For both the boughes doe laughing blossomes beare, And with fresh colours decke the wanton Prime, And eke attonce the heauy trees they clime, Which seeme to labour vnder their fruits lode: The whiles the ioyous birdes make their pastime Emongst the shadie leaues, their sweet abode, And their true loues without suspition tell abrode.

Right in the middest of that Paradise, There stood a stately Mount, on whose round top A gloomy groue of mirtle trees did rise, Whose shadie boughes sharpe steele did neuer lop, Nor wicked beasts their tender buds did crop, But like a girlond compassed the hight, And from their fruitfull sides sweet gum did drop, That all the ground with precious deaw bedight, Threw forth most dainty odours, & most sweet delight.

And in the thickest couert of that shade, There was a pleasant arbour, not by art, But of the trees owne inclination made, Which knitting their rancke braunches part to part, With wanton yuie twyne entrayld athwart, And Eglantine, and Caprifole emong, Fashiond aboue within their inmost part, That nether Phoebus beams could through the throng, Nor Aeolus sharp blast could worke them any wrong.

And all about grew euery sort of flowre, To which sad louers were transformd of yore; Fresh Hyacinthus, Phoebus paramoure, And dearest loue: Foolish Narcisse, that likes the watry shore, Sad Amaranthus, made a flowre but late, Sad Amaranthus, in whose purple gore Me seemes I see Amintas wretched fate, To whom sweet Poets verse hath giuen endlesse date.

There wont faire Venus often to enioy Her deare Adonis ioyous company, And reape sweet pleasure of the wanton boy; There yet, some say, in secret he does ly, Lapped in flowres and pretious spycery, By her hid from the world, and from the skill Of Stygian Gods, which doe her loue enuy; But she her selfe, when euer that she will, Possesseth him, and of his sweetnesse takes her fill.

And sooth it seemes they say: for he may not For euer die, and euer buried bee In balefull night, where all things are forgot; All be he subiect to mortalitie, Yet is eterne in mutabilitie, And by succession made perpetuall, Transformed oft, and chaunged diuerslie: For him the Father of all formes they call; Therefore needs mote he liue, that liuing giues to all.

There now he liueth in eternall blis, Ioying his goddesse, and of her enioyd: Ne feareth he henceforth that foe of his, Which with his cruell tuske him deadly cloyd: For that wilde Bore, the which him once annoyd, She firmely hath emprisoned for ay, That her sweet loue his malice mote auoyd, In a strong rocky Caue, which is they say, Hewen vnderneath that Mount, that none him losen may.

There now he liues in euerlasting ioy, With many of the

Gods in company, Which thither haunt, and with the winged boy Sporting himselfe in safe felicity: Who when he hath with spoiles and cruelty Ransackt the world, and in the wofull harts Of many wretches set his triumphes hye, Thither resorts, and laying his sad darts Aside, with faire Adonis playes his wanton parts.

And his true loue faire Psyche with him playes, Faire Psyche to him lately reconcyld, After long troubles and vnmeet vpbrayes, With which his mother Venus her reuyld, And eke himselfe her cruelly exyld: But now in stedfast loue and happy state She with him liues, and hath him borne a chyld, Pleasure, that doth both gods and men aggrate, Pleasure, the daughter of Cupid and Psyche late.

Hither great Venus brought this infant faire, The younger daughter of Chrysogonee, And vnto Psyche with great trust and care Committed her, yfostered to bee, And trained vp in true feminitee: Who no lesse carefully her tendered, Then her owne daughter Pleasure, to whom shee Made her companion, and her lessoned In all the lore of loue, and goodly womanhead.

In which when she to perfect ripenesse grew, Of grace and beautie noble Paragone, She brought her forth into the worldes vew, To be th'ensample of true loue alone, And Lodestarre of all chaste affectione, To all faire Ladies, that doe liue on ground. To Faery court she came, where many one Admyrd her goodly haueour, and found His feeble hart wide launched with loues cruell wound.

But she to none of them her loue did cast, Saue to the noble knight Sir Scudamore, To whom her louing hart she linked fast In faithfull loue, t'abide for euer more, And for his dearest sake endured sore, Sore trouble of an hainous enimy; Who her would forced haue to haue forlore Her former loue, and stedfast loialty, As ye may elsewhere read that ruefull history.

But well I weene, ye first desire to learne, What end vnto that fearefull Damozell, Which fled so fast from that same foster stearne, Whom with his brethren Timias slew, befell: That was to weet, the goodly Florimell; Who wandring for to seeke her louer deare, Her louer deare, her dearest Marinell, Into misfortune fell, as ye did heare, And from Prince Arthur fled with wings of idle feare.

Cant. VII.

The witches sonne loues Florimell: she flyes, he faines to die. Satyrane saues the Squire of Dames from Gyants tyrannie.

L Ike as an Hynd forth singled from the heard, That hath escaped from a rauenous beast, Yet flyes away of her owne feet affeard, And euery leafe, that shaketh with the least Murmure of winde, her terror hath encreast; So fled faire Florimell from her vaine feare, Long after she from perill was release: Each shade she saw, and each noyse she did heare, Did seeme to be the same, which she escapt whyleare.

All that same euening she in flying spent, And all that night her course continewed: Ne did she let dull sleepe once to relent, Nor wearinesse to slacke her hast, but fled Euer alike, as if her former dred Were hard behind, her readie to arrest: And her white Palfrey hauing conquered The maistring raines out of her weary wrest, Perforce her carried, where euer he thought best.

So long as breath, and hable puissance Did natiue courage vnto him supply, His pace he freshly forward did aduaunce, And carried her beyond all ieopardy, But nought that wanteth rest, can long aby. He hauing through incessant trauell spent His force, at last perforce a downe did ly, Ne foot could further moue: the Lady gent Thereat was suddein strooke with great astonishment.

And forst t'alight, on foot mote algates fare, A traueller vnwonted to such way: Need teacheth her this lesson hard and rare, That fortune all in equall launce doth sway, And mortall miseries doth make her play. So long she trauelled, till at length she came To an hilles side, which did to her bewray A little valley, subiect to the same, All couerd with thick woods, that quite it ouercame.

Through the tops of the high trees she did descry A litle smoke, whose vapour thin and light, Reeking aloft, vprolled to the sky: Which, chearefull signe did send vnto her sight, That in the same did wonne some liuing wight. Eftsoones her steps she thereunto applyde, And came at last in weary wretched plight Vnto the place, to which her hope did guyde, To find some refuge there, and rest her weary syde.

There in a gloomy hollow glen she found A little cottage, built of stickes and reedes In homely wize, and wald with sods around, In which a witch did dwell, in loathly weedes, And wilfull want, all carelesse of her needes; So choosing solitarie to abide, Far from all neighbours, that her deuilish deedes And hellish arts from people she might hide, And hurt far off vnknowne, whom euer she enuide.

The Damzell there arriuing entred in; Where sitting on the flore the Hag she found, Busie (as seem'd) about some wicked gin: Who soone as she beheld that suddein stound, Lightly vpstarted from the dustie ground, And with fell looke and hollow deadly gaze Stared on her awhile, as one astound, Ne had one word to speake, for great amaze, But shewd by outward signes, that dread her sence did daze.

At last turning her feare to foolish wrath, She askt, what deuill had her thither brought, And who she was, and what vnwonted path Had guided her, vnwelcomed, vnsought? To which the Damzell full of doubtfull thought, Her mildly answer'd; Beldame be not wroth With silly Virgin by aduenture brought Vnto your dwelling, ignorant and loth, That craue but rowme to rest, while tempest ouerblo'th.

With that adowne out of her Christall eyne Few trickling teares she softly forth let fall, That like two Orient pearles, did purely shyne Vpon her snowy cheeke; and therewithall She sighed soft, that none so bestiall, Nor saluage hart, but ruth of her sad plight Would make to melt, or pitteously appall; And that vile Hag, all were her whole delight In mischiefe, was much moued at so pitteous sight.

And gan recomfort her in her rude wyse, With womanish compassion of her plaint, Wiping the teares from her suffused eyes, And bidding her sit downe, to rest her faint And wearie limbs a while. She nothing quaint Nor s'deignfull of so homely fashion, Sith brought she was now to so hard constraint, Sate downe vpon the dusty ground anon, As glad of that small rest, as Bird of tempest gon.

Tho gan she gather vp her garments rent, And her loose lockes to dight in order dew, With golden wreath and gorgeous ornament; Whom such whenas the wicked Hag did vew, She was astonisht at her heauenly hew, And doubted her to deeme an earthly wight, But or some Goddesse, or of Dianes crew, And thought her to adore with humble spright; T'adore thing so diuine as beauty, were but right.

This wicked woman had a wicked sonne, The comfort of her age and weary dayes, A laesie loord, for nothing good to donne, But stretched forth in idlenesse alwayes, Ne euer cast his mind to couet prayse, Or ply him selfe to any honest trade, But all the day before the sunny rayes He vs'd to slug, or sleepe in slothfull shade: Such laesinesse both lewd and poore attonce him made.

He comming home at vndertime, there found The fairest creature, that he euer saw, Sitting beside his mother on the ground; The sight whereof did greatly him adaw, And his base thought with terrour and with aw So inly smot, that as one, which had gazed On the bright Sunne vnwares, doth soone withdraw His feeble eyne, with too much brightnesse dazed, So stared he on her, and stood long while amazed.

Softly at last he gan his mother aske, What mister wight that was, and whence deriued, That in so straunge disguizement there did maske, And by what accident she there arriued: But she, as one nigh of her wits depriued, With nought but ghastly lookes him answered, Like to a ghost, that lately is reuiued From Stygian shores, where late it wandered; So both at her, and each at other wondered.

But the faire Virgin was so meeke and mild, That she

to them vouchsafed to embace Her goodly port, and to their senses vild, Her gentle speach applide, that in short space She grew familiare in that desert place. During which time, the Chorle through her so kind And curteise vse conceiu'd affection bace, And cast to loue her in his brutish mind; No loue, but brutish lust, that was so beastly tind.

Closely the wicked flame his bowels brent, And shortly grew into outrageous fire; Yet had he not the hart, nor hardiment, As vnto her to vtter his desire; His caytiue thought durst not so high aspire, But with soft sighes, and louely semblaunces, He ween'd that his affection entire She should aread; many resemblaunces To her he made, and many kind remembraunces.

Oft from the forrest wildings he did bring, Whose sides empurpled were with smiling red, And oft young birds, which he had taught to sing His mistresse prayses, sweetly caroled, Girlonds of flowres sometimes for her faire hed He fine would dight; sometimes the squirell wild He brought to her in bands, as conquered To be her thrall, his fellow seruant vild; All which, she of him tooke with countenance meeke and mild.

But past awhile, when she fit season saw To leaue that desert mansion, she cast In secret wize her selfe thence to withdraw, For feare of mischiefe, which she did forecast Might by the witch or by her sonne compast: Her wearie Palfrey closely, as she might, Now well recouered after long repast, In his proud furnitures she freshly dight, His late miswandred wayes now to remeasure right.

And earely ere the dawning day appeard, She forth issewed, and on her iourney went; She went in perill, of each noyse affeard, And of each shade, that did it selfe present; For still she feared to be ouerhent, Of that vile hag, or her vnciuile sonne: Who when too late awaking, well they kent, That their faire guest was gone, they both begonne To make exceeding mone, as they had bene vndonne.

But that lewd louer did the most lament For her depart,

that euer man did heare; He knockt his brest with desperate intent, And scratcht his face, and with his teeth did teare His rugged flesh, and rent his ragged heare: That his sad mother seeing his sore plight, Was greatly woe begon, and gan to feare, Least his fraile senses were emperisht quight, And loue to frenzy turnd, sith loue is franticke hight.

All wayes she sought, him to restore to plight, With herbs, with charms, with coûsell, & with teares, But tears, nor charms, nor herbs, nor counsell might Asswage the fury, which his entrails teares: So strong is passion, that no reason heares. Tho when all other helpes she saw to faile, She turnd her selfe backe to her wicked leares And by her deuilish arts thought to preuaile, To bring her backe againe, or worke her finall bale.

Eftsoones out of her hidden caue she cald An hideous beast, of horrible aspect, That could the stoutest courage haue appald; Monstrous mishapt, and all his backe was spect With thousand spots of colours queint elect, Thereto so swift, that it all beasts did pas: Like neuer yet did liuing eye detect; But likest it to an Hyena was, That feeds on womens flesh, as others feede on gras.

It forth she cald, and gaue it streight in charge, Through thicke and thin her to pursew apace, Ne once to stay to rest, or breath at large, Till her he had attaind, and brought in place, Or quite deuourd her beauties scornefull grace. The Monster swift as word, that from her went, Went forth in hast, and did her footing trace So sure and swiftly, through his perfect scent, And passing speede, that shortly he her ouerhent.

Whom when the fearefull Damzell nigh espide, No need to bid her fast away to flie; That vgly shape so sore her terrifide, That it she shund no lesse, then dread to die, And her flit Palfrey did so well apply His nimble feet to her conceiued feare, That whilest his breath did strength to him supply, From perill free he her away did beare: But when his force gan faile, his pace gan wex areare.

Which whenas she perceiu'd, she was dismayd At that same last extremitie full sore, And of her safetie greatly grew afrayd; And now she gan approch to the sea shore, As it befell, that she could flie no more, But yield her selfe to spoile of greedinesse. Lightly she leaped, as a wight forlore, From her dull horse, in desperate distresse, And to her feet betooke her doubtfull sickernesse.

Not halfe so fast the wicked Myrrha fled From dread of her reuenging fathers hond: Nor halfe so fast to saue her maidenhed, Fled fearefull Daphne on th'Ægæan strond, As Florimell fled from that Monster yond, To reach the sea, ere she of him were raught: For in the sea to drowne her selfe she fond, Rather then of the tyrant to be caught: Thereto feare gaue her wings, and neede her courage taught.

It fortuned (high God did so ordaine) As she arriued on the roring shore, In minde to leape into the mighty maine, A little boate lay houing her before, In which there slept a fisher old and pore, The whiles his nets were drying on the sand: Into the same she leapt, and with the ore Did thrust the shallop from the floting strand: So safetie found at sea, which she found not at land.

The Monster ready on the pray to sease, Was of his forward hope deceiued quight; Ne durst assay to wade the perlous seas, But greedily long gaping at the sight, At last in vaine was forst to turne his flight, And tell the idle tidings to his Dame: Yet to auenge his deuilish despight, He set vpon her Palfrey tired lame, And slew him cruelly, ere any reskew came.

And after hauing him embowelled, To fill his hellish gorge, it chaunst a knight To passe that way, as forth he trauelled; It was a goodly Swaine, and of great might, As euer man that bloudy field did fight; But in vaine sheows, that wont yongknights bewitch, And courtly seruices tooke no delight, But rather ioyd to be, then seemen sich: For both to be and seeme to him was labour lich.

It was to weete the good Sir Satyrane, That raungd

abroad to seeke aduentures wilde, As was his wont in forrest, and in plaine; He was all armd in rugged steele vnfilde, As in the smoky forge it was compilde, And in his Scutchin bore a Satyres hed: He comming present, where the Monster vilde Vpon that milke-white Palfreyes carkas fed, Vnto his reskew ran, and greedily him sped.

There well perceiu'd he, that it was the horse, Whereon faire Florimell was wont to ride, That of that feend was rent without remorse: Much feared he, least ought did ill betide To that faire Mayd, the flowre of womens pride; For her he dearely loued, and in all His famous conquests highly magnifide: Besides her golden girdle, which did fall From her in flight, he found, that did him sore apall.

Full of sad feare, and doubtfull agony, Fiercely he flew vpon that wicked feend, And with huge strokes, and cruell battery Him forst to leaue his pray, for to attend Him selfe from deadly daunger to defend: Full many wounds in his corrupted flesh He did engraue, and muchell bloud did spend, Yet might not do him dye, but aye more fresh And fierce he still appeard, the more he did him thresh.

He wist not, how him to despoile of life, Ne how to win the wished victory, Sith him he saw still stronger grow through strife, And him selfe weaker through infirmity; Greatly he grew enrag'd, and furiously Hurling his sword away, he lightly lept Vpon the beast, that with great cruelty Rored, and raged to be vnder-kept: Yet he perforce him held, and strokes vpon him hept.

As he that striues to stop a suddein flood, And in strong banckes his violence enclose, Forceth it swell aboue his wonted mood, And largely ouerflow the fruitfull plaine, That all the countrey seemes to be a Maine, And the rich furrowes flote, all quite fordonne: The wofull husbandman doth lowd complaine, To see his whole yeares labour lost so soone, For which to God he made so many an idle boone.

So him he held, and did through might amate: So long he held him, and him bet so long, That at the last his fiercenesse gan abate, And meekely stoup vnto the victour strong: Who to auenge the implacable wrong, Which he supposed donne to Florimell, Sought by all meanes his dolour to prolong, Sith dint of steele his carcas could not quell: His maker with her charmes had framed him so well.

The golden ribband, which that virgin wore About her sclender wast, he tooke in hand, And with it bound the beast, that lowd did rore For great despight of that vnwonted band, Yet dared not his victour to withstand, But trembled like a lambe, fled from the pray, And all the way him followd on the strand, As he had long bene learned to obay; Yet neuer learned he such seruice, till that day.

Thus as he led the Beast along the way, He spide far off a mighty Giauntesse, Fast flying on a Courser dapled gray, From a bold knight, that with great hardinesse Her hard pursewd, and sought for to suppresse; She bore before her lap a dolefull Squire, Lying athwart her horse in great distresse, Fast bounden hand and foote with cords of wire, Whom she did meane to make the thrall of her desire.

Which whenas Satyrane beheld, in hast He left his captiue Beast at liberty, And crost the nearest way, by which he cast Her to encounter, ere she passed by: But she the way shund nathemore for thy, But forward gallopt fast; which when he spyde, His mighty speare he couched warily, And at her ran: she hauing him descryde, Her selfe to fight addrest, and threw her lode aside.

Like as a Goshauke, that in foote doth beare A trembling Culuer, hauing spide on hight An Egle, that with plumy wings doth sheare The subtile ayre, stouping with all his might, The quarrey throwes to ground with fell despight, And to the battell doth her selfe prepare: So ran the Geauntesse vnto the fight; Her firie eyes with furious sparkes did stare, And with blasphemous bannes high God in peeces tare.

She caught in hand an huge great yron mace, Wherewith she many had of life depriued, But ere the stroke could seize his aymed place, His speare amids her sun-broad shield arriued; Yet nathemore the steele a sunder riued, All were the beame in bignesse like a mast, Ne her out of the stedfast sadle driued, But glauncing on the tempred mettall, brast In thousand shiuers, and so forth beside her past.

Her Steed did stagger with that puissaunt strooke; But she no more was moued with that might, Then it had lighted on an aged Oke; Or on the marble Pillour, that is pight Vpon the top of Mount Olympus hight, For the braue youthly Champions to assay, With burning charet wheeles it nigh to smite: But who that smites it, mars his ioyous play, And is the spectacle of ruinous decay.

Yet therewith sore enrag'd, with sterne regard Her dreadfull weapon she to him addrest, Which on his helmet martelled so hard, That made him low incline his lofty crest, And bowd his battred visour to his brest: Wherewith he was so stund, that he n'ote ryde, But reeled to and fro from East to West: Which when his cruell enimy espyde, She lightly vnto him adioyned side to syde;

And on his collar laying puissant hand, Out of his wauering seat him pluckt perforse, Perforse him pluckt, vnable to withstand, Or helpe himselfe, and laying thwart her horse, In loathly wise like to a carion corse, She bore him fast away. Which when the knight, That her pursewed, saw with great remorse, He neare was touched in his noble spright, And gan encrease his speed, as she encreast her flight.

Whom when as nigh approching she espyde, She threw away her burden angrily; For she list not the battell to abide, But made her selfe more light, away to fly: Yet her the hardy knight pursewd so nye, That almost in the backe he oft her strake: But still when him at hand she did espy, She turnd, and semblaunce of faire fight did make; But when he stayd, to flight againe she did her take.

By this the good Sir Satyrane gan wake Out of his dreame, that did him long entraunce, And seeing none in place, he gan to make Exceeding mone, and curst that cruell chaunce, Which reft from him so faire a cheuisaunce: At length he spide, whereas that wofull Squire, Whom he had reskewed from captiuaunce Of his strong foe, lay tombled in the myre, Vnable to arise, or foot or hand to styre.

To whom approching, well he mote perceiue In that foule plight a comely personage, And louely face, made fit for to deceiue Fraile Ladies hart with loues consuming rage, Now in the blossome of his freshest age: He reard him vp, and loosd his yron bands, And after gan inquire his parentage, And how he fell into that Gyaunts hands, And who that was, which chaced her along the lands.

Then trembling yet through feare, the Squire bespake, That Geauntesse Argante is behight, A daughter of the Titans which did make Warre against heauen, and heaped hils on hight, To scale the skyes, and put Ioue from his right: Her sire Typhoeus was, who mad through merth, And drunke with bloud of men, slaine by his might, Through incest, her of his owne mother Earth Whilome begot, being but halfe twin of that berth.

For at that berth another Babe she bore, To weet the mighty Ollyphant, that wrought Great wreake to many errant knights of yore, And many hath to foule confusion brought. These twinnes, men say, (a thing far passing thought) Whiles in their mothers wombe enclosd they were, Ere they into the lightsome world were brought, In fleshly lust were mingled both yfere, And in that monstrous wise did to the world appere.

So liu'd they euer after in like sin, Gainst natures law, and good behauioure: But greatest shame was to that maiden twin, Who not content so fowly to deuoure Her natiue flesh, and staine her brothers bowre, Did wallow in all other fleshly myre, And suffred beasts her body to deflowre: So whot she burned in that lustfull fyre, Yet all that might not slake her sensuall desyre.

But ouer all the countrey she did raunge, To seeke young men, to quench her flaming thurst, And feed her fancy with delightfull chaunge: Whom so she fittest finds to serue her lust, Through her maine strength, in which she most doth trust, She with her brings into a secret Ile, Where in eternall bondage dye he must, Or be the vassall of her pleasures vile, And in all shamefull sort him selfe with her defile.

Me seely wretch she so at vauntage caught, After she long in waite for me did lye, And meant vnto her prison to haue brought, Her lothsome pleasure there to satisfye; That thousand deathes me leuer were to dye, Then breake the vow, that to faire Columbell I plighted haue, and yet keepe stedfastly: As for my name, it mistreth not to tell; Call me the Squyre of Dames that me beseemeth well.

But that bold knight, whom ye pursuing saw That Geauntesse, is not such, as she seemed, But a faire virgin, that in martiall law, And deedes of armes aboue all Dames is deemed, And aboue many knights is eke esteemed, For her great worth; she Palladine is hight: She you from death, you me from dread redeemed. Ne any may that Monster match in fight, But she, or such as she, that is so chaste a wight.

Her well beseemes that Quest (quoth Satyrane) But read, thou Squyre of Dames, what vow is this, Which thou vpon thy selfe hast lately ta'ne? That shall I you recount (quoth he) ywis, So be ye pleasd to pardon all amis. That gentle Lady, whom I loue and serue, After long suit and weary seruicis, Did aske me, how I could her loue deserue, And how she might be sure, that I would neuer swerue.

I glad by any meanes her grace to gaine, Bad her commaund my life to saue, or spill. Eftsoones she bad me, with incessaunt paine To wander through the world abroad at will, And euery where, where with my power or skill I might do seruice vnto gentle Dames, That I the same should faithfully fulfill, And at the twelue monethes end should bring their names And pledges; as the spoiles of my victorious games.

So well I to faire Ladies seruice did, And found such fauour in their louing hartes, That ere the yeare his course had compassid, Three hundred pledges for my good desartes, And thrise three hundred thanks for my good partes I with me brought, and did to her present: Which when she saw, more bent to eke my smartes, Then to reward my trusty true intent, She gan for me deuise a grieuous punishment.

To weet, that I my trauell should resume, And with like labour walke the world around, Ne euer to her presence should presume, Till I so many other Dames had found, The which, for all the suit I could propound, Would me refuse their pledges to afford, But did abide for euer chast and sound. Ah gentle Squire (quoth he) tell at one word, How many foundst thou such to put in thy record?

In deed Sir knight (said he) one word may tell All, that I euer found so wisely stayd; For onely three they were disposd so well, And yet three yeares I now abroad haue strayd, To find them out. Mote I (then laughing sayd The knight) inquire of thee, what were those three, The which thy proffred curtesie denayd? Or ill they seemed sure auizd to bee, Or brutishly brought vp, that neu'r did fashions see.

The first which then refused me (said hee) Certes was but a common Courtisane, Yet flat refusd to haue a do with mee, Because I could not giue her many a Iane. (Thereat full hartely laughed Satyrane.) The second was an holy Nunne to chose, Which would not let me be her Chappellane, Because she knew, she said, I would disclose Her counsell, if he should her trust in me repose.

The third a Damzell was of low degree, Whom I in countrey cottage found by chaunce; Full little weened I, that chastitee Had lodging in so meane a maintenaunce, Yet was she faire, and in her countenance Dwelt simple truth in seemely fashion. Long thus I woo'd her with dew obseruance, In hope vnto my pleasure to haue won; But was as farre at last, as when I first begon.

Safe her, I neuer any woman found, That chastity did for it selfe embrace, But were for other causes firme and sound; Either for want of handsome time and place, Or else for feare of shame and fowle disgrace. Thus am I hopelesse euer to attaine My Ladies loue, in such a desperate case, But all my dayes am like to wast in vaine, Seeking to match the chaste with th'vnchaste Ladies traine.

Perdy, (said Satyrane) thou Squire of Dames, Great labour fondly hast thou hent in hand, To get small thankes, and therewith many blames, That may emongst Alcides labours stand. Thence backe returning to the former land, Where late he left the Beast, he ouercame, He found him not; for he had broke his band, And was return'd againe vnto his Dame, To tell what tydings of faire Florimell became.

Cant. VIII.

The Witch creates a snowy Lady, Like to Florimell, Who wrongd by Carle by Proteus sau'd, Is sought by Paridell.

S O oft as I this history record, My hart doth melt with meere compassion, To thinke, how causelesse of her owne accord This gentle Damzell, whom I wrote vpon, Should plonged be in such affliction, Without all hope of comfort or reliefe, That sure I weene, the hardest hart of stone, Would hardly find to aggrauate her griefe; For misery craues rather mercie, then repriefe. But that accursed Hag, her hostesse late, Had so enranckled her malitious hart, That she desyrd th'abridgement of her fate, Or long enlargement of her painefull smart. Now when the Beast, which by her wicked art Late forth she sent, she backe returning spyde, Tyde with her broken girdle, it a part Of her rich spoyles, whom he had earst destroyd, She weend, and wondrous gladnesse to her hart applyde.

And with it running hast'ly to her sonne, Thought with that sight him much to haue reliued; Who thereby deeming sure the thing as donne, His former griefe with furie fresh reuiued, Much more then earst, and would haue algates riued The hart out of his brest: for sith her ded He surely dempt, himselfe he thought depriued Quite of all hope, wherewith he long had fed His foolish maladie, and long time had misled.

With thought whereof, exceeding mad he grew, And in his rage his mother would haue slaine, Had she not fled into a secret mew, Where she was wont her Sprights to entertaine

The maisters of her art: there was she faine To call them all in order to her ayde, And them coniure vpon eternall paine, To counsell her so carefully dismayd, How she might heale her sonne, whose senses were decayd.

By their aduise, and her owne wicked wit, She there deuiz'd a wondrous worke to frame, Whose like on earth was neuer framed yit, That euen Nature selfe enuide the same, And grudg'd to see the counterfet should shame The thing it selfe. In hand she boldly tooke To make another like the former Dame, Another Florimell, in shape and looke So liuely and so like, that many it mistooke.

The substance, whereof she the bodie made, Was purest snow in massie mould congeald, Which she had gathered in a shadie glade Of the Riphoean hils, to her reueald By errant Sprights, but from all men conceald: The same she tempred with fine Mercury, And virgin wex, that neuer yet was seald, And mingled them with perfect vermily, That like a liuely sanguine it seem'd to the eye.

In stead of eyes two burning lampes she set In siluer sockets, shyning like the skyes, And a quicke mouing Spirit did arret To stirre and roll them, like a womans eyes; In stead of yellow lockes she did deuise, With golden wyre to weaue her curled head; Yet golden wyre was not so yellow thrise As Florimells faire haire: and in the stead Of life, she put a Spright to rule the carkasse dead.

A wicked Spright yfraught with fawning guile, And faire resemblance aboue all the rest, Which with the Prince of Darknesse fell somewhile, From heauens blisse and euerlasting rest; Him needed not instruct, which way were best Himselfe to fashion likest Florimell, Ne how to speake, ne how to vse his gest, For he in counterfeisance did excell, And all the wyles of wemens wits knew passing well.

Him shaped thus, she deckt in garments gay, Which Florimell had left behind her late, That who so then her saw, would surely say, It was her selfe, whom it did imitate, Or fairer then her selfe, if ought algate Might fairer be. And then she forth her brought Vnto her sonne, that lay in feeble state; Who seeing her gan streight vpstart, and thought She was the Lady selfe, whom he so long had sought.

Tho fast her clipping twixt his armes twaine, Extremely ioyed in so happie sight, And soone forgot his former sickly paine; But she, the more to seeme such as she hight, Coyly rebutted his embracement light; Yet still with gentle countenaunce retained, Enough to hold a foole in vaine delight: Him long she so with shadowes entertained, As her Creatresse had in charge to her ordained.

Till on a day, as he disposed was To walke the woods with that his Idole faire, Her to disport, and idle time to pas, In th'open freshnesse of the gentle aire, A knight that way there chaunced to repaire; Yet knight he was not, but a boastfull swaine, That deedes of armes had euer in despaire, Proud Braggadocchio, that in vaunting vaine His glory did repose, and credit did maintaine.

He seeing with that Chorle so faire a wight, Decked with many a costly ornament, Much merueiled thereat, as well he might, And thought that match a fowle disparagement: His bloudie speare eftsoones he boldly bent Against the silly clowne, who dead through feare, Fell streight to ground in great astonishment; Villein (said he) this Ladie is my deare, Dy, if thou it gainesay: I will away her beare.

The fearefull Chorle durst not gainesay, nor doe, But trembling stood, and yielded him the pray; Who finding litle leasure her to wooe, On Tromparts steed her mounted without stay, And without reskew led her quite away. Proud man himselfe then Braggadocchio deemed, And next to none, after that happie day, Being possessed of that spoyle, which seemed The fairest wight on ground, and most of men esteemed.

But when he saw himselfe free from poursute, He gan make gentle purpose to his Dame, With termes of loue and lewdnesse dissolute; For he could well his glozing speaches frame To such vaine vses, that him best became: But she thereto would lend but light regard, As seeming sory, that she euer came Into his powre, that vsed her so hard, To reaue her honor, which she more then life prefard.

Thus as they two of kindnesse treated long, There them by chaunce encountred on the way An armed knight, vpon a courser strong, Whose trampling feet vpon the hollow lay Seemed to thunder, and did nigh affray That Capons courage: yet he looked grim, And fain'd to cheare his Ladie in dismay; Who seem'd for feare to quake in euery lim, And her to saue from outrage, meekely prayed him.

Fiercely that stranger forward came, and nigh Approching, with bold words and bitter threat, Bad that same boaster, as he mote, on high To leaue to him that Lady for excheat, Or bide him battell without further treat. That challenge did too peremptory seeme, And fild his senses with abashment great; Yet seeing nigh him ieopardy extreme, He it dissembled well, and light seem'd to esteeme.

Saying, Thou foolish knight, that weenst with words To steale away, that I with blowes haue wonne, And brought through points of many perilous swords: But if thee list to see thy Courser ronne, Or proue thy selfe, this sad encounter shonne, And seeke else without hazard of thy hed. At those proud words that other knight begonne To wexe exceeding wroth, and him ared To turne his steede about, or sure he should be ded.

Sith then (said Braggadocchio) needes thou wilt Thy dayes abridge, through proofe of puissance, Turne we our steedes, that both in equall tilt May meet againe, and each take happie chance. This said, they both a furlongs mountenance Retyrd their steeds, to ronne in euen race: But Braggadocchio with his bloudie lance Once hauing turnd, no more returnd his face, But left his loue to losse, and fled himselfe apace.

The knight him seeing fly, had no regard Him to poursew, but to the Ladie rode, And hauing her from Trompart lightly reard, Vpon his Courser set the louely lode, And with her fled away without abode. Well weened he, that fairest Florimell It was, with whom in company he yode, And so her selfe did alwaies to him tell; So made him thinke him selfe in heauen, that was in hell.

But Florimell her selfe was farre away, Driuen to great distresse by Fortune straunge, And taught the carefull Mariner to play, Sith late mischaunce had her compeld to chaunge The land for sea, at randon there to raunge: Yet there that cruell Queene auengeresse, Not satisfide so farre her to estraunge From courtly blisse and wonted happinesse, Did heape on her new waues of weary wretchednesse.

For being fled into the fishers bote, For refuge from the Monsters crueltie, Long so she on the mightie maine did flote, And with the tide droue forward careleslie; For th'aire was milde, and cleared was the skie, And all his windes Dan Aeolus did keepe, From stirring vp their stormy enmitie, As pittying to see her waile and weepe; But all the while the fisher did securely sleepe.

At last when droncke with drowsinesse, he woke, And saw his drouer driue along the streame, He was dismayd, and thrise his breast he stroke, For maruell of that accident extreame; But when he saw that blazing beauties beame, Which with rare light his bote did beautifie, He marueild more, and thought he yet did dreame Not well awakt, or that some extasie Assotted had his sense, or dazed was his eie.

But when her well auizing, he perceiued To be no vision, nor fantasticke sight, Great comfort of her presence he conceiued, And felt in his old courage new delight To gin awake, and stirre his frozen spright: Tho rudely askt her, how she thither came. Ah (said she) father, I note read aright, What hard misfortune brought me to the same; Yet am I glad that here I now in safety am.

But thou good man, sith farre in sea we bee, And the great waters gin apace to swell, That now no more we can the maine-land see, Haue care, I pray, to guide the cock-bote well, Least worse on sea then vs on land befell. Thereat th'old man did nought but fondly grin, And said, his boat the way could wisely tell: But his deceiptfull eyes did neuer lin, To looke on her faire face, and marke her snowy skin.

The sight whereof in his congealed flesh, Infixt such secret sting of greedy lust, That the drie withered stocke it gan refresh, And kindled heat, that soone in flame forth brust: The driest wood is soonest burnt to dust. Rudely to her he lept, and his rough hand Where ill became him, rashly would haue thrust, But she with angry scorne him did withstond, And shamefully reproued for his rudenesse fond.

But he, that neuer good nor maners knew, Her sharpe rebuke full litle did esteeme; Hard is to teach an old horse amble trew. The inward smoke, that did before but steeme, Broke into open fire and rage extreme, And now he strength gan adde vnto his will, Forcing to doe, that did him fowle misseeme: Beastly he threw her downe, ne car'd to spill Her garments gay with scales of fish, that all did fill.

The silly virgin stroue him to withstand, All that she might, and him in vaine reuild: She struggled strongly both with foot and hand, To saue her honor from that villaine vild, And cride to heauen, from humane helpe exild. O ye braue knights, that boast this Ladies loue, Where be ye now, when she is nigh defild Of filthy wretch? well may shee you reproue Of falshood or of slouth, when most it may behoue.

But if that thou, Sir Satyran, didst weete, Or thou, Sir Peridure, her sorie state, How soone would yee assemble many a fleete, To fetch from sea, that ye at land lost late; Towres, Cities, Kingdomes ye would ruinate, In your auengement and dispiteous rage, Ne ought your burning fury mote abate; But if Sir Calidore could it presage, No liuing creature could his cruelty asswage.

But sith that none of all her knights is nye, See how the heauens of voluntary grace, And soueraine fauour towards chastity, Doe succour send to her distressed cace: So much high God doth innocence embrace. It fortuned, whilest thus she stifly stroue, And the wide sea importuned long space

With shrilling shriekes, Proteus abroad did roue, Along the fomy waues driuing his finny droue.

Proteus is Shepheard of the seas of yore, And hath the charge of Neptunes mightie heard; An aged sire with head all frory hore, And sprinckled frost vpon his deawy beard: Who when those pittifull outcries he heard, Through all the seas so ruefully resound, His charet swift in haste he thither steard, Which with a teeme of scaly Phocas bound Was drawne vpon the waues, that fomed him around.

And comming to that Fishers wandring bote, That went at will, withouten carde or sayle, He therein saw that yrkesome sight, which smote Deepe indignation and compassion frayle Into his hart attonce: streight did he hayle The greedy villein from his hoped pray, Of which he now did very litle fayle, And with his staffe, that driues his Heard astray, Him bet so sore, that life and sense did much dismay.

The whiles the pitteous Ladie vp did ryse, Ruffled and fowly raid with filthy soyle, And blubbred face with teares of her faire eyes: Her heart nigh broken was with weary toyle, To saue her selfe from that outrageous spoyle, But when she looked vp, to weet, what wight Had her from so infamous fact assoyld, For shame, but more for feare of his grim sight, Downe in her lap she hid her face, and loudly shright.

Her selfe not saued yet from daunger dred She thought, but chaung'd from one to other feare; Like as a fearefull Partridge, that is fled From the sharpe Hauke, which her attached neare, And fals to ground, to seeke for succour theare, Whereas the hungry Spaniels she does spy, With greedy iawes her readie for to teare; In such distresse and sad perplexity Was Florimell, when Proteus she did see thereby.

But he endeuoured with speeches milde Her to recomfort, and accourage bold, Bidding her feare no more her foeman vilde, Nor doubt himselfe; and who he was, her told. Yet all that could not from affright her hold, Ne to recomfort her at all preuayld; For her faint heart was with the frozen cold Benumbd so inly, that her wits nigh fayld, And all her senses with abashment quite were quayld.

Her vp betwixt his rugged hands he reard, And with his frory lips full softly kist, Whiles the cold ysickles from his rough beard, Dropped adowne vpon her yuorie brest: Yet he himselfe so busily addrest, That her out of astonishment he wrought, And out of that same fishers filthy nest Remouing her, into his charet brought, And there with many gentle termes her faire besought.

But that old leachour, which with bold assault That beautie durst presume to violate, He cast to punish for his hainous fault; Then tooke he him yet trembling sith of late, And tyde behind his charet, to aggrate The virgin, whom he had abusde so sore: So drag'd him through the waues in scornefull state, And after cast him vp, vpon the shore; But Florimell with him vnto his bowre he bore.

His bowre is in the bottome of the maine, Vnder a mightie rocke, gainst which do raue The roaring billowes in their proud disdaine, That with the angry working of the waue, Therein is eaten out an hollow caue, That seemes rough Masons hand with engines keene Had long while laboured it to engraue: There was his wonne, ne liuing wight was seene, Saue one old Nymph, hight Panope to keepe it cleane.

Thither he brought the sory Florimell, And entertained her the best he might And Panope her entertaind eke well, As an immortall mote a mortall wight, To winne her liking vnto his delight: With flattering words he sweetly wooed her, And offered faire gifts t'allure her sight, But she both offers and the offerer Despysde, and all the fawning of the flatterer.

Daily he tempted her with this or that, And neuer suffred her to be at rest: But euermore she him refused flat, And all his fained kindnesse did detest. So firmely she had sealed vp her brest. Sometimes he boasted, that a God he hight: But she a mortall creature loued best: Then he would make himselfe a mortall wight; But then she said she lou'd none, but a Faerie knight.

Then like a Faerie knight himselfe he drest; For euery shape on him he could endew: Then like a king he was to her exprest, And offred kingdomes vnto her in vew, To be his Leman and his Ladie trew: But when all this he nothing saw preuaile, With harder meanes he cast her to subdew, And with sharpe threates her often did assaile, So thinking for to make her stubborne courage quaile.

To dreadfull shapes he did himselfe transforme, Now like a Gyant, now like to a feend, Then like a Centaure, then like to a storme, Raging within the waues: thereby he weend Her will to win vnto his wished end. But when with feare, nor fauour, nor with all He else could doe, he saw himselfe esteemd, Downe in a Dongeon deepe he let her fall, And threatned there to make her his eternall thrall.

Eternall thraldome was to her more liefe, Then losse of chastitie, or chaunge of loue: Die had she rather in tormenting griefe, Then any should of falsenesse her reproue, Or loosenesse, that she lightly did remoue. Most vertuous virgin, glory be thy meed, And crowne of heauenly praise with Saints aboue, Where most sweet hymmes of this thy famous deed Are still emongst them song, that far my rymes exceed.

Fit song of Angels caroled to bee; But yet what so my feeble Muse can frame, Shall be t'aduance thy goodly chastitee, And to enroll thy memorable name, In th'heart of euery honourable Dame, That they thy vertuous deedes may imitate, And be partakers of thy endlesse fame. It yrkes me, leaue thee in this wofull state, To tell of Satyrane, where I him left of late.

Who hauing ended with that Squire of Dames A long discourse of his aduentures vaine, The which himselfe, then Ladies more defames, And finding not th'Hyena to be slaine, With that same Squyre, returned backe againe To his first way. And as they forward went, They spyde a knight faire pricking on the plaine, As if he were on some aduenture bent, And in his port appeared manly hardiment.

Sir Satyrane him towards did addresse, To weet, what wight he was, and what his quest: And comming nigh, eftsoones he gan to gesse Both by the burning hart, which on his brest He bare, and by the colours in his crest, That Paridell it was. Tho to him yode, And him saluting, as beseemed best, Gan first inquire of tydings farre abrode; And afterwardes, on what aduenture now he rode.

Who thereto answering, said; the tydings bad, Which now in Faerie court all men do tell, Which turned hath great mirth, to mourning sad, Is the late ruine of proud Marinell, And suddein parture of faire Florimell, To find him forth: and after her are gone All the braue knights, that doen in armes excell, To saueguard her, ywandred all alone; Emongst the rest my lot (vnworthy) is to be one.

Ah gentle knight (said then Sir Satyrane) Thy labour all is lost, I greatly dread, That hast a thanklesse seruice on thee ta'ne, And offrest sacrifice vnto the dead: For dead, I surely doubt, thou maist aread Henceforth for euer Florimell to be. That all the noble knights of Maydenhead, Which her ador'd, may sore repent with me, And all faire Ladies may for euer sory be.

Which words when Paridell had heard, his hew Gan greatly chaunge, and seem'd dismayd to bee; Then said, Faire Sir, how may I weene it trew, That ye doe tell in such vncertaintee? Or speake ye of report, or did ye see Iust cause of dread, that makes ye doubt so sore? For perdie else how mote it euer bee, That euer hand should dare for to engore Her noble bloud? the heauens such crueltie abhore.

These eyes did see, that they will euer rew T'haue seene, (quoth he) when as a monstrous beast The Palfrey, whereon she did trauell, slew, And of his bowels made his bloudie feast: Which speaking token sheweth at the least Her certaine losse, if not her sure decay: Besides, that more suspition encreast, I found her golden girdle cast astray, Distaynd with durt and bloud, as relique of the pray.

Aye me, (said Paridell) the signes be sad, And but God

turne the same to good soothsay, That Ladies safetie is sore to be drad: Yet will I not forsake my forward way, Till triall doe more certaine truth bewray. Faire Sir (quoth he) well may it you succeed, Ne long shall Satyrane behind you stay, But to the rest, which in this Quest proceed My labour adde, and be partaker of their speed.

Ye noble knights (said then the Squire of Dames) Well may ye speed in so praiseworthy paine: But sith the Sunne now ginnes to slake his beames, In deawy vapours of the westerne maine, And lose the teme out of his weary waine, Mote not mislike you also to abate Your zealous hast, till morrow next againe Both light of heauen, and strength of men relate: Which if ye please, to yonder castle turne your gate.

That counsell pleased well; so all yfere Forth marched to a Castle them before, Where soone arriuing, they restrained were Of readie entrance, which ought euermore To errant knights be commun: wondrous sore Thereat displeasd they were, till that young Squire Gan them informe the cause, why that same dore Was shut to all, which lodging did desire: The which to let you weet, will further time require.

Cant. IX.

Malbecco will no straunge knights host, For peeuish gealosie: Paridell giusts with Britomart: Both shew their auncestrie.

R Edoubted knights, and honorable Dames, To whom I leuell all my labours end, Right sore I feare, least with vnworthy blames This odious argument my rimes should shend, Or ought your goodly patience offend, Whiles of a wanton Lady I do write, Which with her loose incontinence doth blend The shyning glory of your soueraigne light, And knighthood fowle defaced by a faithlesse knight. But neuer let th'ensample of the bad Offend the good: for good by paragone Of euill, may more notably be rad, As white seemes fairer, macht with blacke attone; Ne all are shamed by the fault of one; For lo in heauen, whereas all goodnesse is, Emongst the Angels, a whole legione Of wicked Sprights did fall from happy blis; What wonder then, if one of women all did mis?

Then listen Lordings, if ye list to weet The cause, why Satyrane and Paridell Mote not be entertaynd, as seemed meet, Into that Castle (as that Squire does tell.) Therein a cancred crabbed Carle does dwell, That has no skill of Court nor courtesie, Ne cares, what men say of him ill or well; For all his dayes he drownes in priuitie, Yet has full large to liue, and spend at libertie.

But all his mind is set on mucky pelfe, To hoord vp heapes of euill gotten masse, For which he others wrongs, and wreckes himselfe; Yet is he lincked to a louely lasse, Whose beauty doth her bounty far surpasse, The which to him both far vnequall yeares, And also far vnlike conditions has; For she does ioy to play emongst her peares, And to be free from hard restraint and gealous feares.

But he is old, and withered like hay, Vnfit faire Ladies seruice to supply; The priuie guilt whereof makes him alway Suspect her truth, and keepe continuall spy Vpon her with his other blincked eye; Ne suffreth he resort of liuing wight Approch to her, ne keepe her company, But in close bowre her mewes from all mens sight, Depriu'd of kindly ioy and naturall delight.

Malbecco he, and Hellenore she hight, Vnfitly yokt together in one teeme, That is the cause, why neuer any knight Is suffred here to enter, but he seeme Such, as no doubt of him he neede misdeeme. Thereat Sir Satyrane gan smile, and say; Extremely mad the man I surely deeme, That weenes with watch and hard restraint to stay A womans will, which is disposd to go astray.

In vaine he feares that, which he cannot shonne: For who wotes not, that womans subtiltyes Can guilen Argus, when she list misdonne? It is not yron bandes, nor hundred eyes, Nor brasen walls, nor many wakefull spyes, That can withhold her wilfull wandring feet; But fast good will with gentle curtesyes, And timely seruice to her pleasures meet May her perhaps containe, that else would algates fleet.

Then is he not more mad (said Paridell) That hath himselfe vnto such seruice sold, In dolefull thraldome all his dayes to dwell? For sure a foole I do him firmely hold, That loues his fetters, though they were of gold. But why do we deuise of others ill, Whiles thus we suffer this same dotard old, To keepe vs out, in scorne of his owne will, And rather do not ransack all, and him selfe kill?

Nay let vs first (said Satyrane[)] entreat The man by gentle meanes, to let vs in, And afterwardes affray with cruell threat, Ere that we to efforce it do begin: Then if all fayle, we will by force it win, And eke reward the wretch for his mesprise, As may be worthy of his haynous sin. That counsell pleasd: then Paridell did rise, And to the Castle gate approcht in quiet wise.

Whereat soft knocking, entrance he desyrd. The good man selfe, which then the Porter playd, Him answered, that all were now retyrd Vnto their rest, and all the keyes conuayd Vnto their maister, who in bed was layd, That none him durst awake out of his dreme; And therefore them of patience gently prayd. Then Paridell began to chaunge his theme, And threatned him with force & punishment extreme.

But all in vaine; for nought mote him relent, And now so long before the wicket fast They wayted, that the night was forward spent, And the faire welkin fowly ouercast, Gan blowen vp a bitter stormy blast, With shoure and hayle so horrible and dred, That this faire many were compeld at last, To fly for succour to a little shed, The which beside the gate for swine was ordered.

It fortuned, soone after they were gone, Another knight, whom tempest thither brought, Came to that Castle, and with earnest mone, Like as the rest, late entrance deare besought; But like so as the rest he prayd for nought, For flatly he of entrance was refusd, Sorely thereat he was displeasd, and thought How to auenge himselfe so sore abusd, And euermore the Carle of curtesie accusd.

But to auoyde th'intollerable stowre, He was compeld to seeke some refuge neare, And to that shed, to shrowd him from the showre, He came, which full of guests he found whyleare, So as he was not let to enter there: Whereat he gan to wex exceeding wroth, And swore, that he would lodge with them yfere, Or them dislodge, all were they liefe or loth; And so defide them each, and so defide them both.

Both were full loth to leaue that needfull tent, And both full loth in darkenesse to debate; Yet both full liefe him lodging to haue lent, And both full liefe his boasting to abate; But chiefly Paridell his hart did grate, To heare him threaten so despightfully. As if he did a dogge to kenell rate, That durst not barke; and rather had he dy, Then when he was defide, in coward corner ly.

Tho hastily remounting to his steed, He forth issew'd; like as a boistrous wind, Which in th'earthes hollow caues hath long bin hid, And shut vp fast within her prisons blind, Makes the huge element against her kind To moue, and tremble as it were agast, Vntill that it an issew forth may find; Then forth it breakes, and with his furious blast Confounds both land & seas, and skyes doth ouercast.

Their steel-hed speares they strongly coucht, and met Together with impetuous rage and forse, That with the terrour of their fierce affret, They rudely droue to ground both man and horse, That each awhile lay like a sencelesse corse. But Paridell sore brused with the blow, Could not arise, the counterchaunge to scorse, Till that young Squire him reared from below; Then drew he his bright sword, & gan about him throw.

But Satyrane forth stepping, did them stay And with faire treatie pacifide their ire, Then when they were accorded from the fray, Against that Castles Lord they gan conspire, To heape on him dew vengeaunce for his hire. They bene agreed, and to the gates they goe To burne the same with vnquenchable fire, And that vncurteous Carle their commune foe To do fowle death to dye, or wrap in grieuous woe.

Malbecco seeing them resolu'd in deed To flame the gates, and hearing them to call For fire in earnest, ran with fearefull speed, And to them calling from the castle wall, Besought them humbly, him to beare withal, As ignoraunt of seruants bad abuse, And slacke attendaunce vnto straungers call. The knights were willing all things to excuse, Though nought beleu'd, & entrauce late did not refuse.

They bene ybrought into a comely bowre, And seru'd of all things that mote needfull bee; Yet secretly their hoste did on them lowre, And welcomde more for feare, then charitee; But they dissembled, what they did not see, And welcomed themselues. Each gan vndight Their garments wet, and weary armour free, To dry them selues by Vulcanes flaming light, And eke their lately bruzed parts to bring in plight.

And eke that straunger knight emongst the rest; Was for like need enforst to disaray: Tho whenas vailed was her loftie crest, Her golden locks, that were in tramels gay Vpbounden, did them selues adowne display, And raught vnto her heeles; like sunny beames, That in a cloud their light did long time stay, Their vapour vaded, shew their golden gleames, And through the persant aire shoote forth their azure streames.

She also dofte her heauy haberieon, Which the faire feature of her limbs did hyde, And her well plighted frock, which she did won To tucke about her short, when she did ryde, She low let fall, that flowd from her lanck syde Downe to her foot, with carelesse modestee. Then of them all she plainly was espyde, To be a woman wight, vnwist to bee, The fairest woman wight, that euer eye did see.

Like as Minerua, being late returnd From slaughter of the Giaunts conquered; Where proud Encelade, whose wide nosethrils burnd With breathed flames, like to a furnace red, Transfixed with the speare, downe tombled ded From top of Hemus, by him heaped hye; Hath loosd her helmet from her lofty hed, And her Gorgonian shield gins to vntye From her left arme, to rest in glorious victorye.

Which whenas they beheld, they smitten were With great

amazement of so wondrous sight, And each on other, and they all on her Stood gazing, as if suddein great affright Had them surprised. At last auizing right, Her goodly personage and glorious hew, Which they so much mistooke, they tooke delight In their first errour, and yet still anew With wonder of her beauty fed their hungry vew.

Yet note their hungry vew be satisfide, But seeing still the more desir'd to see, And euer firmely fixed did abide In contemplation of diuinitie: But most they meruail[e]d at her cheualree, And noble prowesse, which they had approued, That much they faynd to know, who she mote bee; Yet none of all them her thereof amoued, Yet euery one her likte, and euery one her loued.

And Paridell though partly discontent With his late fall, and fowle indignity, Yet was soone wonne his malice to relent, Through gracious regard of her faire eye, And knightly worth, which he too late did try, Yet tried did adore. Supper was dight; Then they Malbecco prayd of curtesy, That of his Lady they might haue the sight, And company at meat, to do them more delight.

But he to shift their curious request, Gan causen, why she could not come in place; Her crased health, her late recourse to rest, And humid euening ill for sicke folkes cace: But none of those excuses could take place; Ne would they eate, till she in presence came. She came in presence with right comely grace, And fairely them saluted, as became, And shewd her selfe in all a gentle curteous Dame.

They sate to meat, and Satyrane his chaunce Was her before, and Paridell besyde; But he him selfe sate looking still askaunce, Gainst Britomart, and euer closely eyde Sir Satyrane, that glaunces might not glyde: But his blind eye, that syded Paridell, All his demeasnure from his sight did hyde: On her faire face so did he feede his fill, And sent close messages of loue to her at will.

And euer and anone, when none was ware, With speaking lookes, that close embassage bore, He rou'd at her, and told his secret care: For all that art he learned had of yore. Ne was she ignoraunt of that lewd lore, But in his eye his meaning wisely red, And with the like him answerd euermore: She sent at him one firie dart, whose hed Empoisned was with priuy lust, and gealous dred.

He from that deadly throw made no defence, But to the wound his weake hart opened wyde; The wicked engine through false influence, Past through his eyes, and secretly did glyde Into his hart, which it did sorely gryde. But nothing new to him was that same paine, Ne paine at all; for he so oft had tryde The powre thereof, and lou'd so oft in vaine, That thing of course he counted, loue to entertaine.

Thenceforth to her he sought to intimate His inward griefe, by meanes to him well knowne, Now Bacchus fruit out of the siluer plate He on the table dasht, as ouerthrowne, Or of the fruitfull liquor ouerflowne, And by the dauncing bubbles did diuine, Or therein write to let his loue be showne; Which well she red out of the learned line, A sacrament prophane in mistery of wine.

And when so of his hand the pledge she raught, The guilty cup she fained to mistake, And in her lap did shed her idle draught, Shewing desire her inward flame to slake: By such close signes they secret way did make Vnto their wils, and one eyes watch escape; Two eyes him needeth, for to watch and wake, Who louers will deceiue. Thus was the ape, By their faire handling, put into Malbeccoes cape.

Now when of meats and drinks they had their fill, Purpose was moued by that gentle Dame, Vnto those knights aduenturous, to tell Of deeds of armes, which vnto them became, And euery one his kindred, and his name. Then Paridell, in whom a kindly pryde Of gracious speach, and skill his words to frame Abounded, being glad of so fit tyde Him to commend to her, thus spake, of all well eyde.

Troy, that art now nought, but an idle name, And in thine ashes buried low dost lie, Though whilome far much greater then thy fame, Before that angry Gods, and cruell skye Vpon

thee heapt a direfull destinie, What boots it boast thy glorious descent, And fetch from heauen thy great Genealogie,
Sith all thy worthy prayses being blent, Their of-spring hath
embaste, and later glory shent.

Most famous Worthy of the world, by whome That warre
was kindled, which did Troy inflame, And stately towres of
Ilion whilome Brought vnto balefull ruine, was by name Sir
Paris far renowmd through noble fame, Who through great
prowesse and bold hardinesse, From Lacedæmon fetcht the
fairest Dame, That euer Greece did boast, or knight possesse,
Whom Venus to him gaue for meed of worthinesse.

Faire Helene, flowre of beautie excellent, And girlond of
the mighty Conquerours, That madest many Ladies deare
lament The heauie losse of their braue Paramours, Which
they far off beheld from Troian toures, And saw the fieldes of
faire Scamander strowne With carcases of noble warrioures,
Whose fruitlesse liues were vnder furrow sowne, And Xan-
thus sandy bankes with bloud all ouerflowne.

From him my linage I deriue aright, Who long before the
ten yeares siege of Troy, Whiles yet on Ida he a shepheard
hight, On faire Oenone got a louely boy, Whom for remem-
braunce of her passed ioy, She of his Father Parius did name;
Who, after Greekes did Priams realme destroy, Gathred the
Troian reliques sau'd from flame, And with them sayling
thence, to th'Isle of Paros came.

That was by him cald Paros, which before Hight Nausa,
there he many yeares did raine, And built Nausicle by the
Pontick shore, The which he dying left next in remaine To
Paridas his sonne. From whom I Paridell by kin descend; But
for faire Ladies loue, and glories gaine, My natiue soile haue
left, my dayes to spend In sewing deeds of armes, my liues
and labours end.

Whenas the noble Britomart heard tell Of Troian warres,
and Priams Citie sackt, The ruefull story of Sir Paridell, She
was empassiond at that piteous act, With zelous enuy of
Greekes cruell fact, Against that nation, from whose race of

old She heard, that she was lineally extract: For noble Britons sprong from Troians bold, And Troynouant was built of old Troyes ashes cold.

Then sighing soft awhile, at last she thus: O lamentable fall of famous towne, Which raignd so many yeares victorious, And of all Asie bore the soueraigne crowne, In one sad night consumd, and throwen downe: What stony hart, that heares thy haplesse fate, Is not empierst with deepe compassiowne, And makes ensample of mans wretched state, That floures so fresh at morne, and fades at euening late?

Behold, Sir, how your pitifull complaint Hath found another partner of your payne: For nothing may impresse so deare constraint, As countries cause, and commune foes disdayne. But if it should not grieue you, backe agayne To turne your course, I would to heare desyre, What to Aeneas fell; sith that men sayne He was not in the Cities wofull fyre Consum'd, but did him selfe to safetie retyre.

Anchyses sonne begot of Venus faire, (Said he,) out of the flames for safegard fled, And with a remnant did to sea repaire, Where he through fatall errour long was led Full many yeares, and weetlesse wandered From shore to shore, emongst the Lybicke sands, Ere rest he found. Much there he suffered, And many perils past in forreine lands, To saue his people sad from victours vengefull hands.

At last in Latium he did arriue, Where he with cruell warre was entertaind Of th'inland folke, which sought him backe to driue, Till he with old Latinus was constraind, To contract wedlock: (so the fates ordaind.) Wedlock contract in bloud, and eke in blood Accomplished, that many deare complaind: The riuall slaine, the victour through the flood Escaped hardly, hardly praisd his wedlock good.

Yet after all, he victour did suruiue, And with Latinus did the kingdome part. But after when both nations gan to striue, Into their names the title to conuart, His sonne Iulus did from thence depart, With all the warlike youth of Troians bloud, And in long Alba plast his throne apart, Where faire it florished, and long time it stoud, Till Romulus renewing it, to Rome remoud.

There there (said Britomart) a fresh appeard The glory of the later world to spring, And Troy againe out of her dust was reard, To sit in second seat of soueraigne king, Of all the world vnder her gouerning. But a third kingdome yet is to arise, Out of the Troians scattered of-spring, That in all glory and great enterprise, Both first and second Troy shall dare to equalise.

It Troynouant is hight, that with the waues Of wealthy Thamis washed is along, Vpon whose stubborne neck, whereat he raues With roring rage, and sore him selfe does throng, That all men feare to tempt his billowes strong, She fastned hath her foot, which standes so hy, That it a wonder of the world is song In forreine landes, and all which passen by, Beholding it from far, do thinke it threates the skye.

The Troian Brute did first that Citie found, And Hygate made the meare thereof by West, And Ouert gate by North: that is the bound Toward the land; two riuers bound the rest. So huge a scope at first him seemed best, To be the compasse of his kingdomes seat: So huge a mind could not in lesser rest, Ne in small meares containe his glory great, That Albion had conquered first by warlike feat.

Ah fairest Lady knight, (said Paridell) Pardon I pray my heedlesse ouersight, Who had forgot, that whilome I heard tell From aged Mnemon; for my wits bene light. Indeed he said (if I remember right,) That of the antique Troian stocke, there grew Another plant, that raught to wondrous hight, And far abroad his mighty branches threw, Into the vtmost Angle of the world he knew.

For that same Brute, whom much he did aduaunce In all his speach, was Syluius his sonne, Whom hauing slaine, through luckles arrowes glaūce He fled for feare of that he had misdonne, Or else for shame, so fowle reproch to shonne, And with him led to sea an youthly trayne, Where wearie wandring they long time did wonne, And many fortunes prou'd in th'Ocean mayne, And great aduetures found, that now were lõg to sayne.

At last by fatall course they driuen were Into an Island spatious and brode, The furthest North, that did to them appeare: Which after rest they seeking far abrode, Found it the fittest soyle for their abode, Fruitfull of all things fit for liuing foode, But wholy wast, and void of peoples trode, Saue an huge nation of the Geaunts broode, That fed on liuing flesh, & druncke mens vitall blood.

Whom he through wearie wars and labours long, Subdewd with losse of many Britons bold: In which the great Goemagot of strong Corineus, and Coulin of Debon old Were ouerthrowne and layd on th'earth full cold, Which quaked vnder their so hideous masse, A famous history to be enrold In euerlasting moniments of brasse, That all the antique Worthies merits far did passe.

His worke great Troynouant, his worke is eke Faire Lincolne, both renowmed far away, That who from East to West will endlong seeke, Cannot two fairer Cities find this day, Except Cleopolis: so heard I say Old Mnemon. Therefore Sir, I greet you well Your countrey kin, and you entirely pray Of pardon for the strife, which late befell Betwixt vs both vnknowne. So ended Paridell.

But all the while, that he these speaches spent, Vpon his lips hong faire Dame Hellenore, With vigilant regard, and dew attent, Fashioning worlds of fancies euermore In her fraile wit, that now her quite forlore: The whiles vnwares away her wondring eye, And greedy eares her weake hart from her bore: Which he perceiuing, euer priuily In speaking, many false belgardes at her let fly.

So long these knights discoursed diuersly, Of straunge affaires, and noble hardiment, Which they had past with mickle ieopardy, That now the humid night was farforth spent, And heauenly lampes were halfendeale ybrent: Which th'old man seeing well, who too long thought Euery discourse and euery argument, Which by the houres he measured, besought

Them go to rest. So all vnto their bowres were brought.

Cant. X.

Paridell rapeth Hellenore: Malbecco her pursewes:
Findes emongst Satyres, whence with him To turne she doth
refuse.

T He morow next, so soone as Phoebus Lamp Bewrayed
had the world with early light, And fresh Aurora had the
shady damp Out of the goodly heauen amoued quight, Faire
Britomart and that same Faerie knight Vprose, forth on
their iourney for to wend: But Paridell complaynd, that his
late fight With Britomart, so sore did him offend, That ryde
he could not, till his hurts he did amend. So forth they far'd,
but he behind them stayd, Maulgre his host, who grudged
grieuously, To house a guest, that would be needes obayd,
And of his owne him left not liberty: Might wanting measure
moueth surquedry. Two things he feared, but the third was
death; That fierce young mans vnruly maistery; His money,
which he lou'd as liuing breath; And his faire wife, whom
honest long he kept vneath.

But patience perforce he must abie, What fortune and his
fate on him will lay, Fond is the feare, that findes no remedie; Yet warily he watcheth euery way, By which he feareth
euill happen may: So th'euill thinkes by watching to preuent;
Ne doth he suffer her, nor night, nor day, Out of his sight her
selfe once to absent. So doth he punish her and eke himselfe
torment.

But Paridell kept better watch, then hee, A fit occasion
for his turne to find: False loue, why do men say, thou canst
not see, And in their foolish fancie feigne thee blind, That
with thy charmes the sharpest sight doest bind, And to thy
will abuse? Thou walkest free, And seest euery secret of the
mind; Thou seest all, yet none at all sees thee; All that is by
the working of thy Deitee.

So perfect in that art was Paridell, That he Malbeccoes
halfen eye did wyle, His halfen eye he wiled wondrous well,
And Hellenors both eyes did eke beguyle, Both eyes and

hart attonce, during the whyle That he there soiourned his wounds to heale; That Cupid selfe it seeing, close did smyle, To weet how he her loue away did steale, And bad, that none their ioyous treason should reueale.

The learned louer lost no time nor tyde, That least auantage mote to him afford, Yet bore so faire a saile, that none espyde His secret drift, till he her layd abord. When so in open place, and commune bord, He fortun'd her to meet, with commune speach He courted her, yet bayted euery word, That his vngentle hoste n'ote him appeach Of vile vngentlenesse, or hospitages breach.

But when apart (if euer her apart) He found, then his false engins fast he plyde, And all the sleights vnbosomd in his hart; He sigh'd, he sobd, he swownd, he perdy dyde, And cast himselfe on ground her fast besyde: Tho when againe he him bethought to liue, He wept, and wayld, and false laments belyde, Saying, but if she Mercie would him giue That he mote algates dye, yet did his death forgiue.

And otherwhiles with amorous delights, And pleasing toyes he would her entertaine, Now singing sweetly, to surprise her sprights, Now making layes of loue and louers paine, Bransles, Ballads, virelayes, and verses vaine; Oft purposes, oft riddles he deuysd, And thousands like, which flowed in his braine, With which he fed her fancie, and entysd To take to his new loue, and leaue her old despysd.

And euery where he might, and euery while He did her seruice dewtifull, and sewed At hand with humble pride, and pleasing guile, So closely yet, that none but she it vewed, Who well perceiued all, and all indewed. Thus finely did he his false nets dispred, With which he many weake harts had subdewed Of yore, and many had ylike misled: What wonder then, if she were likewise carried?

No fort so fensible, no wals so strong, But that continuall battery will riue, Or daily siege through dispuruayance long, And lacke of reskewes will to parley driue; And Peece, that vnto parley eare will giue, Will shortly yeeld it selfe, and will

be made The vassall of the victors will byliue: That strata-
geme had oftentimes assayd This crafty Paramoure, and now
it plaine displayd.

For through his traines he her intrapped hath, That she
her loue and hart hath wholy sold To him, without regard of
gaine, or scath, Or care of credite, or of husband old, Whom
she hath vow'd to dub a faire Cucquold. Nought wants but
time and place, which shortly shee Deuized hath, and to her
louer told. It pleased well. So well they both agree; So readie
rype to ill, ill wemens counsels bee.

Darke was the Euening, fit for louers stealth, When
chaunst Malbecco busie be elsewhere, She to his closet went,
where all his wealth Lay hid: thereof she countlesse summes
did reare, The which she meant away with her to beare; The
rest she fyr'd for sport, or for despight; As Hellene, when she
saw aloft appeare The Troiane flames, and reach to heauens
hight Did clap her hands, and ioyed at that dolefull sight.

This second Hellene, faire Dame Hellenore, The whiles
her husband ranne with sory haste, To quench the flames,
which she had tyn'd before, Laught at his foolish labour
spent in waste; And ranne into her louers armes right fast;
Where streight embraced, she to him did cry, And call aloud
for helpe, ere helpe were past; For loe that Guest would beare
her forcibly, And meant to rauish her, that rather had to dy.

The wretched man hearing her call for ayd, And readie
seeing him with her to fly, In his disquiet mind was much dismayd: But when againe he backward cast his eye, And saw
the wicked fire so furiously Consume his hart, and scorch his
Idoles face, He was therewith distressed diuersly, Ne wist he
how to turne, nor to what place; Was neuer wretched man in
such a wofull cace.

Ay when to him she cryde, to her he turnd, And left the
fire; loue money ouercame: But when he marked, how his
money burnd, He left his wife; money did loue disclame: Both
was he loth to loose his loued Dame, And loth to leaue his
liefest pelfe behind, Yet sith he n'ote saue both, he sau'd that

same, Which was the dearest to his donghill mind, The God of his desire, the ioy of misers blind.

Thus whilest all things in troublous vprore were, And all men busie to suppresse the flame, The louing couple need no reskew feare, But leasure had, and libertie to frame Their purpost flight, free from all mens reclame; And Night, the patronesse of loue-stealth faire, Gaue them safe conduct, till to end they came: So bene they gone yfeare, a wanton paire Of louers loosely knit, where list them to repaire.

Soone as the cruell flames yslaked were, Malbecco seeing, how his losse did lye, Out of the flames, which he had quencht whylere Into huge waues of griefe and gealosye Full deepe emplonged was, and drowned nye, Twixt inward doole and felonous despight; He rau'd, he wept, he stampt, he lowd did cry, And all the passions, that in man may light, Did him attonce oppresse, and vex his caytiue spright.

Long thus he chawd the cud of inward griefe, And did consume his gall with anguish sore, Still when he mused on his late mischiefe, Then still the smart thereof increased more, And seem'd more grieuous, then it was before: At last when sorrow he saw booted nought, Ne griefe might not his loue to him restore, He gan deuise, how her he reskew mought, Ten thousand wayes he cast in his confused thought.

At last resoluing, like a pilgrim pore, To sea[r]ch her forth, where so she might be fond, And bearing with him treasure in close store, The rest he leaues in ground: so takes in hond To seeke her endlong, both by sea and lond. Long he her sought, he sought her farre and nere, And euery where that he mote vnderstond, Of knights and ladies any meetings were, And of eachone he met, he tydings did inquere.

But all in vaine, his woman was too wise, Euer to come into his clouch againe, And he too simple euer to surprise The iolly Paridell, for all his paine. One day, as he forpassed by the plaine With weary pace, he farre away espide A couple, seeming well to be his twaine, Which houed close vnder a forrest side, As if they lay in wait, or else themselues did hide.

Well weened he, that those the same mote bee, And as he better did their shape auize, Him seemed more their manner did agree; For th'one was armed all in warlike wize, Whom, to be Paridell he did deuize; And th'other all yclad in garments light, Discolour'd like to womanish disguise, He did resemble to his Ladie bright; And euer his faint hart much earned at the sight.

And euer faine he towards them would goe, But yet durst not for dread approchen nie, But stood aloofe, vnweeting what to doe; Till that prickt forth with loues extremitie, That is the father of fowle gealosy, He closely nearer crept, the truth to weet: But, as he nigher drew, he easily Might scerne, that it was not his sweetest sweet, Ne yet her Belamour, the partner of his sheet.

But it was scornefull Braggadocchio, That with his seruant Trompart houerd there, Sith late he fled from his too earnest foe: Whom such when as Malbecco spyed clere, He turned backe, and would haue fled arere; Till Trompart ronning hastily, him did stay, And bad before his soueraine Lord appere: That was him loth, yet durst he not gainesay, And comming him before, low louted on the lay.

The Boaster at him sternely bent his browe, As if he could haue kild him with his looke, That to the ground him meekely made to bowe, And awfull terror deepe into him strooke, That euery member of his bodie quooke. Said he, thou man of nought, what doest thou here, Vnfitly furnisht with thy bag and booke, Where I expected one with shield and spere, To proue some deedes of armes vpon an equall pere.

The wretched man at his imperious speach, Was all abasht, and low prostrating, said; Good Sir, let not my rudenesse be no breach Vnto your patience, ne be ill ypaid; For I vnwares this way by fortune straid, A silly Pilgrim driuen to distresse, That seeke a Lady,---There he suddein staid, And did the rest with grieuous sighes suppresse, While teares stood in his eies, few drops of bitternesse.

What Ladie, man? (said Trompart) take good hart, And tell thy griefe, if any hidden lye; Was neuer better time to shew thy smart, Then now, that noble succour is thee by, That is the whole worlds commune remedy. That cheareful word his weake hart much did cheare, And with vaine hope his spirits faint supply, That bold he said; ô most redoubted Pere, Vouchsafe with mild regard a wretches cace to heare.

Then sighing sore, It is not long (said he) Sith I enioyd the gentlest Dame aliue; Of whom a knight, no knight at all perdee, But shame of all, that doe for honor striue, By treacherous deceipt did me depriue; Through open outrage he her bore away, And with fowle force vnto his will did driue, Which all good knights, that armes do beare this day, Are bound for to reuenge, and punish if they may.

And you most noble Lord, that can and dare Redresse the wrong of miserable wight, Cannot employ your most victorious speare In better quarrell, then defence of right, And for a Ladie gainst a faithlesse knight; So shall your glory be aduaunced much, And all faire Ladies magnifie your might, And eke my selfe, albe I simple such, Your worthy paine shall well reward with guerdon rich.

With that out of his bouget forth he drew Great store of treasure, therewith him to tempt; But he on it lookt scornefully askew, As much disdeigning to be so misdempt, Or a war-monger to be basely nempt; And said; Thy offers base I greatly loth, And eke thy words vncourteous and vnkempt; I tread in dust thee and thy money both, That, were it not for shame,---So turned from him wroth.

But Trompart, that his maisters humor knew, In lofty lookes to hide an humble mind, Was inly tickled with that golden vew, And in his eare him rounded close behind: Yet stoupt he not, but lay still in the wind, Waiting aduauntage on the pray to sease; Till Trompart lowly to the ground inclind, Besought him his great courage to appease, And pardon simple man, that rash did him displease.

Bigge looking like a doughtie Doucepere, At last he thus;

Thou clod of vilest clay, I pardon yield, and with thy rudenesse beare; But weete henceforth, that all that golden pray,
And all that else the vaine world vaunten may, I loath as
doung, ne deeme my dew reward: Fame is my meed, and glory vertues pray. But minds of mortall men are muchell mard,
And mou'd amisse with massie mucks vnmeet regard.

And more, I graunt to thy great miserie Gratious respect,
thy wife shall backe be sent, And that vile knight, who euer
that he bee, Which hath thy Lady reft, and knighthood shent,
By Sanglamort my sword, whose deadly dent The bloud hath
of so many thousands shed, I sweare, ere long shall dearely it
repent; Ne he twixt heauen and earth shall hide his hed, But
soone he shall be found, and shortly doen be ded.

The foolish man thereat woxe wondrous blith, As if the
word so spoken, were halfe donne, And humbly thanked
him a thousand sith, That had from death to life him newly
wonne. Tho forth the Boaster marching, braue begonne His
stolen steed to thunder furiously, As if he heauen and hell
would ouerronne, And all the world confound with cruelty,
That much Malbecco ioyed in his iollity.

Thus long they three together traueiled, Through many
a wood, and many an vncouth way, To seeke his wife, that
was farre wandered: But those two sought nought, but the
present pray, To weete the treasure, which he did bewray,
On which their eies and harts were wholly set, With purpose,
how they might it best betray; For sith the houre, that first
he did them let The same behold, therewith their keene desires were whet.

It fortuned as they together far'd, They spide, where
Paridell came pricking fast Vpon the plaine, the which himselfe prepar'd To giust with that braue straunger knight a
cast, As on aduenture by the way he past: Alone he rode
without his Paragone; For hauing filcht her bels, her vp he
cast To the wide world, and let her fly alone, He nould be
clogd. So had he serued many one.

The gentle Lady, loose at randon left, The greene-wood

long did walke, and wander wide At wilde aduenture, like a forlorne weft, Till on a day the Satyres her espide Straying alone withouten groome or guide; Her vp they tooke, and with them home her led, With them as housewife euer to abide, To milk their gotes, and make them cheese and bred, And euery one as commune good her handeled.

That shortly she Malbecco has forgot, And eke Sir Paridell, all were he deare; Who from her went to seeke another lot, And now by fortune was arriued here, Where those two guilers with Malbecco were: Soone as the old man saw Sir Paridell, He fainted, and was almost dead with feare, Ne word he had to speake, his griefe to tell, But to him louted low, and greeted goodly well.

And after asked him for Hellenore, I take no keepe of her (said Paridell) She wonneth in the forrest there before. So forth he rode, as his aduenture fell; The whiles the Boaster from his loftie sell Faynd to alight, something amisse to mend; But the fresh Swayne would not his leasure dwell, But went his way; whom when he passed kend, He vp remounted light, and after faind to wend.

Perdy nay (said Malbecco) shall ye not: But let him passe as lightly, as he came: For litle good of him is to be got, And mickle perill to be put to shame. But let vs go to seeke my dearest Dame, Whom he hath left in yonder forrest wyld: For of her safety in great doubt I am, Least saluage beastes her person haue despoyld: Then all the world is lost, and we in vaine haue toyld.

They all agree, and forward them addrest: Ah but (said craftie Trompart) weete ye well, That yonder in that wastefull wildernesse Huge monsters haunt, and many dangers dwell; Dragons, and Minotaures, and feendes of hell, And many wilde woodmen, which robbe and rend All trauellers; therefore aduise ye well, Before ye enterprise that way to wend: One may his iourney bring too soone to euill end.

Malbecco stopt in great astonishment, And with pale eyes fast fixed on the rest, Their counsell crau'd, in daunger imminent. Said Trompart, You that are the most opprest With burden of great treasure, I thinke best Here for to stay in safetie behind; My Lord and I will search the wide forrest. That counsell pleased not Malbeccoes mind; For he was much affraid, himselfe alone to find.

Then is it best (said he) that ye doe leaue Your treasure here in some securitie, Either fast closed in some hollow greaue, Or buried in the ground from ieopardie, Till we returne againe in safetie: As for vs two, least doubt of vs ye haue, Hence farre away we will blindfolded lie, Ne priuie be vnto your treasures graue. It pleased: so he did, Then they march forward braue.

Now when amid the thickest woods they were, They heard a noyse of many bagpipes shrill, And shrieking Hububs them approching nere, Which all the forrest did with horror fill: That dreadfull sound the boasters hart did thrill, With such amazement, that in haste he fled, Ne euer looked backe for good or ill, And after him eke fearefull Trompart sped; The old man could not fly, but fell to ground halfe ded.

Yet afterwards close creeping, as he might, He in a bush did hide his fearefull hed, The iolly Satyres full of fresh delight, Came dauncing forth, and with them nimbly led Faire Hellenore, with girlonds all bespred, Whom their May-lady they had newly made: She proud of that new honour, which they red, And of their louely fellowship full glade, Daunst liuely, and her face did with a Lawrell shade.

The silly man that in the thicket lay Saw all this goodly sport, and grieued sore, Yet durst he not against it doe or say, But did his hart with bitter thoughts engore, To see th'vnkindnesse of his Hellenore. All day they daunced with great lustihed, And with their horned feet the greene grasse wore, The whiles their Gotes vpon the brouzes fed, Till drouping Phoebus gan to hide his golden hed.

Tho vp they gan their merry pypes to trusse, And all their goodly heards did gather round, But euery Satyre first did giue a busse To Hellenore: so busses did abound. Now gan the humid vapour shed the ground With perly deaw, and th'Earthes gloomy shade Did dim the brightnesse of the welkin round, That euery bird and beast awarned made, To shrowd themselues, whiles sleepe their senses did inuade.

Which when Malbecco saw, out of his bush Vpon his hands and feete he crept full light, And like a Gote emongst the Gotes did rush, That through the helpe of his faire hornes on hight, And misty dampe of misconceiuing night, And eke through likenesse of his gotish beard, He did the better counterfeite aright: So home he marcht emongst the horned heard, That none of all the Satyres him espyde or heard.

At night, when all they went to sleepe, he vewd, Whereas his louely wife emongst them lay, Embraced of a Satyre rough and rude, Who all the night did minde his ioyous play: Nine times he heard him come aloft ere day, That all his hart with gealosie did swell; But yet that nights ensample did bewray, That not for nought his wife them loued so well, When one so oft a night did ring his matins bell.

So closely as he could, he to them crept, When wearie of their sport to sleepe they fell, And to his wife, that now full soundly slept, He whispered in her eare, and did her tell, That it was he, which by her side did dwell, And therefore prayd her wake, to heare him plaine. As one out of a dreame not waked well, She turned her, and returned backe againe: Yet her for to awake he did the more constraine.

At last with irkesome trouble she abrayd; And then perceiuing, that it was indeed Her old Malbecco, which did her vpbrayd, With loosenesse of her loue, and loathly deed, She was astonisht with exceeding dreed, And would haue wakt the Satyre by her syde; But he her prayd, for mercy, or for meed, To saue his life, ne let him be descryde, But hearken to his lore, and all his counsell hyde.

Tho gan he her perswade, to leaue that lewd And loathsome life, of God and man abhord, And home returne, where all should be renewd With perfect peace, and bandes of fresh accord, And she receiu'd againe to bed and bord, As if no trespasse euer had bene donne: But she it all refused at one word, And by no meanes would to his will be wonne, But chose emongst the iolly Satyres still to wonne.

He wooed her, till day spring he espyde; But all in vaine: and then turnd to the heard, Who butted him with hornes on euery syde, And trode downe in the durt, where his hore beard Was fowly dight, and he of death afeard. Early before the heauens fairest light Out of the ruddy East was fully reard, The heardes out of their foldes were loosed quight, And he emongst the rest crept forth in sory plight.

So soone as he the Prison dore did pas, He ran as fast, as both his feete could beare, And neuer looked, who behind him was, Ne scarsely who before: like as a Beare That creeping close, amongst the hiues to reare An hony combe, the wakefull dogs espy, And him assayling, sore his carkasse teare, That hardly he with life away does fly, Ne stayes, till safe himselfe he see from ieopardy.

Ne stayd he, till he came vnto the place, Where late his treasure he entombed had, Where when he found it not (for Trompart bace Had it purloyned for his maister bad:) With extreme fury he became quite mad, And ran away, ran with himselfe away: That who so straungely had him seene bestad, With vpstart haire, and staring eyes dismay, From Limbo lake him late escaped sure would say.

High ouer hilles and ouer dales he fled, As if the wind him on his winges had borne, Ne banck nor bush could stay him, when he sped His nimble feet, as treading still on thorne: Griefe, and despight, and gealosie, and scorne Did all the way him follow hard behind, And he himselfe himselfe loath'd so forlorne, So shamefully forlorne of womankind; That as a Snake, still lurked in his wounded mind.

Still fled he forward, looking backward still, Ne stayd his flight, nor fearefull agony, Till that he came vnto a rockie hill, Ouer the sea, suspended dreadfully, That liuing creature it would terrify, To looke adowne, or vpward to the hight: From thence he threw himselfe dispiteously, All desperate of his fore-damned spright, That seem'd no helpe for him was left in liuing sight.

But through long anguish, and selfe-murdring thought He was so wasted and forpined quight, That all his substance was consum'd to nought, And nothing left, but like an aery Spright, That on the rockes he fell so flit and light, That he thereby receiu'd no hurt at all, But chaunced on a craggy cliff to light; Whence he with crooked clawes so long did crall, That at the last he found a caue with entrance small.

Into the same he creepes, and thenceforth there Resolu'd to build his balefull mansion, In drery darkenesse, and continuall feare Of that rockes fall, which euer and anon Threates with huge ruine him to fall vpon, That he dare neuer sleepe, but that one eye Still ope he keepes for that occasion; Ne euer rests he in tranquillity, The roring billowes beat his bowre so boystrously.

Ne euer is he wont on ought to feed, But toades and frogs, his pasture poysonous, Which in his cold complexion do breed A filthy bloud, or humour rancorous, Matter of doubt and dread suspitious, That doth with curelesse care consume the hart, Corrupts the stomacke with gall vitious, Croscuts the liuer with internall smart, And doth transfixe the soule with deathes eternall dart.

Yet can he neuer dye, but dying liues, And doth himselfe with sorrow new sustaine, That death and life attonce vnto him giues. And painefull pleasure turnes to pleasing paine. There dwels he euer, miserable swaine, Hatefull both to him selfe, and euery wight; Where he through priuy griefe, and horrour vaine, Is woxen so deform'd, that he has quight Forgot he was a man, and Gealosie is hight.

Cant. XI.

Britomart chaceth Ollyphant, findes Scudamour distrest: Assayes the house of Busyrane, where Loues spoyles are exprest.

O Hatefull hellish Snake, what furie furst Brought thee

from balefull house of Proserpine, Where in her bosome she thee long had nurst, And fostred vp with bitter milke of tine, Fowle Gealosie, that turnest loue diuine To ioylesse dread, and mak'st the louing hart With hatefull thoughts to languish and to pine, And feed it selfe with selfe-consuming smart? Of all the passions in the mind thou vilest art. O let him far be banished away, And in his stead let Loue for euer dwell, Sweet Loue, that doth his golding wings embay In blessed Nectar, and pure Pleasures well, Vntroubled of vile feare, or bitter fell. And ye faire Ladies, that your kingdomes make In th'harts of men, them gouerne wisely well, And of faire Britomart ensample take, That was as trew in loue, as Turtle to her make.

Who with Sir Satyrane, as earst ye red, Forth ryding from Malbeccoes hostlesse hous, Far off aspyde a young man, the which fled From an huge Geaunt, that with hideous And hatefull outrage long him chaced thus; It was that Ollyphant, the brother deare Of that Argante vile and vitious, From whom the Squire of Dames was reft whylere; This all as bad as she, and worse, if worse ought were.

For as the sister did in feminine And filthy lust exceede all woman kind, So he surpassed his sex masculine, In beastly vse that I did euer find; Whom when as Britomart beheld behind The fearefull boy so greedily pursew, She was emmoued in her noble mind, T'employ her puissaunce to his reskew, And pricked fiercely forward, where she him did vew.

Ne was Sir Satyrane her far behinde, But with like fiercenesse did ensew the chace: Whom when the Gyaunt saw, he soone resinde His former suit, and from them fled apace; They after both, and boldly bad him bace, And each did striue the other to out-goe, But he them both outran a wondrous space, For he was long, and swift as any Roe, And now made better speed, t'escape his feared foe.

It was not Satyrane, whom he did feare, But Britomart the flowre of chastity; For he the powre of chast hands might not beare, But alwayes did their dread encounter fly: And now so fast his feet he did apply, That he has gotten to a forrest neare, Where he is shrowded in security. The wood they enter, and search euery where, They searched diuersely, so both diuided were.

Faire Britomart so long him followed, That she at last came to a fountaine sheare, By which there lay a knight all wallowed Vpon the grassy ground, and by him neare His haberieon, his helmet, and his speare; A little off, his shield was rudely throwne, On which the winged boy in colours cleare Depeincted was, full easie to be knowne, And he thereby, where euer it in field was showne.

His face vpon the ground did groueling ly, As if he had bene slombring in the shade, That the braue Mayd would not for courtesy, Out of his quiet slomber him abrade, Nor seeme too suddeinly him to inuade: Still as she stood, she heard with grieuous throb Him grone, as if his hart were peeces made, And with most painefull pangs to sigh and sob, That pitty did the Virgins hart of patience rob.

At last forth breaking into bitter plaintes He said; ô soueraigne Lord that sit'st on hye, And raignst in blis amongst thy blessed Saintes, How suffrest thou such shamefull cruelty, So long vnwreaked of thine enimy? Or hast thou, Lord, of good mens cause no heed? Or doth thy iustice sleepe, and silent ly? What booteth then the good and righteous deed, If goodnesse find no grace, nor righteousnesse no meed?

If good find grace, and righteousnesse reward, Why then is Amoret in caytiue band, Sith that more bounteous creature neuer far'd On foot, vpon the face of liuing land? Or if that heauenly iustice may withstand The wrongfull outrage of vnrighteous men, Why then is Busirane with wicked hand Suffred, these seuen monethes day in secret den My Lady and my loue so cruelly to pen?

My Lady and my loue is cruelly pend In dolefull darkenesse from the vew of day, Whilest deadly torments do her chast brest rend, And the sharpe steele doth riue her hart in tway, All for she Scudamore will not denay. Yet thou vile man, vile Scudamore art sound, Ne canst her ayde, ne canst

her foe dismay: Vnworthy wretch to tread vpon the ground,
For whom so faire a Lady feeles so sore a wound.

There an huge heape of singulfes did oppresse His stru-
gling soule, and swelling throbs empeach His foltring toung
with pangs of drerinesse, Choking the remnant of his plain-
tife speach, As if his dayes were come to their last reach.
Which when she heard, and saw the ghastly fit, Threatning
into his life to make a breach, Both with great ruth and terrour she was smit, Fearing least from her cage the wearie
soule would flit.

Tho stooping downe she him amoued light; Who therewith somewhat starting, vp gan looke, And seeing him behind a straunger knight, Whereas no liuing creature he mistooke, With great indignaunce he that sight forsooke, And
downe againe himselfe disdainefully Abiecting, th'earth with
his faire forhead strooke: Which the bold Virgin seeing, gan
apply Fit medcine to his griefe, and spake thus courtesly.

Ah gentle knight, whose deepe conceiued griefe Well
seemes t'exceede the powre of patience, Yet if that heauenly
grace some good reliefe You send, submit you to high prouidence, And euer in your noble hart prepense, That all the
sorrow in the world is lesse, Then vertues might, and values
confidence, For who nill bide the burden of distresse, Must
not here thinke to liue: for life is wretchednesse.

Therefore, faire Sir, do comfort to you take, And freely
read, what wicked felon so Hath outrag'd you, and thrald
your gentle make. Perhaps this hand may helpe to ease your
woe, And wreake your sorrow on your cruell foe, At least it
faire endeuour will apply. Those feeling wordes so neare the
quicke did goe, That vp his head he reared easily, And lean-
ing on his elbow, these few wordes let fly.

What boots it plaine, that cannot be redrest, And sow
vaine sorrow in a fruitlesse eare, Sith powre of hand, nor
skill of learned brest, Ne worldly price cannot redeeme my
deare, Out of her thraldome and continuall feare? For he
the tyraunt, which her hath in ward By strong enchaunt-

ments and blacke Magicke leare, Hath in a dungeon deepe her close embard, And many dreadfull feends hath pointed to her gard.

There he tormenteth her most terribly, And day and night afflicts with mortall paine, Because to yield him loue she doth deny, Once to me yold, not to be yold againe: But yet by torture he would her constraine Loue to conceiue in her disdainfull brest; Till so she do, she must in doole remaine, Ne may by liuing meanes be thence relest: What boots it then to plaine, that cannot be redrest?

With this sad hersall of his heauy stresse, The warlike Damzell was empassiond sore, And said; Sir knight, your cause is nothing lesse, Then is your sorrow, certes if not more; For nothing so much pitty doth implore, As gentle Ladies helplesse misery. But yet, if please ye listen to my lore, I will with proofe of last extremity, Deliuer her fro thence, or with her for you dy.

Ah gentlest knight aliue, (said Scudamore) What huge heroicke magnanimity Dwels in thy bounteous brest? what couldst thou more, If she were thine, and thou as now am I? O spare thy happy dayes, and them apply To better boot, but let me dye, that ought; More is more losse: one is enough to dy. Life is not lost, (said she) for which is bought Endlesse renowm, that more then death is to be sought.

Thus she at length perswaded him to rise, And with her wend, to see what new successe Mote him befall vpon new enterprise; His armes, which he had vowed to disprofesse, She gathered vp and did about him dresse, And his forwandred steed vnto him got: So forth they both yfere make their progresse, And march not past the mountenaunce of a shot. Till they arriu'd, whereas their purpose they did plot.

There they dismounting, drew their weapons bold And stoutly came vnto the Castle gate; Whereas no gate they found, them to withhold, Nor ward to wait at morne and euening late, But in the Porch, that did them sore amate, A flaming fire, ymixt with smouldry smoke, And stinking

Sulphure, that with griesly hate And dreadfull horrour did all entraunce choke, Enforced them their forward footing to reuoke.

Greatly thereat was Britomart dismayd, Ne in that stownd wist, how her selfe to beare; For daunger vaine it were, to haue assayd That cruell element, which all things feare, Ne none can suffer to approchen neare: And turning backe to Scudamour, thus sayd; What monstrous enmity prouoke we heare, Foolhardy as th'Earthes children, the which made Battell against the Gods? so we a God inuade.

Daunger without discretion to attempt, Inglorious and beastlike is: therefore Sir knight, Aread what course of you is safest dempt, And how we with our foe may come to fight. This is (quoth he) the dolorous despight, Which earst to you I playnd: for neither may This fire be quencht by any wit or might, Ne yet by any meanes remou'd away, So mighty be th'enchauntments, which the same do stay.

What is there else, but cease these fruitlesse paines, And leaue me to my former languishing; Faire Amoret must dwell in wicked chaines, And Scudamore here dye with sorrowing. Perdy not so; (said she) for shamefull thing It were t'abandon noble cheuisaunce, For shew of perill, without venturing: Rather let try extremities of chaunce, Then enterprised prayse for dread to disauaunce.

Therewith resolu'd to proue her vtmost might, Her ample shield she threw before her face, And her swords point directing forward right, Assayld the flame, the which eftsoones gaue place, And did it selfe diuide with equall space, That through she passed; as a thunder bolt Perceth the yielding ayre, and doth displace The soring clouds into sad showres ymolt; So to her yold the flames, and did their force reuolt,

Whom whenas Scudamour saw past the fire, Safe and vntoucht, he likewise gan assay, With greedy will, and enuious desire, And bad the stubborne flames to yield him way: But cruell Mulciber would not obay His threatfull pride, but did the more augment His mighty rage, and with imperious sway Him forst (maulgre) his fiercenesse to relent, And backe retire, all scorcht and pitifully brent.

With huge impatience he inly swelt, More for great sorrow, that he could not pas, Then for the burning torment, which he felt, That with fell woodnesse he effierced was, And wilfully him throwing on the gras, Did beat and bounse his head and brest full sore; The whiles the Championesse now entred has The vtmost rowme, and past the formest dore, The vtmost rowme, abounding with all precious store.

For round about, the wals yclothed were With goodly arras of great maiesty, Wouen with gold and silke so close and nere, That the rich metall lurked priuily, As faining to be hid from enuious eye; Yet here, and there, and euery where vnwares It shewd it selfe, and shone vnwillingly; Like a discolourd Snake, whose hidden snares Through the greene gras his long bright burnisht backe declares.

And in those Tapets weren fashioned Many faire pourtraicts, and many a faire feate, And all of loue, and all of lustyhed, As seemed by their semblaunt did entreat; And eke all Cupids warres they did repeate, And cruell battels, which he whilome fought Gainst all the Gods, to make his empire great; Besides the huge massacres, which he wrought On mighty kings and kesars, into thraldome brought.

Therein was writ, how often thundring Ioue Had felt the point of his hart-percing dart, And leauing heauens kingdome, here did roue In straunge disguize, to slake his scalding smart; Now like a Ram, faire Helle to peruart, Now like a Bull, Europa to withdraw: Ah, how the fearefull Ladies tender hart Did liuely seeme to tremble, wheh she saw The huge seas vnder her t'obay her seruaunts law.

Soone after that into a golden showre Him selfe he chaung'd faire Danaë to vew, And through the roofe of her strong brasen towre Did raine into her lap an hony dew, The whiles her foolish garde, that little knew Of such deceipt, kept th'yron dore fast bard, And watcht, that none should enter nor issew; Vaine was the watch, and bootlesse all the ward, Whenas the God to golden hew him selfe transfard.

Then was he turnd into a snowy Swan, To win faire Leda
to his louely trade: O wondrous skill, and sweet wit of the
man, That her in daffadillies sleeping made, From scorching
heat her daintie limbes to shade: Whiles the proud Bird ruff-
ing his fethers wyde, And brushing his faire brest, did her
inuade; She slept, yet twixt her eyelids closely spyde, How
towards her he rusht, and smiled at his pryde.

Then shewd it, how the Thebane Semelee Deceiu'd of
gealous Iuno, did require To see him in his soueraigne maiestee, Armd with his thunderbolts and lightning fire, Whence
dearely she with death bought her desire. But faire Alcmena
better match did make, Ioying his loue in likenesse more entire; Three nights in one, they say, that for her sake He then
did put, her pleasures lenger to partake.

Twise was he seene in soaring Eagles shape, And with
wide wings to beat the buxome ayre, Once, when he with As-
terie did scape, Againe, when as the Troiane boy so faire He
snatcht from Ida hill, and with him bare: Wondrous delight
it was, there to behould, How the rude Shepheards after
him did stare, Trembling through feare, least down he fallen
should, And often to him calling, to take surer hould.

In Satyres shape Antiopa he snatcht: And like a fire,
when he Aegin' assayd: A shepheard, when Mnemosyne he
catcht: And like a Serpent to the Thracian mayd. Whiles thus
on earth great Ioue these pageaunts playd, The winged boy
did thrust into his throne, And scoffing, thus vnto his mother
sayd, Lo now the heauens obey to me alone, And take me for
their Ioue, whiles Ioue to earth is gone.

And thou, faire Phoebus, in thy colours bright Wast
there enwouen, and the sad distresse, In which that boy thee
plonged, for despight, That thou bewray'dst his mothers wan-
tonnesse, When she with Mars was meynt in ioyfulnesse: For
thy, he thrild thee with a leaden dart, To loue faire Daphne,
which thee loued lesse: Lesse she thee lou'd, then was thy
iust desart, Yet was thy loue her death, & her death was thy

smart.

So louedst thou the lusty Hyacinct, So louedst thou the faire Coronis deare: Yet both are of thy haplesse hand extinct, Yet both in flowres do liue, and loue thee beare, The one a Paunce, the other a sweet breare: For griefe whereof, ye mote haue liuely seene The God himselfe rending his golden heare, And breaking quite his gyrlond euer greene, With other signes of sorrow and impatient teene.

Both for those two, and for his owne deare sonne, The sonne of Climene he did repent, Who bold to guide the charet of the Sunne, Himselfe in thousand peeces fondly rent, And all the world with flashing fier brent; So like, that all the walles did seeme to flame. Yet cruell Cupid, not herewith content, Forst him eftsoones to follow other game, And loue a Shepheards daughter for his dearest Dame.

He loued Isse for his dear est Dame, And for her sake her cattell fed a while, And for her sake a cowheard vile became, The seruant of Admetus cowheard vile, Whiles that from heauen he suffered exile. Long were to tell each other louely fit, Now like a Lyon, hunting after spoile, Now like a Stag, now like a faulcon flit: All which in that faire arras was most liuely writ.

Next vnto him was Neptune pictured, In his diuine resemblance wondrous lyke: His face was rugged, and his hoarie hed Dropped with brackish deaw; his three-forkt Pyke He stearnly shooke, and therewith fierce did stryke The raging billowes, that on euery syde They trembling stood, and made a long broad dyke, That his swift charet might haue passage wyde, Which foure great Hippodames did draw in temewise tyde.

His sea-horses did seeme to sport amayne, And from their nosethrilles blow the brynie streame, That made the sparckling waues to smoke agayne, And flame with gold, but the white fomy creame, Did shine with siluer, and shoot forth his beame. The God himselfe did pensiue seeme and sad, And hong adowne his head, as he did dreame: For priuy loue his brest empierced had, Ne ought but deare Bisaltis ay could make him glad.

He loued eke Iphimedia deare, And Aeolus faire daughter Arne hight. For whom he turnd him selfe into a Steare, And fed on fodder, to beguile her sight. Also to win Deucalions daughter bright, He turnd him selfe into a Dolphin fayre; And like a winged horse he tooke his flight, To snaky-locke Medusa to repayre, On whom he got faire Pegasus, that flitteth in the ayre.

Next Saturne was, (but who would euer weene, That sullein Saturne euer weend to loue? Yet loue is sullein, and Saturnlike seene, As he did for Erigone it proue,) That to a Centaure did him selfe transmoue. So proou'd it eke that gracious God of wine, When for to compasse Philliras hard loue, He turnd himselfe into a fruitfull vine, And into her faire bosome made his grapes decline.

Long were to tell the amorous assayes, And gentle pangues, with which he maked meeke The mighty Mars, to learne his wanton playes: How oft for Venus, and how often eek For many other Nymphes he sore did shreek, With womanish teares, and with vnwarlike smarts, Priuily moystening his horrid cheek. There was he painted full of burning darts, And many wide woundes launched through his inner parts.

Ne did he spare (so cruell was the Elfe) His owne deare mother, (ah why should he so?) Ne did he spare sometime to pricke himselfe, That he might taste the sweet consuming woe, Which he had wrought to many others moe. But to declare the mournfull Tragedyes, And spoiles, wherewith he all the ground did strow, More eath to number, with how many eyes High heauen beholds sad louers nightly theeueryes.

Kings Queenes, Lords Ladies, Knights & Damzels gent Were heap'd together with the vulgar sort, And mingled with the raskall rablement, Without respect of person or of port, To shew Dan Cupids powre and great effort: And round about a border was entrayld, Of broken bowes and arrowes shiuered short, And a long bloudy riuer through them rayld,

So liuely and so like, that liuing sence it fayld.

And at the vpper end of that faire rowme, There was an Altar built of pretious stone, Of passing valew, and of great renowme, On which there stood an Image all alone, Of massy gold, which with his owne light shone; And wings it had with sundry colours dight, More sundry colours, then the proud Pauone Beares in his boasted fan, or Iris bright, When her discolourd bow she spreds through heauens hight.

Blindfold he was, and in his cruell fist A mortall bow and arrowes keene did hold, With which he shot at randon, when him list, Some headed with sad lead, some with pure gold; (Ah man beware, how thou those darts behold) A wounded Dragon vnder him did ly, Whose hideous tayle his left foot did enfold, And with a shaft was shot through either eye, That no man forth might draw, ne no man remedye.

And vnderneath his feet was written thus, Vnto the Victor of the Gods this bee: And all the people in that ample hous Did to that image bow their humble knee, And oft committed fowle Idolatree. That wondrous sight faire Britomart amazed, Ne seeing could her wonder satisfie, But euermore and more vpon it gazed, The whiles the passing brightnes her fraile sences dazed.

Tho as she backward cast her busie eye, To search each secret of that goodly sted, Ouer the dore thus written she did spye Be bold: she oft and oft it ouer-red, Yet could not find what sence it figured: But what so were therein or writ or ment, She was no whit thereby discouraged From prosecuting of her first intent, But forward with bold steps into the next roome went.

Much fairer, then the former, was that roome, And richlier by many partes arayd: For not with arras made in painefull loome, But with pure gold it all was ouerlayd, Wrought with wilde Antickes, which their follies playd, In the rich metall, as they liuing were: A thousand monstrous formes therein were made, Such as false loue doth oft vpon him weare: For loue in thousand monstrous formes doth oft appeare.

And all about, the glistring walles were hong With war-like spoiles, and with victorious prayes, Of mighty Conquer-ours and Captaines strong, Which were whilome captiued in their dayes To cruell loue, and wrought their owne decayes: Their swerds & speres were broke, & hauberques rent; And their proud girlonds of tryumphant bayes Troden in dust with fury insolent, To shew the victors might and mercilesse intent.

The warlike Mayde beholding earnestly The goodly or-dinance of this rich place, Did greatly wonder, ne could sat-isfie Her greedy eyes with gazing a long space: But more she meruaild that no footings trace, Nor wight appear'd, but wastefull emptinesse, And solemne silence ouer all that place: Straunge thing it seem'd, that none was to possesse So rich purueyance, ne them keepe with carefulnesse.

And as she lookt about, she did behold, How ouer that same dore was likewise writ, Be bold, be bold, and euery where Be bold, That much she muz'd, yet could not construe it By any ridling skill, or commune wit. At last she spyde at that roomes vpper end, Another yron dore, on which was writ, Be not too bold; whereto though she did bend Her ear-nest mind, yet wist not what it might intend.

Thus she there waited vntill euentyde, Yet liuing crea-ture none she saw appeare: And now sad shadowes gan the world to hyde, From mortall vew, and wrap in darkenesse dreare; Yet nould she d'off her weary armes, for feare Of se-cret daunger, ne let sleepe oppresse Her heauy eyes with na-tures burdein deare, But drew her selfe aside in sickernesse, And her welpointed weapons did about her dresse.

Cant. XII.

The maske of Cupid, and th'enchaunted Chamber are displayd, Whence Britomart redeemes faire Amoret, through charmes decayd.

T Ho when as chearelesse Night ycouered had Faire heauen with an vniuersall cloud, That euery wight dismayd with darknesse sad, In silence and in sleepe themselues did

shroud, She heard a shrilling Trompet sound aloud, Signe of
nigh battell, or got victory; Nought therewith daunted was
her courage proud, But rather stird to cruell enmity, Expecting euer, when some foe she might descry. With that, an
hideous storme of winde arose, With dreadfull thunder and
lightning atwixt, And an earth-quake, as if it streight would
lose The worlds foundations from his centre fixt; A direfull
stench of smoke and sulphure mixt Ensewd, whose noyance
fild the fearefull sted, From the fourth houre of night vntill
the sixt; Yet the bold Britonesse was nought ydred, Though
much emmou'd, but stedfast still perseuered.

All suddenly a stormy whirlwind blew Throughout the
house, that clapped euery dore, With which that yron wicket
open flew, As it with mightie leuers had bene tore: And forth
issewd, as on the ready flore Of some Theatre, a graue personage, That in his hand a branch of laurell bore, With comely haueour and count'nance sage, Yclad in costly garments,
fit for tragicke Stage.

Proceeding to the midst, he still did stand, As if in mind
he somewhat had to say, And to the vulgar beckning with his
hand, In signe of silence, as to heare a play, By liuely actions
he gan bewray Some argument of matter passioned; Which
doen, he backe retyred soft away, And passing by, his name
discouered, Ease, on his robe in golden letters cyphered.

The noble Mayd, still standing all this vewd, And merue-
ild at his strange intendiment; With that a ioyous fellowship
issewd Of Minstrals, making goodly meriment, With wanton
Bardes, and Rymers impudent, All which together sung full
chearefully A lay of loues delight, with sweet consent: After
whom marcht a iolly company, In manner of a maske, en-
ranged orderly.

The whiles a most delitious harmony, In full straunge
notes was sweetly heard to sound, That the rare sweetnesse
of the melody The feeble senses wholly did confound, And
the fraile soule in deepe delight nigh drownd: And when it
ceast, shrill trompets loud did bray, That their report did
farre away rebound, And when they ceast, it gan againe to

play, The whiles the maskers marched forth in trim aray.

The first was Fancy, like a louely boy, Of rare aspect, and beautie without peare; Matchable either to that ympe of Troy, Whom Ioue did loue, and chose his cup to beare, Or that same daintie lad, which was so deare To great Alcides, that when as he dyde, He wailed womanlike with many a teare, And euery wood, and euery valley wyde He fild with Hylas name; the Nymphes eke Hylas cryde.

His garment neither was of silke nor say, But painted plumes, in goodly order dight, Like as the sunburnt Indians do aray Their tawney bodies, in their proudest plight: As those same plumes, so seemd he vaine and light, That by his gate might easily appeare; For still he far'd as dauncing in delight, And in his hand a windy fan did beare, That in the idle aire he mou'd still here and there.

And him beside marcht amorous Desyre, Who seemd of riper yeares, then th'other Swaine, Yet was that other swayne this elders syre, And gaue him being, commune to them twaine: His garment was disguised very vaine, And his embrodered Bonet sat awry; Twixt both his hands few sparkes he close did straine, Which still he blew, and kindled busily, That soone they life conceiu'd, & forth in flames did fly.

Next after him went Doubt, who was yclad In a discolour'd cote, of straunge disguyse, That at his backe a brode Capuccio had, And sleeues dependant Albanese-wyse: He lookt askew with his mistrustfull eyes, And nicely trode, as thornes lay in his way, Or that the flore to shrinke he did auyse, And on a broken reed he still did stay His feeble steps, which shrunke, when hard theron he lay.

With him went Daunger, cloth'd in ragged weed, Made of Beares skin, that him more dreadfull made, Yet his owne face was dreadfull, ne did need Straunge horrour, to deforme his griesly shade; A net in th'one hand, and a rustie blade In th'other was, this Mischiefe, that Mishap; With th'one his foes he threatned to inuade, With th'other he his friends ment to enwrap: For whom he could not kill, he practizd to entrap.

Next him was Feare, all arm'd from top to toe, Yet thought himselfe not safe enough thereby, But feard each shadow mouing to and fro, And his owne armes when glittering he did spy, Or clashing heard, he fast away did fly, As ashes pale of hew, and wingyheeld; And euermore on daunger fixt his eye, Gainst whom he alwaies bent a brasen shield, Which his right hand vnarmed fearefully did wield.

With him went Hope in rancke, a handsome Mayd, Of chearefull looke and louely to behold; In silken samite she was light arayd, And her faire lockes were wouen vp in gold; She alway smyld, and in her hand did hold An holy water Sprinckle, dipt in deowe, With which she sprinckled fauours manifold, On whom she list, and did great liking sheowe, Great liking vnto many, but true loue to feowe.

And after them Dissemblance, and Suspect Marcht in one rancke, yet an vnequall paire: For she was gentle, and of milde aspect, Courteous to all, and seeming debonaire, Goodly adorned, and exceeding faire: Yet was that all but painted, and purloynd, And her bright browes were deckt with borrowed haire: Her deedes were forged, and her words false coynd, And alwaies in her hand two clewes of silke she twynd.

But he was foule, ill fauoured, and grim, Vnder his eyebrowes looking still askaunce; And euer as Dissemblance laught on him, He lowrd on her with daungerous eyeglaunce; Shewing his nature in his countenance; His rolling eyes did neuer rest in place, But walkt each where, for feare of hid mischaunce, Holding a lattice still before his face, Through which he still did peepe, as forward he did pace.

Next him went Griefe, and Fury matcht yfere; Griefe all in sable sorrowfully clad, Downe hanging his dull head, with heauy chere, Yet inly being more, then seeming sad: A paire of Pincers in his hand he had, With which he pinched people to the hart, That from thenceforth a wretched life they lad, In wilfull languor and consuming smart, Dying each day with inward wounds of dolours dart.

But Fury was full ill appareiled In rags, that naked nigh she did appeare, With ghastly lookes and dreadfull drerihed; For from her backe her garments she did teare, And from her head oft rent her snarled heare: In her right hand a firebrand she did tosse About her head, still roming here and there; As a dismayed Deare in chace embost, Forgetfull of his safety, hath his right way lost.

After them went Displeasure and Pleasance, He looking lompish and full sullein sad, And hanging downe his heauy countenance; She chearefull fresh and full of ioyance glad, As if no sorrow she ne felt ne drad; That euill matched paire they seemd to bee: An angry Waspe th'one in a viall had Th'other in hers an hony-lady Bee; Thus marched these sixe couples forth in faire degree.

After all these there marcht a most faire Dame, Led of two grysie villeins, th'one Despight, The other cleped Cruelty by name: She dolefull Lady, like a dreary Spright, Cald by strong charmes out of eternall night, Had deathes owne image figurd in her face, Full of sad signes, fearefull to liuing sight; Yet in that horror shewd a seemely grace, And with her feeble feet did moue a comely pace.

Her brest all naked, as net iuory, Without adorne of gold or siluer bright, Wherewith the Craftesman wonts it beautify, Of her dew honour was despoyled quight, And a wide wound therein (O ruefull sight) Entrenched deepe with knife accursed keene, Yet freshly bleeding forth her fainting spright, (The worke of cruell hand) was to be seene, That dyde in sanguine red her skin all snowy cleene.

At that wide orifice her trembling hart Was drawne forth, and in siluer basin layd, Quite through transfixed with a deadly dart, And in her bloud yet steeming fresh embayd: And those two villeins, which her steps vpstayd, When her weake feete could scarcely her sustaine, And fading vitall powers gan to fade, Her forward still with torture did constraine, And euermore encreased her consuming paine.

Next after her the winged God himselfe Came riding on a Lion rauenous, Taught to obay the menage of that Elfe, That man and beast with powre imperious Subdeweth to his kingdome tyrannous: His blindfold eyes he bad a while vnbind, That his proud spoyle of that same dolorous Faire Dame he might behold in perfect kind; Which seene, he much reioyced in his cruell mind.

Of which full proud, himselfe vp rearing hye, He looked round about with sterne disdaine; And did suruay his goodly company: And marshalling the euill ordered traine, With that the darts which his right hand did straine, Full dreadfully he shooke that all did quake, And clapt on hie his coulourd winges twaine, That all his many it affraide did make: Tho blinding him againe, his way he forth did take.

Behinde him was Reproch, Repentance, Shame; Reproch the first, Shame next, Repent behind: Repentance feeble, sorrowfull, and lame: Reproch despightfull, carelesse, and vnkind; Shame most ill fauourd, bestiall, and blind: Shame lowrd, Repentance sigh'd, Reproch did scould; Reproch sharpe stings, Repentance whips entwind, Shame burning brond-yrons in her hand did hold: All three to each vnlike, yet all made in one mould.

And after them a rude confused rout Of persons flockt, whose names is hard to read: Emongst them was sterne Strife, and Anger stout, Vnquiet Care, and fond Vnthriftihead, Lewd Losse of Time, and Sorrow seeming dead, Inconstant Chaunge, and false Disloyaltie, Consuming Riotise, and guilty Dread Of heauenly vengeance, faint Infirmitie, Vile Pouertie, and lastly Death with infamie.

There were full many moe like maladies, Whose names and natures I note readen well; So many moe, as there be phantasies In wauering wemens wit, that none can tell, Or paines in loue, or punishments in hell; All which disguized marcht in masking wise, About the chamber with that Damozell, And then returned, hauing marched thrise, Into the inner roome, from whence they first did rise.

So soone as they were in, the dore streight way Fast locked, driuen with that stormy blast, Which first it opened; and bore all away. Then the braue Maid, which all this while was plast, In secret shade, and saw both first and last, Issewed forth, and went vnto the dore, To enter in, but found it locked fast: It vaine she thought with rigorous vprore For to efforce, when charmes had closed it afore.

Where force might not auaile, their sleights and art She cast to vse, both fit for hard emprize; For thy, from that same roome not to depart Till morrow next, she did her selfe auize, When that same Maske againe should forth arize. The morrow next appeard with ioyous cheare, Calling men to their daily exercize, Then she, as morrow fresh, her selfe did reare Out of her secret stand, that day for to out weare.

All that day she outwore in wandering, And gazing on that Chambers ornament, Till that againe the second euening Her couered with her sable vestiment, Wherewith the worlds faire beautie she hath blent: Then when the second watch was almost past, That brasen dore flew open, and in went Bold Britomart, as she had late forecast, Neither of idle shewes, nor of false charmes aghast.

So soone as she was entred, round about She cast her eies, to see what was become Of all those persons, which she saw without: But lo, they streight were vanisht all and some, Ne liuing wight she saw in all that roome, Saue that same woefull Ladie, both whose hands Were bounden fast, that did her ill become, And her small wast girt round with yron bands, Vnto a brasen pillour, by the which she stands.

And her before the vile Enchaunter sate, Figuring straunge characters of his art, With liuing bloud he those characters wrate, Dreadfully dropping from her dying hart, Seeming transfixed with a cruell dart, And all perforce to make her him to loue. Ah who can loue the worker of her smart? A thousand charmes he formerly did proue; Yet thousand charmes could not her stedfast heart remoue.

Soone as that virgin knight he saw in place, His wicked bookes in hast he ouerthrew, Not caring his long labours to deface, And fiercely ronning to that Lady trew, A murdrous knife out of his pocket drew, The which he thought, for villeinous despight, In her tormented bodie to embrew: But the stout Damzell to him leaping light, His cursed hand withheld, and maistered his might.

From her, to whom his fury first he ment, The wicked weapon rashly he did wrest, And turning to her selfe his fell intent, Vnwares it strooke into her snowie chest, That little drops empurpled her faire brest. Exceeding wroth therewith the virgin grew, Albe the wound were nothing deepe imprest, And fiercely forth her mortall blade she drew, To giue him the reward for such vile outrage dew.

So mightily she smote him, that to ground He fell halfe dead; next stroke him should haue slaine, Had not the Lady, which by him stood bound, Dernely vnto her called to abstaine, From doing him to dy. For else her paine Should be remedilesse, sith none but hee, Which wrought it, could the same recure againe. Therewith she stayd her hand, loth stayd to bee; For life she him enuyde, and long'd reuenge to see.

And to him said, Thou wicked man, whose meed For so huge mischiefe, and vile villany Is death, or if that ought do death exceed, Be sure, that nought may saue thee from to dy, But if that thou this Dame doe presently Restore vnto her health, and former state; This doe and liue, else die vndoubtedly. He glad of life, that lookt for death but late, Did yield himselfe right willing to prolong his date.

And rising vp, gan streight to ouerlooke, Those cursed leaues, his charmes backe to reuerse; Full dreadfull things out of that balefull booke He red, and measur'd many a sad verse, That horror gan the virgins hart to perse, And her faire locks vp stared stiffe on end, Hearing him those same bloudy lines reherse; And all the while he red, she did extend Her sword high ouer him, if ought he did offend.

Anon she gan perceiue the house to quake, And all the dores to rattle round about; Yet all that did not her dismaied make, Nor slacke her threatfull hand for daungers dout, But still with stedfast eye and courage stout Abode, to weet what end would come of all. At last that mightie chaine, which round about Her tender waste was wound, adowne gan fall, And that great brasen pillour broke in peeces small.

The cruell steele, which thrild her dying hart, Fell softly forth, as of his owne accord, And the wyde wound, which lately did dispart Her bleeding brest, and riuen bowels gor'd, Was closed vp, as it had not bene bor'd, And euery part to safety full sound, As she were neuer hurt, was soone restor'd: Tho when she felt her selfe to be vnbound, And perfect hole, prostrate she fell vnto the ground.

Before faire Britomart, she fell prostrate, Saying, Ah noble knight, what worthy meed Can wretched Lady, quit from wofull state, Yield you in lieu of this your gratious deed? Your vertue selfe her owne reward shall breed, Euen immortall praise, and glory wyde, Which I your vassall, by your prowesse freed, Shall through the world make to be notifyde, And goodly well aduance, that goodly well was tryde.

But Britomart vprearing her from ground, Said, Gentle Dame, reward enough I weene For many labours more, then I haue found, This, that in safety now I haue you seene, And meane of your deliuerance haue beene: Henceforth faire Lady comfort to you take, And put away remembrance of late teene; In stead thereof know, that your louing Make, Hath no lesse griefe endured for your gentle sake.

She much was cheard to heare him mentiond, Whom of all liuing wights she loued best. Then laid the noble Championesse strong hond Vpon th'enchaunter, which had her distrest So sore, and with foule outrages opprest: With that great chaine, wherewith not long ygo He bound that pitteous Lady prisoner, now relest, Himselfe she bound, more worthy to be so, And captiue with her led to wretchednesse and wo.

Returning backe, those goodly roomes, which erst She saw

so rich and royally arayd, Now vanisht vtterly, and cleane
subuerst She found, and all their glory quite decayd, That
sight of such a chaunge her much dismayd. Thence forth de-
scending to that perlous Porch, Those dreadfull flames she
also found delayd, And quenched quite, like a consumed
torch, That erst all entrers wont so cruelly to scorch.

More easie issew now, then entrance late She found: for
now that fained dreadfull flame, Which chokt the porch of
that enchaunted gate, And passage bard to all, that thither
came, Was vanisht quite, as it were not the same, And gaue
her leaue at pleasure forth to passe. Th'Enchaunter selfe,
which all that fraud did frame, To haue efforst the loue of
that faire lasse, Seeing his worke now wasted deepe engrieued was.

But when the victoresse arriued there, Where late she
left the pensife Scudamore, With her owne trusty Squire,
both full of feare, Neither of them she found where she them
lore: Thereat her noble hart was stonisht sore; But most faire
Amoret, whose gentle spright Now gan to feede on hope,
which she before Conceiued had, to see her owne dear knight,
Being thereof beguyld was fild with new affright.

But he sad man, when he had long in drede Awayted
there for Britomarts returne, Yet saw her not nor signe of
her good speed, His expectation to despaire did turne, Misdeeming sure that her those flames did burne; And therefore
gan aduize with her old Squire, Who her deare nourslings
losse no lesse did mourne, Thence to depart for further aide
t'enquire: Where let them wend at will, whilest here I doe
respire.

STANZAS IN 1590 REPLACED IN 1596 WITH OTH-
ERS.

At last she came vnto the place, where late She left
Sir Scudamour in great distresse, Twixt dolour and despight halfe desperate, Of his loues succour, of his owne redresse, And of the hardie Britomarts successe: There on the
cold earth him now thrown she found, In wilfull anguish,

and dead heauinesse, And to him cald; whose voices knowen sound Soone as he heard, himself he reared light from
ground. There did he see, that most on earth him ioyd, His
dearest loue, the comfort of his dayes, Whose too long ab-
sence him had sore annoyd, And wearied his life with dull
delayes: Straight he vpstarted from the loathed layes, And to
her ran with hasty egernesse, Like as a Deare, that greedily
embayes In the coole soile, after long thirstinesse, Which he
in chace endured hath, now nigh breathlesse.

Lightly he clipt her twixt his armes twaine, And streightly did embrace her body bright, Her body, late the prison of
sad paine, Now the sweet lodge of loue and deare delight:
But she faire Lady ouercommen quight Of huge affection, did
in pleasure melt, And in sweete rauishment pourd out her
spright: No word they spake, nor earthly thing they felt, But
like two senceles stocks in long embracemet dwelt.

Had ye them seene, ye would haue surely thought, That
they had beene that faire Hermaphrodite, Which that rich
Romane of white marble wrought, And in his costly Bath
causd to bee site: So seemd those two, as growne together
quite, That Britomart halfe enuying their b[l]esse, Was much
empassiond in her gentle sprite, And to her selfe oft wisht
like happinesse, In vaine she wisht, that fate n'ould let her
yet possesse.

Thus doe those louers with sweet counteruayle, Each
other of loues bitter fruit despoile. But now my teme begins
to faint and fayle, All woxen weary of their iournall toyle:
Therefore I will their sweatie yokes assoyle, At this same
furrowes end, till a new day: And ye faire swayns, after your
long turmoyle, Now cease your worke, and at your pleasure
play: Now cease your worke; to morrow is an holy day.

THE FOVRTH BOOKE OF THE FAERIE QVEENE.

Containing The Legend of Cambel and Telamond,

OR OF FRIENDSHIP.

The rugged forhead that with graue foresight Welds kingdomes causes, & affaires of state, My looser rimes (I wote) doth sharply wite, For praising loue, as I haue done of late, And magnifying louers deare debate; By which fraile youth is oft to follie led, Through false allurement of that pleasing baite, That better were in vertues discipled, Then with vaine poemes weeds to haue their fancies fed. Such ones ill iudge of loue, that cannot loue, Ne in their frosen hearts feele kindly flame: For thy, they ought not thing vnknowne reproue, Ne naturall affection faultlesse blame, For fault of few that haue abusd the same. For it of honor and all vertue is The roote, and brings forth glorious flowres of fame, That crowne true louers with immortall blis, The meed of them that loue, and do not liue amisse.

Which who so list looke backe to former ages, And call to count the things that then were donne, Shall find, that all the workes of those wise sages, And braue exploits which great Heroes wonne, In loue were either ended or begunne: Witnesse the father of Philosophie, Which to his Critias, shaded oft from sunne, Of loue full manie lessons did apply, The which these Stoicke censours cannot well deny.

To such therefore I do not sing at all, But to that sacred Saint my soueraigne Queene, In whose chast breast all bountie naturall, And treasures of true loue enlocked beene, Boue all her sexe that euer yet was seene; To her I sing of loue, that loueth best, And best is lou'd of all aliue I weene: To her this song most fitly is addrest, The Queene of loue, & Prince of peace frō heauen blest.

Which that she may the better deigne to heare, Do thou dred infant, Venus dearling doue, From her high spirit chase imperious feare, And vse of awfull Maiestie remoue: In sted thereof with drops of melting loue, Deawd with ambrosiall kisses, by thee gotten From thy sweete smyling mother from

aboue, Sprinckle her heart, and haughtie courage soften,
That she may hearke to loue, and reade this lesson often.

Canto I.

Fayre Britomart saues Amoret, Duessa discord breedes
Twixt Scudamour and Blandamour: Their fight and warlike
deedes.

O F louers sad calamities of old, Full many piteous stories
doe remaine, But none more piteous euer was ytold, Then
that of Amorets hart-binding chaine, And this of Florimels
vnworthie paine: The deare compassion of whose bitter fit
My softened heart so sorely doth constraine, That I with
teares full oft doe pittie it, And oftentimes doe wish it neuer
had bene writ.

For from the time that Scudamour her bought In perilous fight, she neuer ioyed day, A perilous fight when he
with force her brought From twentie Knights, that did him
all assay: Yet fairely well he did them all dismay: And with
great glorie both the shield of loue, And eke the Ladie selfe
he brought away, Whom hauing wedded as did him behoue,
A new vnknowen mischiefe did from him remoue.

For that same vile Enchauntour Busyran, The very selfe
same day that she was wedded, Amidst the bridale feast,
whilest euery man Surcharg'd with wine, were heedlesse
and ill hedded. All bent to mirth before the bride was bed-
ded, Brought in that mask of loue which late was showen:
And there the Ladie ill of friends bestedded, By way of sport,
as oft in maskes is knowen, Conueyed quite away to liuing
wight vnknowen.

Seuen moneths he so her kept in bitter smart, Because
his sinfull lust she would not serue, Vntill such time as noble
Britomart Released her, that else was like to sterue, Through
cruell knife that her deare heart did kerue. And now she is
with her vpon the way, Marching in louely wise, that could
deserue No spot of blame, though spite did oft assay To blot
her with dishonor of so faire a pray.

Yet should it be a pleasant tale, to tell The diuerse vsage and demeanure daint, That each to other made, as oft befell. For Amoret right fearefull was and faint, Lest she with blame her honor should attaint, That euerie word did tremble as she spake, And euerie looke was coy, and wondrous quaint, And euerie limbe that touched her did quake: Yet could she not but curteous coūtenance to her make.

For well she wist, as true it was indeed, That her liues Lord and patrone of her health Right well deserued as his duefull meed, Her loue, her seruice, and her vtmost wealth. All is his iustly, that all freely dealth: Nathlesse her honor dearer then her life, She sought to saue, as thing reseru'd from stealth; Die had she leuer with Enchanters knife, Then to be false in loue, profest a virgine wife.

Thereto her feare was made so much the greater Through fine abusion of that Briton mayd: Who for to hide her fained sex the better, And maske her wounded mind, both did and sayd Full many things so doubtfull to be wayd, That well she wist not what by them to gesse, For other whiles to her she purpos made Of loue, and otherwhiles of lustfulnesse That much she feard his mind would grow to some excesse.

His will she feard; for him she surely thought To be a man, such as indeed he seemed, And much the more, by that he lately wrought, When her from deadly thraldome he redeemed, For which no seruice she too much esteemed, Yet dread of shame, and doubt of fowle dishonor Made her not yeeld so much, as due she deemed. Yet Britomart attended duly on her, As well became a knight, and did to her all honor.

It so befell one euening, that they came Vnto a Castell, lodged there to bee, Where many a knight, and many a louely Dame Was then assembled, deeds of armes to see: Amongst all which was none more faire then shee, That many of them mou'd to eye her sore. The custome of that place was such, that hee Which had no loue nor lemman there in store, Should either winne him one, or lye without the dore.

Amongst the rest there was a iolly knight, Who being asked for his loue, auow'd That fairest Amoret was his by right, And offred that to iustifie alowd. The warlike virgine seeing his so prowd And boastfull chalenge, wexed inlie wroth, But for the present did her anger shrowd; And sayd, her loue to lose she was full loth, But either he should neither of them haue, or both.

So foorth they went, and both together giusted; But that same younker soone was ouer throwne, And made repent, that he had rashly lusted For thing vnlawfull, that was not his owne: Yet since he seemed valiant, through vnknowne, She that no lesse was courteous then stout, Cast how to salue, that both the custome showne Were kept, and yet that Knight not locked out: That seem'd full hard t'accord two things so far in dout.

The Seneschall was cal'd to deeme the right, Whom she requir'd, that first fayre Amoret Might be to her allow'd, as to a Knight, That did her win and free from chalenge set: Which straight to her was yeelded without let. Then since that strange Knights loue from him was quitted, She claim'd that to her selfe, as Ladies det, He as a Knight might iustly be admitted; So none should be out shut, sith all of loues were fitted.

With that her glistring helmet she vnlaced; Which doft, her golden lockes, that were vp bound Still in a knot, vnto her heeles downe traced, And like a silken veile in compasse round About her backe and all her bodie wound; Like as the shining skie in summers night, What time the dayes with scorching heat abound, Is creasted all with lines of firie light, That it prodigious seemes in common peoples sight.

Such when those Knights and Ladies all about Beheld her, all were with amazement smit, And euery one gan grow in secret dout Of this and that, according to each wit: Some thought that some enchantment faygned it; Some, that Bellona in that warlike wise To them appear'd, with shield and armour fit; Some, that it was a maske of strange disguise: So diuersely each one did sundrie doubts deuise.

But that young Knight, which through her gentle deed Was to that goodly fellowship restor'd, Ten thousand thankes did yeeld her for her meed, And doubly ouercommen, her ador'd: So did they all their former strife accord; And eke fayre Amoret now freed from feare, More franke affection did to her afford, And to her bed, which she was wont forbeare, Now freely drew, and found right safe assurance theare.

Where all that night they of their loues did treat, And hard aduentures twixt themselues alone, That each the other gan with passion great, And griefull pittie priuately bemone. The morow next so soone as Titan shone, They both vprose, and to their waies them dight: Long wandred they, yet neuer met with none, That to their willes could them direct aright, Or to them tydings tell, that mote their harts delight.

Lo thus they rode, till at the last they spide Two armed Knights, that toward them did pace, And ech of them had ryding by his side A Ladie, seeming in so farre a space, But Ladies none they were, albee in face And outward shew faire semblance they did beare; For vnder maske of beautie and good grace, Vile treason and fowle falshood hidden were, That mote to none but to the warie wise appeare.

The one of them the false Duessa hight, That now had chang'd her former wonted hew: For she could d'on so manie shapes in sight, As euer could Cameleon colours new; So could she forge all colours, saue the trew. The other no whit better was then shee, But that such as she was, she plaine did shew; Yet otherwise much worse, if worse might bee, And dayly more offensiue vnto each degree.

Her name was Ate, mother of debate, And all dissention, which doth dayly grow Amongst fraile men, that many a pub-like state And many a priuate oft doth ouerthrow. Her false Duessa who full well did know, To be most fit to trouble noble knights, Which hunt for honor, raised from below, Out of the dwellings of the damned sprights, Where she in darknes wastes her cursed daies & nights.

Hard by the gates of hell her dwelling is, There whereas

all the plagues and harmes abound, Which punish wicked men, that walke amisse: It is a darksome delue farre vnder ground, With thornes and barren brakes enuirond round, That none the same may easily out win; Yet many waies to enter may be found, But none to issue forth when one is in: For discord harder is to end then to begin.

And all within the riuen walls were hung With ragged monuments of times forepast, All which the sad effects of discord sung: There were rent robes, and broken scepters plast, Altars defyl'd, and holy things defast, Disshiuered speares, and shields ytorne in twaine, Great cities ransackt, and strong castles rast, Nations captiued, and huge armies slaine: Of all which ruines there some relicks did remaine.

There was the signe of antique Babylon, Of fatall Thebes, of Rome that raigned long, Of sacred Salem, and sad Ilion For memorie of which on high there hong The golden Apple, cause of all their wrong, For which the three faire Goddesses did striue: There also was the name of Nimrod strong, Of Alexander, and his Princes fiue, Which shar'd to them the spoiles that he had aliue.

And there the relicks of the drunken fray, The which amongst the Lapithees befell, And of the bloodie feast, which sent away So many Centaures drunken soules to hell, That vnder great Alcides furie fell: And of the dreadfull discord, which did driue The noble Argonauts to outrage fell: That each of life sought others to depriue, All mindlesse of the Golden fleece, which made them striue.

And eke of priuate persons many moe, That were too long a worke to count them all; Some of sworne friends, that did their faith forgoe; Some of borne brethren, prov'd vnnaturall; Some of deare louers, foes perpetuall: Witnesse their broken bandes there to be seene, Their girlonds rent, their bowres despoyled all; The moniments whereof there byding beene, As plaine as at the first, when they were fresh and greene.

Such was her house within; but all without, The barren ground was full of wicked weedes, Which she her selfe had sowen all about, Now growen great, at first of little seedes, The seedes of euill wordes, and factious deedes; Which when to ripenesse due they growen arre, Bring foorth an infinite increase, that breedes Tumultuous trouble and contentious iarre, The which most often end in bloudshed and in warre.

And those same cursed seedes doe also serue To her for bread, and yeeld her liuing food: For life it is to her, when others sterue Through mischieuous debate, and deadly feood, That she may sucke their life, and drinke their blood, With which she from her childhood had bene fed. For she at first was borne of hellish brood, And by infernall furies nourished, That by her monstrous shape might easily be red.

Her face most fowle and filthy was to see, With squinted eyes contrarie wayes intended, And loathly mouth, vnmeete a mouth to bee, That nought but gall and venim comprehended, And wicked wordes that God and man offended: Her lying tongue was in two parts diuided, And both the parts did speake, and both contended; And as her tongue, so was her hart discided, That neuer thoght one thing, but doubly stil was guided.

Als as she double spake, so heard she double, With matchlesse eares deformed and distort, Fild with false rumors and seditious trouble, Bred in assemblies of the vulgar sort, That still are led with euery light report. And as her eares so eke her feet were odde, And much vnlike, th'one long, the other short, And both misplast; that when th'one forward yode, The other backe retired, and contrarie trode.

Likewise vnequall were her handes twaine, That one did reach, the other pusht away, That one did make, the other mard againe, And sought to bring all things vnto decay; Whereby great riches gathered manie a day, She in short space did often bring to nought And their possessours often did dismay. For all her studie was and all her thought, How she might ouerthrow the things that Concord wrought.

So much her malice did her might surpas, That euen th'Almightie selfe she did maligne, Because to man so mercifull he was, And vnto all his creatures so benigne, Sith she her selfe was of his grace indigne: For all this worlds faire workmanship she tride, Vnto his last confusion to bring, And that great golden chaine quite to diuide, With which it blessed Concord hath together tide.

Such was that hag, which with Duessa roade, And seruing her in her malitious vse, To hurt good knights, was as it were her baude, To sell her borrowed beautie to abuse. For though like withered tree, that wanteth iuyce, She old and crooked were, yet now of late, As fresh and fragrant as the floure deluce She was become, by chaunge of her estate, And made full goodly ioyance to her new found mate.

Her mate he was a iollie youthfull knight, That bore great sway in armes and chiualrie, And was indeed a man of mickle might: His name was Blandamour, that did descrie His fickle mind full of inconstancie. And now himselfe he fitted had right well, With two companions of like qualitie, Faithlesse Duessa, and false Paridell, That whether were more false, full hard it is to tell.

Now when this gallant with his goodly crew, From farre espide the famous Britomart, Like knight aduenturous in outward vew, With his faire paragon, his conquests part, Approching nigh, eftsoones his wanton hart Was tickled with delight, and iesting sayd; Lo there Sir Paridel, for your desart, Good lucke presents you with yond louely mayd, For pitie that ye want a fellow for your ayd.

By that the louely paire drew nigh to hond: Whom when as Paridel more plaine beheld, Albee in heart he like affection fond, Yet mindfull how he late by one was feld, That did those armes and that same scutchion weld, He had small lust to buy his loue so deare, But answerd, Sir him wise I neuer held, That hauing once escaped perill neare, Would afterwards afresh the sleeping euill reare.

This knight too late his manhood and his might, I did assay, that me right dearely cost, Ne list I for reuenge prouoke new fight, Ne for light Ladies loue, that soone is lost. The hot-spurre youth so scorning to be crost, Take then to you this Dame of mine (quoth hee) And I without your perill or your cost, Will chalenge yond same other for my fee: So forth he fiercely prickt, that one him scarce could see.

The warlike Britonesse her soone addrest, And with such vncouth welcome did receaue Her fayned Paramour, her forced guest, That being forst his saddle soone to leaue, Him selfe he did of his new loue deceaue: And made him selfe thensample of his follie. Which done, she passed forth not taking leaue, And left him now as sad, as whilome iollie, Well warned to beware with whom he dar'd to dallie.

Which when his other companie beheld, They to his succour ran with readie ayd: And finding him vnable once to weld, They reared him on horsebacke, and vpstayd, Till on his way they had him forth conuayd: And all the way with wondrous griefe of mynd, And shame, he shewd him selfe to be dismayd, More for the loue which he had left behynd, Then that which he had to Sir Paridel resynd.

Nathlesse he forth did march well as he might, And made good semblance to his companie, Dissembling his disease and euill plight; Till that ere long they chaunced to espie Two other knights, that towards them did ply With speedie course, as bent to charge them new. Whom when as Blandamour approching nie, Perceiu'd to be such as they seemd in vew, He was full wo, and gan his former griefe renew.

For th'one of them he perfectly descride, To be Sir Scudamour, by that he bore The God of loue, with wings displayed wide, Whom mortally he hated euermore, Both for his worth, that all men did adore, And eke because his loue he wonne by right: Which when he thought, it grieued him full sore, That through the bruses of his former fight, He now vnable was to wreake his old despight.

For thy, he thus to Paridel bespake, Faire Sir, of friendship let me now you pray, That as I late aduentured for your sake, The hurts whereof me now from battell stay, Ye will me now with like good turne repay, And iustifie my cause on yonder knight. Ah Sir (said Paridel) do not dismay Your selfe for this, my selfe will for you fight, As ye haue done for me: the left hand rubs the right.

With that he put his spurres vnto his steed, With speare in rest, and toward him did fare, Like shaft out of a bow preuenting speed. But Scudamour was shortly well aware Of his approch, and gan him selfe prepare Him to receiue with entertainment meete. So furiously they met, that either bare The other downe vnder their horses feete, That what of them became, themselues did scarsly weete.

As when two billowes in the Irish sowndes, Forcibly driuen with contrarie tydes Do meete together, each abacke rebowndes With roaring rage; and dashing on all sides, That filleth all the sea with fome, diuydes The doubtfull current into diuers wayes: So fell those two in spight of both their prydes, But Scudamour himselfe did soone vprayse, And mounting light his foe for lying long vpbrayes.

Who rolled on an heape lay still in swound, All carelesse of his taunt and bitter rayle, Till that the rest him seeing lie on ground, Ran hastily, to weete what did him ayle. Where finding that the breath gan him to fayle, With busie care they stroue him to awake, And doft his helmet, and vndid his mayle: So much they did, that at the last they brake His slomber, yet so mazed, that he nothing spake.

Which when as Blandamour beheld, he sayd, False faitour Scudamour, that hast by slight And foule aduantage this good Knight dismayd, A Knight much better then thy selfe behight, Well falles it thee that I am not in plight This day, to wreake the dammage by thee donne: Such is thy wont, that still when any Knight Is weakned, then thou doest him ouer-ronne: So hast thou to thy selfe false honour often wonne.

He little answer'd, but in manly heart His mightie indignation did forbeare, Which was not yet so secret, but some part Thereof did in his frouning face appeare: Like as a gloomie cloud, the which doth beare An hideous storme, is by the Northerne blast Quite ouerblowne, yet doth not passe so cleare, But that it all the skie doth ouercast With darknes dred, and threatens all the world to wast.

Ah gentle knight then false Duessa sayd, Why do ye striue for Ladies loue so sore, Whose chiefe desire is loue and friendly aid Mongst gentle Knights to nourish euermore? Ne be ye wroth Sir Scudamour therefore, That she your loue list loue another knight, Ne do your selfe dislike a whit the more; For Loue is free, and led with selfe delight, Ne will enforced be with maisterdome or might.

So false Duessa, but vile Ate thus; Both foolish knights, I can but laugh at both, That striue and storme with stirre outrageous, For her that each of you alike doth loth, And loues another, with whom now she go'th In louely wise, and sleepes, and sports, and playes; Whilest both you here with many a cursed oth, Sweare she is yours, and stirre vp bloudie frayes, To win a willow bough, whilest other weares the bayes.

Vile hag (sayd Scudamour) why dost thou lye? And falsly seekst a vertuous wight to shame? Fond knight (sayd she) the thing that with this eye I saw, why should I doubt to tell the same? Then tell (quoth Blandamour) and feare no blame, Tell what thou saw'st, maulgre who so it heares. I saw (quoth she) a stranger knight, whose name I wote not well, but in his shield he beares (That well I wote) the heads of many broken speares.

I saw him haue your Amoret at will, I saw him kisse, I saw him her embrace, I saw him sleepe with her all night his fill, All manie nights, and manie by in place, That present were to testifie the case. Which when as Scudamour did heare, his heart Was thrild with inward griefe, as when in chace The Parthian strikes a stag with shiuering dart, The beast astonisht stands in middest of his smart.

So stood Sir Scudamour, when this he heard, Ne word he had to speake for great dismay, But lookt on Glauce grim, who woxe afeard Of outrage for the words, which she heard say, Albee vntrue she wist them by assay. But Blandamour,

whenas he did espie His chaunge of cheere, that anguish did
bewray, He woxe full blithe, as he had got thereby, And gan
thereat to triumph without victorie.

Lo recreant (sayd he) the fruitlesse end Of thy vaine
boast, and spoile of loue misgotten, Whereby the name of
knighthood thou dost shend, And all true louers with dishon-
or blotten, All things not rooted well, will soone be rotten. Fy
fy false knight (then false Duessa cryde) Vnworthy life that
loue with guile hast gotten, Be thou, where euer thou do go
or ryde, Loathed of ladies all, and of all knights defyde.

But Scudamour for passing great despight Staid not to
answer, scarcely did refraine, But that in all those knights
and ladies sight, He for reuenge had guiltlesse Glauce slaine:
But being past, he thus began amaine; False traitour squire,
false squire, of falsest knight, Why doth mine hand from
thine auenge abstaine, Whose Lord hath done my loue this
foule despight? Why do I not it wreake, on thee now in my
might?

Discourteous, disloyall Britomart, Vntrue to God, and
vnto man vniust, What vengeance due can equall thy desart, That hast with shamefull spot of sinfull lust Defil'd the
pledge committed to thy trust? Let vgly shame and endlesse
infamy Colour thy name with foule reproaches rust. Yet thou
false Squire his fault shalt deare aby, And with thy punishment his penance shalt supply.

The aged Dame him seeing so enraged, Was dead with
feare, nathlesse as neede required, His flaming furie sought
to haue assuaged With sober words, that sufferance desired,
Till time the tryall of her truth expyred: And euermore sought
Britomart to cleare. But he the more with furious rage was
fyred, And thrise his hand to kill her did vpreare, And thrise
he drew it backe: so did at last forbeare.

Cant. II.

Blandamour winnes false Florimell, Paridell for her striues, They are accorded: Agape doth lengthen her sonnes
liues.

F Irebrand of hell first tynd in Phlegeton, By thousand furies, and from thence out throwen Into this world, to worke confusion, And set it all on fire by force vnknowen, Is wicked discord, whose small sparkes once blowen None but a God or godlike man can slake; Such as was Orpheus, that when strife was growen Amongst those famous ympes of Greece, did take His siluer Harpe in hand, and shortly friends them make. Or such as that celestiall Psalmist was, That when the wicked feend his Lord tormented, With heauenly notes, that did all other pas, The outrage of his furious fit relented. Such Musicke is wise words with time concented, To moderate stiffe minds, disposd to striue: Such as that prudent Romane well inuented, What time his people into partes did riue, Them reconcyld againe, and to their homes did driue.

Such vs'd wise Glauce to that wrathfull knight, To calme the tempest of his troubled thought: Yet Blandamour with termes of foule despight, And Paridell her scornd, and set at nought, As old and crooked and not good for ought. Both they vnwise, and warelesse of the euill, That by themselues vnto themselues is wrought, Through that false witch, and that foule aged dreuill, The one a feend, the other an incarnate deuill.

With whom as they thus rode accompanide, They were encountred of a lustie Knight, That had a goodly Ladie by his side, To whom he made great dalliance and delight. It was to weete the bold Sir Ferraugh hight, He that from Braggadocchio whilome reft The snowy Florimell, whose beautie bright Made him seeme happie for so glorious theft; Yet was it in due triall but a wandring weft.

Which when as Blandamour, whose fancie light Was alwaies flitting as the wauering wind, After each beautie, that appeard in sight, Beheld, eftsoones it prickt his wanton mind With sting of lust, that reasons eye did blind, That to Sir Paridell these words he sent; Sir knight why ride ye dumpish thus behind, Since so good fortune doth to you present So fayre a spoyle, to make you ioyous meriment?

But Paridell that had too late a tryall Of the bad issue

of his counsell vaine, List not to hearke, but made this faire denyall; Last turne was mine, well proued to my paine, This now be yours, God send you better gaine. Whose scoffed words he taking halfe in scorne, Fiercely forth prickt his steed as in disdaine, Against that Knight, ere he him well could torne By meanes whereof he hath him lightly ouerborne.

Who with the sudden stroke astonisht sore, Vpon the ground a while in slomber lay; The whiles his loue away the other bore, And shewing her, did Paridell vpbray; Lo sluggish Knight the victors happie pray: So fortune friends the bold: whom Paridell Seeing so faire indeede, as he did say, His hart with secret enuie gan to swell, And inly grudge at him, that he had sped so well.

Nathlesse proud man himselfe the other deemed, Hauing so peerelesse paragon ygot: For sure the fayrest Florimell him seemed, To him was fallen for his happie lot, Whose like aliue on earth he weened not: Therefore he her did court, did serue, did wooe, With humblest suit that he imagine mot, And all things did deuise, and all things dooe, That might her loue prepare, and liking win theretoo.

She in regard thereof him recompenst With golden words, and goodly countenance, And such fond fauours sparingly dispenst: Sometimes him blessing with a light eye-glance, And coy lookes tempring with loose dalliance; Sometimes estranging him in sterner wise, That hauing cast him in a foolish trance, He seemed brought to bed in Paradise, And prou'd himselfe most foole, in what he seem'd most wise.

So great a mistresse of her art she was, And perfectly practiz'd in womans craft, That though therein himselfe he thought to pas, And by his false allurements wylie draft Had thousand women of their loue beraft, Yet now he was surpriz'd: for that false spright, Which that same witch had in this forme engraft, Was so expert in euery subtile slight, That it could ouerreach the wisest earthly wight.

Yet he to her did dayly seruice more, And dayly more deceiued was thereby; Yet Paridell him enuied therefore, As seeming plast in sole felicity: So blind is lust, false colours to descry. But Ate soone discouering his desire, And finding now fit opportunity To stirre vp strife, twixt loue and spight and ire, Did priuily put coles vnto his secret fire.

By sundry meanes thereto she prickt him forth, Now with remembrance of those spightfull speaches, Now with opinion of his owne more worth, Now with recounting of like former breaches Made in their friendship, as that Hag him teaches: And euer when his passion is allayd, She it reuiues and new occasion reaches: That on a time as they together way'd, He made him open chalenge, and thus boldly sayd.

Too boastfull Blandamour, too long I beare The open wrongs, thou doest me day by day; Well know'st thou, whe͂ we friendship first did sweare, The couenant was, that euery spoyle or pray Should equally be shard betwixt vs tway: Where is my part then of this Ladie bright, Whom to thy selfe thou takest quite away? Render therefore therein to me my right, Or answere for thy wrong, as shall fall out in fight.

Exceeding wroth thereat was Blandamour, And gan this bitter answere to him make; Too foolish Paridell, that fayrest floure Wouldst gather faine, and yet no paines wouldst take: But not so easie will I her forsake; This hand her wonne, this hand shall her defend. With that they gan their shiuering speares to shake, And deadly points at eithers breast to bend, Forgetfull each to haue bene euer others frend.

Their firie Steedes with so vntamed forse Did beare them both to fell auenges end, That both their speares with pitilesse remorse, Through shield and mayle, and haberieon did wend, And in their flesh a griesly passage rend, That with the furie of their owne affret, Each other horse and man to ground did send; Where lying still a while, both did forget The perilous present stownd, in which their liues were set.

As when two warlike Brigandines at sea, With murdrous weapons arm'd to cruell fight, Doe meete together on the watry lea, They stemme ech other with so fell despight, That with the shocke of their owne heedlesse might, Their wooden ribs are shaken nigh a sonder; They which from shore behold the dreadfull sight Of flashing fire, and heare the ordenance thonder, Do greatly stand amaz'd at such vnwonted wonder.

At length they both vpstarted in amaze; As men awaked rashly out of dreme, And round about themselues a while did gaze, Till seeing her, that Florimell did seme, In doubt to whom she victorie should deeme, Therewith their dulled sprights they edgd anew, And drawing both their swords with rage extreme, Like two mad mastiffes each on other flew, And shields did share, & mailes did rash, and helmes did hew.

So furiously each other did assayle, As if their soules they would attonce haue rent Out of their brests, that streames of bloud did rayle Adowne, as if their springes of life were spent; That all the ground with purple bloud was sprent, And all their armours staynd with bloudie gore, Yet scarcely once to breath would they relent, So mortall was their malice and so sore, Become of fayned friendship which they vow'd afore.

And that which is for Ladies most befitting, To stint all strife, and foster friendly peace, Was from those Dames so farre and so vnfitting, As that in stead of praying them sur-cease, They did much more their cruelty encrease; Bidding them fight for honour of their loue, And rather die then La-dies cause release. With which vaine termes so much they did the˜ moue, That both resolu'd the last extremities to proue.

There they I weene would fight vntill this day, Had not a Squire, euen he the Squire of Dames, By great aduenture trauelled that way; Who seeing both bent to so bloudy games, And both of old well knowing by their names, Drew nigh, to weete the cause of their debate: And first laide on those Ladies thousand blames, That did not seeke t'appease their deadly hate, But gazed on their harmes, not pittying their estate.

And then those Knights he humbly did beseech, To stay their hands, till he a while had spoken: Who lookt a little vp at that his speech, Yet would not let their battell so be broken, Both greedie fiers on other to be wroken. Yet he to them so earnestly did call, And them coniur'd by some well knowen token, That they at last their wrothfull hands let fall, Content to heare him speake, and glad to rest withall.

First he desir'd their cause of strife to see: They said, it was for loue of Florimell. Ah gentle knights (quoth he) how may that bee, And she so farre astray, as none can tell. Fond Squire, full angry then sayd Paridell, Seest not the Ladie there before thy face? He looked backe, and her aduizing well, Weend as he said, by that her outward grace, That fayrest Florimell was present there in place.

Glad man was he to see that ioyous sight, For none aliue but ioy'd in Florimell, And lowly to her lowting thus behight; Fayrest of faire, that fairenesse doest excell, This happie day I haue to greete you well, In which you safe I see, whom thousand late, Misdoubted lost through mischiefe that befell; Long may you liue in health and happie state. She litle answer'd him, but lightly did aggrate.

Then turning to those Knights, he gan a new; And you Sir Blandamour and Paridell, That for this Ladie present in your vew, Haue rays'd this cruell warre and outrage fell, Certes me seemes bene not aduised well, But rather ought in friendship for her sake To ioyne your force, their forces to repell, That seeke perforce her from you both to take, And of your gotten spoyle their owne triumph to make.

Thereat Sir Blandamour with countenance sterne, All full of wrath, thus fiercely him bespake; A read thou Squire, that I the man may learne, That dare fro me thinke Florimell to take. Not one (quoth he) but many doe partake Herein, as thus. It lately so befell, That Satyran a girdle did vptake, Well knowne to appertaine to Florimell, Which for her sake he wore, as him beseemed well.

But when as she her selfe was lost and gone, Full many knights, that loued her like deare, Thereat did greatly grudge, that he alone That lost faire Ladies ornament should weare, And gan therefore close spight to him to beare: Which he to shun, and stop vile enuies sting, Hath lately caus'd to be proclaim'd each where A solemne feast, with publike turneying, To which all knights with them their Ladies are to bring.

And of them all she that is fayrest found, Shall haue that golden girdle for reward, And of those Knights who is most stout on ground, Shall to that fairest Ladie be prefard. Since therefore she her selfe is now your ward, To you that ornament of hers pertaines, Against all those, that chalenge it to gard, And saue her honour with your ventrous paines; That shall you win more glory, then ye here find gaines.

When they the reason of his words had hard, They gan abate the rancour of their rage, And with their honours and their loues regard, The furious flames of malice to asswage. Tho each to other did his faith engage, Like faithfull friends thenceforth to ioyne in one With all their force, and battell strong to wage Gainst all those knights, as their professed fone, That chaleng'd ought in Florimell, saue they alone.

So well accorded forth they rode together In friendly sort, that lasted but a while; And of all old dislikes they made faire weather, Yet all was forg'd and spred with golden foyle, That vnder it hidde hate and hollow guyle. Ne certes can that friendship long endure, How euer gay and goodly be the style, That doth ill cause or euill end enure: For vertue is the band, that bindeth harts most sure.

Thus as they marched all in close disguise, Of fayned loue, they chaunst to ouertake Two knights, that lincked rode in louely wise, As if they secret counsels did partake; And each not farre behinde him had his make, To weete, two Ladies of most goodly hew, That twixt themselues did gentle purpose make Vnmindfull both of that discordfull crew, The which with speedie pace did after them pursew.

Who as they now approched nigh at hand, Deeming them doughtie as they did appeare, They sent that Squire afore, to vnderstand, What mote they be: who viewing them more neare Returned readie newes, that those same weare Two of the prowest Knights in Faery lond; And those two Ladies their two louers deare, Couragious Cambell, and stout Triamond, With Canacee and Cambine linckt in louely bond.

Whylome as antique stories tellen vs, Those two were foes the fellonest on ground, And battell made the dreddest daungerous, That euer shrilling trumpet did resound; Though now their acts be no where to be found, As that renowmed Poet them compyled, With warlike numbers and Heroicke sound, Dan Chaucer, well of English vndefyled, On Fames eternall beadroll worthie to be fyled.

But wicked Time that all good thoughts doth waste, And workes of noblest wits to nought out weare, That famous moniment hath quite defaste, And robd the world of threasure endlesse deare, The which mote haue enriched all vs heare. O cursed Eld the cankerworme of writs, How may these rimes, so rude as doth appeare, Hope to endure, sith workes of heauenly wits Are quite deuourd, and brought to nought by little bits?

Then pardon, O most sacred happie spirit, That I thy labours lost may thus reuiue, And steale from thee the meede of thy due merit, That none durst euer whilest thou wast aliue, And being dead in vaine yet many striue: Ne dare I like, but through infusion sweete Of thine owne spirit, which doth in me suruiue, I follow here the footing of thy feete, That with thy meaning so I may the rather meete.

Cambelloes sister was fayre Canacee, That was the learnedst Ladie in her dayes, Well seene in euerie science that mote bee, And euery secret worke of natures wayes, In wittie riddles, and in wise soothsayes, In power of herbes, and tunes of beasts and burds; And, that augmented all her other prayse, She modest was in all her deedes and words, And wondrous chast of life, yet lou'd of Knights & Lords.

Full many Lords, and many Knights her loued, Yet she to none of them her liking lent, Ne euer was with fond affection moued, But rul'd her thoughts with goodly gouernement, For dread of blame and honours blemishment; And eke vnto her lookes a law she made, That none of them once out of order went, But like to warie Centonels well stayd, Still watcht on euery side, of secret foes affrayd.

So much the more as she refusd to loue, So much the more she loued was and sought, That oftentimes vnquiet strife did moue Amongst her louers, and great quarrels wrought, That oft for her in bloudie armes they fought. Which whenas Cambell, that was stout and wise, Perceiu'd would breede great mischiefe, he bethought How to preuent the perill that mote rise, And turne both him and her to honour in this wise.

One day, when all that troupe of warlike wooers Assembled were, to weet whose she should bee, All mightie men and dreadfull derring dooers, (The harder it to make them well agree) Amongst them all this end he did decree; That of them all, which loue to her did make, They by consent should chose the stoutest three, That with himselfe should combat for her sake, And of them all the victour should his sister take.

Bold was the chalenge, as himselfe was bold, And courage full of haughtie hardiment, Approued oft in perils manifold, Which he atchieu'd to his great ornament: But yet his sisters skill vnto him lent Most confidence and hope of happie speed, Conceiued by a ring, which she him sent, That mongst the manie vertues, which we reed, Had power to staunch al wounds, that mortally did bleed.

Well was that rings great vertue knowen to all, That dread thereof, and his redoubted might Did all that youthly rout so much appall, That none of them durst vndertake the fight; More wise they weend to make of loue delight, Then life to hazard for faire Ladies looke; And yet vncertaine by such outward sight, Though for her sake they all that perill tooke, Whether she would them loue, or in her liking brooke.

Amongst those knights there were three brethren bold, Three bolder brethren neuer were yborne, Borne of one mother in one happie mold, Borne at one burden in one happie morne; Thrise happie mother, and thrise happie morne, That bore three such, three such not to be fond; Her name was Agape whose children werne All three as one, the first hight Priamond, The second Dyamond, the youngest Triamond.

Stout Priamond, but not so strong to strike, Strong Diamond, but not so stout a knight, But Triamond was stout and strong alike: On horsebacke vsed Triamond to fight, And Priamond on foote had more delight, But horse and foote knew Diamond to wield: With curtaxe vsed Diamond to smite, And Triamond to handle speare and shield, But speare and curtaxe both vsd Priamond in field.

These three did loue each other dearely well, And with so firme affection were allyde, As if but one soule in them all did dwell, Which did her powre into three parts diuyde; Like three faire branches budding farre and wide, That from one roote deriu'd their vitall sap: And like that roote that doth her life diuide, Their mother was, and had full blessed hap, These three so noble babes to bring forth at one clap.

Their mother was a Fay, and had the skill Of secret things, and all the powres of nature, Which she by art could vse vnto her will, And to her seruice bind each liuing creature; Through secret vnderstanding of their feature. Thereto she was right faire, when so her face She list discouer, and of goodly stature; But she as Fayes are wont, in priuie place Did spend her dayes, and lov'd in forests wyld to space.

There on a day a noble youthly knight Seeking aduentures in the saluage wood, Did by great fortune get of her the sight; As she sate carelesse by a cristall flood, Combing her golden lockes, as seemd her good: And vnawares vpon her laying hold, That stroue in vaine him long to haue withstood, Oppressed her, and there (as it is told) Got these three louely babes, that prov'd three cha~pions bold.

Which she with her long fostred in that wood, Till that to ripenesse of mans state they grew: Then shewing forth signes of their fathers blood, They loued armes, and knighthood did ensew, Seeking aduentures, where they anie knew. Which when their mother saw, she gan to dout Their safetie, least by searching daungers new, And rash prouoking perils all about, Their days mote be abridged through their corage stout.

Therefore desirous th'end of all their dayes To know, and them t'enlarge with long extent, By wondrous skill, and many hidden wayes, To the three fatall sisters house she went. Farre vnder ground from tract of liuing went, Downe in the bottome of the deepe Abysse, Where Demogorgon in dull darknesse pent, Farre from the view of Gods and heauens blis, The hideous Chaos keepes, their dreadfull dwelling is.

There she them found, all sitting round about The direfull distaffe standing in the mid, And with vnwearied fingers drawing out The lines of life, from liuing knowledge hid. Sad Clotho held the rocke, the whiles the thrid By griesly Lachesis was spun with paine, That cruell Atropos eftsoones vndid, With cursed knife cutting the twist in twaine: Most wretched men, whose dayes depend on thrids so vaine.

She them saluting, there by them sate still, Beholding how the thrids of life they span: And when at last she had beheld her fill, Trembling in heart, and looking pale and wan, Her cause of comming she to tell began. To whom fierce Atropos, Bold Fay, that durst Come see the secret of the life of man, Well worthie thou to be of Ioue accurst, And eke thy childrens thrids to be asunder burst.

Whereat she sore affrayd, yet her besought To graunt her boone, and rigour to abate, That she might see her childre͂s thrids forth brought, And know the measure of their vtmost date, To them ordained by eternall fate. Which Clotho graunting, shewed her the same: That when she saw, it did her much amate, To see their thrids so thin, as spiders frame, And eke so short, that seemd their ends out shortly came.

She then began them humbly to intreate, To draw them longer out, and better twine, That so their liues might be prolonged late. But Lachesis thereat gan to repine, And sayd, Fond dame that deem'st of things diuine As of humane, that they may altred bee, And chaung'd at pleasure for those impes of thine. Not so; for what the Fates do once decree, Not all the gods can chaunge, nor Ioue him self can free.

Then since (quoth she) the terme of each mans life For nought may lessened nor enlarged bee, Graunt this, that when ye shred with fatall knife His line, which is the eldest of the three, Which is of them the shortest, as I see, Eftsoones his life may passe into the next; And when the next shall likewise ended bee, That both their liues may likewise be annext Vnto the third, that his may so be trebly wext.

They graunted it; and then that carefull Fay Departed thence with full contended mynd; And comming home, in warlike fresh aray Them found all three according to their kynd: But vnto them what destinie was assynd, Or how their liues were eekt, she did not tell; But euermore, when she fit time could fynd, She warned them to tend their safeties well, And loue each other deare, what euer them befell.

So did they surely during all their dayes, And neuer discord did amongst them fall; Which much augmented all their other praise. And now t'increase affection naturall, In loue of Canacee they ioyned all: Vpon which ground this same great battell grew, Great matter growing of beginning small; The which for length I will not here pursew, But rather will reserue it for a Canto new.

Cant. III.

The battell twixt three brethren, with Cambell for Canacee. Cambina with true friendships bond doth their long strife agree.

O Why doe wretched men so much desire, To draw their dayes vnto the vtmost date, And doe not rather wish them soone expire, Knowing the miserie of their estate, And thousand perills which them still awate, Tossing them like a boate amid the mayne, That euery houre they knocke at deathes gate? And he that happie seemes and least in payne, Yet is as nigh his end, as he that most doth playne. Therefore this Fay I hold but fond and vaine, The which in seeking for her children three Long life, thereby did more prolong their paine. Yet whilest they liued none did euer see More happie creatures, then they seem'd to bee, Nor more ennobled for their courtesie, That made them dearely lou'd of each degree; Ne more renowmed for their cheualrie, That made them dreaded much of all men farre and nie.

These three that hardie chalenge tooke in hand, For Canacee with Cambell for to fight: The day was set, that all might vnderstand, And pledges pawnd the same to keepe a right, That day, the dreddest day that liuing wight Did euer see vpon this world to shine, So soone as heauens window shewed light, These warlike Champions all in armour shine, Assembled were in field, the chalenge to define.

The field with listes was all about enclos'd, To barre the prease of people farre away; And at th'one side sixe iudges were dispos'd, To view and deeme the deedes of armes that day; And on the other side in fresh aray, Fayre Canacee vpon a stately stage Was set, to see the fortune of that fray, And to be seene, as his most worthie wage, That could her purchase with his liues aduentur'd gage.

Then entred Cambell first into the list, With stately steps, and fearelesse countenance, As if the conquest his he surely wist. Soone after did the brethren three aduance, In braue aray and goodly amenance, With scutchins gilt and banners broad displayd: And marching thrise in warlike ordinance, Thrise lowted lowly to the noble Mayd, The whiles shril trompets & loud clarions sweetly playd.

Which doen the doughty chalenger came forth, All arm'd to point his chalenge to abet: Gainst whom Sir Priamond with equall worth: And equall armes himselfe did forward set. A trompet blew; they both together met, With dreadfull force, and furious intent, Carelesse of perill in their fiers affret, As if that life to losse they had forelent, And cared not to spare, that should be shortly spent.

Right practicke was Sir Priamond in fight, And throughly skild in vse of shield and speare; Ne lesse approued was

Cambelloes might, Ne lesse his skill in weapons did appeare, That hard it was to weene which harder were. Full many mightie strokes on either side Were sent, that seemed death in them to beare, But they were both so watchfull and well eyde, That they auoyded were, and vainely by did slyde.

Yet one of many was so strongly bent By Priamond, that with vnluckie glaunce, Through Cambels shoulder it vnwarely went, That forced him his shield to disaduaunce: Much was he grieued with that gracelesse chaunce, Yet from the wound no drop of bloud there fell, But wondrous paine, that did the more enhaunce His haughtie courage to aduengement fell: Smart daunts not mighty harts, but makes them more to swell.

With that his poynant speare he fierce auentred, With doubled force close vnderneath his shield, That through the mayles into his thigh it entred, And there arresting, readie way did yield, For bloud to gush forth on the grassie field; That he for paine himselfe n'ote right vpreare, But too and fro in great amazement reel'd, Like an old Oke whose pith and sap is seare, At puffe of euery storme doth stagger here and theare.

Whom so dismayd when Cambell had espide, Againe he droue at him with double might, That nought mote stay the steele, till in his side The mortall point most cruelly empight: Where fast infixed, whilest he sought by slight It forth to wrest, the staffe a sunder brake, And left the head behind: with which despight He all enrag'd, his shiuering speare did shake, And charging him a fresh thus felly him bespake.

Lo faitour there thy meede vnto thee take, The meede of thy mischalenge and abet: Not for thine owne, but for thy sisters sake, Haue I thus long thy life vnto thee let: But to forbeare doth not forgiue the det. The wicked weapon heard his wrathfull vow, And passing forth with furious affret, Pierst through his beuer quite into his brow, That with the force it backward forced him to bow.

Therewith a sunder in the midst it brast, And in his hand

nought but the troncheon left, The other halfe behind yet
sticking fast, Out of his headpeece Cambell fiercely reft, And
with such furie backe at him it heft, That making way vnto
his dearest life, His weasand pipe it through his gorget cleft:
Thence streames of purple bloud issuing rife, Let forth his
wearie ghost and made an end of strife.

His wearie ghost assoyld from fleshly band, Did not as
others wont, directly fly Vnto her rest in Plutoes griesly land,
Ne into ayre did vanish presently, Ne chaunged was into a
starre in sky: But through traduction was eftsoones deriued,
Like as his mother prayd the Destinie, Into his other brethren, that suruiued, In whom he liu'd a new, of former life
depriued.

Whom when on ground his brother next beheld, Though
sad and sorie for so heauy sight, Yet leaue vnto his sorrow
did not yeeld, But rather stird to vengeance and despight,
Through secret feeling of his generous spright, Rusht fiercely
forth, the battell to renew, As in reuersion of his brothers
right; And chalenging the Virgin as his dew. His foe was
soone addrest: the trompets freshly blew.

With that they both together fiercely met, As if that each
ment other to deuoure; And with their axes both so sorely
bet, That neither plate nor mayle, whereas their powre They
felt, could once sustaine the hideous stowre, But riued were
like rotten wood a sunder, Whilest through their rifts the
ruddie bloud did showre And fire did flash, like lightning after thunder, That fild the lookers on attonce with ruth and
wonder.

As when two Tygers prickt with hungers rage, Haue by
good fortune found some beasts fresh spoyle, On which they
weene their famine to asswage, And gaine a feastfull guerdon of their toyle, Both falling out doe stirre vp strifefull
broyle, And cruell battell twixt themselues doe make, Whiles
neither lets the other touch the soyle, But either sdeignes
with other to partake: So cruelly these Knights stroue for
that Ladies sake.

Full many strokes, that mortally were ment, The whiles were enterchaunged twixt them two; Yet they were all with so good wariment Or warded, or auoyded and let goe, That still the life stood fearelesse of her foe: Till Diamond disdeigning long delay Of doubtfull fortune wauering to and fro, Resolu'd to end it one or other way; And heau'd his murdrous axe at him with mighty sway.

The dreadfull stroke in case it had arriued, Where it was ment, (so deadly it was ment) The soule had sure out of his bodie riued, And stinted all the strife incontinent. But Cambels fate that fortune did preuent: For seeing it at hand, he swaru'd asyde, And so gaue way vnto his fell intent: Who missing of the marke which he had eyde, Was with the force nigh feld whilst his right foot did slyde.

As when a Vulture greedie of his pray, Through hunger long, that hart to him doth lend, Strikes at an Heron with all his bodies sway, That from his force seemes nought may it defend; The warie fowle that spies him toward bend His dreadfull souse auoydes, it shunning light, And maketh him his wing in vaine to spend; That with the weight of his owne weeldlesse might, He falleth nigh to ground, and scarse recouereth flight.

Which faire aduenture when Cambello spide, Full lightly, ere himselfe he could recower, From daungers dread to ward his naked side, He can let driue at him with all his power, And with his axe him smote in euill hower, That from his shoulders quite his head he reft: The headlesse tronke, as heedlesse of that stower, Stood still a while, and his fast footing kept, Till feeling life to fayle, it fell, and deadly slept.

They which that piteous spectacle beheld, Were much amaz'd the headlesse tronke to see Stand vp so long, and weapon vaine to weld, Vnweeting of the Fates diuine decree, For lifes succession in those brethren three. For notwithstanding that one soule was reft, Yet, had the bodie not dismembred bee, It would haue liued, and reuiued eft; But finding no fit seat, the lifelesse corse it left.

It left; but that same soule, which therein dwelt, Streight entring into Triamond, him fild With double life, and griefe, which when he felt, As one whose inner parts had bene ythrild With point of steele, that close his hartbloud spild, He lightly lept out of his place of rest, And rushing forth into the emptie field, Against Cambello fiercely him addrest; Who him affronting soone to fight was readie prest.

Well mote ye wonder how that noble Knight, After he had so often wounded beene, Could stand on foot, now to renew the fight. But had ye then him forth aduauncing seene, Some newborne wight ye would him surely weene: So fresh he seemed and so fierce in sight; Like as a Snake, whom wearie winters teene, Hath worne to nought, now feeling sommers might, Casts off his ragged skin and freshly doth him dight.

All was through vertue of the ring he wore, The which not onely did not from him let One drop of bloud to fall, but did restore His weakned powers, and dulled spirits whet, Through working of the stone therein yset. Else how could one of equall might with most, Against so many no lesse mightie met, Once thinke to match three such on equall cost, Three such as able were to match a puissant host.

Yet nought thereof was Triamond adredde, Ne desperate of glorious victorie, But sharpely him assayld, and sore bestedde, With heapes of strokes, which he at him let flie, As thicke as hayle forth poured from the skie: He stroke, he soust, he foynd, he hewd, he lasht, And did his yron brond so fast applie, That from the same the fierie sparkles flasht, As fast as water-sprinckles gainst a rocke are dasht.

Much was Cambello daunted with his blowes, So thicke they fell, and forcibly were sent, That he was forst from daunger of the throwes Backe to retire, and somewhat to relent, Till th'heat of his fierce furie he had spent: Which when for want of breath gan to abate, He then afresh with new encouragement Did him assayle, and mightily amate, As fast as forward erst, now backward to retrate.

Like as the tide that comes fro th'Ocean mayne, Flowes vp

the Shenan with contrarie forse, And ouerruling him in his owne rayne, Driues backe the current of his kindly course, And makes it seeme to haue some other sourse: But when the floud is spent, then backe againe His borrowed waters forst to redisbourse, He sends the sea his owne with double gaine, And tribute eke withall, as to his Soueraine.

Thus did the battell varie to and fro, With diuerse fortune doubtfull to be deemed: Now this the better had, now had his fo; Then he halfe vanquisht, then the other seemed, Yet victors both them selues always esteemed. And all the while the disentrayled blood Adowne their sides like litle riuers stremed, That with the wasting of his vitall flood, Sir Triamond at last full faint and feeble stood.

But Cambell still more strong and greater grew, Ne felt his blood to wast, ne powres emperisht, Through that rings vertue, that with vigour new, Still when as he enfeebled was, him cherisht, And all his wounds, and all his bruses guarisht, Like as a withered tree through husbands toyle Is often seene full freshly to haue florisht, And fruitfull apples to haue borne awhile, As fresh as when it first was planted in the soyle.

Through which aduantage, in his strength he rose, And smote the other with so wondrous might, That through the seame, which did his hauberk close, Into his throate and life it pierced quight, That downe he fell as dead in all mens sight: Yet dead he was not, yet he sure did die, As all men do, that lose the liuing spright: So did one soule out of his bodie flie Vnto her natiue home from mortall miserie.

But nathelesse whilst all the lookers on Him dead behight, as he to all appeard, All vnwares he started vp anon, As one that had out of a dreame bene reard, And fresh assayld his foe; who halfe affeard Of th'vncouth sight, as he some ghost had seene, Stood still amaz'd, holding his idle sweard; Till hauing often by him stricken beene, He forced was to strike, and saue him selfe from teene.

Yet from thenceforth more warily he fought, As one in

feare the Stygian gods t'offend, Ne followd on so fast, but rather sought Him selfe to saue, and daunger to defend, Then life and labour both in vaine to spend. Which Triamond per-ceiuing, weened sure He gan to faint, toward the battels end, And that he should not long on foote endure, A signe which did to him the victorie assure.

Whereof full blith, eftsoones his mightie hand He heav'd on high, in mind with that same blow To make an end of all that did withstand: Which Cambell seeing come, was noth-ing slow Him selfe to saue from that so deadly throw; And at that instant reaching forth his sweard Close vnderneath his shield, that scarce did show, Stroke him, as he his hand to strike vpreard, In th'arm-pit full, that through both sides the wound appeard.

Yet still that direfull stroke kept on his way, And falling heauie on Cambelloes crest, Strooke him so hugely, that in swowne he lay, And in his head an hideous wound imprest: And sure had it not happily found rest Vpon the brim of his brode plated shield, It would haue cleft his braine downe to his brest. So both at once fell dead vpon the field, And each to other seemd the victorie to yield.

Which when as all the lookers on beheld, They weened sure the warre was at an end, And Iudges rose, and Marshals of the field Broke vp the listes, their armes away to rend; And Canacee gan wayle her dearest frend. All suddenly they both vpstarted light, The one out of the swownd, which him did blend, The other breathing now another spright, And fiercely each assayling, gan afresh to fight.

Long while they then continued in that wize, As if but then the battell had begonne: Strokes, wounds, wards, weap-ons, all they did despise, Ne either car'd to ward, or perill shonne, Desirous both to haue the battell donne; Ne either cared life to saue or spill, Ne which of them did winne, ne which were wonne. So wearie both of fighting had their fill, That life it selfe seemd loathsome, and long safetie ill.

Whilst thus the case in doubtfull ballance hong, Vnsure to

whether side it would incline, And all mens eyes and hearts, which there among Stood gazing, filled were with rufull tine, And secret feare, to see their fatall fine, All suddenly they heard a troublous noyes, That seemd some perilous tumult to desine, Confusd with womens cries, and shouts of boyes, Such as the troubled Theaters oftimes annoyes.

Thereat the Champions both stood still a space, To weeten what that sudden clamour ment; Lo where they spyde with speedie whirling pace, One in a charet of straunge furniment, Towards them driuing like a storme out sent. The charet decked was in wondrous wize, With gold and many a gorgeous ornament, After the Persian Monarks antique guize, Such as the maker selfe could best by art deuize.

And drawne it was (that wonder is to tell) Of two grim lyons, taken from the wood, In which their powre all others did excell; Now made forget their former cruell mood, T'obey their riders hest, as seemed good. And therein sate a Ladie passing faire And bright, that seemed borne of Angels brood, And with her beautie bountie did compare, Whether of them in her should haue the greater share.

Thereto she learned was in Magicke leare, And all the artes, that subtill wits discouer, Hauing therein bene trained many a yeare, And well instructed by the Fay her mother, That in the same she farre exceld all other. Who vnderstanding by her mightie art, Of th'euill plight, in which her dearest brother Now stood, came forth in hast to take his part, And pacifie the strife, which causd so deadly smart.

And as she passed through th'vnruly preace Of people, thronging thicke her to behold, Her angrie teame breaking their bonds of peace, Great heapes of them, like sheepe in narrow fold, For hast did ouer-runne, in dust enrould, That thorough rude confusion of the rout, Some fearing shriekt, some being harmed hould, Some laught for sport, some did for wonder shout, And some that would seeme wise, their wonder turnd to dout.

In her right hand a rod of peace shee bore, About the

which two Serpents weren wound, Entrayled mutually in louely lore, And by the tailes together firmely bound, And both were with one oliue garland crownd, Like to the rod which Maias sonne doth wield, Wherewith the hellish fiends he doth confound. And in her other hand a cup she hild, The which was with Nepenthe to the brim vpfild.

Nepenthe is a drinck of souerayne grace, Deuized by the Gods, for to asswage Harts grief, and bitter gall away to chace, Which stirs vp anguish and contentious rage: In stead thereof sweet peace and quiet age It doth establish in the troubled mynd. Few men, but such as sober are and sage, Are by the Gods to drinck thereof assynd; But such as drinck, eternall happinesse do fynd.

Such famous men, such worthies of the earth, As Ioue will haue aduaunced to the skie, And there made gods, though borne of mortall berth, For their high merits and great dignitie, Are wont, before they may to heauen flie, To drincke hereof, whereby all cares forepast Are washt away quite from their memorie. So did those olde Heroes hereof taste, Before that they in blisse amongst the Gods were plaste.

Much more of price and of more gratious powre Is this, then that same water of Ardenne, The which Rinaldo drunck in happie howre, Described by that famous Tuscane penne: For that had might to change the hearts of men Fro loue to hate, a change of euill choise: But this doth hatred make in loue to brenne, And heauy heart with comfort doth reioyce. Who would not to this vertue rather yeeld his voice?

At last arriuing by the listes side, Shee with her rod did softly smite the raile, Which straight flew ope, and gaue her way to ride. Eftsoones out of her Coch she gan auaile, And pacing fairely forth, did bid all haile, First to her brother, whom she loued deare, That so to see him made her heart to quaile: And next to Cambell, whose sad ruefull cheare Made her to change her hew, and hidden loue t'appeare.

They lightly her requit (for small delight They had as then her long to entertaine.) And eft them turned both againe to

fight; Which when she saw, downe on the bloudy plaine Her
selfe she threw, and teares gan shed amaine; Amongst her
teares immixing prayers meeke, And with her prayers reasons to restraine From blouddy strife, and blessed peace to
seeke, By all that vnto them was deare, did them beseeke.

But when as all might nought with them preuaile, Shee
smote them lightly with her powrefull wand. Then suddenly
as if their hearts did faile, Their wrathfull blades downe fell
out of their hand, And they like men astonisht still did stand.
Thus whilest their minds were doubtfully distraught, And
mighty spirites bound with mightier band, Her golden cup to
them for drinke she raught, Whereof full glad for thirst, ech
drunk an harty draught.

Of which so soone as they once tasted had, Wonder it is
that sudden change to see: Instead of strokes, each other
kissed glad, And louely haulst from feare of treason free, And
plighted hands for euer friends to be. When all men saw this
sudden change of things, So mortall foes so friendly to agree,
For passing ioy, which so great maruaile brings, They all gan
shout aloud, that all the heauen rings.

All which, when gentle Canacee beheld, In hast she from
her lofty chaire descended, To weet what sudden tidings was
befeld: Where when she saw that cruell war so ended, And
deadly foes so faithfully affrended, In louely wise she gan
that Lady greet, Which had so great dismay so well amend-
ed, And entertaining her with curt'sies meet, Profest to her
true friendship and affection sweet.

Thus when they all accorded goodly were, The trumpets
sounded, and they all arose, Thence to depart with glee and
gladsome chere. Those warlike champions both together
chose, Homeward to march, themselues there to repose, And
wise Cambina taking by her side Faire Canacee, as fresh
as morning rose, Vnto her Coch remounting, home did ride,
Admir'd of all the people, and much glorifide.

Where making ioyous feast theire daies they spent In
perfect loue, deuoide of hatefull strife, Allide with bands of

mutuall couplement; For Triamond had Canacee to wife, With whom he ledd a long and happie life; And Cambel tooke Cambina to his fere, The which as life were each to other liefe. So all alike did loue, and loued were, That since their days such louers were not found elswhere.

Cant. IIII.

Satyrane makes a Turneyment For loue of Florimell: Britomart winnes the prize from all, And Artegall doth quell.

IT often fals, (as here it earst befell) That mortall foes doe turne to faithfull frends, And friends profest are chaungd to foemen fell: The cause of both, of both their minds depends; And th'end of both likewise of both their ends. For enmitie, that of no ill proceeds, But of occasion, with th'occasion ends; And friendship, which a faint affection breeds Without regard of good, dyes like ill grounded seeds. That well (me seemes) appeares, by that of late Twixt Cambell and Sir Triamond befell, As als by this, that now a new debate Stird vp twixt Scudamour and Paridell, The which by course befals me here to tell: Who hauing those two other Knights espide, Marching afore, as ye remember well, Sent forth their Squire to haue them both descride, And eke those masked Ladies riding them beside.

Who backe returning, told as he had seene, That they were doughtie knights of dreaded name; And those two Ladies, their two loues vnseene; And therefore wisht them without blot or blame, To let them passe at will, for dread of shame. But Blandamour full of vainglorious spright, And rather stird by his discordfull Dame, Vpon them gladly would haue prov'd his might, But that he yet was sore of his late lucklesse fight.

Yet nigh approching, he them fowle bespake, Disgracing them, him selfe thereby to grace, As was his wont; so weening way to make To Ladies loue, where so he came in place, And with lewd termes their louers to deface. Whose sharpe prouokement them incenst so sore, That both were bent t'auenge his vsage base, And gan their shields addresse them selues afore: For euill deedes may better then bad words be bore.

But faire Cambina with perswasions myld, Did mitigate the fiercenesse of their mode, That for the present they were reconcyld, And gan to treate of deeds of armes abrode, And strange aduentures, all the way they rode: Amongst the which they told, as then befell, Of that great turney, which was blazed brode, For that rich girdle of faire Florimell, The prize of her, which did in beautie most excell.

To which folke-mote they all with one consent, Sith each of them his Ladie had him by, Whose beautie each of them thought excellent, Agreed to trauell, and their fortunes try. So as they passed forth, they did espy One in bright armes, with ready speare in rest, That toward them his course seem'd to apply, Gainst whom Sir Paridell himselfe addrest, Him weening, ere he nigh approcht to haue represt.

Which th'other seeing, gan his course relent, And vaunted speare eftsoones to disaduaunce, As if he naught but peace and pleasure ment, Now falne into their fellowship by chance, Whereat they shewed curteous countenaunce. So as he rode with them accompanide, His rouing eie did on the Lady glaunce, Which Blandamour had riding by his side: Who˜ sure he weend, that he some wher tofore had eide.

It was to weete that snowy Florimell, Which Ferrau late from Braggadochio wonne, Whom he now seeing, her remembred well, How hauing reft her from the witches sonne, He soone her lost: wherefore he now begunne To challenge her anew, as his owne prize, Whom formerly he had in battell wonne, And proffer made by force her to reprize: Which scornefull offer, Blandamour gan soone despize.

And said, Sir Knight, sith ye this Lady clame, Whom he that hath, were loth to lose so light, (For so to lose a Lady, were great shame) Yee shall her winne, as I haue done in fight: And lo shee shall be placed here in sight, Together with this Hag beside her set, That who so winnes her, may her haue by right: But he shall haue the Hag that is ybet, And with her alwaies ride, till he another get.

That offer pleased all the company, So Florimell with Ate forth was brought, At which they all gan laugh full merrily: But Braggadochio said, he neuer thought For such an Hag, that seemed worse then nought, His person to emperill so in fight. But if to match that Lady they had sought Another like, that were like faire and bright, His life he then would spend to iustifie his right.

At which his vaine excuse they all gan smile, As scorning his vnmanly cowardize: And Florimell him fowly gan reuile, That for her sake refus'd to enterprize The battell, offred in so knightly wize. And Ate eke prouokt him priuily, With loue of her, and shame of such mesprize. But naught he car'd for friend or enemy, For in base mind nor friendship dwels nor enmity.

But Cambell thus did shut vp all in iest, Braue Knights and Ladies, certes ye doe wrong To stirre vp strife, when most vs needeth rest, That we may vs reserue both fresh and strong, Against the Turneiment which is not long. When who so list to fight, may fight his fill, Till then your challenges ye may prolong; And then it shall be tried, if ye will, Whether shall haue the Hag, or hold the Lady still.

They all agreed: so turning all to game, And pleasaunt bord, they past forth on their way, And all that while, where so they rode or came, That masked Mock-knight was their sport and play. Till that at length vpon th'appointed day, Vnto the place of turneyment they came; Where they before them found in fresh aray Manie a braue knight, and manie a daintie dame Assembled, for to get the honour of that game.

There this faire crewe arriuing, did diuide Them selues asunder: Blandamour with those Of his, on th'one; the rest on th'other side. But boastfull Braggadocchio rather chose, For glorie vaine their fellowship to lose, That men on him the more might gaze alone. The rest them selues in troupes did else dispose, Like as it seemed best to euery one; The knights in couples marcht, with ladies linckt attone.

Then first of all forth came Sir Satyrane, Bearing that precious relicke in an arke Of gold, that bad eyes might it not prophane: Which drawing softly forth out of the darke, He open shewd, that all men it mote marke. A gorgeous girdle, curiously embost With pearle & precious stone, worth many a marke; Yet did the workmanship farre passe the cost: It was the same, which lately Florimel had lost.

That same aloft he hong in open vew, To be the prize of beautie and of might; The which eftsoones discouered, to it drew The eyes of all, allur'd with close delight, And hearts quite robbed with so glorious sight, That all men threw out vowes and wishes vaine. Thrise happie Ladie, and thrise happie knight, Them seemd, that could so goodly riches gaine, So worthie of the perill, worthy of the paine.

Then tooke the bold Sir Satyrane in hand An huge great speare, such as he wont to wield, And vauncing forth from all the other band Of knights, addrest his maiden-headed shield, Shewing him selfe all ready for the field. Gainst whom there singled from the other side A Painim knight, that well in armes was skild, And had in many a battell oft bene tride, Hight Bruncheual the bold, who fiersly forth did ride.

So furiously they both together met, That neither could the others force sustaine; As two fierce Buls, that striue the rule to get Of all the heard, meete with so hideous maine, That both rebutted, tumble on the plaine: So these two champions to the ground were feld, Where in a maze they both did long remaine, And in their hands their idle troncheons held, Which neither able were to wag, or once to weld.

Which when the noble Ferramont espide, He pricked forth in ayd of Satyran; And him against Sir Blandamour did ride With all the strength and stifnesse that he can. But the more strong and stiffely that he ran, So much more sorely to the ground he fell, That on an heape were tumbled horse and man. Vnto whose rescue forth rode Paridell; But him likewise with that same speare he eke did quell.

Which Braggadocchio seeing, had no will To hasten greatly

to his parties ayd, Albee his turne were next; but stood there still, As one that seemed doubtfull or dismayd. But Triamond halfe wroth to see him staid, Sternly stept forth, and raught away his speare, With which so sore he Ferramont assaid, That horse and man to ground he quite did beare, That neither could in hast themselues againe vpreare.

Which to auenge, Sir Deuon him did dight, But with no better fortune then the rest: For him likewise he quickly downe did smight, And after him Sir Douglas him addrest, And after him Sir Paliumord forth prest, But none of them against his strokes could stand, But all the more, the more his praise increst. For either they were left vppon the land, Or went away sore wounded of his haplesse hand.

And now by this, Sir Satyrane abraid, Out of the swowne, in which too long he lay; And looking round about, like one dismaid, When as he saw the mercilesse affray Which doughty Triamond had wrought that day, Vnto the noble Knights of Maidenhead, His mighty heart did almost rend in tway, For very gall, that rather wholly dead Himselfe he wisht haue beene, then in so bad a stead.

Eftsoones he gan to gather vp around His weapons, which lay scattered all abrode, And as it fell, his steed he ready found. On whom remounting, fiercely forth he rode, Like sparke of fire that from the anduile glode. There where he saw the valiant Triamond Chasing, and laying on them heauy lode, That none his force were able to withstond, So dreadfull were his strokes, so deadly was his hond.

With that, at him his beam-like speare he aimed, And thereto all his power and might applide: The wicked steele for mischiefe first ordained, And hauing now misfortune got for guide, Staid not, till it arriued in his side. And therein made a very griesly wound, That streames of bloud his armour all bedide. Much was he daunted with that direfull stound, That scarse he him vpheld from falling in a sound.

Yet as he might, himselfe he soft withdrew Out of the field, that none perceiu'd it plaine. Then gan the part of

Chalengers anew To range the field, and victorlike to raine, That none against them battell durst maintaine. By that the gloomy euening on them fell, That forced them from fighting to refraine, And trumpets sound to cease did them compell. So Satyrane that day was iudg'd to beare the bell.

The morrow next the Turney gan anew, And with the first the hardy Satyrane Appear'd in place, with all his noble crew: On th'other side, full many a warlike swaine, Assembled were, that glorious prize to gaine. But mongst them all, was not Sir Triamond, Vnable he new battell to darraine, Through grieuaunce of his late receiued wound, That doubly did him grieue, when so himselfe he found.

Which Cambell seeing, though he could not salue, Ne done vndoe, yet for to salue his name, And purchase honour in his friends behalue, This goodly counterfesaunce he did frame. The shield and armes well knowne to be the same, Which Triamond had worne, vnwares to wight, And to his friend vnwist, for doubt of blame, If he misdid, he on himselfe did dight, That none could him discerne, and so went forth to fight.

There Satyrane Lord of the field he found, Triumphing in great ioy and iolity; Gainst whom none able was to stand on ground; That much he gan his glorie to enuy, And cast t'auenge his friends indignity. A mightie speare eftsoones at him he bent; Who seeing him come on so furiously, Met him mid-way with equall hardiment, That forcibly to ground they both together went.

They vp againe them selues can lightly reare, And to their tryed swords them selues betake; With which they wrought such wondrous maruels there, That all the rest it did amazed make, Ne any dar'd their perill to partake; Now cuffling close, now chacing to and fro, Now hurtling round aduantage for to take: As two wild Boares together grapling go, Chaufing and foming choler each against his fo.

So as they courst, and turneyd here and theare, It chaunst Sir Satyrane his steed at last, Whether through foundring or through sodein feare To stumble, that his rider nigh he cast; Which vauntage Cambell did pursue so fast, That ere him selfe he had recouered well, So sore he sowst him on the compast creast, That forced him to leaue his loftie sell, And rudely tumbling downe vnder his horse feete fell.

Lightly Cambello leapt downe from his steed, For to haue rent his shield and armes away, That whylome wont to be the victors meed; When all vnwares he felt an hideous sway Of many swords, that lode on him did lay. An hundred knights had him enclosed round, To rescue Satyrane out of his pray; All which at once huge strokes on him did pound, In hope to take him prisoner, where he stood on ground.

He with their multitude was nought dismayd, But with stout courage turnd vpon them all, And with his brondiron round about him layd; Of which he dealt large almes, as did befall: Like as a Lion that by chaunce doth fall Into the hunters toile, doth rage and rore, In royall heart disdaining to be thrall. But all in vaine: for what might one do more? They haue him taken captiue, though it grieue him sore.

Whereof when newes to Triamond was brought, There as he lay, his wound he soone forgot, And starting vp, streight for his armour sought: In vaine he sought; for there he found it not; Cambello it away before had got: Cambelloes armes therefore he on him threw, And lightly issewd forth to take his lot. There he in troupe found all that warlike crew, Leading his friend away, full sorie to his vew.

Into the thickest of that knightly preasse He thrust, and smote downe all that was betweene, Caried with feruent zeale, ne did he ceasse, Till that he came, where he had Cambell seene, Like captive thral two other Knights atweene, There he amongst them cruell hauocke makes; That they which lead him, soone enforced beene To let him loose, to saue their proper stakes; Who being freed, from one a weapon fiercely takes.

With that he driues at them with dreadfull might, Both in remembrance of his friends late harme, And in reuengement of his owne despight, So both together giue a new allarme, As if but now the battell wexed warme. As when two greedy Wolues doe breake by force Into an heard, farre from the husband farme, They spoile and rauine without all remorse, So did these two through all the field their foes enforce.

Fiercely they followd on their bolde emprize, Till trumpets sound did warne them all to rest; Then all with one consent did yeeld the prize To Triamond and Cambell as the best. But Triamond to Cambell it relest, And Cambell it to Triamond transferd; Each labouring t'aduance the others gest, And make his praise before his owne preferd: So that the doome was to another day differd.

The last day came, when all those knightes againe Assembled were their deedes of armes to shew. Full many deedes that day were shewed plaine: But Satyrane boue all the other crew, His wondrous worth declared in all mens view. For from the first he to the last endured, And though some while Fortune from him withdrew, Yet euermore his honour he recured, And with vnwearied powre his party still assured.

Ne was there Knight that euer thought of armes, But that his vtmost prowesse there made knowen, That by their many wounds, and carelesse harmes, By shiuered speares, and swords all vnder strowen, By scattered shields was easie to be showen. There might ye see loose steeds at randon ronne, Whose luckelesse riders late were ouerthrowen; And squiers make hast to helpe their Lords fordonne. But still the Knights of Maidenhead the better wonne.

Till that there entred on the other side, A straunger knight, from whence no man could reed, In quyent disguise, full hard to be descride. For all his armour was like saluage weed, With woody mosse bedight, and all his steed With oaken leaues attrapt, that seemed fit For saluage wight, and thereto well agreed His word, which on his ragged shield was writ, Saluagesse sans finesse, shewing secret wit.

He at his first incomming, charg'd his spere At him, that first appeared in his sight: That was to weet, the stout Sir

Sangliere, Who well was knowen to be a valiant Knight, Approued oft in many a perlous fight. Him at the first encounter downe he smote, And ouerbore beyond his crouper quight, And after him another Knight, that hote Sir Brianor, so sore, that none him life behote.

Then ere his hand he reard, he ouerthrew Seuen Knights one after other as they came: And when his speare was brust, his sword he drew, The instrument of wrath, and with the same Far'd like a lyon in his bloodie game, Hewing, and slashing shields, and helmets bright, And beating downe, what euer nigh him came, That euery one gan shun his dreadfull sight, No lesse then death it selfe, in daungerous affright.

Much wondred all men, what, or whence he came, That did amongst the troupes so tyrannize; And each of other gan inquire his name. But when they could not learne it by no wize, Most answerable to his wyld disguize It seemed, him to terme the saluage knight. But certes his right name was otherwize, Though knowne to few, that Arthegall he hight, The doughtiest knight that liv'd that day, and most of might.

Thus was Sir Satyrane with all his band By his sole manhood and atchieuement stout Dismayd, that none of them in field durst stand, But beaten were, and chased all about. So he continued all that day throughout, Till euening, that the Sunne gan downward bend. Then rushed forth out of the thickest rout A stranger knight, that did his glorie shend: So nought may be esteemed happie till the end.

He at his entrance charg'd his powrefull speare At Artegall, in middest of his pryde, And therewith smote him on his Vmbriere So sore, that tombling backe, he downe did slyde Ouer his horses taile aboue a stryde: Whence litle lust he had to rise againe. Which Cambell seeing, much the same enuyde, And ran at him with all his might and maine; But shortly was likewise seene lying on the plaine.

Whereat full inly wroth was Triamond, And cast t'auenge the shame doen to his freend: But by his friend himselfe eke soone he fond, In no lesse neede of helpe, then him he weend.

All which when Blandamour from end to end Beheld, he woxe therewith displeased sore, And thought in mind it shortly to amend: His speare he feutred, and at him it bore; But with no better fortune, then the rest afore.

Full many others at him likewise ran: But all of them likewise dismounted were, Ne certes wonder; for no powre of man Could bide the force of that enchaunted speare, The which this famous Britomart did beare; With which she wondrous deeds of arms atchieued, And ouerthrew, what euer came her neare, That all those stranger knights full sore agrieued, And that late weaker band of chalengers relieued.

Like as in sommers day when raging heat Doth burne the earth, and boyled riuers drie, That all brute beasts forst to refraine fro meat, Doe hunt for shade, where shrowded they may lie, And missing it, faine from themselues to flie; All trauellers tormented are with paine: A watry cloud doth ouercast the skie, And poureth forth a sudden shoure of raine, That all the wretched world recomforteth againe.

So did the warlike Britomart restore The prize, to knights of Maydenhead that day, Which else was like to haue bene lost, and bore The prayse of prowesse from them all away. Then shrilling trompets loudly gan to bray, And bad them leaue their labours and long toyle, To ioyous feast and other gentle play; Where beauties prize shold win that pretious spoyle: Where I with sound of trompe will also rest a whyle.

Cant. V.

The Ladies for the Girdle striue of famous Florimell: Scudamour comming to Cares house, doth sleepe from him expell.

I T hath bene through all ages euer seene, That with the praise of armes and cheualrie, The prize of beautie still hath ioyned beene; And that for reasons speciall priuitie: For either doth on other much relie. For he me seemes most fit the faire to serue, That can her best defend from villenie; And she most fit his seruice doth deserue, That fairest is and from her faith will neuer swerue. So fitly now here commeth next in place, After the proofe of prowesse ended well, The controuerse of beauties soueraine grace; In which to her that doth the most excell, Shall fall the girdle of faire Florimell: That many wish to win for glorie vaine, And not for vertuous vse, which some doe tell That glorious belt did in it selfe containe, Which Ladies ought to loue, and seeke for to obtaine.

That girdle gaue the vertue of chast loue, And wiuehood true, to all that did it beare; But whosoeuer contrarie doth proue, Might not the same about her middle weare. But it would loose, or else a sunder teare. Whilome it was (as Faeries wont report) Dame Venus girdle, by her steemed deare, What time she vsd to liue in wiuely sort; But layd aside, when so she vsd her looser sport.

Her husband Vulcan whylome for her sake, When first he loued her with heart entire, This pretious ornament they say did make, And wrought in Lemno with vnquenched fire: And afterwards did for her loues first hire, Giue it to her, for euer to remaine, Therewith to bind lasciuious desire, And loose affections streightly to restraine; Which vertue it for euer after did retaine.

The same one day, when she her selfe disposd To visite her beloued Paramoure, The God of warre, she from her middle loosd, And left behind her in her secret bowre, On Acidalian mount, where many an howre She with the pleasant Graces wont to play. There Florimell in her first ages flowre Was fostered by those Graces, (as they say) And brought with her fro~ thence that goodly belt away.

That goodly belt was Cestus hight by name, And as her life by her esteemed deare. No wonder then, if that to winne the same So many Ladies sought, as shall appeare; For pearelesse she was thought, that did it beare. And now by this their feast all being ended, The iudges which thereto selected were, Into the Martian field adowne descended, To deeme this doutfull case, for which they all cõtended.

But first was question made, which of those Knights That lately turneyd, had the wager wonne: There was it iudged by those worthie wights, That Satyrane the first day best had donne: For he last ended, hauing first begonne. The second was to Triamond behight, For that he sau'd the victour from fordonne: For Cambell victour was in all mens sight, Till by mishap he in his foemens hand did light.

The third dayes prize vnto that straunger Knight, Whom all men term'd Knight of the Hebene speare, To Britomart was giuen by good right; For that with puissant stroke she downe did beare The Saluage Knight, that victour was while-are, And all the rest, which had the best afore, And to the last vnconquer'd did appeare; For last is deemed best. To her therefore The fayrest Ladie was adiudgd for Paramore.

But thereat greatly grudged Arthegall, And much repynd, that both of victors meede, And eke of honour she did him forestall. Yet mote he not withstand, what was decreede; But inly thought of that despightfull deede Fit time t'awaite auenged for to bee. This being ended thus, and all agreed, Then next ensew'd the Paragon to see Of beauties praise, and yeeld the fayrest her due fee.

Then first Cambello brought vnto their view His faire Cambina, couered with a veale; Which being once with-drawne, most perfect hew And passing beautie did eftsoones reueale, That able was weake harts away to steale. Next did Sir Triamond vnto their sight The face of his deare Cana-cee vnheale; Whose beauties beame eftsoones did shine so bright, That daz'd the eyes of all, as with exceeding light.

And after her did Paridell produce His false Duessa, that she might be seene; Who with her forged beautie did seduce The hearts of some, that fairest her did weene; As diuerse wits affected diuers beene. Then did Sir Ferramont vnto them shew His Lucida, that was full faire and sheene, And after these an hundred Ladies moe Appear'd in place, the which each other did outgoe.

All which who so dare thinke for to enchace, Him needeth sure a golden pen I weene, To tell the feature of each goodly face. For since the day that they created beene, So many heauenly faces were not seene Assembled in one place: ne he that thought For Chian folke to pourtraict beauties Queene, By view of all the fairest to him brought, So many faire did see, as here he might haue sought.

At last the most redoubted Britonesse, Her louely Amoret did open shew; Whose face discouered, plainely did expresse The heauenly pourtraict of bright Angels hew. Well weened all, which her that time did vew, That she should surely beare the bell away, Till Blandamour, who thought he had the trew And very Florimell, did her display: The sight of whom once seene did all the rest dismay.

For all afore that seemed fayre and bright, Now base and contemptible did appeare, Compar'd to her, that shone as Phebes light, Amongst the lesser starres in euening cleare. All that her saw with wonder rauisht weare, And weend no mortall creature she should bee, But some celestiall shape, that flesh did beare: Yet all were glad there Florimell to see; Yet thought that Florimell was not so faire as shee.

As guilefull Goldsmith that by secret skill, With golden foyle doth finely ouer spred Some baser metall, which commend he will Vnto the vulgar for good gold insted, He much more goodly glosse thereon doth shed, To hide his falshood, then if it were trew: So hard, this Idole was to be ared, That Florimell her selfe in all mens vew She seem'd to passe: so forged things do fairest shew.

Then was that golden belt by doome of all Graunted to her, as to the fayrest Dame. Which being brought, about her middle small They thought to gird, as best it her became; But by no meanes they could it thereto frame. For euer as they fastned it, it loos'd And fell away, as feeling secret blame. Full oft about her wast she it enclos'd; And it as oft was from about her wast disclos'd.

That all men wondred at the vncouth sight, And each one thought, as to their fancies came. But she her selfe did thinke it doen for spight, And touched was with secret wrath and shame Therewith, as thing deuiz'd her to defame. Then many other Ladies likewise tride, About their tender loynes to knit the same; But it would not on none of them abide, But when they thought it fast, eftsoones it was vntide.

Which when that scornefull Squire of Dames did vew, He lowdly gan to laugh, and thus to iest; Alas for pittie that so faire a crew, As like can not be seene from East to West, Cannot find one this girdle to inuest. Fie on the man, that did it first inuent, To shame vs all with this, Vngirt vnblest. Let neuer Ladie to his loue assent, That hath this day so many so vnmanly shent.

Thereat all Knights gan laugh, and Ladies lowre: Till that at last the gentle Amoret Likewise assayd, to proue that girdles powre; And hauing it about her middle set, Did find it fit, withouten breach or let. Whereat the rest gan greatly to enuie: But Florimell exceedingly did fret, And snatching from her hand halfe angrily The belt againe, about her bodie gan it tie.

Yet nathemore would it her bodie fit; Yet nathelesse to her, as her dew right, It yeelded was by them, that iudged it: And she her selfe adiudged to the Knight, That bore the Hebene speare, as wonne in fight. But Britomart would not thereto assent, Ne her owne Amoret forgoe so light For that strange Dame, whose beauties wonderment She lesse esteem'd, then th'others vertuous gouernment.

Whom when the rest did see her to refuse, They were full glad, in hope themselues to get her: Yet at her choice they all did greatly muse. But after that the Iudges did arret her Vnto the second best, that lou'd her better; That was the Saluage Knight: but he was gone In great displeasure, that he could not get her. Then was she iudged Triamond his one; But Triamond lou'd Canacee, and other none.

Tho vnto Satyran she was adiudged, Who was right glad to gaine so goodly meed: But Blandamour thereat full greatly grudged, And little prays'd his labours euill speed, That for to winne the saddle, lost the steed. Ne lesse thereat did Paridell complaine, And thought t'appeale from that, which was decreed, To single combat with Sir Satyrane. Thereto him Ate stird, new discord to maintaine.

And eke with these, full many other Knights She through her wicked working did incense, Her to demaund, and chalenge as their rights, Deserued for their perils recompense. Amongst the rest with boastfull vaine pretense Stept Braggadochio forth, and as his thrall Her claym'd, by him in battell wonne long sens: Whereto her selfe he did to witnesse call; Who being askt, accordingly confessed all.

Thereat exceeding wroth was Satyran; And wroth with Satyran was Blandamour; And wroth with Blandamour was Eriuan; And at them both Sir Paridell did loure. So all together stird vp strifull stoure, And readie were new battell to darraine. Each one profest to be her paramoure, And vow'd with speare and shield it to maintaine; Ne Iudges powre, ne reasons rule mote them restraine.

Which troublous stirre when Satyrane auiz'd: He gan to cast how to appease the same, And to accord them all, this meanes deuiz'd: First in the midst to set that fayrest Dame, To whom each one his chalenge should disclame, And he himselfe his right would eke releasse: Then looke to whom she voluntarie came, He should without disturbance her possesse: Sweete is the loue that comes alone with willingnesse.

They all agreed, and then that snowy Mayd Was in the middest plast among them all; All on her gazing wisht, and vowd, and prayd, And to the Queene of beautie close did call, That she vnto their portion might befall. Then when she long had lookt vpon each one, As though she wished to haue pleasd them all, At last to Braggadochio selfe alone She came of her accord, in spight of all his fone.

Which when they all beheld they chaft and rag'd, And woxe nigh mad for very harts despight, That from reuenge their willes they scarse asswag'd: Some thought from him her to haue reft by might; Some proffer made with him for her to fight. But he nought car'd for all that they could say:

For he their words as wind esteemed light. Yet not fit place he thought it there to stay, But secretly from thence that night her bore away.

They which remaynd, so soone as they perceiu'd, That she was gone, departed thence with speed, And follow'd them, in mind her to haue reau'd From wight vnworthie of so noble meed. In which poursuit how each one did succeede, Shall else be told in order, as it fell. But now of Britomart it here doth neede, The hard aduentures and strange haps to tell; Since with the rest she went not after Florimell.

For soone as she them saw to discord set, Her list no longer in that place abide; But taking with her louely Amoret, Vpon her first aduenture forth did ride, To seeke her lou'd, making blind Loue her guide. Vnluckie Mayd to seeke her enemie! Vnluckie Mayd to seeke him farre and wide, Whom, when he was vnto her selfe most nie, She through his late disguizeme˜t could him not descrie.

So much the more her griefe, the more her toyle: Yet neither toyle nor griefe she once did spare, In seeking him, that should her paine assoyle; Whereto great comfort in her sad misfare Was Amoret, companion of her care: Who likewise sought her louer long miswent, The gentle Scudamour, whose hart whileare That stryfull hag with gealous discontent Had fild, that he to fell reueng was fully bent.

Bent to reuenge on blamelesse Britomart The crime, which cursed Ate kindled earst, The which like thornes did pricke his gealous hart, And through his soule like poysned arrow perst, That by no reason it might be reuerst, For ought that Glauce could or doe or say. For aye the more that she the same reherst, The more it gauld, and grieu'd him night and day, That nought but dire reuenge his anger mote defray.

So as they trauelled, the drouping night Couered with cloudie storme and bitter showre, That dreadfull seem'd to euery liuing wight, Vpon them fell, before her timely howre; That forced them to seeke some couert bowre, Where they might hide their heads in quiet rest, And shrowd their persons from that stormie stowre. Not farre away, not meete for any guest They spide a little cottage, like some poore mans nest.

Vnder a steepe hilles side it placed was, There where the mouldred earth had cav'd the banke; And fast beside a little brooke did pas Of muddie water, that like puddle stanke; By which few crooked sallowes grew in ranke: Whereto approaching nigh, they heard the sound Of many yron hammers beating ranke, And answering their wearie turnes around, That seemed some blacksmith dwelt in that desert grou˜d.

There entring in, they found the goodman selfe, Full busily vnto his worke ybent; Who was to weet a wretched wearish elfe, With hollow eyes and rawbone cheekes forspent, As if he had in prison long bene pent: Full blacke and griesly did his face appeare, Besmeard with smoke that nigh his eyesight blent; With rugged beard, and hoarie shagged heare, The which he neuer wont to combe, or comely sheare.

Rude was his garment, and to rags all rent, Ne better had he, ne for better cared: With blistred hands emongst the cinders brent, And fingers filthie, with long nayles vnpared, Right fit to rend the food, on which he fared. His name was Care; a blacksmith by his trade, That neither day nor night from working spared, But to small purpose yron wedges made; Those be vnquiet thoughts, that carefull minds inuade.

In which his worke he had sixe seruants prest, About the Andvile standing euermore, With huge great hammers, that did neuer rest From heaping stroakes, which thereon soused sore: All sixe strong groomes, but one then other more: For by degrees they all were disagreed; So likewise did the hammers which they bore, Like belles in greatnesse orderly succeed, That he which was the last, the first did farre exceede.

He like a monstrous Gyant seem'd in sight, Farre passing Bronteus, or Pynacmon great, The which in Lipari doe day and night Frame thunderbolts for Ioues auengefull threate. So dreadfully he did the anduile beat, That seem'd to dust he shortly would it driue: So huge his hammer and so fierce his heat, That seem'd a rocke of Diamond it could riue, And rend a sunder quite, if he thereto list striue.

Sir Scudamour there entring, much admired The manner of their worke and wearie paine; And hauing long beheld, at last enquired The cause and end thereof: but all in vaine; For they for nought would from their worke refraine, Ne let his speeches come vnto their eare. And eke the breathfull bellowes blew amaine, Like to the Northren winde, that none could heare: Those Pensifenesse did moue; and Sighes the bellows weare.

Which when that warriour saw, he said no more, But in his armour layd him downe to rest: To rest he layd him downe vpon the flore, (Whylome for ventrous Knights the bedding best) And thought his wearie limbs to haue redrest. And that old aged Dame, his faithfull Squire, Her feeble ioynts layd eke a downe to rest; That needed much her weake age to desire, After so long a trauell, which them both did tire.

There lay Sir Scudamour long while expecting, When gentle sleepe his heauie eyes would close; Oft chaunging sides, and oft new place electing, Where better seem'd he mote himselfe repose; And oft in wrath he thence againe vprose; And oft in wrath he layd him downe againe. But wheresoeuer he did himselfe dispose, He by no meanes could wished ease obtaine: So euery place seem'd painefull, and ech changing vaine.

And euermore, when he to sleepe did thinke, The hammers sound his senses did molest; And euermore, when he began to winke, The bellowes noyse disturb'd his quiet rest, Ne suffred sleepe to settle in his brest. And all the night the dogs did barke and howle About the house, at sent of stranger guest: And now the crowing Cocke, and now the Owle Lowde shriking him afflicted to the very sowle.

And if by fortune any litle nap Vpon his heauie eye-lids chaunst to fall, Eftsoones one of those villeins him did rap Vpon his headpeece with his yron mall; That he was soone awaked therewithall, And lightly started vp as one affrayd; Or as if one him suddenly did call. So oftentimes he out of sleepe abrayd, And then lay musing long, on that him ill apayd.

So long he muzed, and so long he lay, That at the last his wearie sprite opprest With fleshly weaknesse, which no creature may Long time resist, gaue place to kindly rest, That all his senses did full soone arrest: Yet in his soundest sleepe, his dayly feare His ydle braine gan busily molest, And made him dreame those two disloyall were: The things that day most minds, at night doe most appeare.

With that, the wicked carle the maister Smith A paire of redwhot yron tongs did take Out of the burning cinders, and therewith Vnder his side him nipt, that forst to wake, He felt his hart for very paine to quake, And started vp auenged for to be On him, the which his quiet slomber brake: Yet looking round about him none could see; Yet did the smart remaine, though he himselfe did flee.

In such disquiet and hartfretting payne, He all that night, that too long night did passe. And now the day out of the Ocean mayne Began to peepe aboue this earthly masse, With pearly dew sprinkling the morning grasse: Then vp he rose like heauie lumpe of lead, That in his face, as in a looking glasse, The signes of anguish one mote plainely read, And ghesse the man to be dismayd with gealous dread.

Vnto his lofty steede he clombe anone, And forth vpon his former voiage fared, And with him eke that aged Squire attone; Who whatsoeuer perill was prepared, Both equall paines and equall perill shared: The end whereof and daungerous euent Shall for another canticle be spared. But here my wearie teeme nigh ouer spent Shall breath it selfe awhile, after so long a went.

Cant. VI.

Both Scudamour and Arthegall Doe fight with Britomart: He sees her face; doth fall in loue, and soone from her depart.

VV Hat equall torment to the griefe of mind, And pyning anguish hid in gentle hart, That inly feeds it selfe with thoughts vnkind, And nourisheth her owne consuming smart? What medicine can any Leaches art Yeeld such a sore, that doth her grieuance hide, And will to none her maladie impart? Such was the wound that Scudamour did gride; For which Dan Phebus selfe cannot a salue prouide. Who hauing left that restlesse house of Care, The next day, as he on his way did ride, Full of melancholie and sad misfare, Through misconceipt; all vnawares espide An armed Knight vnder a forrest side, Sitting in shade beside his grazing steede; Who soone as them approaching he descride, Gan towards them to pricke with eger speede, That seem'd he was full bent to some mischieuous deede.

Which Scudamour perceiuing, forth issewed To haue rencountred him in equall race; But soone as th'other nigh approaching, vewed The armes he bore, his speare he gan abase, And voide his course: at which so suddain case He wondred much. But th'other thus can say; Ah gentle Scudamour, vnto your grace I me submit, and you of pardon pray, That almost had against you trespassed this day.

Whereto thus Scudamour, Small harme it were For any knight, vpon a ventrous knight Without displeasance for to proue his spere. But reade you Sir, sith ye my name haue hight, What is your owne, that I mote you requite? Certes (sayd he) ye mote as now excuse Me from discouering you my name aright: For time yet serues that I the same refuse, But call ye me the Saluage Knight, as others vse.

Then this, Sir Saluage Knight (quoth he) areede; Or doe you here within this forrest wonne, That seemeth well to answere to your weede? Or haue ye it for some occasion donne? That rather seemes, sith knowen armes ye shonne. This other day (sayd he) a stranger knight Shame and dishonour hath vnto me donne; On whom I waite to wreake that foule despight, When euer he this way shall passe by day or night.

Shame be his meede (quoth he) that meaneth shame. But what is he, by whom ye shamed were? A stranger knight,

sayd he, vnknowne by name, But knowne by fame, and by
an Hebene speare, With which he all that met him, downe
did beare. He in an open Turney lately held, Fro me the honour of that game did reare; And hauing me all wearie earst,
downe feld, The fayrest Ladie reft, and euer since withheld.

When Scudamour heard mention of that speare, He wist
right well, that it was Britomart, The which from him his
fairest loue did beare. Tho gan he swell in euery inner part,
For fell despight, and gnaw his gealous hart, That thus he
sharply sayd; Now by my head, Yet is not this the first vnknightly part, Which that same knight, whom by his launce
I read, Hath doen to noble knights, that many makes him
dread.

For lately he my loue hath fro me reft, And eke defiled
with foule villanie The sacred pledge, which in his faith was
left, In shame of knighthood and fidelitie; The which ere long
full deare he shall abie. And if to that auenge by you decreed This hand may helpe, or succour ought supplie, It shall
not fayle, when so ye shall it need. So both to wreake their
wrathes on Britomart agreed.

Whiles thus they communed, lo farre away A Knight soft
ryding towards them they spyde, Attyr'd in forraine armes
and straunge aray: Whõ when they nigh approcht, they
plaine descryde To be the same, for whom they did abyde.
Sayd then Sir Scudamour, Sir Saluage knight Let me this
craue, sith first I was defyde, That first I may that wrong to
him requite: And if I hap to fayle, you shall recure my right.

Which being yeelded, he his threatfull speare Gan few-
ter, and against her fiercely ran. Who soone as she him saw
approaching neare With so fell rage, her selfe she lightly gan
To dight, to welcome him, well as she can: But entertaind
him in so rude a wise, That to the ground she smote both
horse and man; Whence neither greatly hasted to arise, But
on their common harmes together did deuise.

But Artegall beholding his mischaunce, New matter
added to his former fire; And eft auentring his steeleheaded

launce, Against her rode, full of despiteous ire, That nought but spoyle and vengeance did require. But to himselfe his felonous intent Returning, disappointed his desire, Whiles vnawares his saddle he forwent, And found himselfe on ground in great amazement.

Lightly he started vp out of that stound, And snatching forth his direfull deadly blade, Did leape to her, as doth an eger hound Thrust to an Hynd within some couert glade, Whom without perill he cannot inuade. With such fell greedines he her assayled, That though she mounted were, yet he her made To giue him ground, (so much his force preuayled) And shun his mightie strokes, gainst which no armes auayled.

So as they coursed here and there, it chaunst That in her wheeling round, behind her crest So sorely he her strooke, that thence it glaunst Adowne her backe, the which it fairely blest From foule mischance; ne did it euer rest, Till on her horses hinder parts it fell; Where byting deepe, so deadly it imprest, That quite it chynd his backe behind the sell, And to alight on foote her algates did compell.

Like as the lightning brond from riuen skie, Throwne out by angry Ioue in his vengeance, With dreadfull force falles on some steeple hie; Which battring, downe it on the church doth glance, And teares it all with terrible mischance. Yet she no whit dismayd, her steed forsooke, And casting from her that enchaunted lance, Vnto her sword and shield her soone betooke; And therewithall at him right furiously she strooke.

So furiously she strooke in her first heat, Whiles with long fight on foot he breathlesse was, That she him forced backward to retreat, And yeeld vnto her weapon way to pas: Whose raging rigour neither steele nor bras Could stay, but to the tender flesh it went, And pour'd the purple bloud forth on the gras; That all his mayle yriu'd, and plates yrent, Shew'd all his bodie bare vnto the cruell dent.

At length when as he saw her hastie heat Abate, and panting breath begin to fayle, He through long sufferance growing now more great, Rose in his strength, and gan her fresh assayle, Heaping huge strokes, as thicke as showre of hayle, And lashing dreadfully at euery part, As if he thought her soule to disentrayle. Ah cruell hand, and thrise more cruell hart, That workst such wrecke on her, to whom thou dearest art.

What yron courage euer could endure, To worke such outrage on so faire a creature? And in his madnesse thinke with hands impure To spoyle so goodly workmanship of nature, The maker selfe resembling in her feature? Certes some hellish furie, or some feend This mischiefe framd, for their first loues defeature, To bath their hands in bloud of dearest freend, Thereby to make their loues beginning, their liues end.

Thus long they trac'd, and trauerst to and fro, Sometimes pursewing, and sometimes pursewed, Still as aduantage they espyde thereto: But toward th'end Sir Arthegall renewed His strength still more, but she still more decrewed. At last his lucklesse hand he heau'd on hie, Hauing his forces all in one accrewed, And therewith stroke at her so hideouslie, That seemed nought but death mote be her destinie.

The wicked stroke vpon her helmet chaunst, And with the force, which in it selfe it bore, Her ventayle shard away, and thence forth glaunst A downe in vaine, ne harm'd her any more. With that her angels face, vnseene afore, Like to the ruddie morne appeard in sight, Deawed with siluer drops, through sweating sore; But somewhat redder, then beseem'd aright, Through toylesome heate and labour of her weary fight.

And round about the same, her yellow heare Hauing through stirring loosd their wonted band, Like to a golden border did appeare, Framed in goldsmithes forge with cunning hand: Yet goldsmithes cunning could not vnderstand To frame such subtile wire, so shinie cleare. For it did glister like the golden sand, The which Pactolus with his waters shere, Throwes forth vpon the riuage round about him nere.

And as his hand he vp againe did reare, Thinking to worke on her his vtmost wracke, His powrelesse arme benumbd with secret feare From his reuengefull purpose shronke abacke, And cruell sword out of his fingers slacke Fell downe to ground, as if the steele had sence, And felt some ruth, or sence his hand did lacke, Or both of them did thinke, obedience To doe to so diuine a beauties excellence.

And he himselfe long gazing thereupon, At last fell humbly downe vpon his knee, And of his wonder made religion, Weening some heauenly goddesse he did see, Or else vnweeting, what it else might bee; And pardon her besought his errour frayle, That had done outrage in so high degree: Whilest trembling horrour did his sense assayle, And made ech member quake, and manly hart to quayle.

Nathelesse she full of wrath for that late stroke, All that long while vpheld her wrathfull hand, With fell intent, on him to bene ywroke, And looking sterne, still ouer him did stand, Threatning to strike, vnlesse he would withstand: And bad him rise, or surely he should die. But die or liue for nought he would vpstand But her of pardon prayd more earnestlie, Or wreake on him her will for so great iniurie.

Which when as Scudamour, who now abrayd, Beheld, whereas he stood not farre aside, He was therewith right wondrously dismayd, And drawing nigh, when as he plaine descride That peerelesse paterne of Dame natures pride, And heauenly image of perfection, He blest himselfe, as one sore terrifide, And turning his feare to faint deuotion, Did worship her as some celestiall vision.

But Glauce, seeing all that chaunced there, Well weeting how their errour to assoyle, Full glad of so good end, to them drew nere, And her salewd with seemely belaccoyle, Ioyous to see her safe after long toyle. Then her besought, as she to her was deare, To graunt vnto those warriours truce a whyle; Which yeelded, they their beuers vp did reare, And shew'd themselues to her, such as indeed they were.

When Britomart with sharpe auizefull eye Beheld the

louely face of Artegall, Tempred with sternesse and stout maiestie, She gan eftsoones it to her mind to call, To be the same which in her fathers hall Long since in that enchaunted glasse she saw. Therewith her wrathfull courage gan appall, And haughtie spirits meekely to adaw, That her enhaunced hand she downe can soft withdraw.

Yet she it forst to haue againe vpheld, As fayning choler, which was turn'd to cold: But euer when his visage she beheld, Her hand fell downe, and would no longer hold The wrathfull weapon gainst his countnance bold: But when in vaine to fight she oft assayd, She arm'd her tongue, and thought at him to scold; Nathlesse her tongue not to her will obayd, But brought forth speeches myld, when she would haue missayd.

But Scudamour now woxen inly glad, That all his gealous feare he false had found, And how that Hag his loue abused had With breach of faith and loyaltie vnsound, The which long time his grieued hart did wound, He thus bespake; Certes Sir Artegall, I ioy to see you lout so low on ground, And now become to liue a Ladies thrall, That whylome in your minde wont to despise them all.

Soone as she heard the name of Artegall, Her hart did leape, and all her hart-strings tremble, For sudden ioy, and secret feare withall, And all her vitall powres with motion nimble, To succour it, themselues gan there assemble, That by the swift recourse of flushing blood Right plaine appeard, though she it would dissemble, And fayned still her former angry mood, Thinking to hide the depth by troubling of the flood.

When Glauce thus gan wisely all vpknit; Ye gentle Knights, whom fortune here hath brought, To be spectators of this vncouth fit, Which secret fate hath in this Ladie wrought, Against the course of kind, ne meruaile nought, Ne thenceforth feare the thing that hethertoo Hath troubled both your mindes with idle thought, Fearing least she your loues away should woo, Feared in vaine, sith meanes ye see there wants theretoo.

And you Sir Artegall, the saluage knight, Henceforth may not disdaine, that womans hand Hath conquered you anew in second fight: For whylome they haue conquerd sea and land, And heauen it selfe, that nought may them withstand, Ne henceforth be rebellious vnto loue, That is the crowne of knighthood, and the band Of noble minds deriued from aboue, Which being knit with vertue, neuer will remoue.

And you faire Ladie knight, my dearest Dame, Relent the rigour of your wrathfull will, Whose fire were better turn'd to other flame; And wiping out remembrance of all ill, Graunt him your grace, but so that he fulfill The penance, which ye shall to him empart: For louers heauen must passe by sorrowes hell. Thereat full inly blushed Britomart; But Artegall close smyling ioy'd in secret hart.

Yet durst he not make loue so suddenly, Ne thinke th'affection of her hart to draw From one to other so quite contrary: Besides her modest countenance he saw So goodly graue, and full of princely aw, That it his ranging fancie did refraine, And looser thoughts to lawfull bounds withdraw; Whereby the passion grew more fierce and faine, Like to a stubborne steede whom strong hand would restraine.

But Scudamour whose hart twixt doubtfull feare And feeble hope hung all this while suspence, Desiring of his Amoret to heare Some gladfull newes and sure intelligence, Her thus bespake; But Sir without offence Mote I request you tydings of my loue, My Amoret, sith you her freed fro thence, Where she captiued long, great woes did proue; That where ye left, I may her seeke, as doth behoue.

To whom thus Britomart, Certes Sir knight, What is of her become, or whether reft, I can not vnto you aread a right. For from that time I from enchaunters theft Her freed, in which ye her all hopelesse left, I her preseru'd from perill and from feare, And euermore from villenie her kept: Ne euer was there wight to me more deare Then she, ne vnto whom I more true loue did beare.

Till on a day as through a desert wyld We trauelled, both

wearie of the way We did alight, and sate in shadow myld;
Where fearelesse I to sleepe me downe did lay. But when as
I did out of sleepe abray, I found her not, where I her left
whyleare, But thought she wandred was, or gone astray. I
cal'd her loud, I sought her farre and neare; But no where
could her find, nor tydings of her heare.

When Scudamour those heauie tydings heard, His hart
was thrild with point of deadly feare; Ne in his face or bloud
or life appeard, But senselesse stood, like to a mazed steare,
That yet of mortall stroke the stound doth beare. Till Glauce
thus; Faire Sir, be nought dismayd With needelesse dread,
till certaintie ye heare: For yet she may be safe though somewhat strayd; Its best to hope the best, though of the worst
affrayd.

Nathlesse he hardly of her chearefull speech Did comfort take, or in his troubled sight Shew'd change of better
cheare: so sore a breach That sudden newes had made into
his spright; Till Britomart him fairely thus behight; Great
cause of sorrow certes Sir ye haue: But comfort take: for by
this heauens light I vow, you dead or liuing not to leaue, Till
I her find, and wreake on him that her did reaue.

Therewith he rested, and well pleased was. So peace being confirm'd amongst them all, They tooke their steeds, and
forward thence did pas Vnto some resting place, which mote
befall, All being guided by Sir Artegall. Where goodly solace
was vnto them made, And dayly feasting both in bowre and
hall, Vntill that they their wounds well healed had, And wearie limmes recur'd after late vsage bad.

In all which time, Sir Artegall made way Vnto the loue
of noble Britomart, And with meeke seruice and much suit
did lay Continuall siege vnto her gentle hart; Which being
whylome launcht with louely dart, More eath was new impression to receiue, How euer she her paynd with womanish
art To hide her wound, that none might it perceiue: Vaine is
the art that seekes it selfe for to deceiue.

So well he woo'd her, and so well he wrought her, With

faire entreatie and sweet blandishment, That at the length vnto a bay he brought her, So as she to his speeches was content To lend an eare, and softly to relent. At last through many vowes which forth he pour'd, And many othes, she yeelded her consent To be his loue, and take him for her Lord, Till they with mariage meet might finish that accord.

Tho when they had long time there taken rest, Sir Artegall, who all this while was bound Vpon an hard aduenture yet in quest, Fit time for him thence to depart it found, To follow that, which he did long propound; And vnto her his congee came to take. But her therewith full sore displeasd he found, And loth to leaue her late betrothed make, Her dearest loue full loth so shortly to forsake.

Yet he with strong perswasions her asswaged, And wonne her will to suffer him depart; For which his faith with her he fast engaged, And thousand vowes from bottome of his hart That all so soone as he by wit or art Could that atchieue, whereto he did aspire, He vnto her would speedily reuert: No longer space thereto he did desire, But till the horned moone three courses did expire.

With which she for the present was appeased, And yeelded leaue, how euer malcontent She inly were, and in her mind displeased. So early in the morrow next he went Forth on his way, to which he was ybent. Ne wight him to attend, or way to guide, As whylome was the custome ancient Mongst Knights, when on aduentures they did ride, Saue that she algates him a while accompanide.

And by the way she sundry purpose found Of this or that, the time for to delay, And of the perils whereto he was bound, The feare whereof seem'd much her to affray: But all she did was but to weare out day. Full oftentimes she leaue of him did take; And eft againe deuiz'd some what to say, Which she forgot, whereby excuse to make: So loth she was his companie for to forsake.

At last when all her speeches she had spent, And new occasion fayld her more to find, She left him to his fortunes gouernment, And backe returned with right heauie mind, To Scudamour, who she had left behind: With whom she went to seeke faire Amoret, Her second care, though in another kind; For vertues onely sake, which doth beget True loue and faithfull friendship, she by her did set.

Backe to that desert forrest they retyred, Where sorie Britomart had lost her late; There they her sought, and euery where inquired, Where they might tydings get of her estate; Yet found they none. But by what haplesse fate, Or hard misfortune she was thence conuayd, And stolne away from her beloued mate, Were long to tell; therefore I here will stay Vntill another tyde, that I it finish may.

Cant. VII.

Amoret rapt by greedie lust Belphebe saues from dread: The Squire her loues, and being blam'd his dayes in dole doth lead.

G Reat God of loue, that with thy cruell darts, Doest conquer greatest conquerors on ground, And setst thy kingdome in the captiue harts Of Kings and Keasars, to thy seruice bound, What glorie, or what guerdon hast thou found In feeble Ladies tyranning so sore; And adding anguish to the bitter wound, With which their liues thou lanchedst long afore, By heaping stormes of trouble on them daily more? So whylome didst thou to faire Florimell; And so and so to noble Britomart: So doest thou now to her, of whom I tell, The louely Amoret, whose gentle hart Thou martyrest with sorow and with smart, In saluage forrests, and in deserts wide, With Beares and Tygers taking heauie part, Withouten comfort, and withouten guide, That pittie is to heare the perils, which she tride.

So soone as she with that braue Britonesse Had left that Turneyment for beauties prise, They trauel'd long, that now for wearinesse, Both of the way, and warlike exercise, Both through a forest ryding did deuise T'alight, and rest their wearie limbs awhile. There heauie sleepe the eye-lids did surprise Of Britomart after long tedious toyle, That did her passed paines in quiet rest assoyle.

The whiles faire Amoret, of nought affeard, Walkt through the wood, for pleasure, or for need; When suddenly behind her backe she heard One rushing forth out of the thickest weed, That ere she backe could turne to taken heed, Had vnawares her snatched vp from ground. Feebly she shriekt, but so feebly indeed, That Britomart heard not the shrilling sound, There where through weary trauel she lay sleeping souˉd.

It was to weet a wilde and saluage man, Yet was no man, but onely like in shape, And eke in stature higher by a span, All ouergrowne with haire, that could awhape An hardy hart, and his wide mouth did gape With huge great teeth, like to a tusked Bore: For he liu'd all on rauin and on rape Of men and beasts; and fed on fleshly gore, The signe whereof yet stain'd his bloudy lips afore.

His neather lip was not like man nor beast, But like a wide deepe poke, downe hanging low, In which he wont the relickes of his feast, And cruell spoyle, which he had spard, to stow: And ouer it his huge great nose did grow, Full dreadfully empurpled all with bloud; And downe both sides two wide long eares did glow, And raught downe to his waste, when vp he stood, More great then th'eares of Elephants by Indus flood.

His wast was with a wreath of yuie greene Engirt about, ne other garment wore: For all his haire was like a garment seene; And in his hand a tall young oake he bore, Whose knottie snags were sharpned all afore, And beath'd in fire for steele to be in sted. But whence he was, or of what wombe ybore, Of beasts, or of the earth, I haue not red: But certes was with milke of Wolues and Tygres fed.

This vgly creature in his armes her snatcht, And through the forrest bore her quite away, With briers and bushes all to rent and scratcht; Ne care he had, ne pittie of the pray, Which many a knight had sought so many a day. He stayed not, but in his armes her bearing Ran, till he came to th'end of all his way, Vnto his caue farre from all peoples hearing, And there he threw her in, nought feeling, ne nought fearing.

For she deare Ladie all the way was dead, Whilest he in armes her bore; but when she felt Her selfe downe soust, she waked out of dread Streight into griefe, that her deare hart nigh swelt, And eft gan into tender teares to melt. Then when she lookt about, and nothing found But darknesse and dread horrour, where she dwelt, She almost fell againe into a swound, Ne wist whether aboue she were, or vnder ground.

With that she heard some one close by her side Sighing and sobbing sore, as if the paine Her tender hart in peeces would diuide: Which she long listning, softly askt againe What mister wight it was that so did plaine? To whom thus aunswer'd was: Ah wretched wight That seekes to know anothers griefe in vaine, Vnweeting of thine owne like haplesse plight: Selfe to forget to mind another, is ouersight.

Aye me (said she) where am I, or with whom? Emong the liuing, or emong the dead? What shall of me vnhappy maid become? Shall death be th'end, or ought else worse, aread. Vnhappy mayd (then answerd she) whose dread Vntride, is lesse then when thou shalt it try: Death is to him, that wretched life doth lead, Both grace and gaine; but he in hell doth lie, That liues a loathed life, and wishing cannot die.

This dismall day hath thee a caytiue made, And vassall to the vilest wretch aliue, Whose cursed vsage and vngodly trade The heauens abhorre, and into darkenesse driue. For on the spoile of women he doth liue, Whose bodies chast, when euer in his powre He may them catch, vnable to gainestriue, He with his shamefull lust doth first deflowre, And afterwards themselues doth cruelly deuoure.

Now twenty daies, by which the sonnes of men Diuide their works, haue past through heuen sheene, Since I was brought into this dolefull den; During which space these sory eies haue seen Seauen women by him slaine, and eaten clene. And now no more for him but I alone, And this old woman here remaining beene; Till thou cam'st hither to augment our mone, And of vs three to morrow he will sure eate one.

Ah dreadfull tidings which thou doest declare, (Quoth she) of all that euer hath bene knowen: Full many great calamities and rare This feeble brest endured hath, but none Equall to this, where euer I haue gone. But what are you, whom like vnlucky lot Hath linckt with me in the same chaine attone? To tell (quoth she) that which ye see, needs not; A wofull wretched maid, of God and man forgot.

But what I was, it irkes me to reherse Daughter vnto a Lord of high degree; That ioyd in happy peace, till fates peruerse With guilefull loue did secretly agree, To ouerthrow my state and dignitie. It was my lot to loue a gentle swaine, Yet was he but a Squire of low degree; Yet was he meet, vnlesse mine eye did faine, By any Ladies side for Leman to haue laine.

But for his meannesse and disparagement, My Sire, who me too dearely well did loue, Vnto my choise by no meanes would assent, But often did my folly fowle reproue. Yet nothing could my fixed mind remoue, But whether willed or nilled friend or foe, I me resolu'd the vtmost end to proue, And rather then my loue abandon so, Both sire, and friends, and all for euer to forego.

Thenceforth I sought by secret meanes to worke Time to my will, and from his wrathfull sight To hide th'intent, which in my heart did lurke, Till I thereto had all things ready dight. So on a day vnweeting vnto wight, I with that Squire agreede away to flit, And in a priuy place, betwixt vs hight, Within a groue appointed him to meete; To which I boldly came vpon my feeble feete.

But ah vnhappy houre me thither brought: For in that place where I him thought to find, There was I found, contrary to my thought, Of this accursed Carle of hellish kind; The shame of men, and plague of womankind, Who trussing me, as Eagle doth his pray, Me hether brought with him, as swift as wind, Where yet vntouched till this present day, I rest his wretched thrall, the sad AEmylia.

Ah sad AEmylia (then sayd Amoret,) Thy ruefull plight I pitty as mine owne. But read to me, by what deuise or wit, Hast thou in all this time, from him vnknowne Thine honor sau'd, though into thraldome throwne? Through helpe (quoth she) of this old woman here I haue so done, as she to me hath showne. For euer when he burnt in lustfull fire, She in my stead supplide his bestiall desire.

Thus of their euils as they did discourse, And each did other much bewaile and mone; Loe where the villaine selfe, their sorrowes sourse, Came to the caue, and rolling thence the stone, Which wont to stop the mouth thereof, that none Might issue forth, came rudely rushing in, And spredding ouer all the flore alone, Gan dight him selfe vnto his wonted sinne; Which ended, then his bloudy banket should beginne.

Which when as fearefull Amoret perceiued, She staid not the vtmost end thereof to try, But like a ghastly Gelt, whose wits are reaued, Ran forth in hast with hideous outcry, For horrour of his shamefull villany. But after her full lightly he vprose, And her pursu'd as fast as she did flie: Full fast she flies, and farre afore him goes, Ne feeles the thorns and thickets pricke her tender toes.

Nor hedge, nor ditch, nor hill, nor dale she staies, But ouerleapes them all, like Robucke light, And through the thickest makes her nighest waies; And euermore when with regardfull sight She looking backe, espies that griesly wight Approching nigh, she gins to mend her pace, And makes her feare a spur to hast her flight: More swift then Myrrh' or Daphne in her race, Or any of the Thracian Nimphes in saluage chase.

Long so she fled, and so he follow'd long; Ne liuing aide for her on earth appeares, But if the heauens helpe to redresse her wrong, Moued with pity of her plenteous teares. It fortuned Belphebe with her peares The woody Nimphs, and with that louely boy, Was hunting then the Libbards and the Beares, In these wild woods, as was her wonted ioy, To banish sloth, that oft doth noble mindes annoy.

It so befell, as oft it fals in chace, That each of them from other sundred were, And that same gentle Squire arriu'd in place, Where this same cursed caytiue did appeare, Pursuing that faire Lady full of feare; And now he her quite ouertaken had; And now he her away with him did beare Vnder his arme, as seeming wondrous glad, That by his grenning laughter mote farre off be rad.

Which drery sight the gentle Squire espying, Doth hast to crosse him by the nearest way, Led with that wofull Ladies piteous crying, And him assailes with all the might he may: Yet will not he the louely spoile downe lay, But with his craggy club in his right hand, Defends him selfe, and saues his gotten pray. Yet had it bene right hard him to withstand, But that he was full light and nimble on the land.

Thereto the villaine vsed craft in fight; For euer when the Squire his iauelin shooke, He held the Lady forth before him right, And with her body, as a buckler, broke The puissance of his intended stroke. And if it chaunst, (as needs it must in fight) Whilest he on him was greedy to be wroke, That any little blow on her did light, Then would he laugh aloud, and gather great delight.

Which subtill sleight did him encumber much, And made him oft, when he would strike, forbeare; For hardly could he come the carle to touch, But that he her must hurt, or hazard neare: Yet he his hand so carefully did beare, That at the last he did himselfe attaine, And therein left the pike head of his speare. A streame of coleblacke bloud thence gusht amaine, That all her silken garments did with bloud bestaine.

With that he threw her rudely on the flore, And laying both his hands vpon his glaue, With dreadfull strokes let driue at him so sore, That forst him flie abacke, himselfe to saue: Yet he therewith so felly still did raue, That scarse the Squire his hand could once vpreare, But for aduantage ground vnto him gaue, Tracing and trauersing, now here, now there; For bootlesse thing it was to think such blowes to beare.

Whilest thus in battell they embusied were, Belphebe raunging in that forrest wide, The hideous noise of their huge strokes did heare, And drew thereto, making her eare her guide. Whom when that theefe approching nigh espide, With bow in hand, and arrowes ready bent, He by his former combate would not bide, But fled away with ghastly dreriment, Well knowing her to be his deaths sole instrument.

Whom seeing flie, she speedily poursewed With winged feete, as nimble as the winde; And euer in her bow she ready shewed The arrow, to his deadly marke desynde, As when Latonaes daughter cruell kynde, In vengement of her mothers great disgrace, With fell despight her cruell arrowes tynde Gainst wofull Niobes vnhappy race, That all the gods did mone her miserable case.

So well she sped her and so far she ventred, That ere vnto his hellish den he raught, Euen as he ready was there to haue entred, She sent an arrow forth with mighty draught, That in the very dore him ouercaught, And in his nape arriuing, through it thrild His greedy throte, therewith in two distraught, That all his vitall spirites thereby spild, And all his hairy brest with gory bloud was fild.

Whom when on ground she groueling saw to rowle, She ran in hast his life to haue bereft: But ere she could him reach, the sinfull sowle Hauing his carrion corse quite sencelesse left, Was fled to hell, surcharg'd with spoile and theft. Yet ouer him she there long gazing stood, And oft admir'd his monstrous shape, and oft His mighty limbs, whilest all with filthy bloud The place there ouerflowne, seemd like a sodaine flood.

Thence forth she past into his dreadfull den, Where nought but darkesome drerinesse she found, Ne creature saw, but hearkned now and then Some litle whispering, and soft groning sound. With that she askt, what ghosts there vnder ground Lay hid in horrour of eternall night? And bad them, if so be they were not bound, To come and shew them-

selues before the light, Now freed from feare and danger of
that dismall wight.

Then forth the sad AEmylia issewed, Yet trembling euery
ioynt through former feare; And after her the Hag, there
with her mewed, A foule and lothsome creature did appeare;
A leman fit for such a louer deare. That mou'd Belphebe her
no lesse to hate, Then for to rue the others heauy cheare; Of
whom she gan enquire of her estate. Who all to her at large,
as hapned, did relate.

Thence she them brought toward the place, where late
She left the gentle Squire with Amoret: There she him found
by that new louely mate, Who lay the whiles in swoune, full
sadly set, From her faire eyes wiping the deawy wet, Which
softly stild, and kissing them atweene, And handling soft the
hurts, which she did get. For of that Carle she sorely bruz'd
had beene, Als of his owne rash hand one wound was to be
seene.

Which when she saw, with sodaine glauncing eye, Her
noble heart with sight thereof was fild With deepe disdaine,
and great indignity, That in her wrath she thought them
both haue thrild, With that selfe arrow, which the Carle had
kild: Yet held her wrathfull hand from vengeance sore, But
drawing nigh, ere he her well beheld; Is this the faith, she
said, and said no more, But turnd her face, and fled away for
euermore.

He seeing her depart, arose vp light, Right sore agrieued
at her sharpe reproofe, And follow'd fast: but when he came in
sight, He durst not nigh approch, but kept aloofe, For dread
of her displeasures vtmost proofe. And euermore, when he
did grace entreat, And framed speaches fit for his behoofe,
Her mortall arrowes she at him did threat, And forst him
backe with fowle dishonor to retreat.

At last when long he follow'd had in vaine, Yet found no
ease of griefe, nor hope of grace, Vnto those woods he turned
backe againe, Full of sad anguish, and in heauy case: And
finding there fit solitary place For wofull wight, chose out

a gloomy glade, Where hardly eye mote see bright heauens face, For mossy trees, which couered all with shade And sad melancholy: there he his cabin made.

His wonted warlike weapons all he broke, And threw away, with vow to vse no more, Ne thenceforth euer strike in battell stroke, Ne euer word to speake to woman more; But in that wildernesse, of men forlore, And of the wicked world forgotten quight, His hard mishap in dolor to deplore, And wast his wretched daies in wofull plight; So on him selfe to wreake his follies owne despight.

And eke his garment, to be thereto meet, He wilfully did cut and shape anew; And his faire lockes, that wont with ointment sweet To be embaulm'd, and sweat out dainty dew, He let to grow and griesly to concrew, Vncomb'd, vncurl'd, and carelesly vnshed; That in short time his face they ouergrew, And ouer all his shoulders did dispred, That who he whilome was, vneath was to be red.

There he continued in this carefull plight, Wretchedly wearing out his youthly yeares, Through wilfull penury consumed quight, That like a pined ghost he soone appeares. For other food then that wilde forrest beares, Ne other drinke there did he euer tast, Then running water, tempred with his teares, The more his weakened body so to wast: That out of all mens knowledge he was worne at last.

For on a day, by fortune as it fell, His owne deare Lord Prince Arthure came that way, Seeking aduentures, where he mote heare tell; And as he through the wandring wood did stray, Hauing espide this Cabin far away, He to it drew, to weet who there did wonne; Weening therein some holy Hermit lay, That did resort of sinfull people shonne; Or else some woodman shrowded there from scorching sunne.

Arriuing there, he found this wretched man, Spending his daies in dolour and despaire, And through long fasting woxen pale and wan, All ouergrowen with rude and rugged haire; That albeit his owne deare Squire he were, Yet he him knew not, ne auiz'd at all, But like strange wight, whom he had seene no where, Saluting him, gan into speach to fall, And pitty much his plight, that liu'd like outcast thrall.

But to his speach he aunswered no whit, But stood still mute, as if he had beene dum, Ne signe of sence did shew, ne common wit, As one with griefe and anguishe ouercum, And vnto euery thing did aunswere mum: And euer when the Prince vnto him spake, He louted lowly, as did him becum, And humble homage did vnto him make, Midst sorrow shewing ioyous semblance for his sake.

At which his vncouth guise and vsage quaint The Prince did wonder much, yet could not ghesse The cause of that his sorrowfull constraint; Yet weend by secret signes of manlinesse, Which close appeard in that rude brutishnesse, That he whilome some gentle swaine had beene, Traind vp in feats of armes and knightlinesse; Which he obseru'd, by that he him had seene To weld his naked sword, and try the edges keene.

And eke by that he saw on euery tree, How he the name of one engrauen had, Which likly was his liefest loue to be, For whom he now so sorely was bestad; Which was by him BELPHEBE rightly rad. Yet who was that Belphebe, he ne wist; Yet saw he often how he wexed glad, When he it heard, and how the ground he kist, Wherein it written was, and how himselfe he blist:

Tho when he long had marked his demeanor, And saw that all he said and did, was vaine, Ne ought mote make him change his wonted tenor, Ne ought mote ease or mitigate his paine, He left him there in languor to remaine, Till time for him should remedy prouide, And him restore to former grace againe. Which for it is too long here to abide, I will deferre the end vntill another tide.

Cant. VIII.

The gentle Squire recouers grace, Sclaunder her guests doth staine: Corflambo chaseth Placidas, And is by Arthure slaine.

W Ell said the wiseman, now prou'd true by this, Which to this gentle Squire did happen late. That the displeasure of the mighty is Then death it selfe more dread and desperate. For naught the same may calme ne mitigate, Till time the tempest doe thereof delay With sufferaunce soft, which rigour can abate, And haue the sterne remembrance wypt away Of bitter thoughts, which deepe therein infixed lay. Like as it fell to this vnhappy boy, Whose tender heart the faire Belphebe had, With one sterne looke so daunted, that no ioy In all his life, which afterwards he lad, He euer tasted, but with penaunce sad And pensiue sorrow pind and wore away, Ne euer laught, ne once shew'd countenance glad; But alwaies wept and wailed night and day, As blasted bloosme through heat doth languish & decay;

Till on a day, as in his wonted wise His doole he made, there chaunst a turtle Doue To come, where he his dolors did deuise, That likewise late had lost her dearest loue; Which losse her made like passion also proue. Who seeing his sad plight, her tender heart With deare compassion deeply did emmoue, That she gan mone his vndeserued smart, And with her dolefull accent beare with him apart.

Shee sitting by him as on ground he lay, Her mournefull notes full piteously did frame, And thereof made a lamentable lay, So sensibly compyld, that in the same Him seemed oft he heard his owne right name. With that he forth would poure so plenteous teares, And beat his breast vnworthy of such blame, And knocke his head, and rend his rugged heares, That could haue perst the hearts of Tigres & of Beares.

Thus long this gentle bird to him did vse, Withouten dread of perill to repaire Vnto his wonne, and with her mournefull muse Him to recomfort in his greatest care, That much did ease his mourning and misfare: And euery day for guerdon of her song, He part of his small feast to her would share; That at the last of all his woe and wrong Companion she became, and so continued long.

Vpon a day as she him sate beside, By chance he certaine miniments forth drew, Which yet with him as relickes did abide Of all the bounty, which Belphebe threw On him, whilst goodly grace she did him shew: Amongst the rest a iewell rich he found, That was a Ruby of right perfect hew, Shap'd like a heart, yet bleeding of the wound, And with a litle golden chaine about it bound.

The same he tooke, and with a riband new, In which his Ladies colours were, did bind About the turtles necke, that with the vew Did greatly solace his engrieued mind. All vnawares the bird, when she did find Her selfe so deckt, her nimble wings displaid, And flew away, as lightly as the wind: Which sodaine accident him much dismaid, And looking after long, did marke which way she straid.

But when as long he looked had in vaine, Yet saw her forward still to make her flight, His weary eie returnd to him againe, Full of discomfort and disquiet plight, That both his iuell he had lost so light, And eke his deare companion of his care. But that sweet bird departing, flew forth right Through the wide region of the wastfull aire, Vntill she came where wonned his Belphebe faire.

There found she her (as then it did betide) Sitting in couert shade of arbors sweet, After late weary toile, which she had tride In saluage chase, to rest as seem'd her meet. There she alighting, fell before her feet, And gan to her her mournfull plaint to make, As was her wont, thinking to let her weet The great tormenting griefe, that for her sake Her gentle Squire through her displeasure did pertake.

She her beholding with attentiue eye, At length did marke about her purple brest That precious iuell, which she formerly Had knowne right well with colourd ribbands drest: Therewith she rose in hast, and her addrest With ready hand it to haue reft away. But the swift bird obayd not her behest, But swaru'd aside, and there againe did stay; She follow'd her, and thought againe it to assay.

And euer when she nigh approcht, the Doue Would flit a litle forward, and then stay, Till she drew neare, and then againe remoue; So tempting her still to pursue the pray, And still from her escaping soft away: Till that at length into that forrest wide, She drew her far, and led with slow delay. In th'end she her vnto that place did guide, Whereas that wofull man in languor did abide.

Eftsoones she flew vnto his fearelesse hand, And there a piteous ditty new deuiz'd, As if she would haue made him vnderstand, His sorrowes cause to be of her despis'd. Whom when she saw in wretched weedes disguiz'd, With heary glib deform'd, and meiger face, Like ghost late risen from his graue agryz'd, She knew him not, but pittied much his case, And wisht it were in her to doe him any grace.

He her beholding, at her feet downe fell, And kist the ground on which her sole did tread, And washt the same with water, which did well From his moist eies, and like two streames procead; Yet spake no word, whereby she might aread What mister wight he was, or what he ment: But as one daunted with her presence dread, Onely few ruefull lookes vnto her sent, As messengers of his true meaning and intent.

Yet nathemore his meaning she ared, But wondred much at his so selcouth case, And by his persons secret seemlyhed Well weend, that he had beene some man of place, Before misfortune did his hew deface: That being mou'd with ruth she thus bespake. Ah wofull man, what heauens hard disgrace, Or wrath of cruell wight on thee ywrake? Or selfe disliked life doth thee thus wretched make?

If heauen, then none may it redresse or blame, Sith to his powre we all are subiect borne: If wrathfull wight, then fowle rebuke and shame Be theirs, that haue so cruell thee forlorne; But if through inward griefe or wilfull scorne Of life it be, then better doe aduise. For he whose daies in wilfull woe are worne, The grace of his Creator doth despise, That will not vse his gifts for thanklesse nigardise.

When so he heard her say, eftsoones he brake His sodaine silence, which he long had pent, And sighing inly deepe, her thus bespake; Then haue they all themselues against me bent: For heauen, first author of my languishment, Enuying my too great felicity, Did closely with a cruell one consent, To cloud my daies in dolefull misery, And make me loath this life, still longing for to die.

Ne any but your selfe, O dearest dred, Hath done this wrong, to wreake on worthlesse wight Your high displesure, through misdeeming bred: That when your pleasure is to deeme aright, Ye may redresse, and me restore to light. Which sory words her mightie hart did mate With mild regard, to see his ruefull plight, That her inburning wrath she gan abate, And him receiu'd againe to former fauours state.

In which he long time afterwards did lead An happie life with grace and good accord, Fearlesse of fortunes chaunge or enuies dread, And eke all mindlesse of his owne deare Lord The noble Prince, who neuer heard one word Of tydings, what did vnto him betide, Or what good fortune did to him afford, But through the endlesse world did wander wide, Him seeking euermore, yet no where him describe.

Till on a day as through that wood he rode, He chaunst to come where those two Ladies late, AEmylia and Amoret abode, Both in full sad and sorrowfull estate; The one right feeble through the euill rate Of food, which in her duresse she had found: The other almost dead and desperate Through her late hurts, and through that haplesse wound, With which the Squire in her defence her sore astound.

Whom when the Prince beheld, he gan to rew The euill case in which those Ladies lay; But most was moued at the piteous vew Of Amoret, so neare vnto decay, That her great daunger did him much dismay. Eftsoones that pretious liquour forth he drew, Which he in store about him kept alway, And with few drops thereof did softly dew Her wounds, that vnto strength restor'd her soone anew.

Tho when they both recouered were right well, He gan of them inquire, what euill guide Them thether brought, and how their harmes befell. To whom they told all, that did them betide, And how from thraldome vile they were vntide Of that same wicked Carle, by Virgins hond; Whose bloudie corse they shew'd him there beside, And eke his caue, in which they both were bond: At which he wondred much, when all those signes he fond.

And euermore he greatly did desire To know, what Virgin did them thence vnbind; And oft of them did earnestly inquire, Where was her won, and how he mote her find. But when as nought according to his mind He could outlearne, he them from ground did reare: No seruice lothsome to a gentle kind; And on his warlike beast them both did beare, Himselfe by them on foot, to succour them from feare.

So when that forrest they had passed well, A litle cotage farre away they spide, To which they drew, ere night vpon them fell; And entring in, found none therein abide, But one old woman sitting there beside, Vpon the ground in ragged rude attyre, With filthy lockes about her scattered wide, Gnawing her nayles for felnesse and for yre, And there out sucking venime to her parts entyre.

A foule and loathly creature sure in sight, And in conditions to be loath'd no lesse: For she was stuft with rancour and despight Vp to the throat, that oft with bitternesse It forth would breake, and gush in great excesse, Pouring out streames of poyson and of gall Gainst all, that truth or vertue doe professe, Whom she with leasings lewdly did miscall, And wickedly backbite: Her name men Sclaunder call.

Her nature is all goodnesse to abuse, And causelesse crimes continually to frame, With which she guiltlesse persons may accuse, And steale away the crowne of their good name; Ne euer Knight so bold, ne euer Dame So chast and loyall liu'd, but she would striue With forged cause them falsely to defame; Ne euer thing so well was doen aliue, But she with blame would blot, & of due praise depriue.

Her words were not, as common words are ment, T'expresse the meaning of the inward mind, But noysome breath, and poysnous spirit sent From inward parts, with cancred malice lind, And breathed forth with blast of bitter wind; Which passing through the eares, would pierce the hart, And wound the soule it selfe with griefe vnkind: For like the stings of Aspes, that kill with smart, Her spightfull words did pricke, & wound the inner part.

Such was that Hag, vnmeet to host such guests, Whom greatest Princes court would welcome fayne; But neede, that answers not to all requests, Bad them not looke for better entertayne; And eke that age despysed nicenesse vaine, Enur'd to hardnesse and to homely fare, Which them to warlike discipline did trayne, And manly limbs endur'd with little care Against all hard mishaps and fortunelesse misfare.

Then all that euening welcommed with cold, And chearelesse hunger, they together spent; Yet found no fault, but that the Hag did scold And rayle at them with grudgefull discontent, For lodging there without her owne consent: Yet they endured all with patience milde, And vnto rest themselues all onely lent, Regardlesse of that queane so base and vilde, To be vniustly blamd, and bitterly reuilde.

Here well I weene, when as these rimes be red With misregard, that some rash witted wight, Whose looser thought will lightly be misled, These gentle Ladies will misdeeme too light, For thus conuersing with this noble Knight; Sith now of dayes such temperance is rare And hard to finde, that heat of youthfull spright For ought will from his greedie pleasure spare: More hard for hungry steed t'abstaine from pleasant lare.

But antique age yet in the infancie Of time, did liue then like an innocent, In simple truth and blamelesse chastitie, Ne then of guile had made experiment, But voide of vile and treacherous intent, Held vertue for it selfe in soueraine awe: Then loyall loue had royall regiment, And each vnto his lust did make a lawe, From all forbidden things his liking to withdraw.

The Lyon there did with the Lambe consort, And eke the Doue sate by the Faulcons side, Ne each of other feared fraud or tort, But did in safe securitie abide, Withouten perill of the stronger pride: But when the world woxe old, it woxe warre old (Whereof it hight) and hauing shortly tride The traines of wit, in wickednesse woxe bold, And dared of all sinnes the secrets to vnfold.

Then beautie, which was made to represent The great Creatours owne resemblance bright, Vnto abuse of lawlesse lust was lent, And made the baite of bestiall delight: Then faire grew foule, and foule grew faire in sight, And that which wont to vanquish God and man, Was made the vassall of the victors might; Then did her glorious flowre wex dead and wan, Despisd and troden downe of all that ouerran.

And now it is so vtterly decayd, That any bud thereof doth scarse remaine, But if few plants preseru'd through heauenly ayd, In Princes Court doe hap to sprout againe, Dew'd with her drops of bountie Soueraine, Which from that goodly glorious flowre proceed, Sprung of the auncient stocke of Princes straine, Now th'onely remnant of that royall breed, Whose noble kind at first was sure of heauenly seed.

Tho soone as day discouered heauens face To sinfull men with darknes ouerdight, This gentle crew gan from their eye-lids chace The drowzie humour of the dampish night, And did themselues vnto their iourney dight. So forth they yode, and forward softly paced, That them to view had bene an vn-couth sight; How all the way the Prince on footpace traced, The Ladies both on horse, together fast embraced.

Soone as they thence departed were afore, That shamefull Hag, the slaunder of her sexe, Them follow'd fast, and them reuiled sore, Him calling theefe, them whores; that much did vexe His noble hart; thereto she did annexe False crimes and facts, such as they neuer ment, That those two Ladies much asham'd did wexe: The more did she pursue her lewd intent, And rayl'd and rag'd, till she had all her poyson spent.

At last when they were passed out of sight, Yet she did not her spightfull speach forbeare, But after them did barke, and still backbite, Though there were none her hatefull words to heare: Like as a curre doth felly bite and teare The stone, which passed straunger at him threw; So she them seeing past the reach of eare, Against the stones and trees did rayle anew, Till she had duld the sting, which in her tongs end grew.

They passing forth kept on their readie way, With easie steps so soft as foot could stryde. Both for great feeblesse, which did oft assay Faire Amoret, that scarcely she could ryde; And eke through heauie armes, which sore annoyd The Prince on foot, not wonted so to fare; Whose steadie hand was faine his steede to guyde, And all the way from trotting hard to spare, So was his toyle the more, the more that was his care.

At length they spide, where towards them with speed A Squire came gallopping, as he would flie; Bearing a litle Dwarfe before his steed, That all the way full loud for aide did crie, That seem'd his shrikes would rend the brasen skie: Whom after did a mightie man pursew, Ryding vpon a Dromedare on hie, Of stature huge, and horrible of hew, That would haue maz'd a man his dreadfull face to vew.

For from his fearefull eyes two fierie beames, More sharpe then points of needles did proceede, Shooting forth farre away two flaming streames, Full of sad powre, that poysonous bale did breede To all, that on him lookt without good heed, And secretly his enemies did slay: Like as the Basiliske of serpents seede, From powrefull eyes close venim doth conuay Into the lookers hart, and killeth farre away.

He all the way did rage at that same Squire, And after him full many threatnings threw, With curses vaine in his auengefull ire: But none of them (so fast away he flew) Him ouertooke, before he came in vew. Where when he saw the Prince in armour bright, He cald to him aloud, his case to rew, And rescue him through succour of his might, From that his cruell foe, that him pursewd in sight.

Eftsoones the Prince tooke downe those Ladies twaine From loftie steede, and mounting in their stead Came to that Squire, yet trembling euery vaine: Of whom he gan enquire his cause of dread; Who as he gan the same to him aread, Loe hard behind his backe his foe was prest, With dread-full weapon aymed at his head; That vnto death had doen him vnredrest, Had not the noble Prince his readie stroke represt.

Who thrusting boldly twixt him and the blow, The bur-den of the deadly brunt did beare Vpon his shield, which lightly he did throw Ouer his head, before the harme came neare. Nathlesse it fell with so despiteous dreare And heauie sway, that hard vnto his crowne The shield it droue, and did the couering reare: Therewith both Squire and dwarfe did tomble downe Vnto the earth, and lay long while in sense-lesse swowne.

Whereat the Prince full wrath, his strong right hand In full auengement heaued vp on hie, And stroke the Pagan with his steely brand So sore, that to his saddle bow thereby He bowed low, and so a while did lie: And sure had not his massie yron mace Betwixt him and his hurt bene happily, It would haue cleft him to the girding place, Yet as it was, it did astonish him long space.

But when he to himselfe returnd againe, All full of rage he gan to curse and sweare, And vow by Mahoune that he should be slaine. With that his murdrous mace he vp did reare, That seemed nought the souse thereof could beare, And therewith smote at him with all his might. But ere that it to him approched neare, The royall child with readie quicke foresight, Did shun the proofe thereof and it auoyded light.

But ere his hand he could recure againe, To ward his bodie from the balefull stound, He smote at him with all his might and maine, So furiously, that ere he wist, he found His head before him tombling on the ground. The whiles his babling tongue did yet blaspheme And curse his God, that did him so confound; The whiles his life ran foorth in bloudie streame, His soule descended downe into the Stygian reame.

Which when that Squire beheld, he woxe full glad To see his foe breath out his spright in vaine: But that same dwarfe right sorie seem'd and sad, And howld aloud to see his Lord there slaine, And rent his haire and scratcht his face for paine. Then gan the Prince at leasure to inquire Of all the accident, there hapned plaine, And what he was, whose eyes did flame with fire; All which was thus to him declared by that Squire.

This mightie man (quoth he) whom you haue slaine, Of an huge Geauntesse whylome was bred; And by his strength rule to himselfe did gaine Of many Nations into thraldome led, And mightie kingdomes of his force adred; Whom yet he conquer'd not by bloudie fight, Ne hostes of men with banners brode dispred, But by the powre of his infectious sight, With which he killed all, that came within his might.

Ne was he euer vanquished afore, But euer vanquisht all, with whom he fought; Ne was there man so strong, but he downe bore, Ne woman yet so faire, but he her brought Vnto his bay, and captiued her thought. For most of strength and beautie his desire Was spoyle to make, and wast them vnto nought, By casting secret flakes of lustfull fire From his false eyes, into their harts and parts entire.

Therefore Corflambo was he cald aright, Though namelesse there his bodie now doth lie, Yet hath he left one daughter that is hight The faire Poeana; who seemes outwardly So faire, as euer yet saw liuing eie: And were her vertue like her beautie bright, She were as faire as any vnder skie. But ah she giuen is to vaine delight, And eke too loose of life, and eke of loue too light.

So as it fell there was a gentle Squire, That lou'd a Ladie of high parentage; But for his meane degree might not aspire To match so high, her friends with counsell sage, Dissuaded her from such a disparage. But she, whose hart to loue was wholly lent, Out of his hands could not redeeme her gage, But firmely following her first intent, Resolu'd with him to wend, gainst all her friends consent.

So twixt themselues they pointed time and place, To which when he according did repaire, An hard mishap and disauentrous case Him chaunst; in stead of his Æmylia faire This Gyants sonne, that lies there on the laire An headlesse heape, him vnawares there caught, And all dismayd through mercilesse despaire, Him wretched thrall vnto his dongeon brought, Where he remaines, of all vnsuccour'd and vnsought.

This Gyants daughter came vpon a day Vnto the prison in her ioyous glee, To view the thrals, which there in bondage lay: Amongst the rest she chaunced there to see This louely swaine the Squire of low degree; To whom she did her liking lightly cast, And wooed him her paramour to bee: From day to day she woo'd and prayd him fast, And for his loue him promist libertie at last.

He though affide vnto a former loue, To whom his faith he firmely ment to hold, Yet seeing not how thence he mote remoue, But by that meanes, which fortune did vnfold, Her graunted loue, but with affection cold To win her grace his libertie to get. Yet she him still detaines in captiue hold Fearing least if she should him freely set, He would her shortly leaue, and former loue forget.

Yet so much fauour she to him hath hight, Aboue the rest, that he sometimes may space And walke about her gardens of delight, Hauing a keeper still with him in place; Which keeper is this Dwarfe, her dearling base, To whom the keyes of euery prison dore By her committed be, of speciall grace, And at his will may whom he list restore, And whom he list reserue, to be afflicted more.

Whereof when tydings came vnto mine eare, Full inly sorie for the feruent zeale, Which I to him as to my soule did beare; I thether went where I did long conceale My selfe, till that the Dwarfe did me reueale, And told his Dame, her Squire of low degree Did secretly out of her prison steale; For me he did mistake that Squire to be; For neuer two so like did liuing creature see.

Then was I taken and before her brought: Who through the likenesse of my outward hew, Being likewise beguiled in her thought, Gan blame me much for being so vntrew, To seeke by flight her fellowship t'eschew, That lou'd me deare, as dearest thing aliue. Thence she commaunded me to prison new; Whereof I glad did not gainesay nor striue, But suffred that same Dwarfe me to her dongeon driue.

There did I finde mine onely faithfull frend In heauy plight and sad perplexitie; Whereof I sorie, yet my selfe did bend, Him to recomfort with my companie. But him the more agreeu'd I found thereby: For all his ioy, he said, in that distresse Was mine and his Æmylias libertie. Æmylia well he lou'd, as I mote ghesse; Yet greater loue to me then her he did professe.

But I with better reason him auiz'd, And shew'd him how through error and mis-thought Of our like persons eath to be disguiz'd, Or his exchange, or freedome might be wrought. Whereto full loth was he, ne would for ought Consent, that I who stood all fearelesse free, Should wilfully be into thraldome brought, Till fortune did perforce it so decree. Yet ouerrul'd at last, he did to me agree.

The morrow next about the wonted howre, The Dwarfe cald at the doore of Amyas, To come forthwith vnto his Ladies bowre. In steed of whom forth came I Placidas, And vndiscerned, forth with him did pas. There with great ioyance and with gladsome glee, Of faire Poeana I receiued was, And oft imbrast, as if that I were hee, And with kind words accoyd, vowing great loue to mee.

Which I, that was not bent to former loue, As was my friend, that had her long refusd, Did well accept, as well it did behoue, And to the present neede it wisely vsd. My former hardnesse first I faire excusd; And after promist large amends to make. With such smooth termes her error I abusd, To my friends good, more then for mine owne sake, For whose sole libertie I loue and life did stake.

Thenceforth I found more fauour at her hand, That to her Dwarfe, which had me in his charge, She bad to lighten my too heauie band, And graunt more scope to me to walke at large. So on a day as by the flowrie marge Of a fresh streame I with that Elfe did play, Finding no meanes how I might vs enlarge, But if that Dwarfe I could with me conuay, I lightly snatcht him vp, and with me bore away.

Thereat he shriekt aloud, that with his cry The Tyrant selfe came forth with yelling bray, And me pursew'd; but nathemore would I Forgoe the purchase of my gotten pray, But haue perforce him hether brought away. Thus as they talked, loe where nigh at hand Those Ladies two yet doubtfull through dismay In presence came, desirous t'vnderstand Tydings of all, which there had hapned on the land.

Where soone as sad Æmylia did espie Her captiue louers friend, young Placidas: All mindlesse of her wonted modestie, She to him ran, and him with streight embras Enfolding said, And liues yet Amyas? He liues (quoth he) and his Æmylia loues. Then lesse (said she) by all the woe I pas, With which my weaker patience fortune proues. But what mishap thus long him fro my selfe remoues?

Then gan he all this storie to renew, And tell the course of his captiuitie; That her deare hart full deepely made to rew, And sigh full sore, to heare the miserie, In which so long he mercilesse did lie. Then after many teares and sorrowes spent, She deare besought the Prince of remedie: Who thereto did with readie will consent, And well perform'd, as shall appeare by his euent.

Cant. IX.

The Squire of low degree release Poeana takes to wife: Britomart fightes with many Knights, Prince Arthur stints their strife.

H Ard is the doubt, and difficult to deeme, When all three kinds of loue together meet, And doe dispart the hart with powre extreme, Whether shall weigh the balance downe; to weet The deare affection vnto kindred sweet, Or raging fire of loue to woman kind, Or zeale of friends combynd with vertues meet. But of them all the band of vertuous mind Me seemes the gentle hart should most assured bind. For naturall affection soone doth cesse, And quenched is with Cupids greater flame: But faithfull friendship doth them both suppresse, And them with maystring discipline doth tame, Through thoughts aspyring to eternall fame. For as the soule doth rule the earthly masse, And all the seruice of the bodie frame, So loue of soule doth loue of bodie passe, No lesse then perfect gold surmounts the meanest brasse.

All which who list by tryall to assay, Shall in this storie find approued plaine; In which these Squires true friendship more did sway, Then either care of parents could refraine, Or loue of fairest Ladie could constraine. For though Poeana were as faire as morne, Yet did this trustie Squire with proud disdaine For his friends sake her offred fauours scorne, And she her selfe her syre, of whom she was yborne.

Now after that Prince Arthur graunted had, To yeeld strong succour to that gentle swayne, Who now long time had lyen in prison sad, He gan aduise how best he mote darrayne That enterprize, for greatest glories gayne. That headlesse tyrants tronke he reard from ground, And hauing ympt the head to it agayne, Vpon his vsuall beast it firmely bound, And made it so to ride, as it aliue was found.

Then did he take that chaced Squire, and layd Before the ryder, as he captiue were, And made his Dwarfe, though with vnwilling ayd, To guide the beast, that did his maister beare, Till to his castle they approched neare. Whom when the watch, that kept continuall ward Saw comming home; all voide of doubtfull feare, He running downe, the gate to him vnbard; Whom straight the Prince ensuing, in together far'd.

There he did find in her delitious boure The faire Poeana playing on a Rote, Complayning of her cruell Paramoure, And singing all her sorrow to the note, As she had learned readily by rote. That with the sweetnesse of her rare delight, The Prince halfe rapt, began on her to dote: Till better him bethinking of the right, He her vnwares attacht, and captiue held by might.

Whence being forth produc'd, when she perceiued Her owne deare sire, she cald to him for aide. But when of him no aunswere she receiued, But saw him sencelesse by the Squire vpstaide, She weened well, that then she was betraide: Then gan she loudly cry, and weepe, and waile, And that same Squire of treason to vpbraide. But all in vaine, her plaints might not preuaile, Ne none there was to reskue her, ne none to baile.

Then tooke he that same Dwarfe, and him compeld To open vnto him the prison dore, And forth to bring those thrals, which there he held. Thence forth were brought to him aboue a score Of Knights and Squires to him vnknowne afore: All which he did from bitter bondage free, And vnto former liberty restore. Amongst the rest, that Squire of low degree Came forth full weake and wan, not like him selfe to bee.

Whom soone as faire AEmylia beheld, And Placidas, they both vnto him ran, And him embracing fast betwixt them held, Striuing to comfort him all that they can, And kissing oft his visage pale and wan. That faire Poeana them beholding both, Gan both enuy, and bitterly to ban; Through iealous passion weeping inly wroth, To see the sight perforce, that both her eyes were loth.

But when a while they had together beene, And diuersly conferred of their case, She, though full oft she both of them had seene A sunder, yet not euer in one place, Began to doubt, when she them saw embrace, Which was the captiue Squire she lou'd so deare, Deceiued through great likenesse of their face. For they so like in person did appeare, That she vneath discerned, whether whether weare.

And eke the Prince, when as he them auized, Their like resemblaunce much admired there, And mazd how nature had so well disguized Her worke, and counterfet her selfe so nere, As if that by one patterne seene somewhere, She had them made a paragone to be, Or whether it through skill, or errour were. Thus gazing long, at them much wondred he, So did the other knights and Squires, which him did see.

Then gan they ransacke that same Castle strong, In which
he found great store of hoorded threasure, The which that
tyrant gathered had by wrong And tortious powre, without
respect or measure. Vpon all which the Briton Prince made
seasure, And afterwards continu'd there a while, To rest him
selfe, and solace in soft pleasure Those weaker Ladies after weary toile; To whom he did diuide part of his purchast
spoile.

And for more ioy, that captiue Lady faire The faire Poeana he enlarged free; And by the rest did set in sumptuous
chaire, To feast and frollicke; nathemore would she Shew
gladsome countenaunce nor pleasaunt glee: But grieued was
for losse both of her sire, And eke of Lordship, with both land
and fee: But most she touched was with griefe entire, For
losse of her new loue, the hope of her desire.

But her the Prince through his well wonted grace, To better termes of myldnesse did entreat, From that fowle rudenesse, which did her deface; And that same bitter corsiue,
which did eat Her tender heart, and made refraine from
meat, He with good thewes and speaches well applyde, Did
mollifie, and calme her raging heat. For though she were
most faire, and goodly dyde, Yet she it all did mar with cruelty and pride.

And for to shut vp all in friendly loue, Sith loue was first
the ground of all her griefe, That trusty Squire he wisely well
did moue Not to despise that dame, which lou'd him liefe,
Till he had made of her some better priefe, But to accept her
to his wedded wife. Thereto he offred for to make him chiefe
Of all her land and lordship during life: He yeelded, and her
tooke; so stinted all their strife.

From that day forth in peace and ioyous blis, They liu'd
together long without debate: Ne priuate iarre, ne spite of
enemis Could shake the safe assuraunce of their state. And
she whom Nature did so faire create, That she mote match
the fairest of her daies, Yet with lewd loues and lust intem-
perate Had it defaste; thenceforth reformd her waies, That
all men much admyrde her change, and spake her praise.

Thus when the Prince had perfectly compylde These paires of friends in peace and setled rest, Him selfe, whose minde did trauell as with chylde, Of his old loue, conceau'd in secret brest, Resolued to pursue his former quest; And taking leaue of all, with him did beare Faire Amoret, whom Fortune by bequest Had left in his protection whileare, Exchanged out of one into an other feare.

Feare of her safety did her not constraine, For well she wist now in a mighty hond, Her person late in perill, did remaine, Who able was all daungers to withstond. But now in feare of shame she more did stond, Seeing her selfe all soly succourlesse, Left in the victors powre, like vassall bond; Whose will her weakenesse could no way represse, In case his burning lust should breake into excesse.

But cause of feare sure had she none at all Of him, who goodly learned had of yore The course of loose affection to forstall, And lawlesse lust to rule with reasons lore; That all the while he by his side her bore, She was as safe as in a Sanctuary; Thus many miles they two together wore, To seeke their loues dispersed diuersly, Yet neither shewed to other their hearts priuity.

At length they came, whereas a troupe of Knights They saw together skirmishing, as seemed: Sixe they were all, all full of fell despight, But foure of them the battell best beseemed, That which of them was best, mote not be deemed. Those foure were they, from whom false Florimell By Braggadochio lately was redeemed. To weet, sterne Druon, and lewd Claribell, Loue-lauish Blandamour, and lustfull Paridell.

Druons delight was all in single life, And vnto Ladies loue would lend no leasure: The more was Claribell enraged rife With feruent flames, and loued out of measure: So eke lou'd Blandamour, but yet at pleasure Would change his liking, and new Lemans proue: But Paridell of loue did make no threasure, But lusted after all, that him did moue. So diuersly these foure disposed were to loue.

But those two other which beside them stoode, Were Britomart, and gentle Scudamour, Who all the while beheld their wrathfull moode, And wondred at their impacable stoure, Whose like they neuer saw till that same houre: So dreadfull strokes each did at other driue, And laid on load with all their might and powre, As if that euery dint the ghost would riue Out of their wretched corses, and their liues depriue.

As when Dan AEolus in great displeasure, For losse of his deare loue by Neptune hent, Sends forth the winds out of his hidden threasure, Vpon the sea to wreake his fell intent; They breaking forth with rude vnruliment, From all foure parts of heauen doe rage full sore, And tosse the deepes, and teare the firmament, And all the world confound with wide vprore, As if in stead thereof they Chaos would restore.

Cause of their discord, and so fell debate, Was for the loue of that same snowy maid, Whome they had lost in Turney-ment of late, And seeking long, to weet which way she straid Met here together; where through lewd vpbraide Of Ate and Duessa they fell out, And each one taking part in others aide, This cruell conflict raised thereabout, Whose dangerous suc-cesse depended yet in dout.

For sometimes Paridell and Blandamour The better had, and bet the others backe, Eftsoones the others did the field recoure, And on their foes did worke full cruell wracke: Yet neither would their fiendlike fury slacke, But euermore their malice did augment; Till that vneath they forced were for lacke Of breath, their raging rigour to relent, And rest them-selues for to recouer spirits spent.

There gan they change their sides, and new parts take; For Paridell did take to Druons side, For old despight, which now forth newly brake Gainst Blandamour, whom alwaies he enuide: And Blandamour to Claribell relide. So all afresh gan former fight renew. As when two Barkes, this caried with the tide, That with the wind, contrary courses sew, If wind and tide doe change, their courses change anew.

Thenceforth they much more furiously gan fare, As if but then the battell had begonne, Ne helmets bright, ne haw-

berks strong did spare, That through the clifts the vermeil
bloud out sponne, And all adowne their riuen sides did ronne.
Such mortall malice, wonder was to see In friends profest,
and so great outrage donne: But sooth is said, and tride in
each degree, Faint friends when they fall out, most cruell fo-
men bee.

Thus they long while continued in fight, Till Scudamour,
and that same Briton maide, By fortune in that place did
chance to light: Whom soone as they with wrathfull eie be-
wraide, They gan remember of the fowle vpbraide, The which
that Britonesse had to them donne, In that late Turney for
the snowy maide; Where she had them both shamefully
fordonne, And eke the famous prize of beauty from them
wonne.

Eftsoones all burning with a fresh desire, Of fell reuenge,
in their malicious mood They from them selues gan turne
their furious ire, And cruell blades yet steeming with whot
bloud, Against those two let driue, as they were wood: Who
wondring much at that so sodaine fit, Yet nought dismayd,
them stoutly well withstood; Ne yeelded foote, ne once abacke
did flit, But being doubly smitten likewise doubly smit.

The warlike Dame was on her part assaid, Of Claribell
and Blandamour attone; And Paridell and Druon fiercely
laid At Scudamour, both his professed fone. Foure charged
two, and two surcharged one; Yet did those two them selues
so brauely beare, That the other litle gained by the lone, But
with their owne repayed duely weare, And vsury withall:
such gaine was gotten deare.

Full oftentimes did Britomart assay To speake to them,
and some emparlance moue; But they for nought their cruell
hands would stay, Ne lend an eare to ought, that might behoue, As when an eager mastiffe once doth proue The tast of
bloud of some engored beast, No words may rate, nor rigour
him remoue From greedy hold of that his blouddy feast: So
litle did they hearken to her sweet beheast.

Whom when the Briton Prince a farre beheld With ods

of so vnequall match opprest, His mighty heart with indignation sweld, And inward grudge fild his heroicke brest: Eftsoones him selfe he to their aide addrest, And thrusting fierce into the thickest preace, Diuided them, how euer loth to rest, And would them faine from battell to surcease, With gentle words perswading them to friendly peace.

But they so farre from peace or patience were, That all at once at him gan fiercely flie, And lay on load, as they him downe would beare; Like to a storme, which houers vnder skie Long here and there, and round about doth stie, At length breakes downe in raine, and haile, and sleet, First from one coast, till nought thereof be drie; And then another, till that likewise fleet; And so from side to side till all the world it weet.

But now their forces greatly were decayd, The Prince yet being fresh vntoucht afore; Who them with speaches milde gan first disswade From such foule outrage, and them long forbore: Till seeing them through suffrance hartned more, Him selfe he bent their furies to abate, And layd at them so sharpely and so sore, That shortly them compelled to retrate, And being brought in daunger, to relent too late.

But now his courage being throughly fired, He ment to make them know their follies prise, Had not those two him instantly desired T'asswage his wrath, and pardon their mesprise. At whose request he gan him selfe aduise To stay his hand, and of a truce to treat In milder tearmes, as list them to deuise: Mongst which the cause of their so cruell heat He did them aske, who all that passed gan repeat.

And told at large how that same errant Knight, To weet faire Britomart, them late had foyled In open turney, and by wrongfull fight Both of their publicke praise had them despoyled, And also of their priuate loues beguyled; Of two full hard to read the harder theft. But she that wrongfull challenge soone assoyled, And shew'd that she had not that Lady reft, (As they supposd) but her had to her liking left.

To whom the Prince thus goodly well replied; Certes sir

Knight[s], ye seemen much to blame, To rip vp wrong, that battell once hath tried; Wherein the honor both of Armes ye shame, And eke the loue of Ladies foule defame; To whom the world this franchise euer yeelded, That of their loues choise they might freedom clame, And in that right should by all knights be shielded: Gainst which me seemes this war ye wrongfully haue wielded.

And yet (quoth she) a greater wrong remaines: For I thereby my former loue haue lost, Whom seeking euer since with endlesse paines, Hath me much sorrow and much trauell cost; Aye me to see that gentle maide so tost. But Scudamour then sighing deepe, thus saide, Certes her losse ought me to sorrow most, Whose right she is, where euer she be straide, Through many perils wonne, and many fortunes waide.

For from the first that I her loue profest, Vnto this houre, this present lucklesse howre, I neuer ioyed happinesse nor rest, But thus turmoild from one to other stowre, I wast my life, and doe my daies deuowre In wretched anguishe and incessant woe, Passing the measure of my feeble powre, That liuing thus, a wretch and louing so, I neither can my loue, ne yet my life forgo.

Then good sir Claribell him thus bespake, Now were it not sir Scudamour to you, Dislikefull paine, so sad a taske to take, Mote we entreat you, sith this gentle crew Is now so well accorded all anew; That as we ride together on our way, Ye will recount to vs in order dew All that aduenture, which ye did assay For that faire Ladies loue: past perils well apay.

So gan the rest him likewise to require, But Britomart did him importune hard, To take on him that paine: whose great desire He glad to satisfie, him selfe prepar'd To tell through what misfortune he had far'd, In that atchieuement, as to him befell. And all those daungers vnto them declar'd, Which sith they cannot in this Canto well Comprised be, I will them in another tell.

Cant. X.

Scudamour doth his conquest tell, Of vertuous Amoret: Great Venus Temple is describ'd, And louers life forth set.

T Rue he it said, what euer man it sayd, That loue with gall and hony doth abound, But if the one be with the other wayd, For euery dram of hony therein found, A pound of gall doth ouer it redound. That I too true by triall haue approued: For since the day that first with deadly wound My heart was launcht, and learned to haue loued, I neuer ioyed howre, but still with care was moued. And yet such grace is giuen them from aboue, That all the cares and euill which they meet, May nought at all their setled mindes remoue, But seeme gainst common sence to them most sweet; As bosting in their martyrdome vnmeet. So all that euer yet I haue endured, I count as naught, and tread downe vnder feet, Since of my loue at length I rest assured, That to disloyalty she will not be allured.

Long were to tell the trauell and long toile, Through which this shield of loue I late haue wonne, And purchased this peerelesse beauties spoile, That harder may be ended, then begonne. But since ye so desire, your will be donne. Then hearke ye gentle knights and Ladies free, My hard mishaps, that ye may learne to shonne; For though sweet loue to conquer glorious be, Yet is the paine thereof much greater then the fee.

What time the fame of this renowmed prise Flew first abroad, and all mens eares possest, I hauing armes then taken, gan auise To winne me honour by some noble gest, And purchase me some place amongst the best. I boldly thought (so young mens thoughts are bold) That this same braue emprize for me did rest, And that both shield and she whom I behold, Might be my lucky lot; sith all by lot we hold.

So on that hard aduenture forth I went, And to the place of perill shortly came. That was a temple faire and auncient, Which of great mother Venus bare the name, And farre renowmed through exceeding fame; Much more then that, which was in Paphos built, Or that in Cyprus, both long since this same, Though all the pillours of the one were guilt, And all the others pauement were with yuory spilt.

And it was seated in an Island strong, Abounding all with delices most rare, And wall'd by nature gainst inuaders wrong, That none mote haue accesse, nor inward fare, But by one way, that passage did prepare. It was a bridge ybuilt in goodly wize, With curious Corbes and pendants grauen faire, And arched all with porches, did arize On stately pillours, fram'd after the Doricke guize.

And for defence thereof, on th'other end There reared was a castle faire and strong, That warded all which in or out did wend, And flancked both the bridges sides along, Gainst all that would it faine to force or wrong. And therein wonned twenty valiant Knights; All twenty tride in warres experience long; Whose office was, against all manner wights By all meanes to maintaine that castels ancient rights.

Before that Castle was an open plaine, And in the midst thereof a piller placed; On which this shield, of many sought in vaine, The shield of Loue, whose guerdon me hath graced, Was hangd on high with golden ribbands laced; And in the marble stone was written this, With golden letters goodly well enchaced, Blessed the man that well can vse his blis: VVhose euer be the shield, faire Amoret be his.

Which when I red, my heart did inly earne, And pant with hope of that aduentures hap: Ne stayed further newes thereof to learne, But with my speare vpon the shield did rap, That all the castle ringed with the clap. Streight forth issewd a Knight all arm'd to proofe, And brauely mounted to his most mishap: Who staying nought to question from aloofe, Ran fierce at me, that fire glaunst from his horses hoofe.

Whom boldly I encountred (as I could) And by good fortune shortly him vnseated. Eftsoones out sprung two more of equall mould; But I them both with equall hap defeated: So all the twenty I likewise entreated, And left them groning there vpon the plaine. Then preacing to the pillour I repeated The read thereof for guerdon of my paine, And taking downe the shield, with me did it retaine.

So forth without impediment I past, Till to the Bridges vtter gate I came: The which I found sure lockt and chained fast. I knockt, but no man aunswred me by name; I cald, but no man answerd to my clame. Yet I perseuer'd still to knocke and call, Till at the last I spide within the same, Where one stood peeping through a creuis small, To whom I cald aloud, halfe angry therewithall.

That was to weet the Porter of the place, Vnto whose trust the charge thereof was lent: His name was Doubt, that had a double face, Th'one forward looking, th'other backeward bent, Therein resembling Ianus auncient, Which hath in charge the ingate of the yeare: And euermore his eyes about him went, As if some proued perill he did feare, Or did mis-doubt some ill, whose cause did not appeare.

On th'one side he, on th'other sate Delay, Behinde the gate, that none her might espy; Whose manner was all passengers to stay, And entertaine with her occasions sly, Through which some lost great hope vnheedily, Which neuer they recouer might againe; And others quite excluded forth, did ly Long languishing there in vnpittied paine, And seeking often entraunce, afterwards in vaine.

Me when as he had priuily espide, Bearing the shield which I had conquerd late, He kend it streight, and to me opened wide. So in I past, and streight he closd the gate. But being in, Delay in close awaite Caught hold on me, and thought my steps to stay, Feigning full many a fond excuse to prate, And time to steale, the threasure of mans day; Whose smallest minute lost, no riches render may.

But by no meanes my way I would forslow, For ought that euer she could doe or say, But from my lofty steede dismounting low, Past forth on foote, beholding all the way The goodly workes, and stones of rich assay, Cast into sundry shapes by wondrous skill, That like on earth no where I recken may:

And vnderneath, the riuer rolling still With murmure soft, that seem'd to serue the workmans will.

Thence forth I passed to the second gate, The Gate of good desert, whose goodly pride And costly frame, were long here to relate. The same to all stoode alwaies open wide: But in the Porch did euermore abide An hideous Giant, dreadfull to behold, That stopt the entraunce with his spacious stride, And with the terrour of his countenance bold Full many did affray, that else faine enter would.

His name was Daunger dreaded ouer all, Who day and night did watch and duely ward, From fearefull cowards, entrance to forstall, And faint-heart-fooles, whom shew of perill hard Could terrifie from Fortunes faire adward: For oftentimes faint hearts at first espiall Of his grim face, were from approaching scard; Vnworthy they of grace, whom one deniall Excludes from fairest hope, withouten further triall.

Yet many doughty warriours, often tride In greater perils to be stout and bold, Durst not the sternnesse of his looke abide, But soone as they his countenance did behold, Began to faint, and feele their corage cold. Againe some other, that in hard assaies Were cowards knowne, and litle count did hold, Either through gifts, or guile, or such like waies, Crept in by stouping low, or stealing of the kaies.

But I though meanest man of many moe, Yet much disdaining vnto him to lout, Or creepe betweene his legs, so in to goe, Resolu'd him to assault with manhood stout, And either beat him in, or driue him out. Eftsoones aduauncing that enchaunted shield, With all my might I gan to lay about: Which when he saw, the glaiue which he did wield He gan forthwith t'auale, and way vnto me yield.

So as I entred, I did backeward looke, For feare of harme, that might lie hidden there; And loe his hindparts, whereof heed I tooke, Much more deformed fearefull vgly were, Then all his former parts did earst appere. For hatred, murther, treason, and despight, With many moe lay in ambushment there, Awayting to entrap the warelesse wight, Which did not them preuent with vigilant foresight.

Thus hauing past all perill, I was come Within the compasse of that Islands space; The which did seeme vnto my simple doome, The onely pleasant and delightfull place, That euer troden was of footings trace. For all that nature by her mother wit Could frame in earth, and forme of substance base, Was there, and all that nature did omit, Art playing second natures part, supplyed it.

No tree, that is of count, in greenewood growes, From lowest Iuniper to Ceder tall, No flowre in field, that daintie odour throwes, And deckes his branch with blossomes ouer all, But there was planted, or grew naturall: Nor sense of man so coy and curious nice, But there mote find to please it selfe withall; Nor hart could wish for any queint deuice, But there it present was, and did fraile sense entice.

In such luxurious plentie of all pleasure, It seem'd a second paradise to ghesse, So lauishly enricht with natures threasure, That if the happie soules, which doe possesse Th'Elysian fields, and liue in lasting blesse, Should happen this with liuing eye to see, They soone would loath their lesser happinesse, And wish to life return'd againe to bee, That in this ioyous place they mote haue ioyance free.

Fresh shadowes, fit to shroud from sunny ray; Faire lawnds, to take the sunne in season dew; Sweet springs, in which a thousand Nymphs did play; Soft rombling brookes, that gentle slomber drew; High reared mounts, the lands about to vew; Low looking dales, disloignd from common gaze; Delightfull bowres, to solace louers trew; False Labyrinthes, fond runners eyes to daze; All which by nature made did nature selfe amaze.

And all without were walkes and alleyes dight, With diuers trees, enrang'd in euen rankes; And here and there were pleasant arbors pight, And shadie seates, and sundry flowring bankes, To sit and rest the walkers wearie shankes, And therein thousand payres of louers walkt, Praysing their god, and yeelding him great thankes, Ne euer ought but of their true loues talkt, Ne euer for rebuke or blame of any balkt.

All these together by themselves did sport Their spotlesse pleasures, and sweet loues content. But farre away
from these, another sort Of louers lincked in true harts consent; Which loued not as these, for like intent, But on chast
vertue grounded their desire, Farre from all fraud, or fayned
blandishment; Which in their spirits kindling zealous fire,
Braue thoughts and noble deedes did euermore aspire.

Such were great Hercules, and Hylas deare; Trew Ion-
athan, and Dauid trustie tryde; Stout Theseus, and Pirithous
his feare; Pylades and Orestes by his syde; Myld Titus and
Gesippus without pryde; Damon and Pythias whom death
could not seuer; All these and all that euer had bene tyde,
In bands of friendship, there did liue for euer, Whose liues
although decay'd, yet loues decayed neuer.

Which when as I, that neuer tasted blis, Nor happie
howre, beheld with gazefull eye, I thought there was none
other heauen then this; And gan their endlesse happinesse
enuye, That being free from feare and gealosye, Might fran-
kely there their loues desire possesse; Whilest I through
paines and perlous ieopardie, Was forst to seeke my lifes
deare patronesse: Much dearer be the things, which come
through hard distresse.

Yet all those sights, and all that else I saw, Might not my
steps withhold, but that forthright Vnto that purposd place
I did me draw, Where as my loue was lodged day and night:
The temple of great Venus, that is hight The Queene of beautie, and of loue the mother, There worshipped of euery liuing
wight; Whose goodly workmanship farre past all other That
euer were on earth, all were they set together.

Not that same famous Temple of Diane, Whose hight all
Ephesus did ouersee, And which all Asia sought with vowes
prophane, One of the worlds seuen wonders sayd to bee, Might
match with this by many a degree: Nor that, which that wise
King of Iurie framed, With endlesse cost, to be th'Almighties
see; Nor all that else through all the world is named To all

the heathen Gods, might like to this be clamed.

I much admyring that so goodly frame, Vnto the porch approcht, which open stood; But therein sate an amiable Dame, That seem'd to be of very sober mood, And in her semblant shewed great womanhood: Strange was her tyre; for on her head a crowne She wore much like vnto a Danisk hood Poudred with pearle and stone, and all her gowne Enwouen was with gold, that raught full low a downe.

On either side of her, two young men stood, Both strongly arm'd, as fearing one another; Yet were they brethren both of halfe the blood, Begotten by two fathers of one mother, Though of contrarie natures each to other: The one of them hight Loue, the other Hate, Hate was the elder, Loue the younger brother; Yet was the younger stronger in his state Then th'elder, and him maystred still in all debate.

Nathlesse that Dame so well them tempred both, That she them forced hand to ioyne in hand, Albe that Hatred was thereto full loth, And turn'd his face away, as he did stand, Vnwilling to behold that louely band. Yet she was of such grace and vertuous might, That her commaundment he could not withstand, But bit his lip for felonous despight, And gnasht his yron tuskes at that displeasing sight.

Concord she cleeped was in common reed, Mother of blessed Peace, and Friendship trew; They both her twins, both borne of heauenly seed, And she her selfe likewise diuinely grew; The which right well her workes diuine did shew: For strength, and wealth, and happinesse she lends, And strife, and warre, and anger does subdew: Of litle much, of foes she maketh frends, And to afflicted minds sweet rest and quiet sends.

By her the heauen is in his course contained, And all the world in state vnmoued stands, As their Almightie maker first ordained, And bound them with inuiolable bands; Else would the waters ouerflow the lands, And fire deuoure the ayre, and hell them quight, But that she holds them with her blessed hands. She is the nourse of pleasure and delight, And vnto Venus grace the gate doth open right.

By her I entring halfe dismayed was, But she in gentle wise me entertayned, And twixt her selfe and Loue did let me pas; But Hatred would my entrance haue restrayned, And with his club me threatned to haue brayned, Had not the Ladie with her powrefull speach Him from his wicked will vneath refrayned; And th'other eke his malice did empeach, Till I was throughly past the perill of his reach.

Into the inmost Temple thus I came, Which fuming all with frankensence I found, And odours rising from the altars flame. Vpon an hundred marble pillors round The roofe vp high was reared from the ground, All deckt with crownes, & chaynes, and girlands gay, And thousand pretious gifts worth many a pound, The which sad louers for their vowes did pay; And all the ground was strow'd with flowres, as fresh as May.

An hundred Altars round about were set, All flaming with their sacrifices fire, That with the steme thereof the Temple swet, Which rould in clouds to heauen did aspire, And in them bore true louers vowes entire: And eke an hundred brasen caudrons bright, To bath in ioy and amorous desire, Euery of which was to a damzell hight; For all the Priests were damzels, in soft linnen dight.

Right in the midst the Goddesse selfe did stand Vpon an altar of some costly masse, Whose substance was vneath to vnderstand: For neither pretious stone, nor durefull brasse, For shining gold, nor mouldring clay it was; But much more rare and pretious to esteeme, Pure in aspect, and like to christall glasse, Yet glasse was not, if one did rightly deeme, But being faire and brickle, likest glasse did seeme.

But it in shape and beautie did excell All other Idoles, which the heathen adore Farre passing that, which by surpassing skill Phidias did make in Paphos Isle of yore, With which that wretched Greeke, that life forlore Did fall in loue: yet this much fairer shined, But couered with a slender veile afore; And both her feete and legs together twyned Were with a snake, whose head & tail were fast cōbyned.

The cause why she was couered with a vele, Was hard to know, for that her Priests the same From peoples knowledge labour'd to concele. But sooth it was not sure for womanish shame, Nor any blemish, which the worke mote blame; But for, they say, she hath both kinds in one, Both male and female, both vnder one name: She syre and mother is her selfe alone, Begets and eke conceiues, ne needeth other none.

And all about her necke and shoulders flew A flocke of litle loues, and sports, and ioyes, With nimble wings of gold and purple hew; Whose shapes seem'd not like to terrestriall boyes, But like to Angels playing heauenly toyes; The whilest their eldest brother was away, Cupid their eldest brother; he enioyes The wide kingdome of loue with Lordly sway, And to his law compels all creatures to obay. ·

And all about her altar scattered lay Great sorts of louers piteously complayning, Some of their losse, some of their loues delay, Some of their pride, some paragons disdayning, Some fearing fraud, some fraudulently fayning, As euery one had cause of good or ill. Amongst the rest some one through loues constrayning, Tormented sore, could not containe it still, But thus brake forth, that all the temple it did fill.

Great Venus, Queene of beautie and of grace, The ioy of Gods and men, that vnder skie Doest fayrest shine, and most adorne thy place, That with thy smyling looke doest pacifie The raging seas, and makst the stormes to flie; Thee goddesse, thee the winds, the clouds doe feare, And when thou spredst thy mantle forth on hie, The waters play and pleasant lands appeare, And heauens laugh, & all the world shews ioyous cheare.

Then doth the dædale earth throw forth to thee Out of her fruitfull lap aboundant flowres, And then all liuing wights, soone as they see The spring breake forth out of his lusty bowres, They all doe learne to play the Paramours; First doe the merry birds, thy prety pages Priuily pricked with thy lustfull powres, Chirpe loud to thee out of their leauy cages,

And thee their mother call to coole their kindly rages.

Then doe the saluage beasts begin to play Their pleasant friskes, and loath their wonted food; The Lyons rore, the Tygres loudly bray, The raging Buls rebellow through the wood, And breaking forth, dare tempt the deepest flood, To come where thou doest draw them with desire: So all things else, that nourish vitall blood, Soone as with fury thou doest them inspire, In generation seeke to quench their inward fire.

So all the world by thee at first was made, And dayly yet thou doest the same repayre: Ne ought on earth that merry is and glad, Ne ought on earth that louely is and fayre, But thou the same for pleasure didst prepayre. Thou art the root of all that ioyous is, Great God of men and women, queene of th'ayre, Mother of laughter, and welspring of blisse, O graunt that of my loue at last I may not misse.

So did he say: but I with murmure soft, That none might heare the sorrow of my hart, Yet inly groning deepe and sighing oft, Besought her to graunt ease vnto my smart, And to my wound her gratious help impart. Whilest thus I spake, behold with happy eye I spyde, where at the Idoles feet apart A beuie of fayre damzels close did lye, Wayting when as the Antheme should be sung on hye.

The first of them did seeme of ryper yeares, And grauer countenance then all the rest; Yet all the rest were eke her equall peares, Yet vnto her obayed all the best. Her name was VVomanhood, that she exprest By her sad semblant and demeanure wyse: For stedfast still her eyes did fixed rest, Ne rov'd at randon after gazers guyse, Whose luring baytes oftimes doe heedlesse harts entyse.

And next to her sate goodly Shamefastnesse, Ne euer durst her eyes from ground vpreare, Ne euer once did looke vp from her desse, As if some blame of euill she did feare, That in her cheekes made roses oft appeare: And her against sweet Cherefulnesse was placed, Whose eyes like twinkling stars in euening cleare, Were deckt with smyles, that all sad humors chaced, And darted forth delights, the which her goodly graced.

And next to her sate sober Modestie, Holding her hand vpon her gentle hart; And her against sate comely Curtesie, That vnto euery person knew her part; And her before was seated ouerthwart Soft Silence, and submisse Obedience, Both linckt together neuer to dispart, Both gifts of God not gotten but from thence, Both girlonds of his Saints against their foes offence.

Thus sate they all a round in seemely rate: And in the midst of them a goodly mayd, Euen in the lap of VVomanhood there sate, The which was all in lilly white arayd, With siluer streames amongst the linnen stray'd; Like to the Morne, when first her shyning face Hath to the gloomy world it selfe bewray'd, That same was fayrest Amoret in place, Shyning with beauties light, and heauenly vertues grace.

Whom soone as I beheld, my hart gan throb, And wade in doubt, what best were to be donne: For sacrilege me seem'd the Church to rob, And folly seem'd to leaue the thing vndonne, Which with so strong attempt I had begonne. Tho shaking off all doubt and shamefast feare, Which Ladies loue I heard had neuer wonne Mongst men of worth, I to her stepped neare, And by the lilly hand her labour'd vp to reare.

Thereat that formost matrone me did blame, And sharpe rebuke, for being ouer bold; Saying it was to Knight vnseemely shame, Vpon a recluse Virgin to lay hold, That vnto Venus seruices was sold. To whom I thus, Nay but it fitteth best, For Cupids man with Venus mayd to hold, For ill your goddesse seruices are drest By virgins, and her sacrifices let to rest.

With that my shield I forth to her did show, Which all that while I closely had conceld; On which when Cupid with his killing bow And cruell shafts emblazond she beheld, At sight thereof she was with terror queld, And said no more: but I which all that while The pledge of faith, her hand engaged held, Like warie Hynd within the weedie soyle, For no intreatie would forgoe so glorious spoyle.

And euermore vpon the Goddesse face Mine eye was fixt, for feare of her offence: Whom when I saw with amiable grace To laugh at me, and fauour my pretence, I was emboldned with more confidence; And nought for nicenesse nor for enuy sparing, In presence of them all forth led her thence: All looking on, and like astonisht staring, Yet to lay hand on her, not one of all them daring.

She often prayd, and often me besought, Sometime with tender teares to let her goe, Sometime with witching smyles: but yet for nought, That euer she to me could say or doe, Could she her wished freedome fro me wooe; But forth I led her through the Temple gate, By which I hardly past with much adoe: But that same Ladie which me friended late In entrance, did me also friend in my retrate.

No lesse did Daunger threaten me with dread, When as he saw me, maugre all his powre, That glorious spoyle of beautie with me lead, Then Cerberus, when Orpheus did recoure His Leman from the Stygian Princes boure. But euermore my shield did me defend, Against the storme of euery dreadfull stoure: Thus safely with my loue I thence did wend. So ended he his tale, where I this Canto end.

Cant. XI.

Marinells former wound is heald, he comes to Proteus hall, Where Thames doth the Medway wedd, and feasts the Sea-gods all.

B Vt ah for pittie that I haue thus long Left a fayre Ladie languishing in payne: Now well away, that I haue doen such wrong, To let faire Florimell in bands remayne, In bands of loue, and in sad thraldomes chayne; From which vnlesse some heauenly powre her free By miracle, not yet appearing playne, She lenger yet is like captiu'd to bee: That euen to thinke thereof, it inly pitties mee. Here neede you to remember, how erewhile Vnlouely Proteus, missing to his mind That Virgins loue to win by wit or wile, Her threw into a dongeon deepe and blind, And there in chaynes her cruelly did bind,

In hope thereby her to his bent to draw: For when as neither gifts nor graces kind Her constant mind could moue at all he saw, He thought her to compell by crueltie and awe.

Deepe in the bottome of an huge great rocke The dongeon was, in which her bound he left, That neither yron barres, nor brasen locke Did neede to gard from force, or secret theft Of all her louers, which would her haue reft. For wall'd it was with waues, which rag'd and ror'd As they the cliffe in peeces would haue cleft; Besides ten thousand monsters foule abhor'd Did waite about it, gaping griesly all begor'd.

And in the midst thereof did horror dwell, And darkenesse dredd, that neuer viewed day, Like to the balefull house of lowest hell, In which old Styx her aged bones alway, Old Styx the Grandame of the Gods, doth lay. There did this lucklesse mayd seuen months abide, Ne euer euening saw, ne mornings ray, Ne euer from the day the night describe, But thought it all one night, that did no houres diuide.

And all this was for loue of Marinell, Who her despysd (ah who would her despyse?) And wemens loue did from his hart expell, And all those ioyes that weake mankind entyse. Nathlesse his pride full dearely he did pryse; For of a womans hand it was ywroke, That of the wound he yet in languor lyes, Ne can be cured of that cruell stroke Which Britomart him gaue, when he did her prouoke.

Yet farre and neare the Nymph his mother sought, And many salues did to his sore applie, And many herbes did vse. But when as nought She saw could ease his rankling maladie, At last to Tryphon she for helpe did hie, (This Tryphon is the seagods surgeon hight) Whom she besought to find some remedie: And for his paines a whistle him behight That of a fishes shell was wrought with rare delight.

So well that Leach did hearke to her request, And did so well employ his carefull paine, That in short space his hurts he had redrest, And him restor'd to healthfull state againe: In which he long time after did remaine There with the Nymph his mother, like her thrall; Who sore against his will did him retaine, For feare of perill, which to him mote fall, Through his too ventrous prowesse proued ouer all.

It fortun'd then, a solemne feast was there To all the Sea-gods and their fruitfull seede, In honour of the spous-alls, which then were Betwixt the Medway and the Thames agreed. Long had the Thames (as we in records reed) Before that day her wooed to his bed; But the proud Nymph would for no worldly meed, Nor no entreatie to his loue be led; Till now at last relenting, she to him was wed.

So both agreed, that this their bridale feast Should for the Gods in Proteus house be made; To which they all repayr'd, both most and least, Aswell which in the mightie Ocean trade, As that in riuers swim, or brookes doe wade. All which not if an hundred tongues to tell, And hundred mouthes, and voice of brasse I had, And endlesse memorie, that mote ex-cell, In order as they came, could I recount them well.

Helpe therefore, O thou sacred imp of Ioue, The noursling of Dame Memorie his deare, To whom those rolles, layd vp in heauen aboue, And records of antiquitie appeare, To which no wit of man may comen neare; Helpe me to tell the names of all those floods, And all those Nymphes, which then as-sembled were To that great banquet of the watry Gods, And all their sundry kinds, and all their hid abodes.

First came great Neptune with his threeforkt mace, That rules the Seas, and makes them rise or fall; His dewy lockes did drop with brine apace, Vnder his Diademe imperiall: And by his side his Queene with coronall, Faire Amphitrite, most diuinely faire, Whose yuorie shoulders weren couered all, As with a robe, with her owne siluer haire, And deckt with pearles, which th'Indian seas for her prepaire.

These marched farre afore the other crew; And all the way before them as they went, Triton his trompet shrill be-fore them blew, For goodly triumph and great iollyment, That made the rockes to roare, as they were rent. And after them the royall issue came, Which of them sprung by lineall descent: First the Sea-gods, which to themselues doe clame

The powre to rule the billowes, and the waues to tame.

Phorcys, the father of that fatall brood, By whom those old Heroes wonne such fame; And Glaucus, that wise southsayes vnderstood; And tragicke Inoes sonne, the which became A God of seas through his mad mothers blame, Now hight Palemon, and is saylers frend; Great Brontes, and Astraeus, that did shame Himselfe with incest of his kin vnkend; And huge Orion, that doth tempests still portend.

The rich Cteatus, and Eurytus long; Neleus and Pelias louely brethren both; Mightie Chrysaor, and Caicus strong; Eurypulus, that calmes the waters wroth; And faire Euphaemus, that vpon them go'th As on the ground, without dismay or dread: Fierce Eryx, and Alebius that know'th The waters depth, and doth their bottome tread; And sad Asopus, comely with his hoarie head.

There also some most famous founders were Of puissant Nations, which the world possest; Yet sonnes of Neptune, now assembled here: Ancient Ogyges, even th'auncientest, And Inachus renowmd aboue the rest; Phoenix, and Aon, and Pelasgus old, Great Belus, Phoeax, and Agenor best; And mightie Albion, father of the bold And warlike people, which the Britaine Islands hold.

For Albion the sonne of Neptune was, Who for the proofe of his great puissance, Out of his Albion did on dry-foot pas Into old Gall, that now is cleeped France, To fight with Hercules, that did aduance To vanquish all the world with matchlesse might, And there his mortall part by great mischance Was slaine: but that which is th'immortall spright Liues still: and to this feast with Neptunes seed was dight.

But what doe I their names seeke to reherse, Which all the world haue with their issue fild? How can they all in this so narrow verse Contayned be, and in small compasse hild? Let them record them, that are better skild, And know the moniments of passed times: Onely what needeth, shall be here fulfild, T'expresse some part of that great equipage, Which from great Neptune do deriue their parentage.

Next came the aged Ocean, and his Dame, Old Tethys, th'oldest two of all the rest, For all the rest of those two parents came, Which afterward both sea and land possest: Of all which Nereus th'eldest, and the best, Did first proceed, then which none more vpright, Ne more sincere in word and deed profest; Most voide of guile, most free from fowle despight, Doing him selfe, and teaching others to doe right.

Thereto he was expert in prophecies, And could the ledden of the Gods vnfold, Through which, when Paris brought his famous prise The faire Tindarid lasse, he him fortold, That her all Greece with many a champion bold Should fetch againe, and finally destroy Proud Priams towne. So wise is Nereus old, And so well skild; nathlesse he takes great ioy Oft-times amõgst the wanton Nymphs to sport and toy.

And after him the famous riuers came, Which doe the earth enrich and beautifie: The fertile Nile, which creatures new doth frame; Long Rhodanus, whose sourse springs from the skie; Faire Ister, flowing from the mountaines hie; Diuine Scamander, purpled yet with blood Of Greekes and Troians, which therein did die; Pactolus glistring with his golden flood, And Tygris fierce, whose streames of none may be withstood.

Great Ganges, and immortall Euphrates, Deepe Indus, and Maeander intricate, Slow Peneus, and tempestuous Phasides, Swift Rhene, and Alpheus still immaculate: Ooraxes, feared for great Cyrus fate; Tybris, renowmed for the Romaines fame, Rich Oranochy, though but knowen late; And that huge Riuer, which doth beare his name Of warlike Amazons, which doe possesse the same.

Ioy on those warlike women, which so long Can from all men so rich a kingdome hold; And shame on you, ô men, which boast your strong And valiant hearts, in thoughts lesse hard and bold, Yet quaile in conquest of that land of gold. But this to you, ô Britons, most pertaines, To whom the right hereof it selfe hath sold; The which for sparing litle cost or paines, Loose so immortall glory, and so endlesse gaines.

Then was there heard a most celestiall sound, Of dainty musicke, which did next ensew Before the spouse: that was Arion crownd; Who playing on his harpe, vnto him drew The eares and hearts of all that goodly crew, That euen yet the Dolphin, which him bore Through the AEgaean seas from Pirates vew, Stood still by him astonisht at his lore, And all the raging seas for ioy forgot to rore.

So went he playing on the watery plaine. Soone after whom the louely Bridegroome came, The noble Thamis, with all his goodly traine, But him before there went, as best became His auncient parents, namely th'auncient Thame. But much more aged was his wife then he, The Ouze, whom men doe Isis rightly name; Full weake and crooked creature seemed she, And almost blind through eld, that scarce her way could see.

Therefore on either side she was sustained Of two smal grooms, which by their names were hight The Churne, and Charwell, two small streames, which pained Them selues her footing to direct aright, Which fayled oft through faint and feeble plight: But Thame was stronger, and of better stay; Yet seem'd full aged by his outward sight, With head all hoary, and his beard all gray, Deawed with siluer drops, that trickled downe alway.

And eke he somewhat seem'd to stoupe afore With bowed backe, by reason of the lode, And auncient heauy burden, which he bore Of that faire City, wherein make abode So many learned impes, that shoote abrode, And with their braunches spred all Britany, No lesse then do her elder sisters broode. Ioy to you both, ye double nourcery Or Arts, but Oxford thine doth Thame most glorify.

But he their sonne full fresh and iolly was, All decked in a robe of watchet hew, On which the waues, glittering like Christall glas, So cunningly enwouen were, that few Could weenen, whether they were false or trew. And on his head like to a Coronet He wore, that seemed strange to common vew, In which were many towres and castels set, That it encompast round as with a golden fret.

Like as the mother of the Gods, they say, In her great iron charet wonts to ride, When to Ioues pallace she doth take her way; Old Cybele, arayd with pompous pride, Wearing a Diademe embattild wide With hundred turrets, like a Turribant. With such an one was Thamis beautifide; That was to weet the famous Troynouant, In which her kingdomes throne is chiefly resiant.

And round about him many a pretty Page Attended duely, ready to obay; All little Riuers, which owe vassallage To him, as to their Lord, and tribute pay: The chaulky Kenet, and the Thetis gray, The morish Cole, and the soft sliding Breane, The wanton Lee, that oft doth loose his way, And the still Darent, in whose waters cleane Ten thousand fishes play, and decke his pleasant streame.

Then came his neighbour flouds, which nigh him dwell, And water all the English soile throughout; They all on him this day attended well; And with meet seruice waited him about; Ne none disdained low to him to lout: No not the stately Seuerne grudg'd at all, Ne storming Humber, though he looked stout; But both him honor'd as their principall, And let their swelling waters low before him fall.

There was the speedy Tamar, which deuides The Cornish and the Deuonish confines; Through both whose borders swiftly downe it glides, And meeting Plim, to Plimmouth thence declines: And Dart, nigh chockt with sands of tinny mines. But Auon marched in more stately path, Proud of his Adamants, with which he shines And glisters wide, as als' of wondrous Bath, And Bristow faire, which on his waues he builded hath.

And there came Stoure with terrible aspect, Bearing his six deformed heads on hye, That doth his course through Blandford plains direct, And washeth Winborne meades in season drye. Next him went Wylibourne with passage slye, That of his wylinesse his name doth take, And of him selfe doth name the shire thereby; And Mole, that like a nousling Mole doth make His way still vnder ground, till Thamis he ouertake.

Then came the Rother, decked all with woods Like a wood God, and flowing fast to Rhy: And Sture, that parteth with his pleasant floods The Easterne Saxons from the Southerne ny, And Clare, and Harwitch both doth beautify: Him follow'd Yar, soft washing Norwitch wall, And with him brought a present ioyfully Of his owne fish vnto their festiuall, Whose like none else could shew, the which they Ruffins call.

Next these the plenteous Ouse came far from land, By many a city, and by many a towne, And many riuers taking vnder hand Into his waters, as he passeth downe, The Cle, the Were, the Grant, the Sture, the Rowne. Thence doth by Huntingdon and Cambridge flit; My mother Cambridge, whom as with a Crowne He doth adorne, and is adorn'd of it With many a gentle Muse, and many a learned wit.

And after him the fatall Welland went, That if old sawes proue true (which God forbid) Shall drowne all Holland with his excrement, And shall see Stamford, though now homely hid, Then shine in learning, more then euer did Cambridge or Oxford, Englands goodly beames. And next to him the Nene downe softly slid; And bounteous Trent, that in him selfe enseames Both thirty sorts of fish, and thirty sundry streames.

Next these came Tyne, along whose stony bancke That Romaine Monarch built a brasen wall, Which mote the feebled Britons strongly flancke Against the Picts, that swarmed ouer all, Which yet thereof Gualseuer they doe call: And Twede the limit betwixt Logris land And Albany: And Eden though but small, Yet often stainde with bloud of many a band Of Scots and English both, that tyned on his strand.

Then came those sixe sad brethren, like forlorne, That whilome were (as antique fathers tell) Six valiant Knights, of one faire Nymphe yborne, Which did in noble deedes of armes excell, And wonned there, where now Yorke people dwell; Still Vre, swift Werfe, and Oze the most of might, High Swale, vnquiet Nide, and troublous Skell; All whom a Scythian king, that Humber hight, Slew cruelly, and in the riuer drowned quight.

But past not long, ere Brutus warlicke sonne Locrinus them aueng'd, and the same date, Which the proud Humber vnto them had donne, By equall dome repayd on his owne pate: For in the selfe same riuer, where he late Had drenched them, he drowned him againe; And nam'd the riuer of his wretched fate; Whose bad condition yet it doth retaine, Oft tossed with his stormes, which therein still remaine.

These after, came the stony shallow Lone, That to old Loncaster his name doth lend; And following Dee, which Britons long ygone Did call diuine, that doth by Chester tend; And Conway which out of his streame doth send Plenty of pearles to decke his dames withall, And Lindus that his pikes doth most commend, Of which the auncient Lincolne men doe call; All these together marched toward Proteus hall.

Ne thence the Irishe Riuers absent were: Sith no lesse famous then the rest they bee, And ioyne in neighbourhood of kingdome nere, Why should they not likewise in loue agree, And ioy likewise this solemne day to see? They saw it all, and present were in place; Though I them all according their degree, Cannot recount, nor tell their hidden race, Nor read the saluage c&utilds;treis, thorough which they pace.

There was the Liffy rolling downe the lea, The sandy Slane, the stony Aubrian, The spacious Shenan spreading like a sea, The pleasant Boyne, the fishy fruitfull Ban, Swift Awniduff, which of the English man Is cal'de Blacke water, and the Liffar deep, Sad Trowis, that once his people ouerran, Strong Allo tombling from Slewlogher steep, And Mulla mine, whose waues I whilom taught to weep.

And there the three renowmed brethren were, Which that great Gyant Blomius begot, Of the faire Nimph Rheusa wandring there. One day, as she to shunne the season whot, Vnder Slewbloome in shady groue was got, This Gyant found her, and by force deflowr'd: Whereof conceiuing, she in time forth brought These three faire sons, which being thece forth powrd In three great riuers ran, and many countreis scowrd.

The first, the gentle Shure that making way By sweet Clonmell, adornes rich Waterford; The next, the stubborne Newre, whose waters gray By faire Kilkenny and Rosseponte boord, The third, the goodly Barow, which doth hoord Great heapes of Salmons in his deepe bosome: All which long sundred, doe at last accord To ioyne in one, ere to the sea they come, So flowing all from one, all one at last become.

There also was the wide embayed Mayre, The pleasaunt Bandon crownd with many a wood, The spreading Lee, that like an Island fayre Encloseth Corke with his deuided flood; And balefull Oure, late staind with English blood: With many more, whose names no tongue can tell. All which that day in order seemly good Did on the Thamis attend, and waited well To doe their duefull seruice, as to them befell.

Then came the Bride, the louely Medua came, Clad in a vesture of vnknowen geare, And vncouth fashion, yet her well became; That seem'd like siluer, sprinckled here and theare With glittering spangs, that did like starres appeare, And wau'd vpon, like water Chamelot, To hide the metall, which yet euery where Bewrayd it selfe, to let men plainely wot, It was no mortall worke, that seem'd and yet was not.

Her goodly lockes adowne her backe did flow Vnto her waste, with flowres bescattered, The which ambrosiall odours forth did throw To all about, and all her shoulders spred As a new spring; and likewise on her hed A Chapelet of sundry flowers she wore, From vnder which the deawy humour shed, Did tricle downe her haire, like to the hore Congealed litle drops, which doe the morne adore.

On her two pretty handmaides did attend, One cald the Theise, the other cald the Crane; Which on her waited, things amisse to mend, And both behind vpheld her spredding traine; Vnder the which, her feet appeared plaine, Her siluer feet, faire washt against this day: And her before there paced Pages twaine, Both clad in colours like, and like array, The Doune & eke the Frith, both which prepard her way.

And after these the Sea Nymphs marched all, All goodly

damzels, deckt with long greene haire, Whom of their sire Nereides men call, All which the Oceans daughter to him bare The gray eyde Doris: all which fifty are; All which she there on her attending had. Swift Proto, milde Eucrate, Thetis faire, Soft Spio, sweete Eudore, Sao sad, Light Doto, wanton Glauce, and Galene glad.

White hand Eunica, proud Dynamene, Ioyous Thalia, goodly Amphitrite, Louely Pasithee, kinde Eulimene, Lifht goote Cymothoe, and sweete Melite, Fairest Pherusa, Phao lilly white, Wondred Agaue, Poris, and Nesæa, With Erato that doth in loue delite, And Panopæ, and wise Protomedæa, And snowy neckd Doris, and milkewhite Galathæa.

Speedy Hippothoe, and chaste Actea, Large Lisianassa, and Pronæa sage, Euagore, and light Pontoporea, And she, that with her least word can asswage The surging seas, when they do sorest rage, Cymodoce, and stout Autonoe, And Neso, and Eione well in age, And seeming still to smile, Glauconome, And she that hight of many heastes Polynome,

Fresh Alimeda, deckt with girlond greene; Hyponeo, with salt bedewed wrests: Laomedia, like the christall sheene; Liagore, much praisd for wise behests; And Psamathe, for her brode snowy brests; Cymo, Eupompe, and Themiste iust; And she that vertue loues and vice detests Euarna, and Menippe true in trust, And Nemertea learned well to rule her lust.

All these the daughters of old Nereus were, Which haue the sea in charge to them assinde, To rule his tides, and surges to vprere, To bring forth stormes, or fast them to vpbinde, And sailers saue from wreckes of wrathfull winde. And yet besides three thousand more there were Of th'Oceans seede, but Ioues and Phoebus kinde; The which in floods and fountaines doe appere, And all mankinde do nourish with their waters clere.

The which, more eath it were for mortall wight, To tell the sands, or count the starres on hye, Or ought more hard, then thinke to reckon right. But well I wote, that these which I descry, Were present at this great solemnity: And there amongst the rest, the mother was Of luckelesse Marinell Cymodoce. Which, for my Muse her selfe now tyred has, Vnto an other Canto I will ouerpas.

Cant. XII.

Marin for loue of Florimell, In languor wastes his life: The Nymph his mother getteth her, And giues to him for wife.

O What an endlesse worke haue I in hand, To count the seas abundant progeny, Whose fruitfull seede farre passeth those in land, And also those which wonne in th'azure sky? For much more eath to tell the starres on hy, Albe they endlesse seeme in estimation, Then to recount the Seas posterity: So fertile be the flouds in generation, So huge their numbers, and so numberlesse their nation. Therefore the antique wisards well inuented, That Venus of the fomy sea was bred; For that the seas by her are most augmented. Witnesse th'exceeding fry, which there are fed, And wondrous sholes, which may of none be red. Then blame me not, if I haue err'd in count Of Gods, of Nymphs, of riuers yet vnred: For though their numbers do much more surmount, Yet all those same were there, which erst I did recount.

All those were there, and many other more, Whose names and nations were too long to tell, That Proteus house they fild euen to the dore; Yet were they all in order, as befell, According their degrees disposed well. Amongst the rest, was faire Cymodoce, The mother of vnlucky Marinell, Who thither with her came, to learne and see The manner of the Gods when they at banquet bee.

But for he was halfe mortall, being bred Of mortall sire, though of immortall wombe, He might not with immortall food be fed, Ne with th'eternall Gods to bancket come; But walkt abrode, and round about did rome, To view the building of that vncouth place, That seem'd vnlike vnto his earthly home: Where, as he to and fro by chaunce did trace, There vnto him betid a disauentrous case.

Vnder the hanging of an hideous clieffe, He heard the lamentable voice of one, That piteously complaind her carefull grieffe, Which neuer she before disclosd to none, But to her selfe her sorrow did bemone. So feelingly her case she did complaine, That ruth it moued in the rocky stone, And made it seeme to feele her grieuous paine, And oft to grone with billowes beating from the maine.

Though vaine I see my sorrowes to vnfold, And count my cares, when none is nigh to heare, Yet hoping griefe may lessen being told, I will them tell though vnto no man neare: For heauen that vnto all lends equall eare, Is farre from hearing of my heauy plight; And lowest hell, to which I lie most neare, Cares not what euils hap to wretched wight; And greedy seas doe in the spoile of life delight.

Yet loe the seas I see by often beating, Doe pearce the rockes, and hardest marble weares; But his hard rocky hart for no entreating Will yeeld, but when my piteous plaints he heares, Is hardned more with my aboundant teares. Yet though he neuer list to me relent, But let me waste in woe my wretched yeares, Yet will I neuer of my loue repent, But ioy that for his sake I suffer prisonment.

And when my weary ghost with griefe outworne, By timely death shall winne her wished rest, Let then this plaint vnto his eares be borne, That blame it is to him, that armes profest, To let her die, whom he might haue redrest. There did she pause, inforced to giue place, Vnto the passion, that her heart opprest, And after she had wept and wail'd a space, She gan afresh thus to renew her wretched case.

Ye Gods of seas, if any Gods at all Haue care of right, or ruth of wretches wrong, By one or other way me woefull thrall, Deliuer hence out of this dungeon strong, In which I daily dying am too long. And if ye deeme me death for louing one, That loues not me, then doe it not prolong, But let me die and end my daies attone, And let him liue vnlou'd, or loue him selfe alone.

But if that life ye vnto me decree, Then let mee liue, as louers ought to do, And of my lifes deare loue beloued be: And if he shall through pride your doome vndo, Do you by duresse him compell thereto, And in this prison put him here with me: One prison fittest is to hold vs two: So had I rather to be thrall, then free; Such thraldome or such freedome let it surely be.

But O vaine iudgement, and conditions vaine, The which the prisoner points vnto the free, The whiles I him condemne, and deeme his paine, He where he list goes loose, and laughes at me. So euer loose, so euer happy be. But where so loose or happy that thou art, Know Marinell that all this is for thee. With that she wept and wail'd, as if her hart Would quite haue burst through great abundance of her smart.

All which complaint when Marinell had heard, And vnderstood the cause of all her care To come of him, for vsing her so hard, His stubborne heart, that neuer felt misfare Was toucht with soft remorse and pitty rare; That euen for griefe of minde he oft did grone, And inly wish, that in his powre it weare Her to redresse: but since he meanes found none He could no more but her great misery bemone.

Thus whilst his stony heart with tender ruth Was toucht, and mighty courage mollifide, Dame Venus sonne that tameth stubborne youth With iron bit, and maketh him abide, Till like a victor on his backe he ride, Into his mouth his maystring bridle threw, That made him stoupe, till he did him bestride: Then gan he make him tread his steps anew, And learne to loue, by learning louers paines to rew.

Now gan he in his grieued minde deuise, How from that dungeon he might her enlarge: Some while he thought, by faire and humble wise To Proteus selfe to sue for her discharge: But then he fear'd his mothers former charge Gainst womens loue, long giuen him in vaine. Then gan he thinke, perforce with sword and targe Her forth to fetch, and Proteus to constraine: But soone he gan such folly to forthinke againe.

Then did he cast to steale her thence away, And with him beare, where none of her might know. But all in vaine: for why he found no way To enter in, or issue forth below: For all about that rocke the sea did flow. And though vnto his will she giuen were, Yet without ship or bote her thence to row, He wist not how her thence away to bere; And daunger well he wist long to continue there.

At last when as no meanes he could inuent, Backe to him selfe he gan returne the blame, That was the author of her punishment; And with vile curses, and reprochfull shame To damne him selfe by euery euill name; And deeme vnworthy or of loue or life, That had despisde so chast and faire a dame, Which him had sought through trouble & lõg strife; Yet had refusde a God that her had sought to wife.

In this sad plight he walked here and there, And romed round about the rocke in vaine, As he had lost him selfe, he wist not where; Oft listening if he mote her heare againe; And still bemoning her vnworthy paine. Like as an Hynde whose calfe is falne vnwares Into some pit, where she him heares complaine, An hundred times about the pit side fares, Right sorrowfully mourning her bereaued cares.

And now by this the feast was throughly ended, And euery one gan homeward to resort. Which seeing Marinell, was sore offended, That his departure thence should be so short, And leaue his loue in that sea-walled fort. Yet durst he not his mother disobay, But her attending in full seemly sort, Did march amongst the many all the way: And all the way did inly mourne, like one astray.

Being returned to his mothers bowre, In solitary silence far from wight, He gan record the lamentable stowre, In which his wretched loue lay day and night, For his deare sake, that ill deseru'd that plight: The thought whereof em-pierst his hart so deepe, That of no worldly thing he tooke delight; Ne dayly food did take, ne nightly sleepe, But pyn'd, &; mourn'd, & languisht, and alone did weepe.

That in short space his wonted chearefull hew Gan fade, and liuely spirits deaded quight: His cheeke bones raw, and eie-pits hollow grew, And brawney armes had lost their kno-wen might, That nothing like himselfe he seem'd in sight.

Ere long so weake of limbe, and sicke of loue He woxe, that lenger he note stand vpright, But to his bed was brought, and layd aboue, Like ruefull ghost, vnable once to stirre or moue.

Which when his mother saw, she in her mind Was troubled sore, ne wist well what to weene, Ne could by search nor any meanes out find The secret cause and nature of his teene, Whereby she might apply some medicine; But weeping day and night, did him attend, And mourn'd to see her losse before her eyne, Which grieu'd her more, that she it could not mend: To see an helpelesse euill, double griefe doth lend.

Nought could she read the roote of his disease, Ne weene what mister maladie it is, Whereby to seeke some meanes it to appease. Most did she thinke, but most she thought amis, That that same former fatall wound of his Whyleare by Tryphon was not throughly healed, But closely rankled vnder th'orifis: Least did she thinke, that which he most concealed, That loue it was, which in his hart lay vnreuealed.

Therefore to Tryphon she againe doth hast, And him doth chyde as false and fraudulent, That fayld the trust, which she in him had plast, To cure her sonne, as he his faith had lent: Who now was falne into new languishment Of his old hurt, which was not throughly cured. So backe he came vnto her patient; Where searching euery part, her well assured, That it was no old sore, which his new paine procured.

But that it was some other maladie, Or griefe vnknowne, which he could not discerne: So left he her withouten remedie. Then gan her heart to faint, and quake, and earne, And inly troubled was, the truth to learne. Vnto himselfe she came, and him besought, Now with faire speches, now with threatnings sterne, If ought lay hidden in his grieued thought, It to reueale: who still her answered, there was nought.

Nathlesse she rested not so satisfide, But leauing watry gods, as booting nought, Vnto the shinie heauen in haste she hide, And thence Apollo King of Leaches brought. Apollo came; who soone as he had sought Through his disease, did by and by out find, That he did languish of some inward thought, The which afflicted his engrieued mind; Which loue he red to be, that leads each liuing kind.

Which when he had vnto his mother told, She gan thereat to fret, and greatly grieue. And comming to her sonne, gan first to scold, And chyde at him, that made her misbelieue: But afterwards she gan him soft to shrieue, And wooe with faire intreatie, to disclose, Which of the Nymphes his heart so sore did mieue. For sure she weend it was some one of those, Which he had lately seene, that for his loue he chose.

Now lesse she feared that same fatall read, That warned him of womens loue beware: Which being ment of mortall creatures sead, For loue of Nymphes she thought she need not care, But promist him, what euer wight she weare, That she her loue to him would shortly gaine: So he her told: but soone as she did heare That Florimell it was, which wrought his paine, She gan a fresh to chafe, and grieue in euery vaine.

Yet since she saw the streight extremitie, In which his life vnluckily was layd, It was no time to scan the prophecie, Whether old Proteus true or false had sayd, That his decay should happen by a mayd. It's late in death of daunger to aduize, Or loue forbid him, that is life denayd: But rather gan in troubled mind deuize, How she that Ladies libertie might enterprize.

To Proteus selfe to sew she thought it vaine, Who was the root and worker of her woe: Nor vnto any meaner to complaine, But vnto great king Neptune selfe did goe, And on her knee before him falling lowe, Made humble suit vnto his Maiestie, To graunt to her, her sonnes life, which his foe A cruell Tyrant had presumpteouslie By wicked doome condemn'd, a wretched death to die.

To whom God Neptune softly smyling, thus; Daughter me seemes of double wrong ye plaine, Gainst one that hath both wronged you, and vs: For death t'adward I ween'd did appertaine To none, but to the seas sole Soueraine. Read therefore who it is, which this hath wrought, And for what cause; the truth discouer plaine. For neuer wight so euill did or thought, But would some rightfull cause pretend, though rightly nought.

To whom she answerd, Then it is by name Proteus, that hath ordayn'd my sonne to die; For that a waift, the which by fortune came Vpon your seas, he claym'd as propertie: And yet nor his, nor his in equitie, But yours the waift by high prerogatiue. Therefore I humbly craue your Maiestie, It to repleuie, and my sonne repriue: So shall you by one gift saue all vs three aliue.

He graunted it: and streight his warrant made, Vnder the Sea-gods seale autenticall, Commaunding Proteus straight t'enlarge the mayd, Which wandring on his seas imperiall, He lately tooke, and sithence kept as thrall. Which she receiuing with meete thankefulnesse, Departed straight to Proteus therewithall: Who reading it with inward loathfulnesse, Was grieued to restore the pledge, he did possesse.

Yet durst he not the warrant to withstand, But vnto her deliuered Florimell. Whom she receiuing by the lilly hand, Admyr'd her beautie much, as she mote well: For she all liuing creatures did excell; And was right ioyous, that she gotten had So faire a wife for her sonne Marinell. So home with her she streight the virgin lad, And shewed her to him, then being sore bestad.

Who soone as he beheld that angels face, Adorn'd with all diuine perfection, His cleared heart eftsoones away gan chace Sad death, reuiued with her sweet inspection And feeble spirit inly felt refection; As withered weed through cruell winters tine, That feeles the warmth of sunny beames reflection, Liftes vp his head, that did before decline And gins to spread his leafe before the faire sunshine.

Right so himselfe did Marinell vpreare, When he in place his dearest loue did spy; And though his limbs could not his bodie beare, Ne former strength returne so suddenly, Yet chearefull signes he shewed outwardly. Ne lesse was she in secret hart affected, But that she masked it with modestie, For feare she should of lightnesse be detected: Which to another place I leaue to be perfected.

[here, in 1609, 'The end of the fourth Booke.']

Made in the USA
Las Vegas, NV
26 July 2021